Rosie Goodwin has worked in [...] children, and lives near Nuneaton with her husband, Trevor, and their four dogs.

Praise for Rosie Goodwin:

'A heart-throbber of a story'

Northern Echo

'A touching and tender story . . . tremendously uplifting and life-affirming. A feel-good read that tugs at the heart strings'

Historical Novels Review

'A gifted writer . . . Not only is Goodwin's characterisation and dialogue compelling, but her descriptive writing is a joy'

Nottingham Evening Post

'Rosie is the real thing – a writer who has something to say and knows how to say it'

Gilda O'Neill

'Goodwin is a born author'

Lancashire Evening Telegraph

'Goodwin is a fabulous writer . . . she reels the reader in surprisingly quickly and her style involves lots of twists and turns that are in no way predictable'

Worcester Evening News

'Rosie is a born storyteller – she'll make you cry, she'll make you laugh, but most of all you'll care for her characters and lose yourself in her story'

Jeannie Johnson

'Her stories are now eagerly awaited by readers the length and breadth of the country'

Heartland Evening News

ROSIE GOODWIN

The Empty Cradle

headline

First published in 2012
by HEADLINE PUBLISHING GROUP

First published in paperback in 2013
by HEADLINE PUBLISHING GROUP

10

Cataloguing in Publication Data is
available from the British Library

ISBN 978 0 7553 8576 8

Typeset in Calisto by Palimpsest Book Production Limited,
Falkirk, Stirlingshire

Printed and bound in Great Britain by
Clays Ltd, Elcograf S.p.A.

Headline's policy is to use papers that are natural, renewable and
recyclable products and made from wood grown in sustainable
forests. The logging and manufacturing processes are expected
to conform to the environmental regulations of the country of origin.

HEADLINE PUBLISHING GROUP
An Hachette UK Company
338 Euston Road
London NW1 3BH

www.headline.co.uk
www.hachette.co.uk

This one is for you, Flora, with gratitude and love for all your care and support xx

Acknowledgements

I would like to say a huge thank you to Flora Rees, who started out as my editor and became a friend, also to Jane Morpeth and all the team at Headline for the care and support you have shown me since I became published. God bless xx

Prologue

June 2011

'So you're saying the poor old soul hasn't spoken a single word since she came here?' the attractive redhead asked her colleague in a hushed voice.

'That's right,' the blonde care assistant answered as she dusted her way across the dressing-table. 'Three months it's been now, and not so much as a peep out of her. She just sits there hugging that doll all day.'

The redhead, who was called Nadine, glanced across at the elderly woman in the neatly made bed and tutted sadly while she gathered up a pile of bedlinen to take to the laundry. 'Doesn't she have any relatives who come to visit her?' she asked.

'No one. At least, not whilst I've been looking after her. Oh, I tell a lie – there *was* someone. A young social worker – Morris or Norris, I think she said her name was. She came a couple of times but the old girl wouldn't even look at her so she stopped coming.' Beth Malone straightened and looked about to see what else needed doing. She removed the plastic bag from the waste-paper basket and replaced it with a fresh one.

'From what I can make of it, no one really knows much about her,' she went on. 'Apparently a neighbour called social services in because they hadn't seen her out and about for a while, and they found her inside her house surrounded by cats and dogs that she'd taken in – and that doll. She clearly wasn't well so they admitted her to hospital, then when they decided that she wasn't capable of looking after herself any more, they sent her here to the home to recuperate.

'And what about the animals?' Nadine asked, aghast. She had pets of her own and would hate to be separated from them. 'Who's looking after them?'

1

'Her solicitor dealt with all of that. They were all well cared-for, as it turned out,' Beth said. 'I believe they have all been rehomed.'

'How sad.' As Nadine looked back towards the bed her heart ached. Both women were very fond of all the patients in The Silas Marner Nursing Home near Bedworth.

Beth rubbed her back, saying, 'Well, I reckon we're done in here for now. We'd best get down to the dining room and start laying up for dinner else we'll have the manageress breathing down our necks.'

Beth crossed to the old woman and stroked her hand. 'I'll be back with your dinner-tray soon, Charlotte,' she told her kindly. 'But if you need anything before, just ring the bell and one of us will come.'

The woman's faded blue eyes stayed firmly fixed on the ceiling, so, with a little sigh, Beth followed Nadine from the room.

Once the door had closed behind them, the woman glanced towards the patch of blue sky that was visible through the window and blinked back tears. The staff at the care home were kind, especially Beth, but they tended to treat her as if she were deaf and dumb now. She knew it was her own fault. She had consciously remained tight-lipped ever since the day the social worker had come into her home and sent her into hospital. They had taken her away from her beloved pets. But now it didn't matter any more. She had nothing left to live for and soon, hopefully, she would join her husband who had passed away ten long years ago.

Thoughts of Joseph made the lump in her throat swell to even larger proportions. He had been such a gentle, sensitive man, but misunderstood, just as she had been for most of her life. She stared harder at the clouds scudding across the sky. Was Joseph really up there waiting for her? Was there a heaven? She could only hope it was so. And soon, very soon now she would go to him and all the pain would end.

Charlotte Branning knew that to the nursing staff here she was just a silly, eccentric old woman – but how she could have enlightened them, had she wished to. Instead, as she cuddled the hard plastic doll to her chest, she prayed for death to come and claim her. It would be nice to go to sleep and never have to wake up again. She closed her eyes and suddenly she was a young girl again as her thoughts drifted back over the years . . .

Chapter One

'Come along, Charlotte. If you don't hurry we shall be late for the service, and you know that will make your father angry.'

'Yes, Mother.' Hastily pulling her gloves on, the girl adjusted her hat before meekly following her mother through the door.

The vicarage, which was the only home Charlotte had ever known, was right next door to St Sebastian's Church in Bedworth, and as they walked down the path leading to the small wooden gate they could see people streaming towards it. Charlotte's father would already be there, going over his notes in the vestry before he began the Sunday morning service, and Charlotte could see that her mother was concerned. The Reverend Bernard Hayes expected his wife and daughter to be there before his flock arrived, and she knew that he would be annoyed. If only I hadn't mislaid my gloves, she thought as she saw the sweat stand out on her mother's forehead, but it was too late to worry about it now, so they hurried on.

Once inside the small church, Charlotte blinked and slowed her steps as she allowed her eyes to adjust. After the bright June sunshine, the church appeared dark and dismal. As they walked down the aisle, people nodded towards them and Charlotte managed to raise a weak smile. No doubt there was yet another boring hour ahead as her father preached about the fire and brimstone that awaited them all, should they stray from the paths of righteousness. Still, she was used to it by now so she sat down without protest at her mother's side in the front pew that was always reserved for them.

A few moments later, Reverend Hayes appeared from the vestry and after casting a glare in their direction, took his place in the pulpit. The church became quiet as he spread his hands and gazed towards heaven with a gentle smile on his face. He then looked towards the congregation and Charlotte stared down at her hands, trying to switch off from it all as her father's voice sliced through the silence and the service began.

When it was over at last, Charlotte and her mother took their places at the church door beside the Reverend as he shook hands with his flock.

'Thank you, Father, that were a lovely service,' old Mrs Hilly told him as he grasped her hand and pumped it up and down. 'And just *look* at your little Charlotte. She ain't so little now an' she's turning into a right beauty, ain't she?'

His lips momentarily tightened, but then he answered cordially enough, 'Yes, they grow up so quickly, don't they, Mrs Hilly? Peace be with you, goodbye.'

Charlotte avoided his eyes as Mrs Hilly tripped past her, but she could feel the disapproval coming off him in waves. Her father could not seem to handle the fact that she was growing up and forming her own opinions, and lately the atmosphere between them had been hostile, to say the least. But she could hardly stop herself from becoming a young woman, could she? She couldn't remain a child forever.

Fifteen minutes later, everyone had gone and the smile slipped from her father's face as he addressed her mother. 'I think you should go and see to the dinner now, Hilary. I have a few things to attend to in the vestry but I shall be along shortly.'

'Yes, dear, of course,' she answered. 'It's roast lamb today – your favourite.' She always tried so hard to please him but he always managed to find something to complain about. Either the meat was overcooked or undercooked or the vegetables were too firm or too soft. Charlotte sometimes wondered why her mother didn't just tell him to cook his own dinner. She made to move on too, but the man caught her arm and told her sharply, 'Just mind you help your mother now. And no slipping out. I expect the family to sit down for their meal together on Sunday. It is not a day for gallivanting about, miss!'

Charlotte opened her mouth to say that the only place she ever went to was her friend Babs's house, where they helped each other with their homework, or to visit her grandmother, but thinking better of it she

4

clamped her lips shut again. There was no point in trying to argue with him. The Reverend Hayes was always right – or at least he thought he was.

'Come along, dear.' Seeing her daughter's set face, her mother gently prodded her out into the bright sunshine. 'Let's get dinner out of the way and then perhaps your father will let you go to see Granny.'

Charlotte plodded along at her side without uttering a word and once inside the vicarage she removed her hat and gloves as her mother scuttled towards the kitchen.

'Don't forget to put those neatly away in your room,' Mrs Hayes threw over her shoulder. 'You know your father hates the place to be untidy.'

Charlotte's eyes stretched wide. *Untidy!* The whole place was spotless, so much so that she often teased her mother that she could have eaten her dinner off the floor. Even so she clumped up the stairs to her bedroom and shoved the gloves and hat into a drawer in her dressing-table. Glancing around the room, she sighed. Even in her own private room she was never allowed to leave a thing out of place. Compared to some of the sprawling vicarages that had been built in the last century, this one was modest. Even so, her mother never seemed to stop cleaning and panicked if everything wasn't just so.

The only room that Mrs Hayes wasn't allowed into was her husband Bernard's dark room. It was a small room that led off his study and no one but himself was allowed in there. He was passionate about photography and liked to develop his own film. Most of the photographs were of wild birds and flowers, and Charlotte had to admit that some of them were stunning. Her mother had dotted them around the vicarage in frames and they had gone a small way towards brightening the place up a little. Her father was inordinately proud of them and showed them off to visiting parishioners at every opportunity. Two of them had even found their way into her own room. One was of a robin digging in the snow and the other was of a family of baby blackbirds feeding on the lawn.

Usually the photographs could make Charlotte smile but today she frowned as her eyes settled on them, and slumping down onto the stool, she gazed towards the open window. It was a beautiful day and she knew that her friends from school would be going for a walk this afternoon. She wished that she could go with them, but knew it would be pointless to ask for permission. Her father considered Barbara, or Babs as she preferred to be called, to be a hussy, ever since he had seen her walking home from school one day hand-in-hand with Tim Hancock from their class.

Babs was Charlotte's best friend, although Charlotte often wondered why Babs even bothered with her. Most of the other girls in her class had given up. They thought she was a snob because Charlotte always turned down invitations to their parties, and because her father was a vicar. Of course, it wasn't from choice, it was because her father wouldn't allow her to go out to socialise, but Charlotte was too proud to explain, and so she tended to keep herself very much to herself.

At that moment, a small bird landed on her bedroom windowsill. 'You don't know how lucky you are,' Charlotte muttered enviously to it. 'It must be so nice to be able to just fly away to anywhere you choose.' She sat watching the tiny creature as it hopped from foot to foot, and once it had flown away she went down to the kitchen to help her mother put the finishing touches to their meal.

It was later that afternoon, when all the dishes had been washed and dried and put away into their proper places that Charlotte dared to ask, 'Would it be all right if I went to visit Granny now, Father? It's such a lovely afternoon, I'd enjoy the walk.'

Looking up from the Bible, which was spread across his lap, he frowned. 'I dare say you may. But I expect you to be back here promptly at five o'clock for your tea. And make sure it is only your Granny's you go to.'

Charlotte bit back a hasty retort. Where else did he think she was going to sidle off to? But she didn't say it. He'd given permission for her to go out for a couple of hours and if she cheeked him she would end up spending the time shut in her room.

'Thank you, Father. I shall be back on time, honestly.' She flashed a smile at her mother who was sitting darning some of Bernard's socks and then shot from the room to get her hat and gloves before he had the chance to change his mind. It wouldn't be the first time he'd done it and she didn't want to give him any excuse to today.

Once clear of the vicarage, the girl heaved a sigh of relief and snatched her hat off, then humming happily to herself she tripped along. Her granny lived a short distance away in a little cottage in Marston Lane and once it came into sight Charlotte immediately felt lighter. Her granny's cottage was the last in a small row, and as usual the garden was a blaze of colour. She opened the gate and set off up the path as the scent of the flowers assailed her, and seconds later she burst into the front room with a broad smile on her face. Her granny was sitting in her rocking chair at the side of the open window with a magazine spread on her lap, and when her eyes lit on Charlotte she beamed.

'Why, this is a lovely surprise,' she said happily. 'But you look all hot an' sweaty, pet. Why don't you sit yerself down while I get you a nice cold drink o' lemonade an' then you can tell me all about what's goin' on at home.'

Kitty Mayoll hauled herself out of the chair, sending the magazine clattering to the floor, but she didn't stoop to pick it up. The cottage was always clean but rarely tidy, which was one of the things Charlotte loved about going there. She didn't have to worry about sitting correctly and not creasing the cushions at Granny's.

Kitty soon scuttled back and pressed a glass into Charlotte's hand before asking, 'So how are things then? An' how is yer mam?'

'Oh, things aren't too bad, and Mum is fine,' Charlotte answered cagily as she sipped at her drink.

'Hmm. Well, I'll believe you but thousands wouldn't.' Kitty frowned as she crossed her arms over her skinny chest.

Charlotte knew that her granny worried about her mum and so she tried to put her mind at rest. Kitty made no secret of the fact that she didn't like the man her daughter had chosen to marry, although she thanked him in her prayers every single day for this granddaughter he had given her. Whenever she looked at Charlotte she saw her daughter Hilary at that age, and she often showed Charlotte photos of her mum.

'You are her double,' she would tell her with a smile, 'an' there weren't a prettier or a happier girl on two legs than our Hilary – till she met that stuck-up bugger. Come here an' swept her off her feet, so he did, an' nothin' I said would change her mind about him. I warned her, "He'll always make you feel as if he married below himself" – an' ain't I been proved right time an' time again? He has her runnin' around after him like a skivvy! Still, it ain't all bad. At least he gave me you.'

She would lean over then and kiss Charlotte affectionately and the girl's heart would melt. She really loved her granny, oh she *did*, and sometimes, even more of late, she felt as if the woman was the only bright spot in her life.

'An' how's that nice little friend of yours – Babs, ain't it?' Granny asked now and Charlotte's face darkened instantly.

'Father doesn't want me to mix with her any more because he saw her walking home from school holding Tim Hancock's hand,' she confided.

'Huh! Why, I ain't never heard anythin' so downright soft,' Granny scoffed. 'It's normal for a young lass that age to get herself a boyfriend. Why, she'll be leavin' school soon. It's only a pity that he don't let you out an' about a bit more.' Glancing at Charlotte's clothes she tutted. 'An' it's about time he treated you to a few more modern clothes an' all,' she commented. 'How about I take you out and buy you a couple of new outfits?'

'I'd love you to,' Charlotte said quickly, 'but I don't think Father would let me wear them. You know what he's like.'

'Oh, I know all right.' Kitty pursed her lips.

Bernard Hayes was fifteen years older than her daughter and had come to Bedworth as the vicar of St Sebastian's when her Hilary had been just seventeen years old. He had instantly charmed his parishioners and had had much the same effect on her daughter. It broke her heart when she thought of it now. Back then, Hilary had looked much as Charlotte did now; tall, slim with natural blonde hair and blue eyes the colour of periwinkles. She had been an outgoing, funloving girl with a zest for life and Kitty was convinced that she could have had any man she set her eye on. But there was something about the handsome older vicar that had appealed to her, and nothing Kitty or Sid, her father, could say managed to sway her decision to marry him.

Kitty's eyes misted as she thought of her beloved Sid. He had been dead for four years now but she still missed him every single day. The placid one in their relationship, he had spent hours patiently pointing out to their daughter what a different life she would lead as a vicar's wife. But Hilary would not listen, and she had married Bernard shortly after her eighteenth birthday. At first Kitty had dared to hope that she might have been wrong about her son-in-law. Hilary had seemed happy and content for a time, but then she suddenly stopped wearing make-up and had her wonderful blonde hair cut short.

Kitty had been devastated. 'But why ever did you do it, love?' she had cried as she fingered the young woman's shorn curls.

Hilary had jerked away from her as if she had been scalded. 'Bernard prefers it like this,' she had informed her tetchily. 'He doesn't think long flowing locks look right on a vicar's wife and of course he's quite right.'

Kitty had held her tongue but next had come the change in the clothes her daughter wore. Gone were the bright colours she had always favoured and in their place she took to wearing long tweedy skirts and up-to-the-neck twinsets that disguised her beautiful figure.

'I'll tell you now, even *I* wouldn't wear some o' the get-ups she's walking around in,' Kitty had complained to her husband.

Sid had puffed quietly on his pipe before saying sensibly, 'Well, me old gel, she's a married woman now an' she won't go thankin' you if you start stickin' your nose in.'

'Hmph!' Kitty had glared back at him but she hadn't argued because she knew deep down that he was quite right. It still hurt though, to see her lovely girl grow so frumpy.

Hilary was the couple's only child and the apple of her mother's eye. And now it seemed that Bernard was beginning to follow the same tack with Charlotte. Whilst she had been a little girl she had been his princess, he would stroke and pet her and sit her on his lap, but now that she was growing into a young woman, Kitty was sure that he would have locked her away if he could. And the worst of it was, there was not a thing that Kitty could do about it. It was then that an idea came to her . . .

'Have you given any thought to what you might like to do when you finish school?' she asked cautiously.

Charlotte had been staring out across the rolling fields in front of the cottage but now she put her head to one side as she considered.

'Not really,' she admitted. 'I think Father expects me to stay at home and help Mum with the chores.'

'Hmm. Well, that wouldn't be much of a life for a young girl,' Kitty said in her usual forthright way. 'How about goin' into nursin'? The thing is, yer grandad left me wi' far more tucked away than I'll ever need, an' I could support you through the trainin'.'

'Oh, I couldn't let you do that, Granny,' Charlotte told her immediately.

'Why not? What else am I goin' to spend me money on?' Kitty retorted. 'I lead a quiet life, as you well know, an' me needs are few. Yer grandad would have been tickled pink if he knew that some o' what he left me was goin' to you. Will you at least think about it? Put the idea to yer mam, but not while *he's* in the room, eh?'

'All right,' Charlotte agreed as she reached over to give her granny a hug, and they then spent the rest of the afternoon talking of other things.

Chapter Two

Charlotte left her gran's at half past four, allowing herself plenty of time to get home. She knew that her father only needed the slightest excuse to stop her visiting the old lady and had no intention of making him angry. The vicarage was less than a fifteen-minute walk away, so she strolled along without haste, deep in thought as she considered her granny's suggestion. A nurse. The idea was appealing, and the more she thought of it, the more excited she became. Surely even Reverend Hayes couldn't object to that career. Nurses were highly regarded, weren't they? And it was a very respectable occupation. She decided she would talk to her mother about it at the first opportunity and her spirits began to lift. She had been dreading leaving school and being stuck in the vicarage all the time, helping out at rummage sales and being at her father's beck and call all the while.

'Lottie!'

The shout made her head snap around, and she saw Babs and Tim hurrying towards her, their hands entwined and broad smiles on their faces. She had known even without turning round that it was Babs. Apart from her granny, Babs was the only one who ever shortened Charlotte's name, which was one of the many reasons why her father was so strongly opposed to the girl.

'*Lottie* indeed!' he had snarled, the first time he had heard Babs address his daughter as such. 'It's so common. Had I wished you to be called Lottie, I would have christened you as such. But then I suppose I should not expect any better from the likes of *her*. She's been dragged up.'

'That's not a very Christian remark to make, Father,' Charlotte had dared to say indignantly and his eyes had blazed with such anger that she had shuddered.

'How *dare* you answer me back, young lady!' he had snapped. 'Have I not raised you with sufficient manners to know that you do not cheek your elders?'

'Sorry, Father,' Charlotte had muttered, keeping her eyes downcast. But she wasn't sorry, not really. She was seething that he could be so judgemental. Babs came from a poor family – it was common knowledge – and Charlotte would have expected her father to have a little more compassion. He was a vicar, after all, and surely they should love *all* mankind?

She tried not to think of it now as Babs skidded to a halt in front of her in a fragrant cloud of Chanel No. 5. She wore a pretty flowered dress that was cinched in tight at the waist and then flowed into a full skirt that reached to mid-calf. The dress had a large collar and wide shoulder-pads, and her hair was done in a bouffant that made Babs look much older than she actually was.

Charlotte cringed as she glanced down at her own drab outfit, and it was then that she noticed Harry, Babs's older brother, ambling along behind her. She instantly felt a flush rise to her cheeks as she fingered her own old-fashioned ponytail. Harry was seventeen years old and ridiculously handsome. He seemed to tower above her, and his dark curly hair, which was heavy with Brylcreem, and his sparkling blue eyes gave him the look of a gypsy. She felt the flush deepen as he grinned at her cheekily.

'So, the old gaffer's let you out, 'as he?' he teased.

'Leave her alone, Harry,' Babs scolded as she took Charlotte's hand. 'Take no notice of him,' she said. 'He's only peeved because you won't go out with him. He's used to the girls queuing up for a date.' And then, 'What are you doing out anyway? I thought His Lordship would 'ave you Bible readin".'

Charlotte couldn't help but chuckle – Babs's sense of humour was very infectious. 'I've just been to see Granny actually,' she explained.

'Well, why don't you come for a walk then?' Babs urged.

Charlotte shook her head regretfully. 'I'd love to, but if I'm not back for five I'll be kept in for a week.'

Babs looked at her sympathetically. She sometimes wondered how Charlotte survived living under such a strict regime, but no doubt a vicar's daughter was supposed to be perfect, if there was such a thing.

12

'Suit yourself,' she responded with a shrug. 'We're off for a walk in the woods, ain't we, Tim? See you tomorrow at school.'

Charlotte watched them go, wishing with all her heart that she could join them, but then, very aware that the time was slipping by, she hurried on her way.

Her mother was in the kitchen preparing a salad when she got in, and after glancing around to make sure that her father wasn't about, Charlotte made up her mind to speak.

'Oh hello, dear,' Hilary smiled, but before she could say any more, Charlotte blurted out, 'Granny asked me what I thought of making nursing my career.'

'Oh . . . did she?' Hilary looked slightly alarmed. 'But I thought you were going to help me and your father with church duties once you left school?'

'Oh, *Mum*,' Charlotte groaned and sank onto one of the chairs arranged around the kitchen table. 'It's you and Father who have assumed that – but I want to *do* something with my life. Granny said she would support me while I did my training, if money is a problem. What do you think?'

'Well, I haven't had much time to think about it, have I? You've taken me a bit by surprise,' Hilary said. 'But I have to admit it would be a good profession to go into. I do think you need to give it a little more thought though. You don't become a fully trained nurse overnight and there's a lot of work to be done if that's what you decide you really want to do.'

Charlotte pouted. She had hoped that her mother would be all for it, but in fairness she supposed she should give her a little time to get used to the idea.

'Just saying I *did* decide that's what I wanted to do, do you think Father would allow it?' she asked.

Hilary paused in the act of slicing up a cucumber. 'I don't know the answer to that, Charlotte,' she said truthfully. 'We would have to talk to him about it – but not until you're absolutely sure this is what you *really* want. You don't do things like this on a whim. But come on now – help me get this all through to the dining room. The evening service starts in an hour and a half, and we don't want to keep your father waiting.'

13

Charlotte rolled her eyes at the thought of having to sit through yet another boring sermon, but nevertheless she lifted the dish of salad and did as she was told.

Once her daughter had disappeared off into the dining room, Hilary chewed on her lip. Charlotte was the one bright spot in her life and she actually liked the idea of her becoming a nurse. At least it would get her away from her father's cold temper and unreasonable behaviour. Every time she looked at Charlotte she saw herself at that age. She had been ambitious too back then, but Bernard had soon knocked all that out of her. Her thoughts drifted back to when she had first met him. He had been so handsome, and being considerably older than her he had appeared so worldly. He had treated her like a princess – as if she was made of the most fragile china – and she had enjoyed the attention. After the boys her own age he seemed so clever and sophisticated, and she had believed that they would live happily ever after. She remembered her wedding day, floating down the aisle on her father's arm in a froth of white lace and Bernard standing waiting for her at the altar with a gentle smile on his face . . . She had felt sure that she would burst with happiness that day but—

'Mum, Father's coming down the path! Is everything ready?' When Charlotte's voice interrupted her reverie, Hilary started and, snatching up the plate of sliced ham, she hurried towards the dining room. Bernard had been over at the church supervising the boys' choir practice, but the second he set foot through the door he would expect his meal to be ready and waiting.

'Coming!' she shouted, and everything else was forgotten for now as she hastened to put the finishing touches to the meal.

It was much later that evening, when Charlotte was helping her mother to wash up the supper pots, that she dared to raise the subject of nursing again.

'I've been thinking really hard about what Granny suggested,' she began tentatively. 'And the more I think about it, the more I like the idea. Would you talk to Father about it for me?'

In actual fact, Hilary had been thinking about it too and now she nodded. 'I will, but let me choose the right moment,' she responded.

'Huh! When *is* the right time with Father?' Charlotte chirped sarcastically, but when she saw the corners of her mother's mouth turn down she was instantly contrite. 'Sorry, Mum,' she apologised. 'But you know what I mean. He's so . . . Well, set in his ways, I suppose. Granny says . . .'

She reddened and her voice trailed away as Hilary lifted her hands from the hot soapy water to stare at her curiously. 'And just *what* does Granny say?'

'She er . . . she said that she doesn't know how you've put up with him all these years and she's surprised that you haven't left him,' Charlotte eventually told her.

'Look, I know Granny means well but you don't just walk away from a marriage,' Hilary said quietly. There was so much more she could have told her daughter but she never would.

Realising that she had probably said too much, Charlotte changed the subject. 'I saw Mr Mason as I was leaving the church this evening. He asked to be remembered to you.'

'Oh. That was nice of him.'

Charlotte stared at her mother curiously. She seemed flustered all of a sudden. 'Granny said that you and Brian Mason were going out together when you met Father. Is that right?'

'Seems to me that Granny has been saying quite a lot,' Hilary said, more sharply than she had intended. 'Yes, I suppose we were seeing each other . . . but that was a very long time ago now.'

'Well, he must have thought a lot of you because he's never married, has he?'

'I'm sure that has nothing to do with me.' Hilary was getting more uncomfortable by the minute. 'I expect he just never met anyone that he wanted to marry enough.'

'Perhaps he wanted to marry *you*,' Charlotte persisted, and at this Hilary slammed another plate into the water, sending soap suds flying everywhere.

'If you don't mind, Charlotte, it's been a long day and I'm really not in the mood for this. I think you have been reading too many of those silly romance magazines. Woe betide you if your father finds you with your head buried in one.'

Sensing that she had upset her mother, Charlotte finished the pots and headed for her bedroom where she sat staring across the lawns of the vicarage garden with her chin in her hands. She wished that her mother *had* married Brian Mason. He was such a nice man and always had a kind word and a smile on his face. She wondered if Hilary regretted the choice she had made. According to Granny, Brian had thought the world of her and had been devastated when she left him for the handsome vicar.

It was funny, now that she came to think of it. Until recently, Granny had never said a bad word about her father, although Charlotte had always sensed that she wasn't at all keen on him. It was only since she herself had begun to confide in her about how strict he was with her and her mum, that old Mrs Mayoll had opened up to her.

If only her father would agree to her nursing training – oh, how wonderful that would be! It would open up a whole new world for her. She would have to leave home while she was training, Charlotte thought dreamily, and then she would be able to put on a little make-up and have some fashionable clothes, the sort that her friends wore – when she wasn't in uniform, that was.

Crossing to the dressing-table mirror, she surveyed herself critically. Granny had always told her that she was pretty but Charlotte always felt so dowdy. Pulling at the ribbon at the nape of her neck, she allowed her hair to fall free around her shoulders. It actually looked quite nice when it was loose but her father always insisted that she wore it tied back. She must be sedate and respectable at all times, as befitted the daughter of a vicar. It had been drummed into her for so long now that she had never really questioned it. Until recently that was, and now there were times when she felt quite resentful towards him. She was never allowed to go out with her friends. Not even allowed to have a record player so that she could listen to modern music. Babs was absolutely mad on Bill Haley and The Comets, but her father said that that sort of music was sinful.

It was as she was sitting there that she saw her father walk across the lawn. He let himself out through the small gate that was a short cut into the cemetery, and then she saw him striding towards the church. He had changed out of his vestments now and was dressed in a smart suit, only his dog collar setting him apart from any other man. At the same time she saw young Andrew Pinnington heading towards the church door too, dragging his feet. Andrew was the soloist in the boys' choir and could do no wrong in her father's eyes. 'He has the voice of an angel,' her father would tell them proudly. 'And with my coaching he could go far.'

Sighing, Charlotte turned away and began to get ready for bed. She was actually thankful for the time her father spent with Andrew. At least it kept him out of the way.

'There's a dance on at the village hall this Saturday,' Babs told Charlotte excitedly as they walked to school together the next day. 'Do you think your dad might let you come? You could stay at my house for the night and I could lend you something to wear.'

'No chance,' Charlotte muttered resentfully. 'You know what he's like.'

'Well, I think he's bein' unreasonable,' Babs said crossly. 'He might as well put a ball an' chain round yer ankles, the way he keeps you in.'

Deeply embarrassed, Charlotte remained silent. There seemed no point in denying it. What Babs had said was true, but what could she do about it?

By the time she trooped out of school that afternoon she was deeply depressed. During break and the lunch-hour, all the other girls had talked about was the upcoming dance and what they were planning to wear, and Charlotte felt severely left out of it.

'So what's up wi' you then?' her granny asked when she popped in to see her on the way home. 'You look like you've lost a bob an' found a sixpence.'

Charlotte knew that she would be in trouble for getting in late but she was past caring. 'There's a dance on at the village hall on Saturday, and Babs has asked me if I'd like to go. She even told me that I could stay at her house for the night,' she told her glumly. 'But there would be no point in asking Father if I'd be allowed. I know what the answer would be.'

'Hmm.' Kitty tapped her lip thoughtfully with her forefinger. 'Perhaps there *is* a way you could go,' she said after a moment.

Charlotte's eyes lit up with hope. 'How?' she asked.

Kitty sighed. 'Well, I know it's dishonest, but a little white lie never hurt nobody. What if I was to say I wasn't feeling too well and I wanted you to spend the night here with me? I'm sure your mam would agree to that, then you could come back here after the dance and stay in the spare room. There's no reason they need ever be any the wiser.'

Charlotte gulped. Could it work? What if someone saw her and told her father? But then the alternative was not to go, and perhaps the risk would be worth it.

'But it doesn't feel right for you to have to lie for me, and Father probably wouldn't let me come here anyway,' she said wretchedly.

Kitty laughed. 'It wouldn't be the first time I'd fibbed, and believe me, he'll let you come,' she assured her. 'Just think – how would it look if he didn't let you keep an eye on your old granny when she was ill? It wouldn't seem very Christian if word got out, would it? And why shouldn't you go out with your friends now and again? If he weren't so bloody strict there wouldn't be any need to lie. You just get off now and keep in his good books for the rest of the week an' leave everythin' up to me.'

Charlotte kissed her soundly on the cheek before racing out and hurrying home with a spring in her step.

It was late on Saturday morning when her mother called her into the kitchen to tell her, 'I've just been round to see your granny, Charlotte, and she's a bit off-colour. I think she may have caught this horrible summer flu bug that's flying around. Anyway, she asked if you might be allowed to go and keep her company tonight. Because she's not feeling well she doesn't fancy being on her own. Would you mind very much?'

'Not at all,' Charlotte answered, keeping her eyes averted from her mother's. 'I could go round there now if you like, and come home in the morning.' She hated lying to her mother, but what else could she do if she wanted to go to the dance? She had already told Babs that she would be going, and her friend had almost swooned with shock.

'Right – then go and pack an overnight bag and get off,' Hilary smiled. 'Thanks, pet. And don't worry – I'll clear it with your father.'

18

Charlotte flew up the stairs as if there were wings on her feet, hardly able to believe that she was really going to her very first dance. It seemed too good to be true and she just wanted to get away before Reverend Hayes returned home. He had been out to visit one of his sick parishioners and she knew that he might be back at any minute. Even if one of his flock was dying he rarely missed a meal.

Once on the landing upstairs she sped past first her mother's room and then her father's. It was only as she had grown older that she had wondered why they slept apart. From what she had heard at school, all the other girls' parents slept together. It didn't really worry her though. In fact, she could quite understand why her mother didn't want to sleep with him. He treated her more like a servant than a wife.

When she entered the kitchen a short time later with a small overnight case in her hand, Charlotte kissed her mother. She thought she detected a twinkle in her mum's eye and wondered briefly if Kitty had confided in her. But she didn't stop to ask. She was too afraid of something going wrong and as she skipped out of the back door she didn't feel a single pang of guilt. This would be *her* night and she was determined to enjoy every single second of it.

Chapter Three

As she hurried past the Old Royal Oak in Collycroft that evening, Charlotte's heart was in her mouth. She expected her father to leap out at her at any minute, but soon she was knocking on the door of Babs's home in Nuneaton Road. It was flung open by the girl's mother, Ivy, who ushered her inside with a welcoming smile. It was like stepping into another world. Babs's younger brother was sprawled across the floor engrossed in a jigsaw, and Harry was lounging in an easy chair with a Woodbine cigarette dangling out of the corner of his mouth. The whole room was disorganised chaos and yet the atmosphere was light.

'Babs is upstairs in her room, love,' Ivy informed her. 'She said as you were comin' here to get ready. Why don't yer go on up to her? Yer know the way. I've got to get a shufty on meself.' She patted her head, which was full of metal curlers, making her flowered wrap-around apron strain across her enormous stomach. 'Me an' Ada from down the road are off to Bingo tonight. That's if that bloody husband o' mine gets back in time to watch the little 'un. I dare say the bugger is still in the Cricketers Arms engrossed in a game o' dominoes. I sometimes wonder why he don't just set up home there. But then I shouldn't grumble. At least he never misses a shift at work an' me housekeepin' money is always on the table regular as clockwork every pay day.'

She lifted a plump arm and idly scratched beneath one of her huge bosoms. Charlotte nodded and sidled past her. Harry had given her no more than a cursory glance and she was grateful for that at least. He usually loved to flirt with her and tease her, but it appeared he'd lost interest now.

She picked her way through the clutter of dirty clothes, newspapers and magazines that were piled on either side of the staircase and seconds later she walked into Babs's bedroom.

Babs's hair was as dark as Charlotte's was fair, and whilst Charlotte was tall and slim, Babs was small and more rounded. She was already dressed and ready to go, and she grinned as Charlotte walked in.

'I've sorted an outfit out for you,' she gabbled as a welcome. 'I don't think any of my dresses would fit yer but I reckon this skirt will.' She pointed to a skirt hanging on the door of an old mahogany wardrobe. 'If it's a bit big round the waist we can always pin it,' she rushed on. 'An' I thought this top would suit you a treat. We can tuck it into the waistband, see?' She gathered the waist of the blouse to show her and crossing to her friend she led her to a stool and unceremoniously plonked her down on it.

'First things first, though. We'll do yer hair an' yer make-up, then you can get into yer glad rags.' She tugged the ribbon from the back of Charlotte's hair and taking up a hairbrush, began to furiously backcomb it. Once or twice Charlotte tried to peep in the mirror, but each time Babs yanked her head away. She was obviously enjoying herself immensely. 'Now – no peepin' till yer done,' she insisted with a giggle.

Ten minutes later, she sprayed Charlotte's hair with lacquer, then stood back and with her head to one side, eyed her critically. 'That should do it,' she said. 'Now let's get crackin' on yer make-up.'

Taking up a tube of Max Factor's Pan Stik, she grinned at Charlotte's horrified expression. 'Don't worry, yer won't need much wi' your lovely skin. I won't make you look like a clown, I promise. Just a bit o' this, a touch of eyeshadow an' mascara an' some lippy, an' you'll look smashin'.'

At last she sighed with satisfaction before saying bossily, 'Right, let's get you into this outfit now. The only problem is you're a shoe size bigger than me so you'll either have to squeeze yer toes into these high heels, else wear those you've got on.'

'I'll squeeze into them,' Charlotte said immediately, glancing with contempt at the dull flat black ones she had been wearing. Ten more minutes and the transformation was complete.

'*Now* you can look.'

Babs twisted the mirror and Charlotte saw a complete stranger staring back at her. Was that really her? The tight waist of the full skirt and shoulder-pads in the blouse gave her an hour-glass figure, and the high heels made her look as if her legs went on forever. Her hair was backcombed on top, making her look inches taller, and Babs had styled it into an elegant pleat on the back of her head. The make-up made her look older too, and suddenly she felt very grown-up and rather self-conscious. She looked at least eighteen years old rather than just fifteen, and if her father could see her now she knew he would have a fit.

'*Wow!*' she gasped.

Babs chuckled. 'All we have to do now is get ourselves off to the dance. Tim's going to meet me there so get a move on an' stop admirin' yerself.'

When they clattered downstairs and entered the small sitting room, Harry's eyes almost popped out of his head. He let out a long, appreciative wolf-whistle, which had Charlotte blushing furiously.

'Blimey O'Riley!' he exclaimed. 'I was plannin' on goin' to the flicks tonight, but wi' you lookin' like that I reckon I'll come along to the dance.'

'You just leave the lass alone an' stick to girls yer own age, me lad,' his mother scolded as she smeared on a thick layer of lipstick in the nicotine-stained mirror above the tiled fireplace. She then looked at Charlotte admiringly. 'Yer look a fair treat, love,' she smiled. 'Our Babs has got a real flair when it comes to hair an' make-up. I've put a word in fer her already at the local hairdressers fer when she leaves school. But you two get off now an' enjoy yourselves – but don't be too late, mind.'

Charlotte felt like a princess as she floated along the street at the side of Babs. She had never felt like this before in her whole life and was sure she would die of excitement.

There was already a queue of young people outside the hall when they got there and the two girls tacked onto the back of it. Charlotte was receiving more than a few admiring glances and could hardly wait to go in. From inside they could hear the group tuning up their instruments and when the doors were opened promptly at seven o'clock she followed Babs eagerly.

Babs nudged her as her eyes scanned the room, 'So what do you want to drink then?' she asked.

'To drink?'

Babs laughed. 'Yes, how about a Babycham or a Cherry B?' She nodded towards the bar in the corner of the room where people were already queuing.

'But we're not old enough to drink alcohol,' Charlotte whispered with a frown.

'Who's to know how old we are, dolled-up like this?' Babs grabbed her hand and dragged her towards the bar, and minutes later Charlotte had her first taste of a Babycham.

The band was playing by then and Babs's foot was tapping in time to the beat. 'So what do you think of it then?'

Charlotte's smile stretched from ear to ear. 'It's quite nice.' She took another sip, enjoying the way it warmed her throat as it went down. 'It's not much different to lemonade really.'

'You won't think that when you've had two or three,' Babs chuckled. 'But come on – let's have a dance, eh?'

Charlotte just had time to balance her drink on the edge of the table before Babs dragged her onto the dance floor, and before she knew it they were moving to the beat. The lights were dimmed and the music throbbed, and soon she was enjoying herself immensely. She had been afraid that she wouldn't know how to jive, never having done it before except in the privacy of her room, but it was easy enough to follow what Babs was doing. Within minutes, Tim and one of his friends came to join them, and Charlotte blushed prettily as her new partner twirled her round with an appreciative expression on his face. At the end of that number, another young man appeared to take his place and Charlotte found herself suddenly very popular. Babs watched what was going on with an amused twinkle in her eye, pleased to see her friend enjoying herself so much, but eventually she took Charlotte's hand and yanked her off the dance floor, much to the annoyance of the young man who was awaiting his turn.

'Phew, it's gettin' hot in here,' she panted. 'Come on, let's have another drink. It's Tim's round. You can try a Cherry B this time.'

They were standing by the bar sipping their drinks when Charlotte glanced up to see Harry sauntering towards her. Her heart skipped a beat. His lovely dark hair was slicked back and he looked very handsome. She was aware of girls' heads turning to watch his progress and she gulped at her drink feeling totally out of her depth. What was she supposed to say to him? She needn't have worried though because Harry had enough to say for the both of them.

'Hello, gorgeous.' His eyes raked up and down her. 'How about another drink?'

'I've just had—' But he was already heading for the bar, so she fell silent as Tim led Babs onto the dance floor for a slow number.

Harry was back in seconds and he pressed yet another glass into her hand.

'What is it?' she asked dubiously. It didn't look anything like the Babycham or the Cherry B she had already tried.

'It's a G and T.' He grinned as he took a long swallow of his beer. Believing that it would be rude not to try it, Charlotte sipped at the drink. She was feeling curiously light-headed by now and as if she didn't have a care in the world, which at that moment in time she didn't. Harry waited until she had finished it, then as another slow song began he led her onto the dance floor and she found herself pressed tightly against him. Her heart began to beat faster as she leaned her head on his shoulder, smelling soap and aftershave.

'Did I tell you yet that you look stunning tonight?' he muttered into her hair, and her heart beat faster still. 'How about we go outside and get a bit of fresh air?'

Charlotte nodded, suddenly feeling a bit nauseous, and she let him lead her towards the exit like a lamb to the slaughter. There were a number of young people outside, smoking and laughing. Others were standing in the shadows of the hall with their arms around each other.

'I er . . . I don't feel so well,' Charlotte mumbled, and suddenly she leaned over and was violently sick into a nearby hedge.

'Oh *great*,' Harry snorted as he stood well back from her. 'How many drinks have you had?'

'Th-three.' Everything was spinning now and Charlotte leaned heavily against the wall, sure that she was going to die.

'Three, eh? And have you ever had a drink before?' Harry sounded mildly amused.

'N-no.'

'All right. Stay there an' I'll go and tell Babs I'm going to take you home. The best thing you can do now is sleep it off.'

As he strode away, Charlotte cursed beneath her breath. Trust her to go and make a complete idiot of herself. She had been really enjoying the evening, but what would Harry think of her now?

'I'm so sorry,' she said dejectedly when he appeared and took her elbow.

He chuckled. 'Don't worry about it. We all have to start somewhere. But where are you going now? I don't think it would go down too well if the old Vic was to see you in this state.'

'I'm staying at my granny's tonight,' Charlotte told him, still feeling wobbly, and she leaned on him as he began to lead her along.

'Is Babs very angry at me?' she asked ashamedly when they had gone some way. Her legs seemed to have developed a life of their own and she was glad that she had Harry there to support her.

'She's too busy hangin' around Tim's neck to worry about much else,' he assured her. 'Now then, which is yer granny's house?'

'It's that one there.'

When they stopped at the gate, Charlotte looked shyly up at him. 'Thanks for bringing me home, Harry. And I'm sorry if I've spoiled your night.'

'There'll be plenty of others.' He leaned towards her and kissed her cheek and she felt as if she had died and gone to heaven.

''Night, Lottie,' he shouted over his shoulder as he walked away, and she watched him until he was out of sight before turning to enter the cottage.

Kitty's eyebrows rose into her hairline when she saw the way Charlotte was dolled up, but then as the girl tottered unsteadily into the small cosy lounge she became truly concerned.

'Good Lord, whatever happened to you, lass?' she asked. 'Yer look as if you've been pulled through a hedge backwards.'

'Sorry, Granny.' Charlotte sat down heavily on the nearest chair. 'I er . . . I think I had too much to drink.' She expected the old lady to be annoyed with her, but instead Kitty smiled indulgently.

'Well, it happens to all of us at some time or another,' she stated. 'Mebbe next time you'll know to take it a bit slower, eh? Now let me make you a nice cup o' coffee. You look a bit green about the gills.'

As she pottered away, Charlotte's hand rose to finger the cheek that Harry had kissed. He had walked her home and kissed her. Could this mean that he wanted her to be his girl? But then, suddenly, all thoughts of him were wiped out as she clapped her hand across her mouth and shot off to the bathroom as if the devil was at her heels.

Kitty grinned as she watched her granddaughter's retreating figure. She could only imagine what her son-in-law would have said if he had seen the girl in this state. He would probably have kept her locked away for at least a month. But to her mind, young people learned by their mistakes and Charlotte should be allowed to have a little fun, even if she was paying the price for it now. Not that she condoned drinking, of course, but she had a funny feeling that Charlotte would be more careful the next time she got let off the leash. Chuckling to herself, she spooned some Camp coffee into a mug and waited for the girl's return.

When Charlotte came down to breakfast the next morning she was looking grey and more than a little sorry for herself.

'So how are you feelin' today then?' Kitty asked as she expertly flipped the bacon she was frying.

Charlotte grimaced as the smell wafted towards her. 'Not too good,' she admitted. 'I didn't get to sleep for ages. When I lay down, the room started to spin and I daren't close my eyes.'

'That's the demon drink for you,' Kitty answered stoically. 'Now – do you fancy a nice fry-up? You need to get somethin' inside you an' line yer stomach.'

'No thanks,' Charlotte squeaked. 'Perhaps just a slice of dry toast?'

Half an hour later she was dressed and ready to go back to Babs's house. She would need to collect her own clothes before going home, otherwise she would face an inquisition from her father. Actually she was glad of the excuse and excited at the thought of seeing Harry again.

'Thanks for having me, Granny.' She kissed Kitty before asking anxiously, 'You won't mention to Mum that I had a drink, will you?'

'Of course I won't,' Kitty assured her. 'But make sure you're back there in plenty of time for dinner. Your dad will already be narked because you've missed the morning service.'

'I will,' Charlotte promised, and she set off with the items of clothing she had borrowed from Babs the night before safely folded in a brown carrier bag with string handles. She had left her small overnight case at her friend's but had thought to sneak another of her own outfits to her granny's beforehand.

When she arrived at Babs she was disappointed to see no sign of Harry, and as Babs saw her staring about she laughed. 'If you're lookin' fer our Harry, you're out o' luck,' she told her. 'He always goes up the Cricketers of a Sunday mornin' wi' me dad fer a pint before dinner. But never mind that. Did you enjoy goin' to your first dance?'

'Oh yes.' Charlotte's face was animated as she thought back to it. 'I think I overdid it a bit on the drinks though. But anyway, now I've returned your things I ought to get going. You know what my father's like. Thanks, Babs.'

She set off with a spring in her step, wondering when she might be able to wangle another night out.

Chapter Four

It was three weeks later before Charlotte got the chance to escape again. She came home from school one afternoon to find her mother packing a basket of food up.

'Who is that for?' Charlotte asked.

'It's for Granny,' Hilary told her, her face a mask of concern. 'She's had a fall and sprained her ankle, so she's going to need a little help for a while until she can get about properly again. I was hoping you might volunteer, as I'm rather busy at the moment. Your father has a wedding on Saturday and I've got to get all the flowers ready for the church. That's besides getting everything sorted out for the rummage sale on Friday.'

'Of course I'll help – do you want me to take that along to her now?' Charlotte offered.

Her mother nodded and she shot off to get changed. Half an hour later she was at her granny's cottage and she saw instantly that Kitty was not going to be a good patient. She was sitting in a chair with her heavily bandaged foot propped up on a stool, and the moment Charlotte arrived she began to complain.

'I must be goin' senile to trip over like that,' she grumbled.

'Anyone can have an accident,' Charlotte pointed out as she straightened the cushion behind her. 'Now you just sit there and tell me what you need doing. But first I'll pop this cottage pie Mum made you for tea into the oven to warm.'

'Well, the garden will need a good watering for a start-off.' Kitty looked longingly towards the open door. She loved pottering about in her garden and was deeply frustrated.

'Very well, I'll do that first,' Charlotte told her as she came back out of the kitchen.

'Just make sure as you give me roses a good soakin',' Kitty shouted after her.

Charlotte grinned. 'Yes, Granny.'

Later on, when they were sitting sharing the pie that Hilary had cooked, Kitty said, 'You know, we might be able to use this to get you another night out. Seein' as I'm housebound, yer dad might let you stay here again at the weekend – and I don't need you at me beck an' call every minute. There'd be nothin' to stop you goin' to the dance on Saturday night with Babs, would there? I don't want you rollin' in drunk again, mind.'

'Oh, I wouldn't, Granny!' Charlotte promised, as her mind raced ahead. It would be another chance to see Harry and she could hardly wait.

'Right, then in that case I'll have a word with your mum when she comes round in the mornin',' Kitty answered, and for now the subject was dropped.

On Saturday evening, Babs once again worked her magic on Charlotte and when the two girls were finally dolled-up to the nines they set off for the dance arm-in-arm. Up to now there had been no sign of Harry and Charlotte was slightly disappointed.

'Has Harry gone out?' she asked, and wondered why Babs seemed to hesitate before answering her.

'Actually, he's been seein' this girl from All Saints Square fer the last couple o' weeks,' she told her eventually. 'I think her dad has a shop there an' the family live in the flat above it.'

Charlotte felt as if the bottom had dropped out of her world, and seeing her downcast face, Babs squeezed her arm.

'I know you've got a bit of a soft spot for him, but don't worry – none of his girlfriends last fer long,' she said. 'Our Harry is a right ladies' man. One sniff of a petticoat an' he's like a dog after a bitch in heat. But he soon loses interest. If I were you I'd look elsewhere fer a boyfriend. The lads were queuin' up to dance wi' you the last time we went out, so why don't you look a bit further afield?'

'I might just do that,' Charlotte muttered, but she knew that she wouldn't. No one else could hold a candle to Harry as far as she was concerned.

Somehow tonight, the evening didn't seem quite so exciting, especially as she insisted on sticking to soft drinks. But then at just after ten o'clock, Harry strolled in with a very pretty girl hanging on his arm. Charlotte's heart sank and all at once she wanted to go home. Tim had already put in an appearance by now and Babs was so taken with him that Charlotte was sure she wouldn't mind her slipping away.

'Babs?' She shook her friend's arm gently and Bab's turned her attention from Tim to look at her. 'I'm sorry but I've got a bit of a headache. Would you mind if I went home?'

'But the night is young!' Babs looked shocked that anyone would want to go home so early. 'Why don't you go an' stand outside fer a few minutes an' see if that makes you feel better, first.'

Never one to argue or stand up for herself, Charlotte nodded miserably and rising, she picked her way through the tables towards the exit. She had almost reached the door when Harry stopped her.

'You're off early, ain't yer?' He was grinning and Charlotte felt humiliated when she thought of how she had let him walk her home the last time she'd come to the dance. He must be laughing at her now.

'I er . . . I've got a bit of a headache,' she said weakly, then hurried on as her cheeks flamed. Once outside she took great gulps of air and leaned heavily against the wall. She had borrowed Babs's shoes again and her feet were killing her. It was funny now she came to think of it, the last time she'd worn them she'd had such a great time she hadn't even noticed the discomfort.

Suddenly Harry appeared in front of her and placed his hands on the wall on either side of her.

'W-won't your girlfriend wonder where you've gone?' Charlotte stuttered.

He chuckled as he leaned in closer. She could feel his breath on her cheek and was experiencing a feeling that hovered somewhere between panic and ecstasy.

'She ain't me girlfriend,' he whispered. 'Well, not officially anyway . . . but I wish you were.' And then suddenly he kissed her fully on the lips and a thousand fireworks seemed to explode behind her eyes.

When he eventually drew away her legs had turned to jelly and she was afraid that she might just slither down the wall.

'Now then, if you ain't feelin' so good, how about I walk you home? We could go through the park seein' as it's such a nice night.'

Charlotte stared back at him, dumbstruck. Harry had said he wanted her to be his girl. But what would her father say if he ever saw them together? Harry had a bit of a reputation, to say the least. And what would her granny say? She'd been happy enough to wangle things so that Charlotte could come to the dance but she doubted that she'd be very happy to hear that she'd been into the park with a young man.

'All right,' she heard herself say, and tucking her arm through his he began to lead her away.

'Sh-shouldn't I just pop back in and say goodbye to Babs?' she croaked, hardly believing that this was really happening. 'And what about the girl you came with? Won't she wonder where you've gone?'

'Aw, let 'em think what they like,' Harry responded as he swaggered along, so Charlotte fell silent.

Once in the park, Harry led her to a bench and suddenly he was like an octopus with hands everywhere. Charlotte was terrified and delighted all at once as she tried to correct his straying hands. Feelings that she had never known were suddenly springing to life and she didn't know if she was more afraid of him or herself.

'Why don't we go and lie on the grass over by them bushes,' he breathed heavily into her neck, and although she was sorely tempted she shook her head and managed to draw away from him.

'No, I er . . . think I should be getting home now.'

He turned away abruptly and lit a cigarette before shrugging. 'Have it your own way. Will you be all right on your own? I may as well get back to the dance.'

Charlotte had to stifle the urge to cry but she nodded. 'Yes, I'll be fine.'

'Night then.' Harry rose and walked away without looking back, leaving Charlotte to set off alone in the opposite direction feeling totally mortified.

Her granny was listening to the wireless when she got in and she stared at her smudged lipstick with a frown before asking, 'Did you have a good night?' Charlotte seemed very subdued and she sensed that something wasn't quite right.

When the girl merely nodded she went on, 'Come back on your own, did you?'

'Yes. Well, part of the way.' Charlotte avoided her eyes as Kitty continued to stare at her.

'A lad, was it, that walked you the rest of the way?'

Charlotte nodded as Kitty pursed her lips. She'd been expecting this for some time. After all, Charlotte was a pretty girl and she was bound to have the lads after her, dressed up as she was at present. But it would be God help them both if Bernard ever got a whiff of it. 'And who is this lad?' she asked now.

'It was Harry. Babs's brother,' Charlotte admitted in a small voice.

Mrs Mayall looked horrified for a moment before saying, 'Not Harry Bradford? Aw lass, I think you can do a bit better than that. Harry's a right little hell-raiser, always in trouble wi' the police, an' he's had more young lasses than hot dinners. Lads like him are only after one thing, an' you don't need me to spell out what I mean, do yer?'

'Actually he's really nice,' Charlotte shot back defensively. 'He told me he wants me to be his girl.'

'Hmm, till he's had your knickers round yer ankles then he'll drop yer like a ton o' hot bricks,' Kitty snapped. As Charlotte lowered her head, the old lady instantly softened. 'Look, love, I don't mean to be a spoilsport but believe me, he ain't the one fer you. Try castin' yer net a bit wider, eh? An' now come on an' help me up the stairs. We can talk some more in the mornin'. You're back safe an' sound, an' that's all that matters.'

Charlotte helped Kitty up to bed and kissed her goodnight before going to the little bedroom that her granny always kept ready for her. It had been Charlotte's mother's room once, and as Charlotte got undressed she tried to imagine her mother as a young girl. Had she felt about her father as she herself felt about Harry now? It was hard to think of her mum with butterflies in her stomach and all lovesick, but she must have been once. Sighing heavily, she pulled her nightdress over her head, then tweaking down the candlewick bedspread, she clambered into bed and tunnelled beneath the blankets.

Until recently her life had been so straightforward but she was growing up now and at that moment she wasn't sure if she liked it. It had been so much easier being a child.

The next morning, after making sure that her granny was settled in her chair with everything she needed to hand, Charlotte rushed around to Babs's house to collect her things. Her friend was still in bed when she got there and none too pleased at being disturbed.

'What're you doin' here so early?' she growled after her mother had directed Charlotte upstairs.

'Sorry to disturb you but I promised Father I'd be back in time for the morning service.' Charlotte hastily collected her clothes together. Needless to say they were still where she'd left them, along with piles of Babs's clothing. Charlotte wondered how she ever managed to find anything in such a mess, but it didn't seem to bother the other girl in the slightest.

'Right, I'm off now, you go back to sleep,' she told the lump in the bed, and was rewarded with a grunt as she slipped away.

She made it back to the vicarage with only minutes to spare, to find her mother pacing the kitchen.

'Oh, thank goodness you're back,' Hilary sighed with relief. 'Now hurry up and put your hat and gloves on. Your father will be furious if we're late.'

Charlotte grudgingly did as she was told and soon they were seated in the front-row pew in their usual position.

Most of the service went over Charlotte's head as she thought back to the evening before. Should she have let Harry go a little further? Every instinct she had screamed that she had done right – and yet a little part of her had wanted to feel his hands on her breasts. She blushed at her thoughts and tried harder to concentrate on what her father was saying, without any success.

As soon as the service was over, Charlotte and her mother returned to the vicarage to prepare the Sunday lunch, leaving her father talking to an elderly churchgoer at the door. Miss Straight was a spinster, and although she professed to be a devout Christian it was well known that she had a tongue like a viper and enjoyed nothing more than a good gossip.

'I wonder who she's tearing to shreds this morning,' Hilary said as she and Charlotte worked side by side in the kitchen, and then, 'Are you listening to me, Charlotte? You've been miles away ever since you got back. Your granny is OK, isn't she?'

'What? Oh yes, Granny's fine,' Charlotte replied, then mustering up her courage she asked, 'Mum, how old were you when you had your first boyfriend?'

'What a question to ask.' Hilary looked distinctly uncomfortable. 'And why would you want to know that?' Then as she glanced at Charlotte her hands became still and she frowned. '*You* haven't gone and got yourself a boyfriend, have you?'

Charlotte squirmed. 'Not exactly,' she said in a hushed voice. 'But there *is* a boy who would like to go out with me.'

'Oh, I see.' For a moment Hilary was lost for words but then she asked, 'Don't you think you're a little young to be thinking of boys?' Even as she asked the question she felt a complete hypocrite. Charlotte was merely weeks away from being sixteen, and she herself had had at least three or four harmless boyfriends by then, including Brian Mason. He had been The One until Bernard came on the scene, but she tried not to think of what might have been now. It was all in the past. She would have said more, but at that precise moment Bernard stormed into the room with a face like thunder.

'And just where were *you* last night, miss?' he asked threateningly.

Charlotte paled. 'I . . . I was at Granny's – you know I was,' she gulped.

'I know that's where you were *supposed* to be,' he snapped back. 'But Miss Straight just told me that she thought she saw you walking along Nuneaton Road with Barbara Bradford. Was she correct?'

Charlotte's mouth went dry. She had never lied to her father before but now she told him, 'N-no, Father. She must have been mistaken.'

'Hmm. Well, I hope she was because if I thought you were going about with that brazen little hussy I'd lock you up in your room and throw away the key. Nothing good can come from mixing with people like that.'

Charlotte knew that he meant every word he said and she lowered her eyes as she tried to stop her hands from trembling. Her father was a bully of the worst kind – but not in a physical sense. She could never remember him so much as raising a finger to herself or her mother. Somehow she sensed that she could have coped with that, but her father bullied them mentally with harsh words and glares that could have them both quaking in their shoes.

Hilary had remained silent throughout the exchange but now she laid her hand gently on her husband's arm. 'I'm sure Miss Straight must have been mistaken, dear,' she said in a timid voice.

He shook her off roughly. 'Keep out of this, will you! I'll deal with it my way! As for *you*,' he turned his attention back to Charlotte, 'I think I have been remiss in allowing you too much time at your grandmother's. From now on, your mother will have to fit in seeing to her welfare around her church duties.'

'But, Bernard,' Hilary objected, 'there are not enough hours in the day as it is, and Mother so looks forward to seeing Char—'

'Be *quiet*, woman!' he roared. 'And *you* – get to your room.' As he pointed a finger towards the staircase Charlotte shot off like a bullet from a gun. She knew better than to answer her father back. It was when she was halfway up the stairs that for the first time she heard her mother arguing with him.

'Bernard, I think you are being a little harsh with her,' she heard her say – and then there was a sickening thud, and suddenly her mother was silent. Charlotte turned without thinking and ran back down the stairs, and as she entered the room she had just left she was shocked to see her mother with her hand to her cheek and her father standing threateningly over her with his fist raised. Seeing Charlotte seemed to bring him back to his senses and he lowered his fist and strode out of the room as Charlotte rushed to her mother's side.

'Are you all right, Mum? Did he hit you?' She was so shocked she could barely get the words out, and when her mother removed her hand and Charlotte saw the angry red mark on her cheek she began to cry.

'He *did* hit you!' she choked.

They both listened to the front door slam. 'It's my fault, I shouldn't have answered him back,' Hilary mumbled.

'B-but he's never hit you before!'

'Huh! That's what *you* think.' Instantly regretting her words, Hilary placed an arm about her daughter's shoulders. 'Your father doesn't mean it. He just has a short temper,' she said quietly. 'Now forget you ever saw this and go and unpack your bag. He'll be back shortly and we don't want to upset him any more, do we?'

Shocked to the very core, Charlotte shuffled away. She had lived with her father's mental cruelty all her life, but never in her wildest dreams had she believed that he would stoop to hitting either of them. From what her mother had let slip, it wasn't the first time he had been violent towards her, but this time Charlotte had been the cause of it. Suddenly she saw her life stretching ahead of her. Long, empty days living under her father's strict rules with nothing to look forward to. Giving in to despair, she wept bitter tears.

Chapter Five

November 1956

The time since Charlotte had left school had passed slowly. Her days were spent helping her mother to organise the church rummage sales, running errands for those of her father's parishioners who were sick and infirm, and decorating the church with flowers. She rarely got to see Babs any more. Her friend was now happily working at a hairdresser's in Bedworth town centre, and her visits to her granny were limited to once a week.

Sometimes it broke Kitty's heart to see the misery in her granddaughter's eyes.

'Why don't you come an' live here with me?' she suggested one day, but Charlotte shook her head. How could she go and leave her mother, now that she knew that the Reverend could be violent towards her? She didn't tell Kitty that, of course, but sometimes the offer was sorely tempting.

On this particular day, Charlotte was sitting across the kitchen-table from her granny sipping tea and looking as miserable as sin.

Kitty had just rented a black and white television set from a shop in town and was the envy of all her neighbours.

'I was watchin' *I Love Lucy* last night,' she said as she topped her own mug up. 'That telly is a godsend. I don't know how I managed without it now.'

Charlotte smiled as she listened to the Four Aces singing 'Three Coins in the Fountain' on the wireless. It was the only time she was allowed to listen to popular music and just one of the reasons she loved visiting her granny. The latest rage was an American singer called Elvis Presley who had burst onto the scene singing rock 'n' roll, and Charlotte couldn't hear enough of him.

'I bumped into your friend Babs the other day up town,' Kitty told her. 'Seems she's gettin' engaged to young Tim Hancock on her eighteenth birthday. Nice lad he is, from what I can make out. Have you seen anythin' of her lately?'

Charlotte shook her head regretfully. Many of the girls she had gone to school with were getting engaged, some of them were even married. She wished Babs well. She was just about the only friend Charlotte had ever had, and she still missed her. She missed Harry too and wondered if he ever thought of her, not that it would have made any difference if he had. Her father would never have allowed her to have a boyfriend, and she sometimes feared that she was going to end up a withered old spinster like Miss Straight, her father's most devout admirer.

Charlotte and Kitty enjoyed a pleasant hour together, chatting and listening to the wireless, but eventually Charlotte glanced at the clock on the mantelpiece and rose.

'I'd better get going now, Granny. You know what Father is like if I'm late.'

Kitty forced herself to remain silent. The way she saw it, things were hard enough for this girl without her adding her two penn'orth.

'All right, love. You mind how you go now an' I'll look forward to seein' you next week.' She kissed her granddaughter affectionately and saw her on her way before returning to the jumper she was knitting.

Although it was only four o'clock in the afternoon the light was fast fading and Charlotte shuddered as she hurried along. The frost was already forming on the pavements and she pulled her coat collar up. Soon she was passing the churchyard. The church was in darkness and looked cold and dismal, but the vicarage was in sight. Lights spilled from the kitchen window and it looked inviting – but Charlotte knew differently. The atmosphere in there was as cold as the air outside. And then she saw the police car parked on the road outside and she frowned. Why would the police be visiting her mother and father?

Once in the hall, she hung her coat up and drew her gloves off before heading for the kitchen where she knew her mother would normally have been preparing the evening meal. Finding the kitchen empty, she made for the parlour, where she saw her mother with her head bent, softly crying into a tiny white handkerchief. Two policemen were deep in conversation with her father but they stopped talking when Charlotte entered and glanced at him enquiringly.

'Th-this is my daughter, Charlotte,' her father introduced her and the older of the two policemen nodded at her as she hurried to her mother and placed her arm protectively about her waist. Her father was as white as a sheet and looked deeply shocked, but turning his attention to Charlotte he told her, 'I'm afraid something terrible has happened. It-it's Andrew.'

Charlotte assumed that he meant Andrew Pinnington, his pet choir boy, as she secretly thought of him. Her father went on, 'These gentlemen have called to tell me that he is dead.'

'Dead!' Charlotte's eyes stretched wide. 'But why? How? He was fine last night. You were in the church practising with him.'

'I know.' Her father mopped at his brow. 'But apparently someone walking their dog found him dangling from a tree down by the canal in Marston Lane earlier this afternoon. It seems that he has hung himself.'

Charlotte sat down heavily, hardly able to take it in, and now the policeman turned his attention back to her father.

'So you are saying, sir, that he appeared to be perfectly happy when he left you last night?'

'Oh yes.' Her father nodded vigorously. 'He seemed to be fine. We had made arrangements for his next choir practice on Tuesday evening after school, but now . . .' His voice trailed away and the younger of the policemen who had been furiously scribbling in his notebook snapped it shut.

'Thank you for your time, sir. I'm sorry to be the bearer of such bad news. Andrew's parents are in a terrible state as you can imagine, and now we have to try and find out why their lad would have done such a thing.'

'Perhaps someone else did it to him,' Charlotte blurted out, but the policeman shook his head.

'No, miss. We have already ruled out foul play. Andrew's mother has informed us that he had been becoming increasingly nervy and depressed for some time. Now it is our job to learn the reason for

39

this. There didn't appear to be any problems at school, although his friends have told us that he hadn't been his usual happy-go-lucky self for a while. But thank you again for your time. Goodbye. If we need to speak to you again we shall be in touch.'

'Of course.' Bernard rose and saw the officers to the door as Charlotte clung to her mother who was now sobbing brokenheartedly.

'Don't cry, Mum,' she said softly. She always addressed Hilary as Mum when out of her father's earshot. She hated to see her so upset, although she could quite understand why. It was such a waste of a young life and Andrew had been such a lovely young boy, only twelve years old, too. She could not begin to imagine how devastated his parents must be.

'Come on,' she urged, nudging her mother towards the kitchen. 'I'll make you a nice hot cup of sweet tea. Granny always says it's good for shock.'

She led her mother along the hallway just as her father closed the door after the policemen, but then she was further shocked when her mother glared at him and snapped accusingly, 'Happy now, are you?' She pointed a trembling finger at him. 'You pushed the child too hard – the poor lad never had a minute to himself.'

'Hilary, pull yourself together,' he answered as his hands clenched into fists. 'What has happened is most regrettable, but you really must control yourself. Andrew loved being the lead chorister.'

Charlotte gaped from one to the other in total bewilderment. She had never heard her mother say so much as a wrong word to her father before, let alone shout at him like that. Her parents stared at each other for what seemed like forever but then her father turned abruptly and slammed off into his study.

'What was all that about?' Charlotte asked as she manoeuvred her mother into the kitchen and hurried away to fill the kettle.

Her mother massaged her forehead as she replied, 'Oh, nothing. Just forget I ever said it.'

'But you must have meant *something*,' Charlotte persisted.

'I told you – I didn't mean anything,' Hilary said in a small voice. 'I suppose it was just the shock of hearing such tragic news.'

'Oh, Mum.' Suddenly Charlotte plucked up the courage to ask the question that she'd wanted to put to her for so long. 'Why do you stay with him? You're obviously not happy and Granny would have you back to stay with her like a shot.'

'How could you even suggest such a thing, my girl?' Hilary gasped as she clutched her throat with one hand. 'This is your father you're talking about!'

Charlotte shrugged. The way she saw it, it was in for a penny in for a pound. 'But he doesn't treat you right,' she pointed out. 'And don't shake your head like that, Mum. I know he's been hitting you now. I didn't, not for a long time. He's a hypocrite, that's what he is. He stands there in the pulpit telling everyone else how to behave, when you and I are little more than his skivvies!'

'Charlotte, that is quite enough.' Hilary rose from her seat. 'There are things you couldn't understand at your age. Marriage is something you enter into for life.'

'Not in this day and age it isn't,' Charlotte snorted. 'We're not living in the Dark Ages now, Mum.' But her words fell on deaf ears as Hilary marched out of the room.

Charlotte sighed as she turned the kettle off and sat down at the table. She knew that she had probably had no right to speak out like that, but it hurt to see her mum looking so wretched all the while. Her thoughts moved on to Andrew and she shuddered. Poor lad. He must have been desperately unhappy to commit suicide, but what could have caused it? She glanced around the sparse kitchen then after turning off the lights she made her way to her room.

Andrew was buried the following week in the churchyard adjoining the vicarage. Her father conducted the service and the church was full to overflowing of people who had come to pay their last respects to the boy. His poor parents were inconsolable but still it seemed that no one was any nearer to knowing why he had chosen to take his own life, and it was beginning to look like they never would. Charlotte's heart ached as his small coffin was lowered into the ground. And then it was done and everyone walked away and life went on.

It was three weeks later when they were all sitting at dinner that her father informed them, 'I have asked young Tommy Webster to take

41

Andrew's place in the choir. His voice has great promise and I feel with a little tuition he could do really well. It is most regrettable, of course, about Andrew but life must go on.'

Charlotte frowned as she watched her mother's face drop. Then without a word Hilary rose and left her meal to go cold.

'Sh-should I go and fetch her?' she asked her father falteringly.

'No.' He lifted his knife and fork and went on eating. 'I'm sure your mother will come back if she's hungry. If she doesn't, you are more than capable of serving the dessert and clearing away yourself.'

'Yes, Father.' Charlotte watched as he picked up a snow-white napkin and dabbed at his lips, and a flood of resentment rushed through her. Andrew was barely cold in his grave and here he was telling them that he was replacing him already. No wonder her mother had walked away.

When everything was tidied away to the Reverend's satisfaction, Charlotte got a chance to sneak up to her mother's room. She tapped on the door and when she opened it she found Hilary lying on the bed staring up at the ceiling. Her mother's room, like every other in the house, was furnished with only the barest essentials and it looked cold and uninviting.

'Are you all right, Mum?' She hovered in the doorway uncertainly.

Hilary nodded. 'Yes, dear, I just have a headache, that's all. I shall be fine in a little while.'

'Is there anything I can get for you?'

'No, nothing. But thank you. I just need to be quiet for a while.'

Charlotte slunk away to her own room. From her window she could just see Andrew's grave, covered in frost. It was sparkling in the moonlight, and again it struck her how strange life was. People passed away, but life went on just as if they had never been. Already her father was talking of replacing him with Tommy Webster. It was a sobering thought.

As Christmas raced towards them, Hilary developed a heavy cold and took to her bed. Charlotte ran up and downstairs and took care of her as well as running the house. She had been hoping to speak to her mother again about the possibility of going into nursing, but now she decided that she would wait until after Christmas when her mother was well again. Charlotte was very concerned about her. Hilary seemed to have gone into herself since Andrew's death, and didn't seem at all concerned about what went on around her. Charlotte cooked her tempting meals and encouraged her to eat, but Hilary refused them all.

Finally one evening over dinner, Charlotte plucked up the courage to tell her father, 'I'm worried about Mother. She doesn't seem to be getting any better and she's lost a lot of weight.'

He loaded his fork with the roast lamb she had cooked for him and said, 'I'm sure there is nothing to concern yourself about. It's only a head cold.'

Charlotte laid her knife and fork down. As far as she was aware, he hadn't visited her mother's room once since she had fallen ill to enquire how she was, and it appeared that as long as the house was running smoothly and his meals were on the table, he didn't much care.

'All the same, I think I shall get the doctor to call in and take another look at her.'

Reverend Hayes sighed heavily. 'Very well, if you think it is absolutely necessary but personally I see no need. It's most inconvenient of your mother to become ill when there's so much to do at the church in the lead-up to Christmas. The tree is being delivered tomorrow and it will need to be decorated, so could you put that on your list of things to do? You'll find the dressings for it in a box in the vestry. The congregation do like to see the tree looking nice. And now what is for dessert? I have a choir practice this evening and it wouldn't do to keep young Tommy waiting.'

Charlotte felt resentment bubble up inside her and before she could stop herself she blurted out, 'It must be awful for Andrew's parents. He should have been leading the choir during the Christmas Day service.'

Her father's face set. 'Yes, but Andrew isn't here, is he?' he responded unfeelingly. 'The family should just think themselves lucky that he was allowed to be buried in hallowed ground. Years ago, anyone who committed suicide would have been buried outside of the churchyard. It is a sin to take one's own life.'

Charlotte silently fumed as she lifted his empty plate and headed for the kitchen to fetch the treacle sponge pudding. Despite being a vicar, she was sure her father was the most uncaring man she knew, and in that moment what she felt for him bordered on hate.

It was the following morning as Charlotte was straightening the blankets on her mother's bed that Hilary asked, 'Do you think you could find time to nip around and see how your granny is sometime today, dear? I usually go around on Friday but I don't feel up to it and I don't want her worrying.'

'Of course I will, but I doubt I'll get time to go until this evening,' Charlotte answered. 'Father has asked me to decorate the Christmas tree in the church when it's delivered, and he's given me a list of errands to run as long as your arm.'

'I'm so sorry,' Hilary replied as tears started to her eyes.

'It's all right, really,' Charlotte quickly assured her. 'It will be nice to see Granny. You know I love going round there. Now is there anything I can get for you?'

When Hilary shook her head, Charlotte quietly left the room, closing the door softly behind her. The doctor had promised to call around and see Mrs Hayes after the morning surgery, so the girl set to to get the housework done and out of the way. Even with his wife ill in bed, her father insisted that everywhere was just so – and she knew that it would be woe betide her if she let her mother's standards slip.

Dr Mortimer arrived just before lunchtime following a hectic morning surgery looking harassed and frazzled. He was a small portly man with bushy eyebrows and a bulbous nose. He had been the family doctor for as long as Charlotte could remember and she was very fond of him.

'Half the population of Bedworth is down with the flu,' he complained as he shrugged his coat off and passed it to Charlotte. 'But is your mum no better?'

When the girl looked solemn he smiled reassuringly. 'Well, not to worry. If she's a bit run down, this cold will have a tendency to hang on. But now how about I go up and have a look at her while you make me a nice strong cup of tea, eh? I've been so run off my feet this morning I haven't had time for a break and my mouth is as dry as a bone.'

Charlotte grinned as she headed for the kitchen. Dr Mortimer was a lovely, kind man and he could always manage to make her smile.

She had his tea waiting for him when he entered the kitchen a short while later and she peered at him anxiously.

'Don't look so worried,' he urged as he took up the cup and slurped at the steaming tea. 'Ah, that was just what the doctor ordered,' he quipped, then, 'It's as I thought. She's a little low and run-down so I'm going to prescribe her a tonic. That should do the trick and before you know it she'll be fighting fit again.'

'Oh.' Charlotte looked relieved as she hastily filled his cup again. Minutes later, the doctor was on his way and she immediately shot off to the chemist's to get the tonic the doctor had prescribed. The rest of the day passed in a blur as Charlotte saw to her mother's needs and tackled all the jobs on the list that her father had given her. But then at last the evening meal was out of the way and once she had tidied the kitchen she set off to her granny's.

'By, you'll be bad next,' Kitty scolded as Charlotte entered the cosy kitchen. 'You look frozen through and dead on your feet, my girl. Come an' sit down while I make you a nice cup o' cocoa.'

Charlotte chuckled. 'I'm supposed to be checking that *you're* all right,' she joked as she peeled her gloves off.

'Never better,' Kitty assured her as she heated some milk in a pan on the stove. 'But now you get yourself over by the fire.'

Charlotte obediently sank down into the fireside chair and sighed with contentment as she looked around at her granny's little home. Most of the furniture in there was secondhand pieces that Kitty had collected over the years, and it was far from grand, but even so it was homely and welcoming and nothing at all like the vicarage. She felt herself beginning to relax and stretched her stockinged feet out to the flames that were licking up the chimney as she settled down for a chat.

Eventually, she glanced at the clock and rose reluctantly. 'I really ought to be getting back or else Father will be worried,' she muttered.

'I suppose you should,' Kitty agreed, looking at the frost beyond the little leaded window. 'But make sure you don't loiter about. It's bitter out there. Goodbye now, love. I'll see you on Saturday.'

Charlotte was in a slightly happier frame of mind and as she picked her way along the icy pavements her mood further improved when she looked up to see Harry walking towards her with his hands tucked into his overcoat pockets. As always her heart raced at the sight of him. It had been so long since she had last seen him that she had forgotten how handsome he was.

'Hello, Harry,' she said shyly as he drew closer.

He peered at her, his lovely black hair shining in the glow from the streetlamp, and then as he recognised her, his face broke into a grin. 'Why if it ain't little Lottie. How are yer nowadays? We don't get to see much of yer any more.'

'Oh, my father tends to keep me quite busy.' Charlotte lowered her eyes, ashamed of the feelings that were flooding through her.

'So where you off to then?'

'I've just called round to see my granny but I'm on my way home now,' she told him.

'Hmm. Well, why don't yer let me buy you a drink? We could do wi' sommat to warm us up this weather.'

There was nothing Charlotte would have liked more, but she shook her head. 'I'm afraid I'll be late if I don't get on,' she apologised.

'Then I'll walk yer part o' the way back,' Harry offered. 'We could take a short-cut through the park.'

Charlotte hesitated. There were no lights on in the park at night and she usually avoided going that way if she was alone. But then what harm could come to her if she was with Harry? she reasoned.

'All right – I'd like that,' she agreed shyly, and he fell into step with her, drawing her arm through his and holding her hand. Charlotte felt as if she had died and gone to heaven and by the time they turned into the park gates she was floating. The further into the park they got the darker it became as they left the streetlights behind, and soon Charlotte was straining her eyes into the darkness to make sure that they stayed to the path.

Eventually they came to a bench and when Harry drew her down onto it she didn't object. Nor did she object when his lips came down on hers and she gave herself up to the pleasure of the moment. But then after a while his hands began to stray and she became slightly uneasy. One of his hands had slipped beneath her coat, and as he fondled her breast through the thick jumper she was wearing she was shocked to feel her nipple grow erect.

'I er . . . think we should be getting on now,' she panted breathlessly as she tried to move his hand. Her only answer was a loud grunt as Harry manoeuvred her further back onto the bench. The first feelings of panic fluttered to life as his breath became fast and loud.

'Don't be such a fuckin' prick-tease,' he groaned in her ear. 'Yer know this is what you've wanted since the first time yer set eyes on me.'

'N-no, it isn't.' Alarm bells were going off in her head now and she tried harder to push him away, but her strength was no match for his and soon he had her lying lengthways on the bench as his hands found their way beneath her skirt. Her fingernails scraped along the back of the bench as she tried to sit up, but it was useless.

'Harry, NO!' Charlotte felt as if she had been douched in cold water as his hands raked her thick stockings down and then he was tearing at her knickers and she began to cry as she struggled beneath him.

'Harry, please stop!'

Her words fell on deaf ears. Harry was beyond pleas and suddenly he was on top of her and now she really began to fight him. And then suddenly he lunged into her and her screams stopped abruptly as the air was knocked out of her lungs. She felt as if she was being rent in two as he pounded into her, and when she found her breath she began to scream. But there was no one to hear her and tears coursed down her cheeks. It seemed to go on forever, but then Harry suddenly stiffened and let out a loud animal cry before dropping limply on top of her. When his breathing returned to something of a more normal rhythm, he rolled off her and laughed.

'That were great, Lottie. I didn't realise it were yer first time though. Did yer enjoy it?'

She stared at him in horrified disbelief as he calmly stood up and began to button up his trousers. She felt dirty and humiliated and lost for words. Never in a million years had she ever imagined that the sex act could be as awful and painful as this. It was certainly nothing like it had been described in the odd romance magazines that she had managed to read now and again. It was sordid and degrading and she knew that she would never feel clean again.

47

'Right then.' Harry smoothed his hair. 'I'd best be off else I'll be late meetin' me mates in the pub. See yer about, Lottie.' He then strolled away without a care in the world while Charlotte curled into a ball and sobbed as if her heart would break.

Chapter Six

Charlotte had no idea how long she lay there but eventually she was so cold that her teeth began to chatter. Prising herself up, she straightened her clothes as best she could and got shakily to her feet. She headed unsteadily towards the park entrance and after glancing up and down the road to make sure that no one was coming, she stumbled towards home. Despite being bitterly cold her cheeks flamed with shame and she was sure that if anyone saw her they would know instantly what had happened.

When the lights of the vicarage came into sight she slowed her steps and gulped deep in her throat. How could she face her father now? As she drew closer she saw that the light was on in his study, so she quietly walked around to the back of the house and let herself in at the kitchen door. The room was thankfully in darkness, so she closed the door quietly behind her and crept into the hallway. No one was about and she hurried up the stairs, avoiding the ones that creaked. Once in the privacy of her room she breathed a sigh of relief, and after snapping the light on she sank onto the side of her bed and hugged herself as she rocked back and forth. *What am I going to do?* she asked herself as tears coursed down her pale cheeks. Harry, who she had always placed on a pedestal, had raped her and she didn't know how she would ever face going out of the door again.

Should she tell her mother? Charlotte rejected that idea instantly. Hilary was low enough as it was, and if she were to discover what had happened, it might make her condition even worse. And of course she could never confide something like this to her father. He would probably end up blaming her. He'd say that she had tempted Harry or something and Charlotte knew that she wouldn't be able to bear that. There was her granny – she would believe her – but

Kitty would probably want to kill Harry, and then everyone would find out about it and the girl knew that she would never be able to live with the shame.

Eventually, Charlotte realised that the only thing to do was to try and put it behind her, although she knew that it would be easier said than done. Taking a deep breath she pulled herself together as best she could. She would have a nice hot bath. Surely that would help? She soon found out that it didn't. She had the water as hot as she could bear it and scrubbed every inch of herself until her skin felt raw, but still she felt dirty and now she feared that she always would.

Back in her room once more, she burrowed down under the blankets. Bruises were appearing on her arms and her inner thighs, and every bone in her body ached. She tossed and turned for hours as she tried to come to terms with what had happened, but then thankfully she eventually cried herself to sleep.

The following morning, Charlotte had to drag herself out of bed. A glance in the mirror showed that her arms were black and blue, but there were no bruises on her face so she supposed that was something to be thankful for. Once she was dressed no one would see them. Wearing a calf-length skirt and thick stockings, she then pulled a long-sleeved sweater over her head before tying her hair back into a ribbon at the nape of her neck. One last peep in the mirror asssured her that to anyone else she looked just the same, but she knew that she would never be the same again. Straightening her shoulders, she forced herself to go and check on her mother before going downstairs to prepare breakfast for her father.

'Are you feeling all right, Charlotte? You look very pasty,' her mother fretted, the instant she set foot in the room.

'I'm fine,' Charlotte lied as she hurried over to the window and swished the curtains aside. 'Do you want me to bring you a bowl of water and a towel up so you can wash now, or would you rather wait until after breakfast?' Crossing to the bed she began to straighten the blankets as her mother shook her head.

'I'll wash later and I don't really feel like any breakfast,' she replied.

'But you *have* to eat. You heard what the doctor said,' Charlotte told her sternly. 'How about if I do you a nice soft-boiled egg and some bread and butter soldiers like you used to make for me when I was a little girl?'

Hilary smiled at her fondly as memories rushed back. She didn't bother to argue. Charlotte could be as stubborn as a mule when she set her mind to something; Hilary supposed she had inherited that trait from her father.

Charlotte now walked towards the door again, saying over her shoulder, 'I'll just go and see to Father's breakfast and then I'll be back up with yours.' Once out on the landing her shoulders sagged and she leaned heavily against the wall for a moment. The events of the night before were still very fresh in her mind and she had no idea how she had managed to appear so normal in front of her mother. But the worst part was yet to come. Her father seemed to be able to see into her very soul, and it was going to be even harder to act normally in front of him.

He was sitting at the table reading the newspaper when she entered the kitchen and he looked pointedly towards the clock. Charlotte followed his gaze. It was three minutes past seven.

'Sorry I'm a few minutes late,' she mumbled. 'I just went in to check on Mother before I came down.'

Avoiding his eyes, she filled the kettle and put it on to boil before getting the frying pan out. Her father expected a full English breakfast with all the trimmings be it summer or winter.

'So how is she this morning?'

Ignoring the trace of disapproval in his voice, Charlotte concentrated on melting the lard in the pan. 'About the same, I should say, but the tonic the doctor prescribed will help.'

'Hmm, let's hope you are right,' he said unfeelingly. 'She really couldn't have chosen a worse time to take to her bed.'

Charlotte bit her lip and got on with the breakfast, and it was as she was placing a loaded plate full of bacon, sausage, tomatoes and eggs in front of him that he mentioned, 'Oh, I had a letter from your Aunt Edith yesterday. She has decided she's going to come and stay with us over Christmas. She will be arriving on Christmas Eve in time for the midnight carol service. That will be nice, won't it?'

Charlotte nodded numbly. She'd been convinced that things couldn't get any worse than they already were, but they just had. Her nickname for her aunt was 'The Dragon' and as far as Charlotte was concerned the title suited her perfectly. Edith was thirty-five, ten years younger than her brother, and was a schoolteacher. She had moved to Ireland in her twenties, and she had lived there, in a small village just outside Cork, ever since. Charlotte had visited her once or twice over the years with her parents and had hated every minute of it. A tall, thin spinster, with eyes as cold as snow and a nature to match, she struck terror into the girl's heart every time she so much as looked at her. Her pupils must be scared stiff of her; the girl pitied them.

Her mother had once confided that Aunt Edith had actually been quite nice when she had first met Bernard. Edith had been engaged to be married to the headmaster at the school where she taught, but he had run off with the school secretary, never to be seen again, and from that day on Edith had become a bitter and twisted woman with a chip on her shoulder the size of a house brick. She had bought the rambling old house she still lived in with an inheritance she had received from an aunt, with the intentions of restoring it to its former glory once she and her fiancé were married, but it still remained as it had been the day she purchased it.

Charlotte suppressed a shudder as she thought of it now. The windows shook in their rotting frames every time the wind blew, and the place was even draughtier and less inviting than the vicarage. Her aunt didn't believe in 'frills and furbelows' as she termed them, and Charlotte had often wondered how she managed to exist in such a bleak place. Set on the very edge of the village, it was at least half a mile to the nearest neighbours, and surrounded by trees that tapped at the windows in the wind as if they were trying to gain entry. Her aunt had no modern appliances whatsoever, and when Hilary had once suggested that it might be beneficial and timesaving for her to get some, she had told her in a very cold voice that this was the way she liked it. Hilary had never been brave enough to suggest such a thing again and Charlotte had a sneaky suspicion that her mother feared Edith almost as much as she did.

A picture of her aunt flashed in front of her eyes and panic began to set in. Her aunt never failed to pick fault with everything that Hilary did when she came to Bedworth to stay with them, but this time it would be even worse than usual. Unless her mother made a miraculous recovery, it would be left up to Charlotte to cater to her aunt's needs.

With this in mind, Charlotte plucked up every ounce of courage she had and said, 'Do you think this is a good idea, Father? What I mean is, with Mother ill in bed I'm rushed off my feet as it is and—

'Do you *really* expect me to tell your aunt that she is not welcome here?' Reverend Hayes glared. 'Why, Charlotte, I am *shocked* at you. Your dear Aunt Edith is no trouble at all, and if she doesn't come to stay with us, she will be all alone over Christmas. I am astonished that you could harbour such uncharitable thoughts.'

'I'm sorry, Father, I'm sure I shall manage,' Charlotte choked.

'Hmm, I should think so too,' he growled as he tucked into his breakfast and Charlotte scuttled away to prepare her mother's tray with a sinking feeling in her stomach. It seemed that no matter what she said, it was decided.

By the time Charlotte tumbled into bed late that night, she was exhausted. She had cleaned the house from top to bottom, raced up and downstairs looking after her mother's needs, run errands for her father as well as cooking the meals, and now she wasn't sure where she ached the most. By now the full horror of what had happened with Harry the night before had fully sunk in and she wasn't sure how she had managed to get through the day. Perhaps it was just as well she had been so busy and hadn't had much time to brood on things . . . but now it all came back to her and she just made it to the toilet where she was violently sick.

Despair ran through her like iced water. Her father had always drummed it into her that nice girls did not have anything to do with boys before marriage. Admittedly, he had never talked openly about sex but Charlotte had heard enough from the girls she had gone to school with to know what he meant. But who would want her now? Not that she could ever envisage wanting to be married now. Harry had brutally raped her, and suddenly the rose-coloured glasses through which she had always viewed him had disappeared and she saw him for what he was: a no-good layabout with no thought for anyone but himself. Worse still, she blamed herself for what had happened – up to a point. She had always encouraged Harry's attentions and had even enjoyed it when he kissed her. It was only when he had gone further than she had wanted him to that she had started to object, so perhaps she had unwittingly given him the wrong messages?

Dragging herself back to bed, she lay watching the flickering shadows on the ceiling. If only she had left her granny's earlier the night before, she would never have bumped into him. If only she had refused to let him walk her home. But it was too late for *if only* now. What was done was done, and somehow she was going to have to try and come to terms with it and put it behind her.

A loud knocking at the front door announced the arrival of Aunt Edith mid-afternoon on Christmas Eve, and after a quick glance around to make sure that everywhere was spotless, Charlotte fixed a smile on her face and hurried to answer it.

'Aunt Edith,' she greeted her. 'Do come in.'

Edith swept past her, leaving Charlotte to lug her case into the hallway.

'Where are your mother and father?' she demanded. 'I expected them to be at the station to greet me. I have had to take a cab.'

'Mother is ill in bed and Father is over at the church,' Charlotte explained as she dropped the heavy case to the floor and shut the door. 'But he said he will be here as soon as possible. He's been looking forward to you coming.'

'Hmm.' Edith ran her finger along the hall-table inspecting for dust before taking a lethal-looking hatpin out of her hat and handing it to Charlotte. 'And what is wrong with your mother?'

'She's had a heavy cold and it's left her very run-down.'

'Run-down indeed,' Edith said disapprovingly. 'Some people don't know when they are well off. She's never done a day's work since she married your father. She obviously doesn't know how fortunate she is. But never mind that for now. I've come a very long way and a cup of tea wouldn't go amiss.'

Charlotte gritted her teeth before saying falsely, 'Of course, come through to the kitchen. I'll put the kettle on and I've made you a sponge cake too.'

'A sandwich wouldn't go amiss either,' Edith informed her. 'Just to keep me going until dinnertime.' She then straightened her hair, which was scraped back into an unbecoming bun, and running her hands down her tweed skirt she followed her niece along the hallway.

Once in the kitchen she glanced around as if she was looking for something to find fault with and Charlotte hurriedly asked, 'Why don't you sit down, Aunt? You must be tired after your long journey.'

Thankfully she was saved from having to think of anything further to say when the back door opened and her father appeared.

'Edith, my dear.' He held his arms out to his sister, looking genuinely pleased to see her, then after giving her a perfunctory hug he scolded, 'Charlotte, where are your manners, girl? You do not serve refreshments to guests in the kitchen. Bring a tray through to the parlour. Come along, Edith, we have a lot of catching up to do.'

Charlotte breathed a sigh of relief as her father led her aunt away. The last couple of weeks had taken their toll on her but now she would have to run around after her aunt too, and there would certainly be no help from her father. All she could do was hope that her aunt wasn't planning on staying for too long. *Her looks certainly haven't improved,* she thought to herself as she prepared a plate of sandwiches and placed them on the tray. Edith was so thin that if she turned sideways, she might slip through a crack in the pavement. She was very tall for a woman too, and Charlotte had to look up to her. Of course, these things could have been acceptable had she been attractive, but the truth of the matter was that Edith was one of the ugliest women Charlotte had ever seen. She had a large hooked nose and thin lips that always looked disapproving, and her eyes were a pale watery grey that missed nothing. All this, added to the fact that she had a most disagreeable personality, did nothing to endear her to her niece at all.

As Charlotte put the finishing touches to the tea tray, she wondered how she was going to get through the days ahead. She suddenly thought of the brother or sister she had always longed for. At school she had listened enviously to the other children as they gabbled on excitedly about their latest sibling and wondered when it would be her turn. But the years had passed by and she had remained an only child until eventually she had been forced to accept that it was highly unlikely things would change. But oh, how much better things might have been, had it turned out differently!

Her heart ached. It would have been so nice to have someone else to love. She had her gran, of course, and her mother too – although Hilary never dared to show her feelings when Reverend Hayes was present. Giving herself a mental shake, Charlotte began to lift the tray. She would just have to get on with things and make the best of her aunt's visit. She didn't have much choice, did she?

Chapter Seven

Christmas Day found the family sitting around the dining-room table whilst Bernard made a great show of carving an enormous turkey. Charlotte was painfully aware that some of her father's parishioners would be lucky to be sitting down to a chicken leg, but it didn't seem to trouble him. Still, at least Granny was there to lighten the atmosphere, or at least to try to. Kitty and Bernard made no secret of the fact that there was no love lost between them, but Charlotte supposed that he would look uncharitable if it became common knowledge that Kitty was forced to spend Christmas Day alone, so each year the old lady was invited to dinner. Now as she glanced across at her, Charlotte saw that her granny's eyes were fastened on her mother.

'You're still lookin' peaky, love,' she commented, sounding concerned.

Hilary smiled. 'Oh, I'm feeling much better,' she assured her mother. 'It's done me good to get up. I think lying in bed has weakened me.' Then, hoping to change the subject, she remarked, 'Hasn't Charlotte done a wonderful job of the Christmas dinner? I really don't know what I would have done without her over the last few weeks. She's been an absolute angel.'

'Angels only exist in heaven,' Bernard said sharply as he placed a slice of turkey onto his wife's plate.

'Even so, what Hilary says is right,' Kitty snapped. 'Our Charlotte is a lovely cook. Takes after her mam fer that, she does.'

'Roast potatoes, Granny?' Charlotte hastily pushed the dish across the table, sensing that a row was brewing. 'And how about some Brussels sprouts? I know you're partial to them.'

'Don't mind if I do.' Kitty glared at Bernard before loading some onto her plate.

Edith watched her with distaste. As far as she was concerned, the woman was as common as clouts and she could never understand how her dear brother had ever become entangled with her daughter, who in her eyes wasn't much better. Bernard could have done so well for himself, although in fairness, Hilary *had* calmed down over the years. In fact, she was downright dowdy now. But a right flightly little piece she had been when he had first met her. Still, there was no accounting for taste.

'So, Kitty, how are you keeping nowadays?' Edith asked politely. She supposed she should make an effort.

'Oh, I can't complain, yer know.' Kitty added some peas and carrots to the food already on her plate. 'And how about you, Edith?'

The other woman sniffed as she lifted a linen napkin and smoothed it across her lap. 'Like you I can't complain, but then I keep myself busy. Idle hands make work for the devil, so they say, don't they? I'm still working at the school. Have you taken any form of employment yet?'

Kitty knew that she was trying to goad her, but refusing to rise to the bait, she merely chuckled and said, 'I ain't got no need to work. My old man left me well provided for, God rest his soul. An' anyway, I'm a bit long in the tooth to be startin' work now. No, I'm happy enough potterin' about me cottage an' me garden, an' I can't see that changin' any day soon.'

'How fortunate you are.' Disapproval was coming off Edith in waves and Charlotte had to gaze down at her plate so that no one would see her smiling. It would take a far better woman than Aunt Edith to get one over on her granny, that was for sure.

Once everyone had helped themselves to food, Reverend Hayes said piously, 'Let us say Grace.'

They all bowed their heads as Bernard intoned, 'For what we are about to receive, may the Lord make us truly thankful. Amen.'

The meal passed in silence as they all concentrated on their food, but once everyone was finished, Charlotte quickly rose and began to gather together the dirty pots. 'I'll just get these into the kitchen and then I'll bring the pudding through,' she told them, glad of a chance to escape the strained atmosphere.

'I'll help you,' Hilary offered, making to rise, but the girl pressed her back into her seat.

'No, it's all right. I can manage,' she promised, as she scuttled away with the first handful of plates.

Ten minutes later, she placed a large steaming Christmas pudding and a jug of thick creamy custard in the centre of the table and once again Bernard began to fill everyone's dishes.

'I think the pudding could have done with a little more brandy,' he commented after taking the first mouthful.

'Well, *I* reckon it's lovely,' Kitty chipped in resentfully. Trust him to pick fault. Nothing was ever right for him.

Charlotte smiled at her gratefully, wondering what she would ever do without her.

'I think it's lovely too,' Hilary dared to say, but then as her husband glared at her she quickly lowered her eyes.

Charlotte was grateful when the meal was finally over and she could lock herself away in the kitchen to wash the dirty pots, whilst the adults all retired to the sitting room.

Leaning heavily on the edge of the sink, she stared off across the garden. Kitty had always been able to read her like a book, and throughout the meal, Charlotte had caught her watching her more than once. What if she's guessed what's happened to me? she fretted, but then she shook her head. How *could* Kitty know what Harry had done to her? She had been cosily sitting by the fire in the kitchen at the time and wasn't even aware that Charlotte had met Harry. Sighing, she filled the sink with hot soapy water and set to on the mountain of pots. Once everything was washed, dried and put away, she began to prepare a tray of tea. When it was ready, she carried it through to the sitting room, where she found the family listening to the wireless.

'Ah, here she is,' Kitty said brightly, clearing a space for the tray on a small table. 'Come an' have a sit-down now, love.' She patted the seat at the side of her on the overstuffed settee. 'You've worked yer socks off today an' a right good job you've done of everythin'.'

Aunt Edith accepted a dainty china cup and saucer and sipped at it delicately while Kitty eyed her with amusement.

'These farty cups are pretty enough, but they ain't as good as a decent solid mug, are they?' she remarked.

59

Edith's lips compressed into a thin line. 'Personally I think these are so much more refined,' she answered.

'Well, it's each to his own.' Kitty took a large swig of tea and again Charlotte had to stop herself from smiling. There was no chance of her granny and her auntie ever becoming friends, that was for sure.

Once the tea was drunk, the Reverend then began to read a piece from the Bible – and by the time he had done, Kitty was almost yawning with boredom.

'It's been very nice but I reckon I'll be makin' tracks back to me own fireside now,' she told them. 'Why don't you come back wi' me an' have yer tea at my house, pet?' she addressed Charlotte.

When Charlotte looked hopefully at her father, Hilary piped up, 'I was hoping you'd stay and have tea here with us, Mother.'

Kitty shook her head. 'I appreciate the offer but there's no place like home at Christmas. Thanks all the same though, love.' She saw the disappointment in her daughter's face and hardened her heart to it. She would have had her daughter back home to live with her like a shot and had made that exact offer numerous times over the years, but each time Hilary had made an excuse to stay with her husband, so Kitty had given up asking her now.

'May I go with Granny, Father?' Charlotte asked.

Bernard scowled. Even so, he did not wish to appear to be unreasonable in front of his sister so he said grudgingly, 'You may see your grandmother home and have half an hour with her, but then I would like you back here for teatime. Your mother isn't up to preparing it yet.'

Thankful for small mercies, Charlotte slipped away to fetch their coats, and soon she and her granny were heading away from the vicarage arm-in-arm.

'Phew, thank Christ that's over,' Kitty breathed. 'I'd have had more fun in a flea-pit. I don't know how yer put up wi' it, I really don't.'

'You know why I put up with it,' Charlotte said in a small voice. 'I could hardly leave Mum on her own with him, could I? He'd run her into the ground.'

'And whose fault would that be, eh?' Kitty said indignantly. 'She could come home today and bring you with her, if she'd a mind to.

Trouble is, she's a stubborn little bugger. But it's you I worry about most. Yer should be out enjoyin' yerself at your age.'

'Oh, I'm all right.'

'Hmm, but *are* you?' Kitty peered at her closely, causing colour to speed into the girl's cheeks. 'You seem nervy an' upset. Has somethin' happened?'

'What could have happened?' Charlotte avoided the woman's eyes. 'I've just been a bit busy, that's all.'

'That's as maybe, but just remember there's always a bed at my place.' Kitty paused. 'As it happens, I've been meanin' to have a word wi' you.'

'What about?'

'Well . . .' Kitty coughed to clear her throat. 'The thing is, I ain't gettin' any younger an' I've been thinkin' it's time I set me house in order, so I've been to see a solicitor. I know by rights anythin' I have should go to yer mam after I'm gone, 'cos she's officially me next-o'-kin, but we both know what would happen if I left everythin' to her, don't we? Yer dad would get his holy mitts on it an' no doubt all me worldly goods would be sold off to pay fer a new church roof or sommat. Not that I've got anythin' against the church,' she rushed on hastily, 'but I'd rather think of me money doin' me own flesh an' blood a bit o' good. So actin' on that, I've told Mr Collins, me solicitor in the town square, that once I'm gone everythin' I own goes to you, lock stock an' barrel. Happen then you'll be able to have a few nice things.' She thought in disgust of earlier in the day when they had all exchanged presents and the dowdy thick woollen stockings Charlotte had received from her parents. What sort of a gift was that for a young girl, eh? The year before, it had been a Bible.

Deeply dismayed, Charlotte implored, 'Don't talk like that, Granny! Nothing is going to happen to you for a long, long time. I can't bear to think of it, so don't talk about it any more, please.'

'All right,' Kitty sighed. 'But just remember, when it does, you go to Mr Collin's office. He's got everythin' written down in black an' white. You just go to him an' he'll put yer right. Will yer promise me you'll do that?'

When Charlotte nodded she squeezed her hand. 'That's good enough then. I'll not mention it again. An' now we'll go an' watch a bit o' telly an' have a slice o' that nice Christmas cake I made, eh? I noticed you hardly ate anythin' at dinner.'

Charlotte got home shortly before teatime and immediately began to prepare the evening meal. It was a dismal affair, much as the Christmas dinner had been, and she was relieved when it was over and she could excuse herself and retire to her room.

Once there, she sank onto the edge of her bed and lowered her face into her hands. Luckily she had been too busy to think much throughout the day, but now that she was alone again the enormity of what had happened to her crept up on her again, and she bit down so hard on her lip that she tasted blood.

Eventually she rose and crossed to the window, just in time to see her father, accompanied by Tommy Webster, disappearing through the church door. Charlotte sighed. It seemed that even on Christmas Day her father preferred the company of his choir boys to that of his own family. Wearily, she began to prepare for bed. It had been a long day and she was glad that Christmas was over for another year.

When Aunt Edith departed two days after New Year's Day, Charlotte was glad to see the back of her. For the whole of her stay she had treated Charlotte as little more than a lackey, and although the girl had done all she could to please her, her aunt had picked fault with everything. *This egg is too runny*, or *This bacon is too crispy*, or, *You didn't make my bed correctly*. So it had gone on until Charlotte had felt close to screaming. But now, thankfully, things might get back to some sort of normality. Hilary had managed to get up for a little longer each day during Aunt Edith's stay, but she was still far from well and so for now the running of the house was still firmly down to Charlotte, although her mother did try to help as much as she could.

Charlotte found that she dreaded being asked to run errands for her father, whereas before she had quite enjoyed it. It was the fear of bumping into Harry – since she didn't have a clue what she would say to him. Half of her still wanted to throw herself into her mother's arms and sob out the truth. The other half was too ashamed to do that and so she kept her secret close, although by now Hilary had sensed that something was wrong.

'Is there anything worrying you? Are you feeling unwell?' she asked constantly, but Charlotte would just shake her head and tell her she was fine.

It was towards the end of January when the whole world was carpeted beneath a thick blanket of snow that Charlotte's worst nightmare came true. She missed a period. She checked and re-checked her diary, praying that she was wrong – but each time the result was the same. She was definitely a week overdue. Added to that, her breasts felt tender and sore and she found that she could no longer face breakfast each morning.

'Not going to see Granny today?' Hilary asked one Saturday afternoon. Charlotte usually couldn't wait to get round there, but lately she seemed to be staying in more and more.

'Oh, I think I may be coming down with a cold, so I don't think it's fair to go today in case I give it to her,' Charlotte answered lamely.

'I see.' Hilary stared at her searchingly for a heart-stopping moment before walking away.

Charlotte breathed a sigh of relief. But the relief was shortlived. What was she going to do if she was . . . she couldn't even bring herself to say the word, as if by saying it, it would come true. There was no one with whom she could share her fears. She couldn't confide in her mother and certainly not Granny; the old lady would be heartbroken. There was Babs, but she rarely saw her any more and anyway, it was her brother who had got her into this position, so what would she say?

The end of February came, and when Charlotte missed her second period, she was beside herself with fear. What would her father do when he found out? He would probably throw her out on the streets.

It was Hilary who brought things to a head when she was doing the laundry one day and commented, 'I haven't noticed any of your monthly rags left to soak in the bucket for a while, Charlotte.'

The girl's face crumpled and Hilary's stomach sank. 'Is there anything you want to tell me?' she asked softly, and suddenly Charlotte was in her arms, sobbing as if her heart would break. Painfully aware of her husband, who was in the study, Hilary quickly dried her daughter's cheeks on her apron and whisked her away up the stairs to the privacy of her room where she rounded on her and said, 'You're pregnant, aren't you?'

When Charlotte nodded miserably, Hilary sank onto the dressing-table stool as every bit of colour drained from her cheeks. 'Oh my dear God,' she said dully. 'Your father mustn't know about this. Whose is it?'

'I . . . I can't tell you,' Charlotte hiccuped.

'Well, have you been sneaking out to meet someone?' Hilary was desperate to find out.

'N-no, I haven't. It happened one night before Christmas when I was on my way home from Granny's. I was going through the park to take the short-cut and someone—'

Hilary gasped with horror. 'Are you telling me that you were *raped*?' she asked.

When Charlotte nodded, Hilary's hand flew to her throat then she was across the room and holding Charlotte protectively to her. 'Oh, you poor lamb,' she soothed. 'For this to happen to you . . . But why didn't you tell me?'

'I didn't say anything because you were poorly,' Charlotte wept. 'And there was nothing you could have done about it. But what am I going to do when Father finds out? He'll throw me out on the streets.'

'Oh no he won't, because he's not going to find out,' Hilary said with a rare show of strength.

'But I can't hide it forever,' Charlotte said fearfully.

'You won't have to because we're going to get rid of it.'

Charlotte's head snapped up. 'What do you mean, *get rid of it*?' she squeaked.

'I'm going to take you for an abortion,' Hilary told her and Charlotte's mouth gaped open.

'An *abortion*? But how do you know about these things?' she asked incredulously.

'You'd be surprised what I know,' Hilary told her, and then she studied Charlotte closely for a second as she wrestled with her conscience before going on: 'I know about abortions because I once had one. It was an unwanted pregnancy so I had a back-street abortion to get rid of it.'

Chapter Eight

Once the full significance of what her mother had just told her had sunk in, Charlotte edged closer to her and took her hand. Her mother was shaking now but even so she stared back bravely at Charlotte. 'I don't regret it,' she said steadfastly. 'And I would do it again if I had to.'

'But *why*?' Charlotte was totally confused. It wasn't as if her mother hadn't been married – and she had thought that she had wanted another child? Or had this happened before her mother was married?

'It's a long story,' her mother sighed. 'And not one that I can tell you right now, but let's just say that there was no way on this earth I wanted another child to have to live as you do.'

This statement answered Charlotte's unspoken question.

'But my life isn't *that* bad,' the girl replied.

'Huh! I don't agree with that.' Hilary tossed her head. 'At least I *had* a life before I met your father. You're a virtual prisoner here. How do you think it makes me feel when I see young women your age going out and enjoying themselves, when your father monitors everywhere you go? But enough about that for now. Do you want to keep this baby?'

The girl shook her head without even having to think about it. The baby had been forced upon her and she knew that she would never be able to love it. It would just be a constant reminder of what Harry had done to her. Even so, the thought of an abortion was terrifying and Hilary saw the fear in her eyes.

'It'll be all right,' she promised, squeezing her hand, although her own face was deathly pale. 'Just keep out of your father's way as much as you can and leave everything to me.'

'Where will we go?' Charlotte asked tremulously.

'I know someone in Coventry who will do it, but you must promise me you won't say a word to anyone. Do you understand? Not even your granny.'

Charlotte's head bobbed as her mother stood up and began to pace the floor.

'I shall tell your father that I am taking you shopping for some new clothes,' Hilary said after a while. 'God knows you've grown out of almost everything you own so he may well believe that.'

'W-will it hurt?' Charlotte asked.

Her mother stared at her for a moment before saying honestly, 'Yes, it will, I'm afraid. But it's over very quickly. Once it's done I shall bring you home and tell your father that you've caught a cold and then you can stay in bed for a couple of days whilst you recover.'

'When will we go?' Charlotte asked next.

'As soon as I can arrange it,' Hilary answered, and she suddenly looked so old and weary that Charlotte's heart went out to her. This would have been her first grandchild and she guessed that it wouldn't be easy for her mother. But then what alternative was there? They both knew that Reverend Hayes would never allow his daughter to bring shame on him and he would disown her at the very least.

'Try and rest now,' Hilary said as she walked towards the door and Charlotte was left alone with her thoughts.

On a cold morning in early March, Hilary and Charlotte caught the bus into Coventry. Charlotte was shaking with nerves and Hilary looked haggard with worry.

'Whereabouts are we going?' Charlotte whispered once they were seated and the conductor had taken their fare.

'We're going to Cherryfields,' Hilary whispered back. 'I should warn you it isn't a particularly nice area, but hopefully we won't be there for long.' She squeezed Charlotte's hand reassuringly.

Mrs Hayes had agonised for days, wondering if she was doing the right thing, but she could see no other way out of the predicament. Even so, she knew that what they were planning was morally wrong, and she wondered how she would live with herself once the deed was done. It had been bad enough, going through it herself, all those years ago – but to see Charlotte in the same situation hurt even more.

Charlotte nodded and stared out of the window as she chewed on her lip, trying to envisage the horror that lay ahead.

Eventually her mother tapped her arm and brought her thoughts sharply back to the present. 'We get off at the next stop,' she told her.

Once they had climbed down from the bus, Charlotte looked about in dismay. They were in a very rundown area which consisted mainly of rows of terraced houses whose doors all opened directly onto the pavement. Groups of women in turban-style head squares and wrap-around aprons were standing about gossiping, cigarettes dangling from the corners of their mouths, and they watched Charlotte and Hilary curiously as they passed them. Charlotte had always been painfully aware that her clothes were far from the height of fashion, but compared to these women she and her mother looked positively well-dressed.

'Is it far?' Charlotte asked as they rounded a corner. Her teeth were chattering and she knew that it was from fear rather than from the cold.

'Just a couple more streets away now,' Hilary answered and they hurried on. The further they went, the more confused Charlotte became. She had no idea at all where they were and just hoped that her mother knew where they were going.

Eventually the woman drew to a halt outside a terraced house with dirty lace curtains hanging at the equally grimy windows.

'This is it, love.' She stared into Charlotte's face before asking, 'Are you all right?'

Charlotte nodded. 'Yes. I just want to get it over with now.'

'Good, and just remember – I shall be with you the whole time.' Hilary took a deep breath then raised her hand and rapped at the door. Almost instantly it was opened by an elderly lady. She looked them up and down, then after quickly glancing around to make sure that no one was watching, she ushered them into a small front room and hastily slammed the door behind them.

The old woman looked positively filthy, and Charlotte grimaced when she noticed that her fingernails were caked with dirt. The room she was in wasn't much better. An old settee stood against one wall with a number of cats asleep on it, and every available surface was strewn with old newspapers and unwashed pots.

'Which one on yer is it then?' the old woman asked and Charlotte started as she looked back at her. Her head was clad in small metal curlers and when she spoke Charlotte saw that her teeth were rotting and black.

'I . . . It's my daughter,' Hilary answered as she took Charlotte's elbow.

The woman nodded. 'Fair enough. 'Ave yer got the cash?'

Hilary fumbled in her handbag and handed the woman a five-pound note which she instantly stuffed deep into the front pocket of her stained pinafore.

'An' how far along is she?'

'Going on three months,' Hilary answered in a small voice.

'Good. Well, let's go an' get it over wi' then. But remember, should owt go wrong it were nowt to do wi' me. Is that quite clear?'

Hilary seemed incapable of speech now, so she merely nodded as the old woman shooed them into the next room. This was just as dirty as the front room and Charlotte gulped as she saw a large metal bowl with a number of evil-looking objects inside it. One of them was what looked like an oversized crocheting hook and suddenly she guessed what lay ahead and terror coursed through her.

'Get yer knickers an' yer stockin's off an' lay on that settee there.'

Without being able to stop herself Charlotte started to cry as Hilary looked helplessly on. Charlotte took her coat off and handed it to her mother as the old woman pottered away to return with a bowl of hot water and a very grubby-looking towel.

'Come on then,' she said sharply as she rolled her sleeves up. 'We ain't got all day, yer know!'

Charlotte was crying so hard now that she could scarcely see what she was doing, and as she slid her thick woollen stockings down, Hilary began to cry too. As her knickers followed her stockings, shame brought colour flooding into the girl's cheeks and she began to doubt whether she could go through with it.

'I don't think I can do it, Mum,' she sobbed and the old woman rolled her eyes.

'Well, make yer bloody mind up,' she snapped coldly. 'Whether yer do or whether yer don't, you ain't getting' yer bleedin' money back now. I ain't here to be messed about.'

Charlotte stared at the grubby settee for a moment, then after taking a shuddering breath, she slowly walked over to it and lay down with her heart hammering in her chest.

'I should think so an' all,' the old woman grumbled. 'You young 'uns are all the bloody same. Yer don't think o' this bit when yer havin' yer fun. Now pull yer knees up an' let yer legs drop open.' She swiped her sleeve along her nose then lifting the metal hook from the dish she bent towards Charlotte.

'Aren't you going to wash your hands?' Hilary asked, panicking now. 'What about the risk of infection?'

'Gawd love us.' The old woman shook her head. 'Do yer want me to do this or what?'

Hilary chewed on her knuckles as the woman once again turned her attention to Charlotte. The girl felt something cold and a sharp stabbing pain. Screaming, she rolled away to land in an undignified heap on the floor with her skirt rolled up around her waist.

'I can't do it! I can't do it!'

Hilary raced across to her, and dropping to her knees, she gathered her into her arms.

'But I only just started,' the old woman objected as she stood there with blood dripping from the hook onto the carpet.

'It doesn't matter,' Hilary said, pushing Charlotte's under-clothing towards her. 'I'm taking her home.'

'Please yerself.' The crone threw the hook back into the bowl. 'But don't blame me if it ain't worked.'

Already Hilary was greatly regretting her decision to bring Charlotte here and could hardly wait to get her away from the place. *Whatever was I thinking of?* she asked herself as she helped the girl to dress.

Within minutes they were outside on the pavement with the door firmly banged shut behind them and Charlotte slumped against the wall as she clutched at her stomach.

'I . . . I'm sorry, Mum,' she sobbed as pain ripped at her insides. 'But I was so frightened.'

'Don't apologise,' Hilary soothed. 'I should never have brought you here. Let's just get you back home into the warm.'

Linking her arm through her daughter's, she helped her along as

Charlotte leaned heavily on her. It seemed to take forever to find their way back through the labyrinth of streets but at last they reached the bus stop and Hilary prayed that a bus would come along soon. Charlotte looked in danger of fainting at any moment. She was deathly pale and sweat was standing out in beads on her forehead despite the coldness of the day.

When a bus pulled finally up, Hilary helped Charlotte to board it, and once they were seated Charlotte leaned her head against her mother's shoulder.

The conductor clucked his tongue with concern when he came to take their fare. 'Lawdy, she don't look so good, missus,' he commented as he handed Hilary her tickets.

'Oh, she's er . . . just a bit under the weather. She'll be fine when I get her home to bed.'

'Best place for her, by the looks of it,' he answered, and whistling merrily he moved on.

As they entered the hallway of the vicarage some time later, Bernard, who had been preparing a sermon, was just leaving his study.

'That was a quick shopping trip, wasn't it?' he remarked.

'Charlotte wasn't feeling so good so we decided to come home and leave the shopping until another day,' Hilary told him as she helped Charlotte to take her coat off. 'It's women's problems.'

'Oh.' He flushed and to her relief he quickly moved on. Bernard couldn't abide to speak of personal things.

'Right, let's get you up to bed now,' Hilary told the girl softly and once upstairs she helped her to undress and get into bed after fetching a clean monthly towel from the drawer. Charlotte was bleeding profusely and now a feeling of dread settled around Hilary as she wondered how long it would be before her daughter lost the child.

'I'll go and get you a nice hot drink,' she soothed as she pulled the blankets around her. 'And I'll make you a hot water bottle too, shall I?'

Charlotte rolled into a ball, clutching her stomach as she prayed for the pain to stop, and Hilary bustled away.

The following morning, Hilary found Charlotte burning up with a high temperature and in agony. She rushed away to fetch a bowl of cool water and bathed her forehead, deeply concerned. Charlotte was still bleeding but not heavily, and as yet there was no sign of her losing the baby. Panic set in. If Charlotte didn't improve soon, Hilary would have no choice but to fetch the doctor in – and then once Bernard found out what was really wrong, she dreaded to think of what might happen.

'I'll just go and do your father's breakfast and then I'll be right back,' she promised the girl.

When Bernard saw his wife frying bacon on the stove he raised his eyebrows and asked, 'Where is Charlotte?'

'She's come down with a heavy cold now too so I've persuaded her to have the day in bed,' Hilary lied. She flustered about, avoiding his eyes as much as was possible, and once his meal was in front of him she prepared a tray and carried it upstairs to her daughter.

'How is the pain now?' she asked as she tenderly wiped the damp hair from Charlotte's brow.

'I think it's easing a little,' the girl said weakly. She had tossed and turned all night and was worn out. 'What will happen now, Mum?'

Hilary gulped as she drew the curtains, allowing grey light to filter into the room. It had stopped snowing some days ago and now that the thaw had set in, everywhere looked slushy and dirty.

'You'll go to the toilet and everything should come away soon,' she told her. 'And then hopefully you will be able to put all this behind you. But come on now, you must keep your strength up. Try to eat a little of this porridge. I've put some honey in it for you so it will be nice and sweet.'

Charlotte obediently tried to do as she was told, but she had only taken a couple of spoonfuls when she leaned over the side of the bed and was violently sick all over the linoleum. She was absolutely mortified. It was something she hadn't done since she was a very little girl but Hilary brushed aside her apologies.

'It doesn't matter, really. I'll go and get a bowl and I'll have it cleaned up in no time,' she said kindly.

Half an hour later, she helped Charlotte along the landing to the bathroom, thankful today for the one luxury that the vicarage boasted. Most of Bernard's parishioners were still bathing in tin baths in front

71

of the fire and using an outside toilet, but here they had one upstairs with hot and cold running water.

Thankfully, Bernard had locked himself away in his dark room, so as Charlotte limped along, Hilary told her, 'If you're no better by this afternoon I shall be fetching the doctor in. I shan't ever forgive myself if anything happens to you. I should *never* have taken you to that dreadful dump in the first place, but I didn't know what else to do. I was desperate.'

'No!' Charlotte choked out, stark terror shining in her eyes. 'You mustn't call the doctor, Mum. Promise me you won't! If Father ever found out what was wrong with me, there would be no living with him. You only did what you thought was best and I'll be fine soon.'

Once the bathroom door had closed behind her daughter, Hilary hurried away to wash up the pots, with strict instructions to Charlotte to call out if she needed her. The girl had refused to let her go into the bathroom with her and Hilary respected her request for some privacy. But once she reached the kitchen she leaned heavily against the table and openly wept. Right at this very minute her first grand-child could be being flushed away, and she wondered how she was ever going to be able to look in the mirror or live with herself ever again.

It was well over half an hour later that Charlotte emerged from the bathroom looking as weak as a kitten. Hilary was waiting for her at the top of the stairs and she immediately went over to her daughter, asking, 'Has anything happened?'

When Charlotte nodded, her mother gulped before helping her back to her room. It was over, and Hilary silently prayed that God would forgive her for what she had done.

Chapter Nine

Charlotte slowly recovered but Hilary was still seriously concerned about her. She avoided leaving the house and seemed to take no pride in herself whatsoever. She stopped washing her hair and took to wearing the same clothes for days on end until Hilary would gently suggest that it was time she had a bath and got changed.

It was one evening in April when Bernard was in the church that Hilary came across his sermon lying on the kitchen table.

'Oh dear.' She waved it at Charlotte who was slumped at the table. 'Your father has gone without this. You wouldn't run it across to him for me, would you, love?' She was quite capable of doing it herself but seeing that Charlotte hadn't stepped out of the house for days, she thought it would do her good to get out into the fresh air, even if it was for only a few minutes.

Charlotte reluctantly picked the sermon up and fetched her coat from the hall cupboard. She hated going into the church in the daytime let alone the night, but she didn't want to refuse her mother. It wasn't the night for the weekly service, so she guessed that her father would be with the choirboys.

'I shan't be long,' she mumbled as she slipped away, and Hilary watched her go with a frown on her face. She was well aware that her poor girl had gone through hell, but surely she should be picking up a little by now?

Outside a blustery wind was blowing and Charlotte shuddered as she pulled the collar of her coat up around her ears. She was so sick with fear that it was an effort to get through each day, and with every one that passed, her fear intensified. She had lied to her mother. The baby was miraculously still there, growing inside her despite what the old woman had done to her. She had pretended it was gone because she was terrified that her mother would fetch the doctor to her – but now she realised that she had been a fool. There was no way she would be able to hide her condition for much longer and then her father would find out about it anyway. Head bent, she struggled through the churchyard, starting as the yew trees bent towards her in the wind.

The church was in darkness as she slipped inside and she glanced nervously around. As she felt her way down the empty aisle she noticed a light shining from beneath the vestry door and, guessing that her father must be in there, she headed towards it with the sermon clutched close to her chest.

She pushed the door open, and as she stepped into the room she began, 'Father, Mother asked me to bring this over—' She stopped abruptly and gasped at the sight in front of her. Her father was leaning against his desk with his trousers around his ankles and young Tommy Webster was kneeling in front of him doing unspeakable things to him. Her father's head was thrown back and he was panting, but when he heard the door open he looked towards her and shock replaced the look of ecstasy.

'*Damn and blast you, girl!* Haven't you ever heard of knocking before you enter a room?' Her father's face reddened as he stooped and yanked his trousers up in one motion, sending Tommy sprawling across the floor. Charlotte's head wagged from side-to-side in disbelief and she had to swallow the bile that rose in her throat. And then her father took a step towards her with his arms outstretched and a false smile on his face.

'I . . . it's not what it looked like,' he whined, but Charlotte didn't stop to hear any more. Slinging his sermon onto the floor she turned and fled, and didn't slow her steps until she almost fell into the kitchen back at the vicarage.

'Good grief!' Hilary stared at her daughter's waxen face. 'Whatever has happened?'

Charlotte gulped as she tried to get her breath. 'It's – it's Father,' she managed to splutter. 'I just caught him in the vestry with Tommy Webster and he was . . .' Unable to go on, she buried her face in her hands as sobs shook her body. Hilary hurried over and put her arms around her, and they were still standing there when they heard footsteps on the path outside and the door crashed open.

'Charlotte, let me explain.' The Reverend held his hand out to her but she slapped it away as she stared at him with hate shining in her eyes.

'How *could* you?' she spat with loathing loud in her voice. 'Tommy is just a child – and to make him do such despicable things!'

'What despicable things?' Hilary was staring from one to the other of them as if they had both gone mad. 'Would someone *please* explain to me what's going on!'

Charlotte pointed a wavering finger at her father. 'He had his trousers down and Tommy was kneeling in front of him and he was . . .' Unable to go on she looked away as Hilary stood frozen to the spot. But then comprehension dawned, and surprisingly calmly, she told her daughter, 'Go up to your room. I shall be with you in a minute.'

'But—' Charlotte made to protest but then one look at her mother's livid face made her change her mind and she scuttled away like a frightened rabbit. As she took the stairs two at a time she could hear raised voices but she didn't stop to listen.

It was ten minutes later when Hilary joined her. 'I'm sorry you had to see that,' she said quietly.

Confused, Charlotte stared back at her. 'Aren't you shocked?' she asked.

Hilary sighed. 'Not really,' she admitted dully. 'I've suspected for a long time that your father had unnatural tendencies. He seemed obsessed with the choirboys, and as I said when young Andrew died, he never let the poor child have an evening off if he could help it. But I never dreamed it had gone this far.'

'So why have you stayed with him then?' Charlotte demanded. 'I know you're not happy. You don't even sleep in the same room.'

'Let's just say that I haven't been entirely blameless since we got married.'

Hilary sat down heavily on the candlewick bedspread and clasped her hands together. After a while she said quietly, 'I suppose you're old enough to be told now, so I may as well get it out of the way.' She licked her dry lips before going on. 'I was very young when I met your father. He is older than me, as you know, and he appeared very wise and sophisticated compared to the boys that I had been going out with. Not that there had been many. By the time I met your father I was courting Brian Mason, and I think I broke his heart when I dropped him for Bernard. It's something that I've lived to regret, but we all make mistakes, I suppose.'

Hilary wiped away a tear before continuing. 'On the day that your father and I were married, I was the happiest girl on earth and this place appeared to be a little palace. I could hardly believe that I was going to really move in here and I thought we'd live happily ever after. Huh! That thought didn't last long. On our wedding night I came to bed and got ready, then lay waiting for your father to join me but he didn't come and eventually I went in search of him. He was in the bedroom he still sleeps in, fast asleep, and being young and naïve I didn't like to disturb him. This went on for weeks until eventually I confessed to your granny and told her what was – or *wasn't* – going on.'

Hilary smiled ruefully at this point. 'You know what your granny is like. She hit the roof and said it wasn't natural. So I came back home and the first opportunity I got, I broached the subject. Your father was furious and he called me a whore. He said that the only reason for marriage was to create children and not for lust, and when I broke down and said that I wanted children, he . . . he raped me.' Hilary bowed her head in shame as she remembered, and Charlotte looked on in silence, too horrified to comment.

'It was like that for a long time,' Hilary whispered. 'Every now and again he would come to my room and . . . Well, eventually I found out that I was having you and thankfully that was the end of it. Your father thought he had proved his manliness and he never touched me again. But you were the best thing that ever happened to me, and your father loved showing you off.'

'But if he never touched you again, how could you have got pregnant with another baby?' Charlotte asked.

Hilary seemed to be battling with herself but eventually she admitted, 'The baby I aborted wasn't your father's . . . it was Brian Mason's. I realised soon after I married your father that I still loved Brian and we've seen each other whenever we could, ever since. It broke my heart to get rid of it, but I knew that Bernard would make the child's life hell if it was born. There was nothing else I could do.'

'Oh, *Mum*!' Charlotte was speechless for a while but then she asked, 'Why didn't you just run away with Brian?'

'How could I?' Hilary replied brokenly. 'What would it have done to you and your granny?'

'But I could have come with you, and Granny would have understood.'

Hilary shook her head. 'It isn't as simple as that. You see, I hoped I'd never have to tell you this, but your granny is very poorly. I found out just after I discovered that I was pregnant, that she had angina and the doctor told me that a shock could kill her. I couldn't take that risk.'

This second revelation was almost too much for Charlotte to take in and she rocked back on her heels as things began to fall into place. This must have been why her gran had told her about leaving all her money for her in her will. She rubbed her face in stunned disbelief as Hilary caught her hands.

'You have to try and forget what you saw tonight for your granny's sake,' she urged. 'We must go on as if nothing has happened.'

'Is there anything else I should know?' Charlotte managed to ask.

'I don't think so.'

'Then perhaps it's time I told *you* something.' Charlotte swallowed as the words she knew she must say stuck in her throat, but then she ploughed on. 'I didn't lose the baby, Mum . . . I'm still pregnant. What on earth am I going to do?'

The two women put their arms around each other and stayed that way for a long time, each drawing comfort from the other.

Chapter Ten

Life went on as if nothing untoward had happened until the following week when Charlotte was cleaning. Her father had gone out to see a parishioner who was ill and her mother had gone food shopping, so time hung heavy on her hands. She opened the door to her father's study and stepped inside, wrinkling her nose at the smell. Reverend Hayes was very partial to a glass of whisky, and the room smelled of whisky and stale air. Crossing to the window, she threw it open, then after tidying and polishing his desk her eyes were drawn towards the door of the dark room. She had never so much as set foot in there, but now curiosity consumed her. Nervously wiping her hands down either side of her skirt, Charlotte gently tried the door. The handle gave beneath her touch and after glancing across her shoulder, she slowly inched it open. A blackout blind hung at the window, blocking out every vestige of light, and a dull red lamp was the only illumination. She stood, letting her eyes adjust, before tentatively stepping inside. Sheets of photographic paper were strewn across the work-top, and a string that had a number of photos attached to it with little pegs was stretched across the ceiling from corner to corner, like a miniature clothesline. She peered at the first photograph. It was quite beautiful: her father had photographed a mother blackbird feeding her baby in the garden. The second was of the sun, setting across the roof of the church, making the colours in the stained-glass windows sparkle like jewels. Again it was quite beautiful, and she had to admit that her father had a talent.

And then she noticed another photo lying face down on the floor. It must have fallen off the line so she bent to pick it up, and as she looked at it, her stomach heaved with shock. The image was so shocking that she screwed her eyes tight shut for a moment, convinced that she had made a mistake. But then she opened them again, and the evidence was still there in front of her. It was a picture of her father doing disgusting things to young Andrew Pinnington. Vomit rose in her throat as she staggered backwards, upsetting a bowl of some solution that immediately spread across the floor.

'*No!*' She clamped her hand across her mouth. The young boy's face was contorted as if in agony, and as an idea occurred to her it was almost more than she could bear. Was this why the poor child had committed suicide? Had her father forced him into performing these unnatural acts until the boy felt that he couldn't do it any more? And if the photo was of her father and Andrew, then who could have taken it? There must have been a third person present – but who could be so sick-minded as to participate in such perverted activities? A quick scout-around revealed a number of other photos spread hidden beneath a blotter on a small table, and the girl felt her stomach revolt at the sight of them.

She felt her way to the door, unable to look at any more, and once back in the study she took great gulps of air to try and calm herself. But then making a hasty decision, she crept back into the dark room and, lifting one of the photos, she slipped it into her pocket before quickly shifting the others about so that it wouldn't be immediately apparent that one was missing. Her father had a terrible temper as she knew to her cost, and if he were to discover the theft, he would make both her and her mother's lives hell.

The sound of the front door closing brought her thoughts crashing back to the present, and snatching up the polish and duster, she headed for the hallway where she almost collided with her father who had just come in.

'What's the matter with you?' he asked as she barged past but she ignored him and headed to the kitchen. Once there she gripped the edge of the sink until her trembling subsided. Anger began to pulse through her. Here she was, terrified to tell her father that she was pregnant after being raped, when he was no more than a vile, disgusting beast . . . But perhaps she would be able to use this new knowledge to her advantage? She would talk to her mother about it as soon as she came in.

* * *

79

In actual fact it was late evening before Charlotte managed to get Hilary alone. There had been a steady stream of visitors to the vicarage all afternoon and her mother had been kept busy carrying trays of tea to and fro. But now the supper was over and at last Charlotte had her mother to herself as they washed up the supper pots.

She bit hard on her lip wondering how to begin before saying, 'Mum . . .?'

'Yes, love?' As Hilary looked at her expectantly, Charlotte's courage failed her. Her mother was a bag of nerves nowadays, jumping at her own shadow, and Charlotte couldn't add to her concerns. Perhaps it would be better to have this out with her father alone and not involve her mother.

'Oh, I was just thinking that we won't be able to put off telling Father about the baby for much longer,' she said lamely. 'My clothes are getting very tight and he's bound to realise what's wrong. Do you think we should tell him and get it over with?'

Hilary hung her head for a moment before nodding. 'I dare say we should. As you say, it's not something we can hide forever – and what can he do, when all is said and done? When do you think we should do it?'

'I'll do it,' Charlotte replied with quiet determination. 'There's no reason for you to be there. This is my problem.'

'Charlotte! You shouldn't have to do this on your own,' Hilary objected. 'It's not as if it's even your fault. You were *raped*, for God's sake.'

'No, Mum. I want to – *really*,' Charlotte said softly. 'And there's no time like the present. Is he in his study?'

Hilary's eyes were wide with fear now as she nodded numbly. Charlotte pecked her on the cheek, then drawing herself up to her full height she left the room before her courage deserted her. Once in the hallway her steps faltered but she forced herself to move on until she was standing in front of her father's study door. She rapped, then without waiting for him to answer, she swung the door open just in time to see her father coming out of the dark room. Inside she was quaking but outwardly she was calm as she remembered the dish of fluid she had disturbed when she had first glimpsed the appalling photograph. He would know that someone had been in there and would be on his guard.

'Father, I need to speak to you.' After closing the door firmly behind her she went to stand in front of his desk as he sat down in his leather chair. He steepled his fingers and peered at her over the top of them. He could never remember Charlotte asking to speak to him before.

'What is it that is so important it couldn't wait until morning?' he asked coldly.

'I'm afraid I have something to tell you that you aren't going to be too happy about.'

'Go on then.'

Charlotte took a deep breath before saying quickly, 'Just before Christmas as I was on my way home from Granny's one night I went into the park and I was raped.' She saw his eyebrows disappear into his hairline but before he could say anything she rushed on, 'The consequence of that is I am pregnant.'

'You are *what*?' He jumped to his feet and, leaning his knuckles heavily on the desk, he loomed over her menacingly. 'You mean you have waited all this time to tell me? I find that a little strange.'

'It's quite true,' she said calmly, glad that the desk was between them. 'And the reason I didn't tell you sooner is because I knew that you would react like this.'

'Are you *quite* sure that this hasn't come about through some sordid liaison?' he roared.

Charlotte felt anger course through her veins. 'I'm quite sure. Although how *you* dare accuse anyone of being sordid, I don't know. As Granny would say, it would be like the pot calling the kettle black, wouldn't it?'

'And just what is that supposed to mean?'

When Charlotte pointed towards the dark room, the colour drained from his face and he sank heavily into his chair. 'You had no business to go in there,' he muttered.

'No, I didn't, but I'm glad that I did,' Charlotte shot back as her lip curled with contempt. 'I am in this predicament through no fault of my own. What excuse do you have for what you've done? I just wonder what your parishioners would think if they knew.

And what about poor Andrew? No wonder he took his own life. The poor child probably couldn't face what you were doing to him any more!'

'How *dare* you speak to me like this!' Bernard ground out but he felt very vulnerable. Somehow he had to shut his daughter up. 'Let's leave my er . . . well, let's speak about your condition first. What do you propose to do about it? Of course there is no possible way you can keep the child. The scandal would be . . .' His voice trailed away as he saw the hatred on Charlotte's face.

'I don't want to keep the child,' she informed him, thinking what a hypocrite he was. 'And I did consider a termination but I couldn't go through with it.'

'I see.' He stared off into space, his mind in turmoil. He had worked so hard to cover his fetish and he was a well-respected member of the community, but should Charlotte ever expose him for what he was, he would be hounded out of the town with his reputation in tatters, and his career finished. He shuddered at the thought. And then it came to him in a blinding flash.

'I think I might be able to help you,' he said cautiously. 'But first you must promise me that you will tell no one of what you saw in there.' He jerked his head towards the dark room. 'It was, of course, a single moment of madness.'

Charlotte didn't believe him for a moment but she stood silently, enjoying seeing him squirm. Judging by the number of photographs she had seen, it was much more than that.

'I think the best thing for all concerned would be for you to go away until after the child is born.'

'Where would I go and what would I do with the baby afterwards?' she asked coolly.

'I shall phone your Aunt Edith and ask her if you can stay with her until after the birth, and then she could arrange for the child to be adopted. I can tell people that she is unwell and that you have gone to nurse her until she is better and no one will be any the wiser. What do you think of the idea?'

'I suppose it *could* work,' Charlotte admitted ungraciously, although the thought of spending months cooped up in the back of beyond with her aunt filled her with dread.

'And if I do this for you, are you prepared to remain silent about what you saw in there?' Reverend Hayes asked now. 'I must advise you to think of the consequences if you don't. Just think of the shame it would bring onto your mother and granny.'

'Not to mention *you*, of course,' Charlotte said.

He had the grace to bow his head and a silence fell between them until Charlotte eventually grudgingly muttered, 'I suppose it would be for the best. Mother has told me that Granny has angina and I don't want to make her ill.'

'Good, good. Now run along and leave it with me,' he urged, looking vastly relieved. 'I'm sure everything will look better in the morning after a good night's sleep.'

Charlotte threw him one last withering glance before turning on her heel and marching from the room. Sleep, he had said. *Huh!* She doubted that she would ever rest easy again. She was sure that every time she closed her eyes, an image of her father and young Andrew would flash behind them.

Hilary was pacing anxiously up and down the kitchen when Charlotte appeared, and she asked instantly, 'How did he take it?'

'Better than I'd thought he would,' Charlotte lied. 'He's going to ask Aunt Edith if I can go and stay with her until after the baby is born and then she will arrange for it to be adopted.'

'And how do you feel about that?'

'I suppose it would be for the best, and then at least I could try and put it behind me,' Charlotte replied. She didn't want to keep the child, after all, so perhaps this was the best option.

Hilary wrung her hands. Part of her was relieved that Bernard had taken it so well, another part of her dreaded Charlotte going away for the birth. She felt that she should have been with her – but what could she do?

Charlotte, meanwhile, was wrestling with her conscience. Should she tell her mother what she had seen in the dark room? It was obvious from Hilary's confession that she didn't love her husband any more, and as far as Charlotte was concerned, she wished her mother would leave him and find happiness with the man she really *did* love. But if she confided what she had discovered about the dark room photographs, her granny would be bound to find out about it, and if she was as ill as they said, what would it do to her? The shock might kill her, and Charlotte knew that she wouldn't be able to live with herself if that happened.

Suddenly the events of the evening caught up with her and she was so tired that she could barely stand. She felt as if her whole world had been ripped apart and all she wanted to do was escape to her room and think.

'Look, Mum,' she said wearily, 'it's been a long day. Would you mind if I went up for an early night?'

'Of course not, pet.' Hilary stroked her daughter's smooth cheek as tears clogged her throat. It broke her heart to think of what lay ahead for her but she was powerless to do anything about it. 'I suppose we should at least be thankful that your father knows about the baby now,' she said. 'He's taken it so much better than I'd thought he would. Go on, you go up to bed. Things will work out, you'll see.'

Charlotte managed a weak smile before heading for the stairs, but once in her room her mind gave her no rest. What was her father doing with the disgusting picture he had taken? Was he taking them purely for his own pleasure? But then commonsense told her that he couldn't be. There *had* to be at least one other person involved – the person who was holding the camera. Somehow she would find out who it was before she was shipped off to Ireland.

Two days later, on her way home from the town where she had done a little shopping for her mother, Charlotte bumped into Bab's. They hadn't seen each other for ages and Charlotte had an idea that Bab's had been avoiding her, but the other girl seemed pleased enough to see her.

'Hello, stranger,' Babs greeted her cheerily. 'Long time no see, eh? How is life treatin' yer?'

Charlotte could hardly blurt out, 'Well, your brother raped me and I'm pregnant, and oh, by the way, my father is a pervert!' Instead she raised a smile and told her, 'Not too badly, and how are you? you're certainly looking well.'

Babs grinned. 'I ain't never been better,' she confided. 'I suppose yer heard that me an' Tim got married last month? It were only a

84

quiet Register Office do, mind.' She pointed to her stomach. 'It were all done a bit quick, if yer get me drift.'

'What – you mean you're pregnant?' Charlotte answered incredulously.

'Well, I don't reckon this is wind.' Babs laughed, patting her stomach, and the two girls fell into step together. Then, looking a little guilty, she added, 'I would have invited yer, but from what I've been hearin' you've had a lot on yer plate lately what wi' yer mam an yer granny both bein' poorly.'

'It's all right,' Charlotte answered, and then before she could stop herself she asked, 'How is Harry?'

Babs' face became solemn. 'Huh – you tell me! I don't see much of him nowadays.' She made sure no one was in earshot and then lowering her voice, she confided, 'Between you an' me, me mam chucked him out on his ear, which were a bit of a shock to say the least 'cos she always thought the sun shone out of our Harry's arse.'

'Why ever did she do that?' Charlotte asked curiously.

'Well . . .' Babs hesitated for a moment before saying, 'Let's just say she found sommat in his room as she didn't approve of. Don't get me wrong,' she rushed on, 'we've always known that our Harry were sailin' close to the wind wi' some of the things he got up to, but even me mam couldn't condone this.'

'What was it?'

'It were . . .' Babs gulped. 'It were pictures. *Nasty* pictures. Yer know? Of little kids doin' dirty things. It seems he sells 'em on an' makes a mint out of 'em.'

Charlotte's stomach performed a somersault as she recalled her father talking to Harry outside the church. Could it be that Harry was the person who had taken the photos? It certainly appeared that way, and now as she thought of the life growing inside her, she was even more repulsed.

'Where has he gone?' she asked eventually when she had managed to pull herself together.

Babs shrugged. 'I've heard he's still about, but I doubt he'll show his face round at me mam's again. She told him in no uncertain terms that if he did, she'd shop him to the coppers. An' good on her, that's what I say! I mean, there's a difference between petty crime an' that sort o' thing, ain't there? An' yer have to draw the line somewhere. Me mam does have *some* principles, even if she's turned a blind eye to the odd bit o' knocked-off stuff.'

Babs grimaced with disgust as Charlotte stared blankly ahead. It really felt in that moment that things simply couldn't get any worse.

Chapter Eleven

'I would like you to be ready to leave tomorrow morning at seven o'clock. We shall be taking a bus to the docks and from there we shall board a ferry to Ireland. From there it will be the train to County Cork, so it will be a long day.'

'Yes, Father.' Charlotte felt like a naughty child summoned to the headmaster's office as she stood in front of her father, but then he had always managed to make her feel like that. Part of her was glad that she was finally going away, but the other half was terrified of what lay ahead. She had no qualms about giving the baby away once it was born, but she knew that she would miss her mother and her granny. Still, she consoled herself, it wouldn't be forever and when the birth was over she could try to get on with her life. In fact, once she was home again, she fully intended to look into a career in nursing as her granny had suggested.

'Does my aunt expect us?' she asked now.

'Of course. And once we have arrived I shall stay overnight and then the next morning I shall return here,' he told her.

Charlotte nodded and turned away. There was little more to be said and she didn't wish to stay in her father's presence for a second longer than was necessary. She left the room without another word to find her mother hovering in the hallway.

'What did he want you for?' she asked anxiously.

Charlotte put her arm around Hilary's shoulders and steered her towards the kitchen. 'He wanted to tell me that we will be leaving for Aunt Edith's first thing in the morning. Didn't you know?'

'Since when does he tell *me* anything?' Hilary retorted. 'I'm just the unpaid help around here.' Her shoulders sagged. 'I don't know what I'm going to do without you for all that time,' she muttered brokenly. She had known that the day when Charlotte would have to leave was fast approaching, but now that it was almost there she felt bereft.

'Look, the sooner I go the sooner I'll be back,' Charlotte told her reassuringly. 'But now I'd better go and do some packing. Father wants us to leave at seven in the morning so I won't have time to do it tomorrow.'

'Do you want me to come and help you?' her mother offered.

Charlotte shook her head. 'No, really, I'd rather do it myself. I shan't be taking that much anyway. I've very little left that fits me. You go and put your feet up. You look all in.'

Despite her brave words, Charlotte was crying inside. She would have liked to have had time to say goodbye to her granny, but then commonsense took over and she knew that it was better this way. If she were to see her, she might well break down and confess why she was really going, and that would be no good for either of them. Far better for Hilary to tell her the story they had decided on, that her aunt was ill and she had gone to Ireland to nurse her until she was better.

She climbed the stairs on legs that felt like lead. Once inside her room she stared around her. The room was quite austere by any standards and yet it had been Charlotte's own little sanctuary for so long that she couldn't imagine sleeping anywhere else. Crossing to the wardrobe she dragged out an old brown leather suitcase, and trying to close her mind to what lay ahead, she began to pack her few meagre possessions.

She slept very little that night and it was as she was lying there that she felt the child inside her kick; really kick for the first time. This was no gentle flutter but a tiny person making their presence felt. Her eyes welled with tears as her hand dropped unconsciously to her stomach and she felt an overwhelming sadness. It wasn't the child's fault, after all, and all she could do now was hope that her aunt would find it a good home once it was born. She owed her baby that much at least.

Early the next morning found Charlotte and her mother standing face to face in the kitchen as her mother fiddled with the buttons on her daughter's coat and turned her collar up. 'You'd never believe it was the end of April,' she grumbled, glancing towards the window where the rain was hurling itself against the panes as if it was trying to gain entry. 'And are you quite sure that you've got everything that you need?'

She had already asked the same question at least a dozen times but Charlotte smiled at her patiently as she struggled to hold back tears. 'Yes, Mum, I'm quite sure. Now stop fussing.'

Leaning forward, she kissed her mother's cheek and Hilary hugged her fiercely, wondering how she was going to get through the next few months without her. It was then that they heard Bernard coming down the stairs and they jumped apart.

'All ready, are we?' he asked as he entered the kitchen and began to do up the buttons on his own heavy topcoat.

When Charlotte nodded he glanced towards the clock.

'Good. The taxi that I've ordered to take us to the bus station in Nuneaton should be here any moment.' Scarcely before the words had left his lips the sound of a car's horn reached them and he smiled with satisfaction. 'That will be it then, right on time just as I like it. Come along, Charlotte, say goodbye to your mother. We have a very long journey ahead of us.'

Now that the moment had arrived, Charlotte could find nothing to say. Words seemed so inadequate.

'Now you will ring me as soon as you get to Aunt Edith's, won't you?' Hilary fretted.

'I probably won't get a chance,' Charlotte answered. 'Father says it will be very late before we get there, so I'll ring you first thing tomorrow.'

Hilary's eyes were like saucers as she nodded mutely, desperately trying to keep the tears at bay. And then Bernard had hold of Charlotte's elbow and was ushering her towards the door with her suitcase in his other hand and all Hilary could do was watch helplessly.

In no time at all they were heading towards Nuneaton and now Charlotte dared to ask, 'Where will we be sailing from, Father?'

'Swansea,' he informed her curtly. 'But it will be two bus journeys and one train journey before we get there, then we'll be taking the overnight ferry to Cork.'

Charlotte nodded and lapsed into silence as she stared miserably from the window at the passing scenery.

By the time they arrived at the docks late that afternoon, Charlotte was tired and hungry and not looking forward to the ride on the ferry at all. The sea looked black and choppy, and the ferry seemed to be swaying about alarmingly on the waves.

'I think we've just about got time to get something to eat and drink before we board,' her father commented as he looked about. 'I dare say we ought to get something into our stomachs before we sail. It doesn't look like we're going to have a calm crossing. Look, there's a café there. That will do.'

He hastened towards a seedy-looking establishment that appeared to be half-full of seamen, and as he pushed the door open and ushered Charlotte past him, curious eyes glanced in their direction. The place was full of cigarette smoke and stale cooking smells, but even so Charlotte sank down gratefully at the nearest available table as her father hurried towards the counter. She watched a heavily made-up, blowsy-looking woman serve him and minutes later he was back carrying a wooden tray.

'There we are,' he said, placing a heavy mug in front of Charlotte. She eyed it dubiously. The china was cracked and a film of grease was floating on the top of what looked like very weak tea. Her father began to spoon sugar into one of the mugs from a pressed-glass sugar bowl in the centre of the table, and then he handed her a bread roll.

'It's bacon,' he informed her, and seeing her grimace, he said crossly, 'It may not be Cordon Bleu but at least it's edible. We should be grateful for small mercies.'

Charlotte took a bite. The bacon was dripping in fat and the bread was so stale that it was curling at the edges, but even so she understood it would help if there was something in her stomach when she went onto the boat, so she forced it down. Surprisingly enough she did feel a little better after she had eaten and she even managed a few sips of the lukewarm tea.

'Right, I think we should board now,' her father said when they had finished. He rose from the table. 'Come along, Charlotte.'

She followed him outside meekly. Thankfully he had said very little to her on the journey. In fact, now that she came to think of it, he had said very little to her since the night she had discovered the photographs. She sometimes felt that they were skirting around each other like two opponents in a boxing ring. She was still in an agony of indecision on whether or not she had done the right thing by not exposing him for what he was. Even now he could be abusing young Tommy in the same brutal manner as he had abused Andrew, but then what would have been the repercussions on her mother and her gran if she had told them what she had found? Perhaps it was as well that she was going away for a while.

It was bitterly cold on the dock with a cruel wind blowing in from the sea. Once they had boarded the ferry, her father led her inside to a row of hard wooden seats. He hadn't felt that it was worth getting them a sleeping cabin and she knew that there was an uncomfortable night ahead. After what seemed like a very long time the ferry rumbled into life and as Charlotte peeped through the window she saw the docks slipping away from them. The boat began to roll ominously. The further out to sea they got the worse it became until she was gripping the edge of her seat and feeling very nauseous.

'I – I think I might just go out on deck for a while,' she gasped after a time and her father shrugged and continued to read his newspaper as she staggered through the rows of seats and out onto the deck. She headed for the railings and leaning over them, promptly emptied the contents of her stomach into the heaving sea. A glimpse to either side of her soon showed that she wasn't the only one who was being sea-sick. There were a number of passengers leaning across the railings and they looked equally as ill as she felt, not that it gave her any comfort. Soon the lights of the docks had disappeared as night fell, and there was nothing but ocean on either side as far as the eye could see. The ship was rising and dipping alarmingly and Charlotte suddenly wondered if they were all going to drown. Right at that moment she didn't much care.

That night was the longest that Charlotte had ever spent. She alternated between trying to sit on the hard wooden seat and leaning over the rails, and at one point she almost wished that she could die. But then at last early the next morning, she saw land in the distance and felt her spirits rise. Reverend Hayes had somehow managed to nap with his chin resting on his chest but she hadn't slept a wink and her eyes felt gritty and were red-rimmed.

'Father, I think I see the port ahead.' She gently shook his arm and he started awake and peered through the window.

'Yes, I believe you are right,' he conceded. 'Start to gather your things together then.'

Charlotte sat back down. There was nothing to gather apart from her battered old suitcase. At last the ferry pulled into the port and they went on deck as they watched the deck hands manhandling the gangplanks into place. Once it was done people began to stream off the ferry and Charlotte noted that the majority of them looked as grateful to be back on dry land as she felt. It had certainly been an awful crossing and she was just glad that it was behind them.

'Right,' her father said, once they were back on terra firma. 'We need to find out what time the next bus to Tipperary is now.'

His sister Edith lived just outside the town and Charlotte knew that they would have a good walk ahead of them, once the bus had dropped them off. Two hours later found them trundling through the lanes past emerald-green fields and peatlands, with the Galtee Mountains in the background. Ireland really was a beautiful place but today Charlotte was too tired to appreciate it and she dozed off in no time.

Eventually the bus drew to a halt and she woke and rubbed the sleep from her eyes.

'This is as far as it goes,' her father informed her. 'I'm afraid it's Shanks's pony from here.'

Charlotte groaned as she toted her case off the bus. There was a long walk ahead of them now and she didn't feel up to it, not that she had much choice. As they moved along the lanes a number of enormous hooded crows flew past them and Charlotte grimaced as she swiped the rain out of her eyes. They were huge birds, common to this area and known to occasionally prey on small lambs. The coastline was also well-known for sightings of fin whales, basking sharks, pilot whales, and minke whales, and was a major attraction for tourists – not that Charlotte much cared at that moment in time.

They moved on, the case becoming heavier by the minute, and soon there was nothing to be seen but the odd solitary cottage with smoke curling from its chimneys. Charlotte wished that her father would offer to carry her case for her, but he strode ahead, almost as if he had forgotten she was there until at last they rounded a bend in a lane and her aunt's house came into view.

The girl shuddered involuntarily at the sight of it. At one time it must have been a beautiful house, but now it looked cold and forbidding – much like the woman who lived inside it. It struck Charlotte afresh that this would be her home for the foreseeable future, and she gulped to stop the tears that were threatening to erupt.

The house stood alone with no neighbours within sight and Charlotte felt isolated already. It was quite a large property with tall chimney pots surrounded by overgrown gardens with not a single flower in sight. Bernard hurried up the path and rang the bell on the door. They heard the sound echo throughout the house followed by the soft thud of footsteps, and seconds later Aunt Edith drew back the bolts and the enormous oak door swung open. She was dressed in a shapeless black cardigan, a calf-length black skirt, thick black stockings and flat black shoes, and she looked as if she was in mourning.

'So you are here then,' she said unnecessarily.

'Yes, and I'm afraid we haven't had the best of journeys. The sea crossing was terribly rough,' Bernard answered as he stepped past her into the hall.

'And are you coming in too, or are you just going to stand there gawping like an idiot?' her aunt barked.

Charlotte shot past her and placed the case down on the tiled floor in the hallway, her heart sinking to new depths.

'So, this is a fine state of affairs, isn't it?' her aunt said scathingly, looking her niece up and down. 'I should think you are ashamed of yourself, my girl, bringing scandal on the family like this.'

Charlotte didn't even bother to argue. She knew that there would be no point. Had it been left to her aunt, she would probably have had her tarred and feathered and run out of town on a donkey. As it was, the girl supposed that she should just be grateful that the woman had agreed to help her, so she merely hung her head and didn't reply.

'I dare say you'll both be tired and hungry,' the woman said now, addressing her brother. 'I wasn't sure what time you would arrive so I've made a large pot of stew. It will only need heating up. But first give me your coats.'

Charlotte and her father obediently slid out of their wet coats and handed them to her, and after she had hung them on an old-fashioned coat-stand they followed her through to the kitchen. It was absolutely enormous and so out-dated that it looked as if it belonged in the last century. There was no running water here, but a large wooden pump on the sink pumped in water from a well in the garden that was fed by a freshwater spring. An old oven stood against another wall and Aunt Edith crossed to it now and placed a large blackened pot on it to heat through the contents. She then filled the kettle at the deep stone sink and after placing it on a large metal bracket that hung above the fire, she pushed it into the heart of the flames to boil.

'We'll have tea whilst we wait for the stew to warm up,' she informed them. 'I expect you'll be ready for a hot drink.'

'That would be wonderful.' Bernard crossed to the fire and held his hands out to the blaze as Charlotte slid onto one of the hard-backed chairs that stood next to the scrubbed pine table.

Soon they had steaming mugs in front of them and as Charlotte sipped at hers, warmth began to seep through her again and she felt slightly better. The beef stew was surprisingly tasty and Bernard had two large bowls full before patting his stomach contentedly. It was early evening by then and the light outside was fading. The kitchen was situated at the back of the house and all that could be seen beyond the windows were trees that were bowing in the wind and rain.

'Right, you can wash the dishes up now while your father and I go into the drawing room to have a chat,' her aunt informed her imperiously, as if Charlotte was the hired help. 'You'll find hot water in the kettle. And just make sure that you clean them properly. I cannot be doing with half measures. If a job is worth doing, it is worth doing well.'

Charlotte was tempted to stick her tongue out at her but she merely nodded as her aunt and her father left the room.

Half an hour later the kitchen was tidy again and Charlotte yawned. All she wanted to do right then was sleep, so she walked along the hallway and tapped on the door of the drawing room before entering. Her aunt and her father stopped talking immediately and her aunt glared at her. 'Yes? What do you want?'

'I'm really tired and I'd like to go to bed. Could you tell me which room I'm in, please?'

Her aunt sighed. 'The third on the right at the top of the stairs,' she said curtly.

Charlotte scuttled away. She hefted her suitcase up the steep dog-leg staircase and when she came to the room her aunt had directed her to, she opened the door and clicked on the light. The room was sparsely furnished and lacking in comfort, but the bed looked so inviting that Charlotte immediately began to strip her clothes off as she rummaged in her case for her nightdress. Her clothes were still damp from the long walk in the rain and she shivered as she looked about the room more closely. Drab brown curtains hung at an enormous sash-cord window and the floorboards were bare save for a peg rug that was placed next to the bed. The latter was a large wooden affair with no decoration of any sort, and on it was a faded patchwork quilt. Next to it was a washstand on which stood a plain pottery jug and bowl, a battered chest of drawers and what appeared to be an old kitchen chair stood against the other wall. There was no room for a wardrobe but then Charlotte knew that she wouldn't need one. She had only brought essentials but tonight she was just too tired to unpack them. She was even too tired to wash so she pulled her nightdress on, closed the curtains and slithered between the cold cotton sheets.

The first night in what was to be her home for some time to come had begun.

Chapter Twelve

'Come along, girl. Idle hands make work for the devil.'

Charlotte started awake as her aunt roughly shook her arm. She looked groggily at the small clock on the chest of drawers. It was six o'clock in the morning and she felt as if she had only just gone to sleep.

Her aunt meanwhile crossed to the curtains and swished them aside, allowing the cold early-morning light to flood into the room. As always she was dressed from head to foot in black and her grey hair was pulled into a severe bun on the back of her head.

'You can come and help me to cook the breakfast,' she barked as she marched back towards the door.' And then we shall be going out.'

'Where to?' Charlotte dared to ask but her only answer was the slamming of the door as her aunt left the room.

Once she was washed and dressed and had tied her hair neatly back with a ribbon she went down to the kitchen where she found her aunt cooking bacon and her father drinking his second cup of tea.

'Lay the table,' her aunt ordered, and Charlotte began to fetch plates from the large dresser that stood against one wall.

They had scrambled eggs and bacon for breakfast and then once again Charlotte washed the pots up while her aunt and her father took a tray of fresh tea into the drawing room. She noticed that her father seemed to be a little preoccupied, but supposed that it was because he wasn't looking forward to the return journey.

Once everything was washed, dried and returned to its rightful place, her father came back into the kitchen and told her, 'You may telephone your mother now to let her know that we arrived safely. But your aunt and I have decided that this should be the last call until . . . well, until the birth is over.'

When Charlotte went to protest he held his hand up. 'No arguing, please. Phone calls are expensive and besides, this has all been very distressing for your mother and you wouldn't want to make things worse for her, would you? Let the next call you make be the one to tell her that all this is behind you and you are coming home.'

Put that way, Charlotte supposed that he was right, but it would be very hard not to be able to hear her mother's voice.

'Very well,' she said meekly, and seconds later she got through to the telephone exchange and waited whilst the operator put her call through to the vicarage.

'Are you all right, dear?' Hilary wanted to know, when Charlotte finally managed to speak to her.

Charlotte swallowed. 'Yes, I'm absolutely fine,' she managed to say brightly. 'We had an awful crossing on the ferry but we got here safely in the end. I'll let Father tell you all about it when he comes home.'

'And how is your aunt?'

'Oh, she seems well enough,' Charlotte said vaguely. She was fighting the urge to cry but she held herself together for her mother's sake. Hilary suddenly seemed to be a million miles away and although the girl wanted to tell her how much she loved and missed her, she knew that this would only make things worse.

They talked for another few minutes about everyday things, but after telling her mother that she would not be ringing her again until the baby had been born, the conversation was stilted. Neither of them really knew quite what to say to each other, so Charlotte was almost relieved when she put the receiver down.

Half an hour later, her father emerged from the drawing room with her aunt and told her, 'Get your coat on. A cab will be coming in a minute to take us out.'

'Out where?' Charlotte asked. She had thought that her father would be leaving shortly to begin the journey home. He had a service in the church the next day and she knew that he wouldn't want to miss that.

'We're taking you to meet the people who will be helping with the adoption of the child once it is born,' he said, avoiding her eyes and looking vaguely uncomfortable.

Charlotte would have liked to ask more questions but instead she went upstairs and got her shoes, then after putting her coat on, her aunt told her to go to the kitchen and wait until the cab arrived.

Ten minutes later, her father came to collect her. She followed him outside to where one of the oldest cars that Charlotte had ever seen was waiting. It looked as if it was only the rust on it holding it together, and she wondered how far it would get them.

Her father sat in the front with the driver, a wizened old man who looked to be even older than the car, whilst Charlotte sat in the back with her aunt, and soon they were rolling along the winding lanes. Under other circumstances, Charlotte would have enjoyed the drive because the countryside was breathtakingly beautiful, but today she saw nothing to be happy about. She had no idea at all where they might be going and soon she was helplessly lost. They seemed to have left all the cottages and houses behind them but eventually a huge wall loomed ahead.

'Is this some sort of stately home?' Charlotte asked innocently.

'No, it's a convent,' her aunt snapped and Charlotte fell silent again.

They drew up outside some enormous wooden gates that were at least ten foot high, and her father got out to rap on them. Almost immediately they swung open, and as they drove through them Charlotte saw an elderly nun closing and locking them behind them.

'It feels as if we're going into a prison,' she said before she could stop herself, and Reverend Hayes glared at her as they set off down a long driveway that was overhung with trees. Eventually the convent came into sight and Charlotte suppressed a shudder. It looked like every haunted house she had ever read about, grim and foreboding. In the centre of the house was an enormous arched door; on either side of it stretched dark windows with no adornment of any kind. There was not a soul in sight and the girl began to feel uneasy.

The cab drew up at the door and the driver asked them in a broad Irish brogue, 'Will yer be wantin' me to wait fer yer then, mister?'

'Yes, we shouldn't be long,' her father replied as he climbed out of the car and marched up the three curved stone steps that led to the doorway.

'Right'y' are, mister.' The old man doffed his cap and sank back into his seat as her father rang the bell at the side of the door. Just for an instant the old man caught Charlotte's eye and she thought she saw pity there, but she thought that she must have been mistaken and looked away. There was nothing to be heard except the sound of birdsong and Charlotte stared around. The grounds surrounding the house looked just as bleak as the exterior, and she shuddered as a cold hand closed around her heart.

Eventually, they all heard the sound of a key in the lock and bolts being drawn back, and as the door creaked open they found themselves staring at a solemn-faced nun.

'This is Charlotte Hayes,' her father said as he hastily removed his hat, and the nun inclined her head as she stepped aside to allow them entry.

'Sister Magdalene is expecting you. Come this way, please.' She then relocked the door and fastened the bolts again before tucking her hands into the sleeves of her long black habit and gliding away from them.

As they followed her through the austere, spotlessly clean corridors Charlotte spotted a young, heavily pregnant girl further along the hallway, down on her knees polishing the parquet flooring. She briefly raised her head to glance at them and when Charlotte saw the utter despair mirrored in them she gulped deeply. She would have liked to go across and speak to her but she didn't have a chance because the nun who had admitted them suddenly stopped in front of one of the many closed doors that led off the hallway and tapped on it.

'Enter,' a voice called from the other side and the nun ushered them inside. They were confronted by another nun, a much older one this time, who was seated at a large desk to one side of a deep bay window. An enormous brass crucifix hung on the wall beside her and a number of hard-backed chairs were placed in front of the desk, but other than a large metal filing cabinet there was nothing else at all in the room.

'Reverend Hayes?' the nun enquired as she rose to greet them, and Charlotte saw that her eyes were cold.

'Yes, Sister,' her father answered falteringly. 'I have brought Charlotte as arranged.'

Charlotte glanced at him questioningly but he studiously avoided her eyes as the elderly nun looked her up and down. She then lifted a bell on her desk and after ringing it she told them, 'I shall get Sister Brigid to show you to the admittance room.'

Charlotte's eyes stretched wide. 'Wh-what do mean?' she asked fearfully.

'You will be staying here until after your confinement – possibly even longer depending on how you behave,' the sour-faced nun informed her.

Charlotte's head wagged from side to side. 'N-no, you must be mistaken,' she stammered. 'I'm staying with my aunt until the baby is born.'

At that moment the young nun who had admitted them appeared with two others on either side of her and beckoned to her. Charlotte glanced down and saw that they had her suitcase with them and panic began to set in. What was happening? Her father had told her that she would be staying with Aunt Edith.

'Oh no, I'm not staying *here*,' she said loudly, but when she made to leave the room, two of the nuns caught her arms and began to march her further along the corridor. Charlotte looked imploringly at her aunt but the woman only stared coldly back at her before going to stand at the side of the entrance door. Her father meanwhile followed them along the corridor until the nuns shoved her none too gently into another room, telling her, 'You have two minutes to say your goodbyes.' They then left, closing the door behind them.

Charlotte was crying now as she rounded on her father. 'What's going on?' she asked. 'Why have you brought me here?'

He rose to his full height and she saw him smirk as he told her, 'You didn't *really* think I was going to let you threaten everything I have ever worked for, did you?'

When Charlotte stared back at him open-mouthed, he went on, 'From the second that you stumbled across my . . . shall we say, "little hobby" . . . you have left me in no doubt at all that you could expose me and destroy me at any second. Well, now it won't be so easy, will it, my dear?'

'I shall tell Mother what you've done,' Charlotte retaliated, but he smiled – a chilly smile that turned her blood to water.

'I'm afraid you won't have a chance. Your aunt and I have

organised all this very carefully, you see. Your mother isn't expecting to hear from you anyway until after the birth, and then your aunt and I will tell her that you have met an Irish boy and run away with him. She will never be any the wiser and you will stay here for the rest of your life.'

'No!' Charlotte keened as she realised how easily she had fallen into his trap. Now she could see why he had been so accepting of her condition. It had made it all the easier for him to dispose of her in this godforsaken place. And her aunt must have sent her to wait in the kitchen that morning in order to give them time to take her suitcase out to the boot of the cab without her seeing it.

He turned now and headed to the door, but Charlotte grabbed at his sleeve. 'Please, Father, don't leave me here,' she begged as tears spurted from her eyes, momentarily blinding her. 'I will never tell anyone what I saw in your dark room, I promise.'

'Promises were made to be broken,' he told her as he fastidiously shook her off. 'Goodbye, my dear. I doubt that our paths will ever cross again.'

As he made to leave the room she rushed after him, but the two nuns who were waiting in the hallway once again caught her arms and although she struggled she was no match for them.

'Father!' she screamed as he walked away without a second glance to join her aunt at the door, but she was already being dragged in the opposite direction. Seconds later, she heard the front door clang shut behind her last link with the world and she began to sob soundlessly as the nuns pulled her up an uncarpeted staircase. The sound of her shoes on the bare wooden floor echoed around her, but Charlotte was oblivious to everything except the panic that was building inside her.

At the top of the stairs she came to yet another locked door, on which one of the nuns knocked briskly. It swung open and she was propelled along a narrow corridor with numerous doors leading off either side of it. From behind some of them came the sound of subdued crying, and Charlotte's terror increased.

At last, a nun pushed one of the doors open with her foot and flung Charlotte inside. She found herself in what appeared to be a huge shower room. It was covered from floor to ceiling in plain white tiles, many of which were cracked, and all along one wall shower heads dangled from the ceiling. There were no separate cubicles or privacy of any sort, and Charlotte cringed at the thought of having to shower there with other girls. Along the opposite wall were a number of plain chairs and one of the nuns pointed to them now as she told her unfeelingly, 'Get undressed and put your clothes on there.'

'What?' Charlotte stared at her as if she had taken leave of her senses.

'Do as you are told, girl, otherwise it will be the worse for you,' the nun answered.

'B-but I washed this morning, thoroughly,' Charlotte objected as she wrapped her arms protectively across her chest.

The two nuns advanced on her and in seconds she was standing naked in front of them.

'Now sit down here,' the older one shouted at her, and realising now that it was useless to argue, Charlotte did as she was told, her cheeks burning with humiliation.

The nun then produced a pair of scissors from the depths of the pocket in her habit and advanced on Charlotte. 'What are you going to do with them?' the girl asked in terror.

'I am going to shear your vanity, girl,' she answered coldly. 'It is vanity that has got you into this condition.'

Before Charlotte had time to object, the woman grabbed a handful of her beautiful long blonde hair and began to hack at it. The girl watched in horror as her fair tresses floated to the floor, but was so shocked that for now she could say or do nothing to stop it. She felt as if she was caught in the grip of a nightmare and prayed that she would soon wake up.

When the nun finally stepped away from her, Charlotte raised her hand to feel the stubbly growth that was all that was left of her lovely hair.

'Now get under this shower here,' the nun directed, switching the tap on, and when Charlotte once more did as she was told the freezing cold water took her breath away. The nun handed her a bar of foul-smelling carbolic soap and ordered, 'Now scrub every inch of yourself. We must wash away your sins.'

When Charlotte emerged some minutes later, her teeth were chattering with cold and she was crying so hard that she was incapable of saying anything.

The other nun threw her a shapeless grey shift dress, a huge pair of knickers with a drawstring around the waist and elasticated legs, and a pair of down-at-heel shoes. 'Put these on,' she told her.

'B-but I have my own clothes in my suitcase,' Charlotte protested.

'They will be put away for when – or *if* – you ever leave here.' The nun's eyes were as cold as glass marbles. 'But we shall allow you to take out any personal things in it you may wish to keep first,' she went on as if she was bestowing some great gift.

Charlotte had always considered that her clothes were drab compared to those of her friends, but in that moment she would have given anything to have them back again.

Once she was clad in the awful outfit that the nun had handed her she bowed her head. Everything had happened so quickly, and all the fight had gone out of her. She was little more than a prisoner and she knew it. *But somehow*, she vowed to herself, *when I'm feeling stronger again I shall get out of this hellhole!*

The nuns now led her back out into the corridor and into what appeared to be a large dormitory with three wooden beds spaced down either side of it. By each bed was a small wooden chest of drawers and a chair. A blanket was neatly folded on the end of each bed, and on the top of that was a Bible.

'The other girls are either working or at prayer,' one of the nuns informed her, stopping at the bed nearest to the window. There were no curtains but a fine meshwork of metal bars covered the glass. 'This will be your bed and whilst you wait for lunch you may read your Bible and consider your sins. You have far to go before you are cleansed, I fear. After lunch you will be told what your duties are to be.'

She then began to walk away, only to pause to say, 'And do not think of trying to escape. All the doors within the convent are kept locked, and should we discover you trying to leave, you will be severely punished.'

As the door closed behind her, Charlotte sank onto the end of the bed and stroked her shorn hair in despair. She had suspected for a

103

long time that her father had no time for her, but now she realised that he must really hate her to lock her away in this place. And what would her mother and granny think, when she failed to keep in touch with them?

Lowering her head into her hands, she wept brokenheartedly.

Chapter Thirteen

Eventually Charlotte curled into a ball on the hard lumpy mattress and cried herself to sleep. She was woken by the sound of someone else in the room, and when she blearily opened her eyes she was confronted by a young, heavily pregnant girl.

'Sorry to disturb you,' the girl apologised, 'but Sister Brigid sent me to fetch you down to lunch.'

'Oh.' Charlotte eyed the girl warily as she swung her legs over the side of the bed. She ached everywhere and wondered how she would survive a whole night on the mattress. It was like sleeping on a door. As she pushed her feet into the drab shoes that she had been supplied with, she studied the girl more closely. She was very young, probably no more than fifteen or sixteen, and quite short and stockily built. It was obvious that at some time she had suffered the same indignity as Charlotte and had all her hair cut off, but it was chin-length again now and a lovely deep auburn colour. That, added to her bright blue eyes, made her quite attractive, although she was very pale and she looked tired.

'I'm Cathleen,' the girl introduced herself. 'At least, that's what I'm called here.' There was a soft Irish lilt to her voice and Charlotte felt herself warming to her, although she was slightly confused now.

'Isn't that your real name then?' she asked.

Cathleen shook her head. 'No, it's Mary really.' She looked fearfully towards the door before lowering her voice and confiding, 'They take everything away from you here – even your name. I dare say they'll give you another one too.'

'Oh. Well, I'm Charlotte – do you sleep in this room too?'

'Yes, that's my bed there.' Cathleen pointed to the bed next but one to Charlotte's then urged, 'We'd better be off. The Sisters don't like it if we're late.'

They went out of the room and down a narrow back staircase that Charlotte hadn't seen before. At the bottom of the stairs, Cathleen turned left and led her to a large room that was obviously the dining room, but like the rest of the place it was very austere.

Long trestle tables stood in rows with the minimum of cutlery placed next to a number of plain plates. At the top of the room was another table that faced the others and as Cathleen saw Charlotte looking towards it, she explained, 'That's where the Sisters sit. They eat like queens, but the muck they serve us here is little better than pigswill.'

Just then a bell sounded and Cathleen instantly dropped onto a chair and bowed her head. 'You'd best sit down,' she whispered, and Charlotte did as she was told.

Seconds later, a number of girls began to file into the room although there was not a sound to be heard except that of their footsteps. Many of them were pregnant but they all looked pale and unhappy as they silently took their seats, some of them glancing at Charlotte curiously from the corners of their eyes.

A line of Sisters then filed into the room to take their places at the top table. The girls hastily stood up, folded their hands and bowed their heads.

Charlotte recognised Sister Magdalene and it was she who took the centre place at the top table and addressed the girls.

'We shall now say Grace.'

The prayers went on for at least ten minutes and then the girls lifted their plates and formed an orderly queue at a side table where nuns covered in huge white aprons were serving them food. As Charlotte passed the table where the nuns were seated, her mouth watered; they were being served with thick slices of beef swimming in gravy, crispy roast potatoes and vegetables. She fell into line beside Cathleen and soon it was their turn to be served. The first nun dropped a single boiled potato onto her plate and Charlotte moved on to the next, who gave her a single spoonful of peas. The third and final nun dropped something that vaguely resembled a slice of meat onto her plate and then Charlotte followed Cathleen back to their seats.

The potato was hard in the middle and barely digestible, and the meat was so tough that Charlotte feared she would break her teeth on it, but she struggled to eat it all the same. If what Cathleen had told her was true, then it was a case of either eat what was put in front of you or starve.

Their pudding consisted of a rather mushy apple and the only drink available was water which was placed in a large jug on each table.

Under other circumstances, Charlotte knew that she would have left the table hungry, but today she was so upset that she forced the food down. And throughout it all, not a single word was spoken. The silence became oppressive. Occasionally she risked peeking to either side of her, but all she saw was the same blank look of hopelessness on every girl's face.

Immediately the girls had finished eating, Sister Magdalene then led them in yet more prayers, thanking the Lord for what they had received and then the girls slowly began to file out of the room.

'Charlotte, follow me,' Sister Magdalene ordered when the last girl had gone, and she reluctantly did as she was told. The Sister led her back to the office where she had first met her, and pointing at Charlotte's case she told her, 'You may take out any photographs or anything that is important to you, and then I shall get Sister Maeve to take you to your duties.'

Charlotte snapped open the clasps on her case and lifted out a picture of her mum and her granny standing together in the garden at the vicarage. It had been taken in happier times, and just seeing their beloved smiling faces almost broke her heart. Who knew if she would ever see them again?

It was while the nun was turning to ring the bell to summon Sister Maeve that Charlotte quickly dipped her hand into the case again and pulled out a sock that she hastily dropped into the pocket of the drab dress she was wearing.

'Right,' said Sister Magdalene, turning back to her. 'You may leave the picture with me and I shall see that it is taken to your room. The rest of your things will be locked away.' Then, as yet another nun entered the room she told her, 'You may go now. Sister Maeve will show you what to do. We shall decide on a new name for you by tomorrow.'

'But I like the one I've got,' Charlotte told her boldly as her eyes flashed.

'Because it is your first day I shall ignore that,' the nun said coldly.

Charlotte followed the younger nun from the room, through a maze of corridors that all looked the same until they came to the back of the house where a huge laundry was situated.

'This is where you will be working,' Sister Maeve informed her and when Charlotte looked into her face she saw that her eyes were kindly.

Another nun who was swathed in an enormous white apron that almost completely covered her flowing black habit came hurrying towards them, and taking Charlotte's elbow she rapped out: 'Come along then. We don't waste time in here.'

Charlotte coughed as the damp steamy atmosphere closed in around her. Sweat broke out on her forehead and she wondered how anyone could work in such uncomfortable conditions.

She was led to a large tub with a scrubbing board in it.

'You'll find a scrubbing brush there.' The nun pointed. 'And there is the washing.'

Charlotte looked in alarm at a huge pile of soiled white sheets.

'You are to scrub each one until it is spotless,' the nun instructed. 'I will then come and check them, and it will be woe betide you if I find so much as a single mark on them.'

'And what do I do with them then?' Charlotte enquired.

'That isn't your concern,' the nun said nastily. 'Someone will come and move them to the rinsing tubs once you have done your job, so just get on with it. And make sure that you change the water regularly. You'll find it in the boilers over there and buckets to bring it across in. You may empty the dirty water down that drain there.'

She then turned and glided away, and Charlotte glared at her retreating figure as the young woman at the tub next to her whispered fearfully, 'I should do as she says, if I were you. You don't mess with Sister Agatha.'

'Why n—'

'Ssh,' the girl hissed frantically. 'If she catches us talking we won't eat again today and we get pitifully little as it is.'

'*What?* You mean we're not even allowed to speak?' Charlotte said incredulously.

The girl lowered her head and continued to frantically scrub at the sheet she was washing so Charlotte started to do the same. Within an hour she felt as if her hands were on fire and they were red and swollen. Her back was aching too from bending over the tub and she was wet through with sweat, but then thankfully a bell sounded from deep within the house and one by one the girls in the laundry room slowly straightened up.

'Form an orderly queue now, girls,' Sister Agatha ordered as she walked amongst them swishing a large cane in her hands. It was then that a girl who looked to be heavily pregnant slid to the floor in a faint. Sister Agatha tutted with disapproval.

'You two,' she said to the two girls nearest to her. 'Take her to the sick room and tell them I need her ready for evening prayers. She will have to miss dinner if she's going to be so melodramatic.'

Charlotte was horrified. The poor girl on the floor looked desperately ill and pale, but it was obvious there would be no sympathy forthcoming from the nun in charge.

The girls then filed from the room, and before going into dinner, the ones that needed to go to the lavatory were led to a row of open latrines where they were at least left alone for a few minutes.

'What sort of a place *is* this?' Charlotte whispered to the girl who had worked next to her.

'It's a home for unmarried mothers,' the girl answered. 'But there are a lot of women who've been here for years since they had their babies. You can only get out if a relative comes to fetch you after the birth, and some of them were just abandoned so they had to stay. Oh, and I'm Miriam, by the way – at least, that's what I'm known as here.'

'I can't believe they even take our names away from us,' Charlotte said incredulously. Having to use open toilets in front of all the other girls had stained her cheeks red although they all seemed to be used to it now. 'It's as if they're trying to take away our identity,' she went on. 'Let alone our dignity.'

'Huh! Dignity flies out of the window the second you set foot in this place,' Miriam remarked.

'And what will happen to that poor girl who fainted?' Charlotte asked now. 'She looked worn out and absolutely enormous.'

'That's because she's due to have her baby any day now. But she'll be back at work tomorrow, you just watch.'

Charlotte shook her head. Her own baby wasn't due for some months yet and she was exhausted after only a short time, so she could only imagine how hard the work must be when you were nine months' pregnant, and surely all that bending over couldn't be good for the baby?

It was then that a nun appeared, and when she clapped her hands the girls instantly stood, righted their clothes and followed her silently to the dining room.

This time, Charlotte saw that there were tin dishes and spoons placed in rows on the tables and after lifting her dish she joined the other girls in the queue, pleased to see that she was standing next to Cathleen again. The windows in this room were set high in the wall and when Charlotte looked up, all she could see was the light fading from the sky. It only added to her feelings of loneliness.

Eventually it was her turn and she held her dish out to a nun who was serving food from a great blackened cooking pot. She placed one ladleful of some disgusting-looking concoction in Charlotte's dish and then the next nun gave her a slice of hard bread.

Once back at the table, Charlotte stared at her meal in dismay. 'What is this supposed to be?' she breathed to Cathleen from the side of her mouth.

'Beef stew,' Cathleen responded.

They were then made to stand to say Grace, and by the time they sat down again the food was only tepid and a film of grease had appeared on the top of it. A few pieces of vegetable floated in the clear liquid but Charlotte could see no sign of any beef. She soon discovered that it tasted just as disgusting as it looked, but she forced it down anyway. She had no idea what the time was but guessed that it must be well after six now. The meal this time was swilled down with watery milk that made her retch, and then they stood to thank the Lord for what they had received before forming a queue down the side of the room again.

'We'll be going to the chapel now,' Cathleen whispered and Charlotte quietly groaned. She ached everywhere and just longed to lie down, not that she would have any chance to do so.

Soon the girls were all packed into the chapel, which was surprisingly beautiful. Stained-glass windows lined the walls and a huge statue of the Virgin Mother stood against one wall. The girls were ushered onto wooden pews before the service began. Charlotte had always considered that her father's sermons were somewhat lengthy and boring, but she soon found out that his were nothing compared to this. The service lasted for two whole hours and by that time she was almost passing out, and even the thought of the hard lumpy mattress was welcoming.

At last they were led to their separate dormitories and a nun told them, 'Ten minutes till lights out. Get yourselves changed, girls.'

Charlotte saw that someone had placed a plain white nightgown on her bed so she stripped off her dress and slid it on. It was huge and she had to roll the sleeves up but it still trailed on the floor. As the girl in the opposite bed got changed, Charlotte noticed that she had angry red marks all across her back and hastily averted her eyes. It was as she was folding the drab grey dress that she remembered the sock she had taken from her suitcase. She hastily took it from her pocket and hid it in her hand as she spread her blanket out on the bed and slipped it beneath it. She would figure out where she could hide it when the other girls were asleep. Once they were all changed, the girls stood silently at the sides of their beds and when the nun reappeared she nodded in approval before clapping her hands.

'Right, into bed now, girls. And no talking.'

Once they had done as they were told she snapped off the bare overhead bulb and left the room. The atmosphere instantly relaxed a little as Charlotte leaned up on her elbow.

'So what happened to your back then?' she whispered to the girl opposite.

The girl shrugged as a tear slid down her cheek. 'I left a mark on one of the sheets in the laundry and Sister Agatha caned me.'

Charlotte scowled in horror. 'But where does all that washing come from?' she asked.

'From the local hospital,' Cathleen told her. 'A van comes to collect it twice a week when it's all been washed and pressed, and then the nuns are paid for us doing it.'

'I see.' Charlotte chewed on her lip as she looked around at her

111

four roommates. Only one of the beds was empty and already she felt sorry for the poor soul that would eventually come to fill it. This place was turning out to be hell on earth.

'I'm Ruby,' the girl in the bed opposite introduced herself. She was a very pretty girl with natural blonde hair that had received the same treatment as Charlotte's, and she had lovely brown eyes.

'And when is your baby due?' Charlotte asked.

'In about four weeks,' Ruby told her in a small voice.

The girl in the bed next to her then piped up, 'I'm Rachel.' Rachel was quite tall for a girl with mousy brown hair and soft grey eyes. She seemed to be very timid and shy and Charlotte smiled at her.

'And I'm Joan,' the final girl told her. 'Or at least that's what I'm called here. The bastards won't allow me to be called by me real name.'

Unlike the other girls who had distinctly Irish accents, Joan had a Cockney accent. She was obviously the rebel of the pack and Charlotte liked her immediately. It seemed that all of the girls' babies were due before hers and she asked them what happened once the infants were born.

'We're taken up onto the next floor,' Joan informed her, running her hand across her shorn dark hair. 'An' then we're allowed to feed 'em an' care fer 'em fer a little while till adopters come an' take 'em away.'

Charlotte scowled at the horrible picture Joan was painting. She would have liked to ask more, but suddenly she yawned and lay back onto her pillows. She was desperately tired but she knew that she mustn't allow herself to fall asleep just yet. Slowly the dormitory became silent and the sounds of the girls' snores echoed around her. Charlotte glanced at each of them in turn to make sure that they were asleep, then she sat up and slowly emptied the sock she had hidden earlier beneath her blanket. Inside it was almost twenty pounds. Her life savings. Most of it had been given to her by Kitty and as she thought of her granny now, tears clogged her throat. Now this money was more important than ever because somehow, when she managed to get out of this place, it would pay for her passage home.

She considered the scratched chest of drawers next to her bed but instantly dismissed the idea of hiding her money in there. It would be too easy for the nuns to find. And then her fingers ran along the edge of her mattress and an idea occurred to her. Painstakingly slowly, she began to unpick the threads that bound it until there was a hole just big enough to push the sock into. By the time she had done, her already sore fingers felt as if they were on fire but at least she knew that the money was safe now, or at least as safe as it could be.

A quick look around assured her that the rest of the girls were still sound asleep so once more she settled down beneath the blanket and before she knew it, had dropped into an exhausted sleep as her first night in the Convent of the Sacred Mother began.

Chapter Fourteen

At five o'clock the next morning the sound of a loud bell clanging made Charlotte jump awake. For a moment she wondered where she was, but then as it all rushed back she swiped the sleep from her eyes and leaned up on her elbow.

The other girls were already up and taking old scratchy towels from the drawers at the side of their beds.

'Come on, mate,' Joan urged. 'Sister Hag will be here any minute, an' if you ain't ready to go into the showers it'll be the worse fer you.'

Sister Hag, as Charlotte soon discovered, was the nickname given to Sister Agatha, the most dreaded of the nuns.

She quickly did as Joan advised and with not a second to spare, for the door then banged open and Sister Agatha stood there staring at them each in turn until Charlotte felt as if she could see into their very souls.

'Come along,' she snapped, clapping her hands as if she were about to herd cattle. 'Into the showers now, girls. Cleanliness is next to godliness, as you should all know.'

Charlotte cringed at the thought of the ordeal ahead. It had been bad enough the day before, having to shower in front of the nuns, but today she would stand naked amongst all the girls as well.

Once again it struck her how quiet it was as the nun shepherded them all along the corridor to the shower block. There were at least eighteen girls lining up for their turns beneath the cold water, but not one of them was uttering so much as a single word.

Eventually it came to Charlotte's turn. Gritting her teeth, she stripped off her nightshirt and stepped beneath the water. At the same time, Rachel stepped under the faucet next to her and as the icy cold water played across her skin the girl gasped involuntarily and took a step away. Sister Agatha bore down on her like a great black raven and the cane she was holding whistled through the air before connecting soundly with the girl's buttocks.

'Get *back* under there and wash away your sins. You are unclean! To think of the shame you have brought down on your poor father's head – and him a man of the cloth too!' the nun hissed unfeelingly as tears spurted from Rachel's eyes.

So her father must be a vicar or priest too, Charlotte thought. Her first instinct was to offer sympathy, but she knew already that would simply bring herself into the firing line as well, so instead she bit down hard on her lip and continued to wash herself with the strip of cotton she had been issued with. It was hard and scratchy against her skin and she felt her unborn child move uneasily inside her but at last the ordeal was over and the nun beckoned the girls out as yet another lot of girls took their places.

They were led naked back to their room where they dressed quickly under Sister Agatha's watchful eye. Then once they were dressed they were taken to the chapel where an hour of prayers took place. At six thirty they were led to the dining room where Sister Magdalene again said Grace and the girls were served with something that vaguely resembled watery porridge whilst the nuns ate bacon and eggs and fat juicy sausages.

Charlotte's stomach revolted as she forced the glutinous mess down but she had already learned that if she left it there would be nothing else so she made herself eat every spoonful.

When the meal and prayers were finally over, Sister Agatha bore down on her like an avenging black angel.

'Come with me,' she ordered, her hands tucked deep into the sleeves of her habit. 'Sister Magdalene wishes to see you.'

Charlotte trod dejectedly after her, knowing that she had little choice, and eventually they came to the room that she had first been taken to when she arrived at the convent.

Sister Magdalene was sitting at her desk writing something in a large ledger and she looked up when Charlotte was shown into the room.

'Ah, I wished to see you because I have chosen the name you shall be known as during your stay here,' she said.

'I already have a name,' Charlotte said stubbornly. 'It's Charlotte Hayes.'

'No one has a last name here,' the nun informed her imperiously. 'And from now on you shall be known as Eilish.'

'But that's an Irish name and I am English,' Charlotte objected.

The woman looked at Sister Agatha who was standing close to Charlotte's side. 'I think this young lady needs a little lesson in humility,' she said quietly. 'And perhaps then later she can visit me again and tell me what her new name is.'

When Sister Agatha nodded she turned her attention back to the ledger in front of her as Charlotte was bundled from the room. They had no sooner entered the corridor and closed the door behind them when Sister Agatha produced her dreaded cane with the speed of lightning from the sleeve of her habit.

'*What* is your name, girl?' she hissed.

'Charlotte!' The girl's chin jutted with defiance as the cane whistled through the air and slapped her cruelly across the knuckles.

'*What* is it?' Again and again the cane whistled down as Charlotte wept and screamed and tried to cover herself. And then eventually, when she realised that she could not win, she sobbed, 'I-it's . . . Eilish!'

'That's better,' Sister Agatha said breathlessly. 'Now get back in there and tell that to Sister Magdalene.'

Large red welts were popping up on Charlotte's arms and legs and she felt sick and faint, but all the same she tapped at the door and staggered back into Sister Magdalene's room.

'Ah.' There was a cruel glint in the older nun's eyes. 'Are you ready to tell me your name now, girl?'

'It is Eilish, Sister,' Charlotte choked out, avoiding her eyes.

The nun smirked. 'That's better – and don't you forget it. Now go about your duties.'

Charlotte tottered from the room. Some of the strokes of the cane had broken the skin and now thin rivers of blood were beginning to trickle down her arms and legs. She felt sick and giddy, and asked Sister Agatha, 'May I clean myself up a little before I go to work?'

'No, you may not.' The nun hauled her along the hallway in the direction of the laundry room. 'You girls are all the same – keen to sin, but slow to work.'

In no time at all, Charlotte was back in the stifling atmosphere of the laundry and bending over a huge steaming bowl of water.

'Now see that you do a good job of those sheets or it will be the worse for you,' the nun told her as she turned and glided away in a flurry of black skirts. Charlotte slowly lifted the brush, and as she began to scrub at the linen her tears plopped into the water and a wave of helplessness washed over her.

By the time the girls were returned to their dormitories that night, Charlotte was so stiff and sore that she wished she could just curl up and die. Surely death would be preferable to this living hell? The blood on the wounds that Sister Agatha had inflicted on her had dried, and once the lights were out Joan whispered, 'Don't cry, Eilish. As soon as everything is quiet I'll sneak off to the bathroom and get a cold cloth to bathe your cuts. That might ease them a bit.'

Eilish, Joan had called her, and resentment coursed through her. Her name was Charlotte and always would be, as far as she was concerned. True to her word, some time later Joan sneaked off to the bathroom and returned with a cold wet cloth.

'Try an' lie still,' she urged as she gently dabbed at the dried caked blood. 'This might make yer feel a bit easier.'

Charlotte winced but managed a weak smile as the girl tried to ease her suffering. At least I've got one friend in this hole, she thought, and she was slightly comforted and didn't feel quite so alone then.

As the week progressed the weather grew hotter and Sister Agatha began to leave the door to the laundry open, which was bliss to Charlotte. At least now she could see outside, even if it was only to glimpse the wet washing flapping on the clotheslines.

'Don't we *ever* get to go outside?' she asked the other girls one night when they were in the dormitory.

'Oh yeah, we get an hour outside on a Sunday afternoon if we're good. Big deal, eh?' scoffed Joan.

Charlotte chewed on her lip. At that moment, even half an hour in the fresh air sounded like heaven. She then glanced across at Ruby and frowned. The girl had her head tucked beneath her blanket but they could all hear her softly crying. She had complained of feeling unwell for two days now but Sister Agatha had shown her no mercy and insisted that she still did her work in the laundry. Ruby was struggling to bend across the tubs now that she was so enormous but she was doing her best to carry on. It was only at night when she was in the privacy of the dormitory that she gave vent to her feelings and Charlotte's heart ached for her.

Joan had confided that it was Ruby's brother who had abused her and got her pregnant, and the family had stuck her in the home rather than face the shame of it.

'Do you think they'll come to fetch her once she's had the baby?' Charlotte had asked with concern.

'Who knows?' Joan had shrugged. 'There's some poor buggers 'ave been stuck in 'ere fer years, an' it's 'ighly unlikely they'll ever get out now.'

Charlotte had wanted to scream at the injustice of it all, but with each day that passed now her resolve to escape grew stronger and she knew that somehow she must find a way. She had decided to behave rather than rebel. That way at least the nuns wouldn't know what she was planning and she hoped that would increase her chances of success. It would also lessen the chances of being beaten and having her hair shorn off again. But first she had to get to know her way about the place. It was like a maze and she accepted that she must also get to know the routines right down to the smallest detail.

Now she dared to get out of bed and padding across to Ruby, she asked, 'Are you all right?' What a stupid question, she silently scolded herself. Of course she wasn't all right – but Ruby's head appeared from beneath the blankets and she managed a weak smile.

'It's my back,' she muttered. 'It's throbbing as if there are hot irons in there and I can't seem to get comfortable. I haven't felt the baby move either today,' she added fearfully. 'Do you think bending over the tub has harmed it?'

'I shouldn't think so,' Charlotte said reassuringly as she gently rubbed Ruby's back for her. 'But surely now that you're so close to your time they'll let you stop work?'

Ruby shook her head miserably. 'No, they won't. You work till you go into labour here. One girl actually had her baby on the laundry floor a couple of weeks back.'

Charlotte was appalled. 'Goodness me, was she all right?'

'We didn't get to find out,' Ruby mumbled. 'But we never saw her again and the next day we saw the gardeners carrying a coffin around to the back of the house. There's a small graveyard there but none of the graves are marked.'

Charlotte shuddered. 'How many graves are there?' she dared to ask.

Again, Ruby shrugged. 'I wouldn't like to guess.' She then broke into a fresh torrent of tears.

'Are you worried about your baby?' Charlotte asked gently.

'Well . . .' Ruby gulped deeply. 'I don't want it, yet it's not the baby's fault, is it? So I wouldn't want anything to happen to it. I just want the nuns to find it a good home so that I can go back to my family.'

Charlotte understood. She felt exactly the same way about the baby she was carrying. She had been raped just like Ruby and the knowledge made her feel even closer to the girl.

Ruby arched her back then and groaned with pain and Charlotte asked, 'Do you want me to fetch someone for you?'

'No – it's better if you don't,' Ruby gasped, looking tired and worried. 'It'll go off in a minute, no doubt. You go back to bed. If Sister Agatha catches you over here, you'll feel the cane again.'

Charlotte reluctantly did as she was told, but as she tried to get comfortable on the lumpy mattress her determination to escape increased. She would watch and listen and make her move when the time was right.

When Sunday came around, Charlotte's hands were so sore that she didn't know what to do with them. But at least they didn't work on a Sunday so that was something to be grateful for. However, the three hours she was forced to spend at morning Mass in prayer and quiet meditation were almost worse.

Today, a man led the prayers with the Reverend Mother. Charlotte thought he might be somewhere in his early forties. He was quite a good-looking man with dark hair that was silver at the temples, and he was tall with striking grey eyes that seemed to look right through you. However, having to sit for so long on the hard wooden pews was agony and by the time they were allowed to leave she ached all over. The Sunday lunch, although far from tasty, was a little more palatable than the rest of the meals she'd had before, and her spirits lifted a little. Until the meal was over, that was, when Sister Agatha approached her table.

'It is this table's turn to do the washing-up today,' she informed them imperiously and then, turning her attention to Ruby, she told her, 'You may start to clear the tables. You know what to do.'

'Yes, Sister Agatha,' Ruby replied meekly as she rose and began to gather the plates together.

The Sister then clapped her hands as she turned back to the other girls. 'The rest of you may now go into the gardens for your recreation time.'

Charlotte watched enviously as the other girls hurried away towards the sunshine whilst she helped Ruby and Joan to carry the dirty crockery to the kitchen. Once inside it her mouth gaped open. It was an enormous room with a long row of sinks. On the other wall were two gigantic cookers. Two large oak tables took centre place in the room, but like the rest of the rooms in the convent there was nothing to brighten the place whatsoever, apart from a large brass crucifix placed high on one wall. The other girls seemed to know what was expected of them, so Charlotte took her place at the sink next to Ruby and began to scrub the numerous plates and dishes and place them on the wooden draining-board while a nun walked up and down watching them closely.

'That's Sister Breda,' Ruby whispered. 'She's the cook here and she acts as midwife as well. Apparently she was a midwife before she joined the Order.'

'Oh.' Charlotte glanced across her shoulder to make sure that Sister Breda wasn't in earshot before asking, 'And who was that priest?'

'Huh!' Ruby snorted in disgust. 'That's Father O'Leary. He leads the Mass every Sunday with the Reverend Mother. He won't leave until late afternoon though. He'll be too busy giving religious instruction to Colleen – that's when the nuns have stopped fawning over him.'

'Isn't she the pretty blonde girl with the long hair?' Charlotte asked innocently. She had seen her about and wondered about her slender figure and beautiful hair. She seemed to be a favourite with the nuns and Charlotte had never seen her in the laundry, or doing any other job for that matter, now that she came to think about it.

Just then a bell on the wall tinkled and Sister Breda tutted with annoyance. 'It seems I am needed up on the first floor,' she said. 'One of the girls must be ready to deliver, so I shall have to trust you to do your jobs properly.' She swept towards the door where she paused to threaten, 'I shall be back as soon as possible – now get to it!'

Once she had left, all the girls sighed with relief and the gloomy atmosphere in the room instantly lifted as they relaxed.

'So who is this Colleen?' Charlotte asked. 'I've seen her about and she doesn't look as if she's having a baby.'

'She ain't,' Joan snorted. 'She were brought up in an orphanage but by all accounts she were a hot-arsed little sod so they stuck her in here out of temptation's way. Not that it did much good.'

'What do you mean?'

Joan chuckled. 'Well, let's put it this way. I doubt it's religious instruction she's gettin' right this minute from Father O'Leary.'

When Charlotte's eyes stretched wide she went on, 'Why do yer fink she ain't never had her hair chopped off? An' why do yer fink she gets all the cushy jobs to do?'

'What? You mean she and Father O' Leary are . . .' Charlotte couldn't bring herself to say what she was thinking and Joan laughed aloud.

'That's *exactly* what I mean.' Joan slammed an empty meat tin onto the draining-board and rubbed the sleeve of her dress across her dripping nose. 'The nuns wouldn't dare to upset her 'cos they know it would upset the Father,' she confided. 'Personally though I'd rather work in the laundry all day than 'ave 'im gropin' me.'

'Good grief!' Charlotte was shocked. 'But I thought this was supposed to be a house of God.'

'More like a den o' vice,' Joan muttered with contempt. 'An' the nuns ain't no better. They make a fortune from all the work we do. I was in the Reverend Mother's office one day an' she had the safe open. It's behind the large cross on the wall an' I'm tellin' yer, it was crammed wiv more money than you or me could spend in a bleedin' lifetime! She nearly bit me bloody head off fer goin' in before I was told to.'

Joan would have said more but at that moment, Ruby groaned and leaned against the sink as a pool of water splashed onto the floor between her legs.

'Oh Jesus, it looks like her waters have broke,' Joan said, as she hastily wiped her wet hands on her dress and rushed over to the girl.

Ruby had gone deathly pale and was gritting her teeth now as she doubled over with pain.

'Run an' fetch one of the Sisters,' Joan ordered bossily to anyone who would listen. 'Seems like there's more than one little 'un gonna come today.'

'B-but it's too soon,' Ruby sobbed as she clutched her distended stomach.

One of the girls had already fled through the door and seconds later she was back with Sister Agatha, who eyed the girl with no pity as she roughly took her arm.

'Now we shall see if your little bit of pleasure was worth it, won't we?' she said as she dragged Ruby towards the door.

'But you can't expect her to climb stairs,' Charlotte objected hotly. 'She can hardly walk.'

Sister Agatha silenced her with a stare that would have curdled milk. 'We are *hardly* a luxury hotel,' she said coldly. 'How else is she supposed to get upstairs if she doesn't walk? Now get back to work, the lot of you – this instant!'

Charlotte turned back to the sinkful of hot water with a mutinous expression on her face. Ruby looked absolutely terrified of the ordeal ahead but it seemed she would have to face it alone. One thing was for sure: she would get no sympathy from the nuns.

Chapter Fifteen

When the kitchen was clean again the girls were finally allowed outside and Charlotte gazed up at the sky and breathed in the fresh air deeply. She felt as if she had been locked away forever and wondered how she would bear to stay here until her baby was born. The thought of even that long was terrifying, but beyond that was unthinkable. The place was more like a harsh prison than a convent and she wondered at the cruelty of the nuns and their complete and utter indifference to the girls' suffering. They didn't seem to have an ounce of compassion between them. Joan had told her that the girls she had managed to speak to who had already had their babies had confided that the nuns had been just as unfeeling during their labours, showing no sympathy whatsoever. It seemed barbaric to Charlotte but she already knew that there was nothing she could do about it. The nuns were a law unto themselves and it was woe betide anyone who stepped out of line.

As she wandered along the small enclosed grass area where they were allowed to walk she gazed longingly towards the high brick walls in the distance. Tall trees grew all around the wall and she looked carefully to see if there would be any way she could climb one and escape that way. Of course, that method of escape would be out of the question until the baby was born, but then . . .

'Penny for 'em?' Joan piped up, pulling Charlotte's thoughts sharply back to the present.

'I was just wondering how Ruby is doing,' Charlotte answered.

'Poor little cow.' Joan sighed as she rubbed her own aching back. 'Let's just hope she 'as a short labour.'

They sat down on the grass then as Charlotte stared thoughtfully towards the high walls again. They were enclosed in an area that was surrounded by a low wire fence. As well as being their recreation area it was also used for drying the washing and lines were strung here and there like the lines on a map. Today they were empty but Charlotte knew that tomorrow there would be wet sheets flapping on them again. Already she envied the girls who hung them out. At least they got to be out in the fresh air, if even for a short time. She then glanced towards the windows on the first floor but they gave away nothing of the agony that must be going on behind them. It seemed that none of the girls ever got to go up there until they were in labour – and then they stayed there with their babies until someone came to take them away and adopt them.

She studied her sore hands again before asking, 'So how does the laundry get transported to and from the hospital?'

'A big van comes early on Monday mornin' with all the dirty stuff, then it comes again to take it back when it's been washed late on Friday.' Joan grinned as if she could read Charlotte's mind. 'But don't go thinkin' you'll escape that way. One of the gels tried it not so long ago, but she soon got dragged back. They had the Gardai out lookin' fer her in no time, an' when she got back she felt the length of Sister Hag's cane and had her head shaved. Poor cow was in the sick bay fer days before she got packed off back to the laundry.' Joan pointed to an area near the laundry door. 'The van parks there but the Sisters watch us like hawks till it's been an' gone.'

Charlotte nodded and closed her eyes, determined to enjoy the few minutes of freedom. Joan had told her that soon they would be led to the chapel for yet another Mass, and she dreaded it.

It was as they were being herded back in again like cattle that Charlotte managed to sidle up to Sister Maeve and whisper, 'Have you heard how Ruby is doing, Sister?'

Of all the nuns, Sister Maeve seemed to be the kindliest, and luckily because Sister Agatha had been called away to the first floor, she was now in charge of the girls for the time being.

'It's very doubtful anything would have happened yet with a first baby, Eilish,' she answered, giving her the name Charlotte would be forced to answer to whilst she was in the convent. 'Ruby could be in labour for hours, but I'm sure she'll be fine.'

She then went back to ushering the girls towards the chapel and as Charlotte entered the building she sighed and looked back

124

regretfully just once at the blue sky. It was funny how she had always taken it for granted before.

At teatime the girls were served with coarse bread that had been scraped with marge and tin mugs full of watered-down milk. Even so, Charlotte drained her mug and ate every crumb. There would be nothing else until breakfast and she knew that she had to keep her strength up.

As she lay in bed that night listening to the snores of the other girls, tears coursed down her cheeks. She had never felt so alone in her whole life and at that moment she desperately wanted her mother and her granny. Her Aunt Edith would probably have informed them by now that she had run away, and she was sad to think how upset they would be. Anger then replaced her sorrow as her thoughts turned to her father. He and her aunt had obviously had it all planned before she had even set foot on the ferry. He had betrayed her but one day, somehow, she silently vowed to have her revenge on him. And with that thought uppermost in her mind, she eventually fell asleep with the tears still wet on her cheeks.

The next day Charlotte looked desperately for a sight of Sister Maeve as she worked in the laundry, but Sister Agatha was back in charge once more. It was some time before Charlotte plucked up enough courage to ask, 'Sister, may I enquire how Ruby is today?'

The sister looked enraged but eventually she muttered, 'If you *must* know, she gave birth to a baby boy early this morning.'

'Oh, and are they both well?'

The Sister glowered at her before barking, 'That is really none of your business, Eilish. Now get back to work this instant!'

Charlotte sighed as she wiped the sweat from her forehead before bending back over the huge tub of steamy water. It was so hot in the laundry that she felt ill and would have given anything for a drink of water, but already she knew better than to ask

It was shortly afterwards, when Charlotte was manoeuvring the sheet she had just scrubbed into another large bowl for swilling that she glanced up to see that Rachel, her roommate, was in distress. She was leaning heavily over the tub she was working at and she had gone alarmingly pale despite the heat in the room.

Charlotte instantly straightened and would have risked Sister Agatha's wrath and gone to her, but before she had the chance, Rachel gave a cry and pitched backwards to land in an unconscious heap on the wet floor.

Sister Agatha tutted with annoyance as she strode over to the girl. 'Get her on her feet right now!' she snapped.

It was as they were struggling to do as they were told that they noticed a pool of blood spreading on the floor beneath their friend. Charlotte chewed on her lip with consternation. Rachel's baby wasn't due for another three months.

As the girls managed to heave her up, Rachel came round then gasped as she doubled over with pain.

'We need to get her up to the first floor,' Sister Agatha told them unfeelingly.

'But her baby isn't due yet. Shouldn't she go to the hospital?' Charlotte dared to ask. She knew from the other girls how pitifully restricted the medical amenities were at the convent.

The Sister ignored her as the two girls half-carried Rachel from the room, and after exchanging a worried glance with Joan, Charlotte had no choice but to return to her work.

It was after the evening meal as they were being led to the chapel for Mass that Charlotte managed to sidetrack Sister Maeve and ask, 'How is Rachel, Sister?'

The woman looked back at her gravely then after quickly glancing around she whispered, 'I'm afraid she didn't make it, Eilish. The child was premature and she haemorrhaged badly. Unfortunately, despite Sister Breda's best efforts, we lost both mother and child.'

Charlotte stared disbelievingly back at the nun. It couldn't be true. Just that morning Rachel had been working in the laundry with her and now the nun was telling her that she was dead.

Sister Maeve patted her arm sympathetically before urging, 'Come along, Eilish. We mustn't be late for Mass. It was God's will. She is at peace now.'

AT PEACE! The words rattled around in Charlotte's head as she thought of Rachel. She had been such a timid, inoffensive girl and now she was gone.

That night when they were in their dormitory, Joan cried as she

126

spoke of Rachel. 'I can't believe she's gone,' she sobbed, showing a softer side that Charlotte had never seen before. 'Me an' her come in here within days of each other an' 'cos she was a timid little soul I sort of looked out fer her.' She swiped the snot and tears from her face on the sleeve of her nightdress as she gazed at Rachel's empty bed.

'What will happen now? Will they tell her family?' Charlotte enquired as she placed a comforting arm around Joan's shoulder.

Cathleen, who had said little up to now, snorted. 'Huh! They'll tell them but I bet the sods don't do anything about it,' she said. 'Poor little devil will probably be buried around the back with the rest of them in an unmarked grave.'

Cathleen, who was remarkably well-spoken, came from London. The child of wealthy parents, she had attended a private school there, but following a liaison with a boy from the school next door she had found herself pregnant and her parents had put her into the convent to avoid a scandal. Even so, Charlotte considered that Cathleen was fortunate. Her parents had every intention of coming to fetch her once her baby was born, whereas she and Joan had no idea how long they might be incarcerated there. It will be forever if it's left up to my father, she thought gloomily, and turned her attentions back to Joan.

Just as they had all feared, the next morning as they made their way to Mass before starting work they caught a glimpse of the gardeners carrying a plain pine coffin out of the back entrance. Joan instantly broke into a fresh torrent of tears before being painfully poked in the back by Sister Agatha's cane. She moved on and the day progressed just like all the others. There was no mention of Rachel and it was just as if she had never existed.

Two days later, the girls sat down to their evening meal to see an attractive woman seated at the nuns' table. A ripple of interest went through the room until Sister Hag silenced it with one of her famous glares.

They all wondered if she was someone from the Welfare Department who had come to talk to them about their unborn babies.

The nuns had always told them that the babies were adopted through this channel and she certainly looked the part. But then no one had ever been known to come and talk to them before, so they all decided it was highly unlikely. The woman actually looked very out of place sitting with the nuns. She was immaculately dressed and very pretty. Surely she couldn't be an unmarried mother, one girl murmured – but no, she couldn't be; a quick glance showed a gold band gleaming on the fourth finger of her left hand.

'Who do yer reckon she is?' Joan whispered to Charlotte curiously.

'I've no idea, but I dare say we'll find out soon enough,' Charlotte whispered back. She was so tired that all she wanted to do was eat and go to bed. But first she would have to sit through yet another long-drawn-out evening Mass.

Charlotte's next encounter with the mystery woman came later that evening as they all trooped wearily to their dormitory to see her just disappearing into a room at the end of the long landing.

'That's the posh room,' Joan muttered, and when Charlotte raised an eyebrow, she giggled. 'I've only known one other person go in there since I've been stayin' 'ere, an' she were a right toff,' she enlarged. 'She were a lady or summink like that, or at least her mother was, an' the nuns treated her like a queen. She didn't stay long, mind. She was about ready to drop her kid when she arrived, an' the day after it was born, a chauffeur-driven car come an' whipped her away.'

Charlotte was too utterly fagged-out to care and simply nodded as she headed for her bed and began to strip her clothes off. Perhaps tomorrow she would be glad of the distraction, but for now all she wanted to do was sleep.

The woman was there again at the nuns' table the next morning, and once when Charlotte caught her eyes she smiled at her before Charlotte hastily looked away. During the day whilst Charlotte was leaning over the hot tub, she caught a glimpse of the woman strolling around the grounds and she felt envious. Whoever she was, she was certainly being given preferential treatment. Again, she was immaculately dressed in clothes that might have come straight from the pages of a magazine. Charlotte judged her to be somewhere in her mid to late thirties, although she was aware that she had never been very good at gauging people's ages.

That night, when the girls retired to their dormitory they were surprised to find the woman perched on the end of Charlotte's bed waiting for them.

'Hello, I'm Mari— or should I say Sheila, as I have to be known whilst I'm here. I thought it was time I came and introduced myself, seeing as we're going to be neighbours for a time.'

The others stared at her curiously. This was certainly no young girl who had been abandoned there by her parents, and as if she could read what they were all thinking, she explained, 'I'm a solicitor and I work in Dublin.' She grinned ruefully as she wiped the beautifully styled dark hair from her forehead with a carefully manicured hand.

Joan asked bluntly, 'So why are yer here then?'

Sheila had the grace to blush. 'Well, let's just say I needed a little rest.'

'Hmm!' As Joan stared at the woman's rounded stomach, she was not fooled for a single second. It would take a better liar than this woman to pull the wool over her eyes.

Sheila crossed one leg elegantly over the other. Charlotte noticed that they were clad in silk stockings which shimmered in the dull light filtering in through the window.

The woman meantime was also solemnly surveying them, and realising that she would probably never see any of the girls again after she left the convent, she saw no reason to lie to them. They were all in the same boat, after all.

'I'm afraid I had a little fling with one of the partners in the business and this is the result.' She patted her tummy, her eyes sad. 'The man I had the affair with is married and so am I, so we decided this would be the best thing to do: to come here, have the baby and let it go for adoption. My husband is away at sea for at least another eight months – he's the captain of a cruise liner – and by the time he comes home, all this will be over and done with and we can go on as before.'

When she saw the confused looks on the girls' faces she laughed softly. 'I know it all sounds rather odd, but in actual fact both the man I had the affair with and I really do love our spouses. It was just a silly, mad fling. Call it a mid-life crisis, if you like. I already

129

have two children who are in their late teens and both at university and I wouldn't like them to know about this. So, I told them that I was going to take some time off work and travel the world for a few months and booked myself into here.'

'Booked *yourself* in?' Charlotte was even more confused now. 'But we all got dumped in here against our will. How will you get out after you've had the baby?'

'Let's just say that the nuns have been handsomely rewarded for my board and their discretion,' Sheila answered. 'I shall have the baby, it will go for adoption and then I shall leave and resume my life. I know it sounds heartless but it's better this way. My children would never forgive me if they knew that I had cheated on their father, and I have to put them first. I fear I've been rather foolish.' She gave them a guilty grin and Charlotte warmed to the woman.

'Will you have to work whilst you are here?' she asked next.

Sheila shook her head. 'No, this place will be more of a refuge from prying eyes,' she admitted, then glancing around the sparsely furnished room, she shuddered. 'I must admit that my room is a little more comfortable than this but only fractionally. I had hoped for slightly more luxurious accommodation, but then it isn't forever, is it? And if you girls can put up with it then I'm sure that I shall. Now come along and tell me all about yourselves.'

And so for the next ten minutes the girls did just that as Sheila listened sympathetically. Joan was clutching her sore breasts by then, and glancing towards her with concern, Sheila asked, 'Are you in pain, dear?' These young girls were so close to the age of her own daughter that her heart ached to see them in such a dilemma.

'The nuns won't let us wear brassières,' Joan muttered. 'An' after hangin' over the hot tubs all day our breasts hurt somethin' bloody terrible.'

'How awful.' Sheila looked appalled. She herself was still dressed in a very smart blue dress and jacket, having refused to don the uniform the girls were forced to wear. After all, considering the ridiculous sum of money she had paid the nuns to give her refuge, she believed she should be given preferential treatment – and to her surprise, the Reverend Mother had agreed.

'What will you do wiv yourself all day if you ain't got to work?' Joan now enquired.

Sheila nodded towards the door. 'I have an enormous suitcase in my room that is half-full of books, so I shall read,' she answered. 'Or I shall stroll around the grounds and make the most of not having to go to work for a while.'

'But we ain't allowed to wander about except for an hour on Sunday afternoon, an' even then the nuns keep their eyes on us,' Joan told her solemnly.

Sheila gently patted her leg. 'Well, they're hardly going to need to keep their eye on me, are they, seeing as I admitted myself to the place,' she pointed out. 'And all of you are quite welcome to borrow any of the books you fancy.'

'That's right kind of you, but I doubt we'd be able to stay awake long enough to read 'em.' Joan yawned. 'By the time we've done a shift in the laundry an' sat at Mass fer hours on end, on them hard bloody pews, all we wanna do when we get back here is close our eyes. But thanks all the same.'

'Then feel free to come along to my room any time you like for a chat,' Sheila offered kindly. 'At least I have a comfy chair in there.' She felt so sorry for the girls. They all looked so worn out. Rising, she said, 'I shall go now and let you all get some rest. Goodnight, my dears.' And with that she departed in a waft of expensive French perfume.

Once the woman had left they all hastily got changed into their unbecoming nightdresses and clambered into their own beds. It was already apparent that there was going to be one set of rules for Sheila and another for them, but despite that fact they still liked her. She was such a warm person it would have been hard not to. Charlotte decided that she would try to stay awake and sneak along to Sheila's room to talk to her for a little longer – but in no time at all she was fast asleep and snoring softly.

Chapter Sixteen

Charlotte found life in the convent slightly easier once Sheila had moved in and looked forward to their chats together each evening. She would creep along the landing to Sheila's room whenever she could, once the nuns had retired, and she always received a warm welcome. Sheila proved to be a highly intelligent woman who seemed able to have a conversation on any topic, but she was also remarkably kind and often she would massage the girl's aching back for her. At mealtimes she continued to sit at the nuns' table and dine with them, but often she would smuggle a part of her meal back to the dormitory in a serviette for the girls to share, and they were grateful for it.

She and Charlotte formed a special bond as the older woman realised that Charlotte had been brought up much as her own children had, and her heart went out to the girl. Charlotte had told her the whole sorry story of how she had ended up at the Convent of the Sacred Mother, and Sheila felt it was unfair. She shuddered at the thought of her own daughter being in Charlotte's position, but knew that she would have stood by her no matter what, and she quickly formed the opinion that Charlotte's father must be a monster, which wasn't far from the truth. Even so, she realised how foolish it would be to become overly involved. There were so many young girls incarcerated there, each with their own sad story to tell, and she was wise enough to know that she couldn't help them all.

In no time at all they were into July and the heat in the laundry became unbearable. Charlotte was waddling around like a duck by then and beginning to fret as the birth of her baby drew closer. She was suffering from heartburn and cramps, and without the support of a bra her heavy breasts were very painful.

Sheila had become her port in a storm and within no time at all even the nuns left the woman well alone. They had soon realised that Sheila was a law unto herself and was not prepared to conform to their rules. If they tried any of their threats on her she would just stare at them coldly and draw herself up to her full height, and inevitably it was the nuns who backed down. This was no young frightened girl that they could bully, and so in a very short time they left her to her own devices. She had a quiet kind of authority about her and Charlotte could just imagine her in a courtroom pleading her clients' cases.

Each morning, whilst the rest of the girls got up for a hurried cold shower, Sheila would lie in bed and then go along to the bathroom when she had the room to herself. If she did not feel like eating with the Reverend Mother and the rest of the nuns, she would then wander down to breakfast late – but unlike the girls, she was never scolded. She was always dressed immaculately and was more than generous when it came to giving away her expensive shampoos and hand creams to Charlotte and her room-mates. Whilst the Sisters continued to berate the girls for being sinful, Charlotte could never remember hearing them say a wrong word to Sheila. The latter attended the chapel services if and when she felt like it, and again the nuns said nothing. Throughout the days, whilst the girls were hard at work, Sheila would drift about the grounds or spend her time reading. Charlotte often envied Sheila for being able to wear her own clothes, even if the pretty twinsets and skirts she favoured now strained across her bulging stomach. But then Sheila had paid an extortionate amount of money to find refuge there, and Charlotte had realised that money could buy almost anything. Not that she held it against Sheila in any way.

It was when they were sitting together one Sunday afternoon in the small enclosed garden that fenced in the laundry that Sheila asked, 'How are you going to get out of here once your baby is born, Eilish?'

Charlotte shrugged. She felt she could trust Sheila. 'I'm going to escape somehow,' she confided, then nodding towards the trees she told her, 'I'm going to try and climb one of them and get over the wall.'

Sheila frowned with dismay as she followed the girl's eyes. The

133

high wall behind the trees was topped with barbed wire and it sounded like a dangerous idea to her. The nuns had done all they could to keep her away from the girls and the laundry, but Sheila had seen enough to know that the way the girls were treated was appalling and she was shocked to her roots. The convent might have been a sanctuary for her, but it certainly wasn't for the girls whose families had dumped them here. Her own baby was due in less than two weeks now and she knew that she would probably be gone by the time Charlotte gave birth to hers. The thought disturbed her, because despite the fact that she had tried not to get overly familiar, she had become fond of the girl.

'And what will you do when you get out of here?' she asked. 'Do you have any money?'

'A little,' Charlotte admitted, glancing around warily to make sure that they couldn't be overheard. 'I have it hidden and it would probably be just about enough to get me home. It's getting out that will be the problem. I know my father will never come to fetch me, and my mother doesn't even know I am here, so unless I do manage to escape I could be stuck in here forever.'

They would have gone on with the conversation but just then they noticed a car coming down the drive with a young couple in it. Charlotte shuddered. They were probably coming to take away one of the babies on the first floor. She'd seen many such couples over the time she had been there. Noticing the girl shudder, Sheila asked, 'What's wrong?'

Charlotte shook her head. 'Nothing really, but I don't mind betting they're adopters come to take one of the babies.' She knew that this outcome was inevitable and yet she still felt sympathy for the girls who were about to say goodbye to their babies. Most of them appeared back downstairs the following day to resume work, and nine times out of ten their eyes were red and swollen from crying.

Both women fell silent now as they tried to imagine how they would feel when it was their turn. It wasn't a nice thought, but then neither of them felt that they were in a position to keep their child, so it was probably for the best.

Sheila patted her hand. 'I'm sure the nuns make sure that the little ones go to good homes,' she said softly.

Charlotte nodded in agreement. 'I'm sure they do, but it's still sad, isn't it?'

It was then that one of the Sisters appeared and clapped her hands. 'Come along,' she shouted, glaring disapprovingly towards Charlotte and Sheila. 'It is time to make our way to chapel now.'

Everyone except Sheila instantly rose and followed her, and soon Charlotte's head was bowed in prayer as she sat on a hard wooden pew with her baby kicking away inside her.

Later, as they were being led to the dining room for their evening meal, Charlotte spotted the young couple she had seen on the drive coming down the stairs with Sister Breda close behind them. The young woman was carrying a baby swaddled in a snow-white shawl and the look on her face was joyous.

At least it looks as if that one is going to a good home, Charlotte thought to herself, and silently prayed that the same sort of couple would come forward for her child.

They were all preparing for bed that evening when the door to their room opened and Ruby appeared.

'Ruby!' Delighted to see her again, Charlotte raced across to give her a hug. 'What are you doing here?'

The girl swiped at the tears that were silently streaming down her ashen cheeks with the back of her hand. 'A couple came for my baby this afternoon, so I'm back to work tomorrow.'

'Oh!' Charlotte guessed that this must be the couple she had seen earlier and she stroked Ruby's hand sympathetically. 'I think I saw them leaving with him,' she admitted. 'And I have to say, the woman looked so happy. I'm sure they'll be good to him.'

'I hope so.' Ruby looked thoroughly miserable as she sank down onto the end of the bed that had been hers until the birth. 'You know, it's funny,' she confided in a small voice. 'The baby was forced on me and I never wanted him – and yet, when he was born . . .' She gulped before going on, 'I just sort of loved him without being able to stop myself. He was so little and defenceless, and it wasn't his fault, was it? He didn't ask to be born. I called him Patrick although I've no doubt his new mum and dad will change it. That's their prerogative.'

As she broke into a fresh torrent of tears, Charlotte cuddled her close as she asked, 'And what will happen to you now?'

Ruby sniffed. 'Well, hopefully the nuns will get word to me mam an' dad that it's over an' they'll come for me. If not . . .' Her voice trailed away as she thought of the other option. What if they *didn't* come for her and she ended up locked away in this place for the rest of her life? She knew that she would rather die.

'They'll come,' Charlotte told her confidently, seeing the fear in the other girl's eyes.

Ruby nodded as she kneaded her rock-hard breasts with the heels of her hands. They were full of milk and as she thought of the son who would never suckle from them again she began to cry afresh as Charlotte looked helplessly on.

The days passed in a monotonous blur and soon it was nearing the end of July. Sheila was spending a lot of time lying on her bed by then but she didn't complain. She just wanted the birth to be over and done with now so that she could return to her family and her life.

'How long will you stay here after the baby is born?' Charlotte asked one night as they lay in the darkness of her room. She had popped in to see Sheila after lights out.

'I've already said that I don't even want to see the child,' Sheila said sadly. 'It would make things even harder if I bonded with it, so it's best that I leave as soon as I can once it's arrived.'

The sad fact was that, as the months had progressed, her maternal instincts had come to the fore again and she had begun to quite like the idea of having another child. But of course, under these circumstances that was quite impossible. How would she ever explain it to her husband or the children that she already had? It would tear her family apart and she couldn't risk that for anything.

'I suppose the sisters will be bringing in a doctor for your delivery, won't they?' Charlotte now asked, thinking of all the preferential treatment Sheila had already received.

'Oh no.' Sheila's head bobbed from side to side. 'I don't want to risk anyone from outside here knowing about this so I shall receive the same treatment as you girls do from choice.' Even as she spoke

136

she rubbed her back, which had been aching all day. The baby's head had been engaged for some time and Sheila knew from past experience that the birth was imminent. In one way she longed for it to be over, but another part of her felt guilty about leaving Charlotte there.

'Will you keep in touch once you've gone?' Charlotte whispered as if she could read the woman's mind.

'No, the Sisters would never allow it,' Sheila said regretfully. 'But perhaps it's for the best. I've no doubt you'll get home to your mammy somehow and then you'll forget all about me, so you will.'

'I won't,' Charlotte retorted. 'You've kept me sane in here and I'll always be thankful to you for that.'

Deeply touched, Sheila sought for an answer, but finding none she gently wished Charlotte goodnight then turned on her side as she tried to find escape in sleep from the niggling pains in her back.

The clanging of the bell from deep within the convent woke the girls as usual the next morning, and yawning, Charlotte padded down to Sheila's room to find that her bed was empty with the blanket thrown back.

She raced back to the dormitory. 'Have you seen Sheila this morning?' she asked Joan, who was struggling out of bed.

Before the other girl could answer, Sister Agatha swept into the room in a swish of black skirts, clapping her hands. 'Come along now, girls,' she ordered. 'Off to the shower room. It's time to wash away your sins again, although I'm thinking it will take a lot more than cold water to do that, so I am.'

Joan glared at her as Charlotte asked politely, 'Sister, where is Sheila?'

'And just what business would that be of yours now?' the nun snapped, then, 'If you must know, she went into labour during the night and she's up on the first floor.'

Charlotte frowned as she snatched up the thin towel they were each allotted. She hadn't heard a thing, but then she was so exhausted each night when she went to bed that she could probably have slept through an earthquake. As she stood shivering beneath the ice-cold water she wondered if Sheila had delivered her baby yet.

It was late that evening as the girls were once more changing into their scratchy nightdresses that the door opened and Sheila appeared looking pale, worn out, and considerably slimmer.

Charlotte's face lit up as she hurled herself towards the older woman and clutched her hand. 'Oh Sheila, I've been so worried about you. What's happened and why are up and about so quickly?' Her eyes then fell to the case that Sheila was carrying and her face dropped.

'I had a little girl early this morning,' Sheila told her, her voice heavy with regret. 'She's fine and healthy by all accounts, although I haven't seen her. A taxi will be here in a minute to take me to a hotel for a few days where I shall rest before I go home, but I wanted to come and see you first to say goodbye.'

The breath caught in Charlotte's throat as she stared up at this kindly woman whom she now regarded as a friend.

'I – I shall miss you,' she forced herself to say past the lump in her throat.

'I shall miss you too,' Sheila answered, and then she turned as Sister Agatha appeared in the doorway.

'Your cab is here,' the nun told the woman disapprovingly, and Sheila nodded before turning back to Charlotte again.

'Take care of yourself and I hope everything turns out well for you,' she whispered, then she planted a gentle kiss on the girl's cheek, smiled at Joan and she was gone.

Charlotte stared at the door forlornly as tears trickled down her cheeks unheeded. She was very fond of Joan, her one remaining roommate, but somehow over the time they had been thrown together, Sheila had become like a substitute mother to her and she knew that it would be even harder for her again now that she was gone.

Crossing quickly to the high window, she balanced precariously on a chair and peered out of it just in time to see Sheila climbing into the back of an old black cab. She watched it drive away and at that moment she would have sold her soul to the devil to be in the cab with her.

Chapter Seventeen

Joan gave birth to a baby boy two days after Sheila left the convent and suddenly the loneliness pressed down on Charlotte like a heavy weight. A new arrival soon joined her in the dormitory, a young girl of fifteen who never seemed to stop crying. Rebecca had startling red hair, dark eyes that were flecked with green, and a spattering of freckles across her nose. She confided that a boy in the next village to the one where she lived outside Cork had got her pregnant. She was so naïve that Charlotte quickly guessed that it wouldn't have been difficult. Rebecca had been brought up by an elderly grandmother after losing both her parents in a tragic accident when she was little more than a baby. Sadly, once her grandmother had found out that she was pregnant the shock of the disclosure had caused her to have a stroke and so she had no choice but to send Rebecca to the convent. There was no way that she could have coped with a new baby in the house. Especially an illegitimate one. And so Rebecca found herself incarcerated there with all the other unmarried mothers and she wasn't coping well at all.

She began to rely heavily on Charlotte, which Charlotte supposed wasn't wholly a bad thing. She was so busy soothing Rebecca and drying her tears that she didn't have time to dwell too much on the fact that her own baby's birth was drawing closer.

The work in the laundry had become unbearable now and Charlotte was struggling to lean across the tubs of steaming water each day. By the time she retired to her room each night she ached in every limb and her feet were swollen. The child inside her never seemed to be still and Charlotte vowed to herself that she would never go through this again. Nor would she ever trust another man.

Joan joined her back in the dormitory two weeks after giving birth late on one Sunday afternoon.

'Joan!' Charlotte's face lit up at the sight of her and she hurried across the room to place her arms about her shoulders. 'How are you?'

Joan shrugged, looking depressed and despondent.

'Well, it ain't been no picnic, I don't mind tellin' you,' she answered moodily as she threw her few possessions onto her bed. 'A couple came an' fetched the baby this afternoon.'

'What were they like?' Charlotte asked cautiously.

The other girl grimaced. 'Very la-di-da. I weren't that keen on 'em, to tell the truth – but then we don't 'ave no say in the matter, do we? I dare say my boy'll want for nuffink though. They certainly didn't seem to be short of a bob or two. She was drippin' in gold an' diamonds an' she told me that they'd already 'ired a nanny to take care of 'im.'

'Did they give you any idea where they were from?'

'No, but from their accents I reckon they were American,' Joan responded. 'Which rather does away wiv the idea that the nuns work wiv the Welfare Department, don't it? Between you an' me, I reckon they're sellin' the babies. It's just like we're so much dirt an' they can do what they want wiv us!'

'No!' Charlotte was horrified at the very idea, although there was no way of finding out if Joan's suspicions were correct. However, she knew exactly what the girl meant about the nuns treating them like dirt. After the treatment she had received at the hands of Harry and the nuns, Charlotte doubted that she would ever feel clean again – but that was something she would worry about when she eventually got out of the place. That day couldn't come soon enough now.

'Well, at least the worst part is over now,' Charlotte soothed as Joan swung her legs onto the bed and lay down. Then she asked tentatively, 'What was the baby like?'

A tear trickled from the corner of Joan's eye as she stroked her swollen breasts. 'He was a dear little feller,' she said huskily, and when she lapsed into silence Charlotte held her tongue and went back to her own bed. It was obviously too painful for Joan to talk about right now and she didn't want to make her feel any worse than she already did.

She herself had very mixed feelings about the baby she was

carrying. Sometimes she would feel sympathy for the child that had never asked to be born and worried about what sort of life it would have. At other times she felt nothing but resentment for it and this made her feel guilty. Above all though, she just longed for the whole thing to be over so that she could resume her life. She had so many plans for when she got out of the convent. First she would return home and expose her father for the pervert that he really was. She would never forgive him now for what he had done to her; or her aunt, for that matter. They had lied to her and tricked her, and someday soon she would have her revenge. Then she fully intended to take up the nursing career she had dreamed of. But for now all she could do was bide her time – and that grew more difficult by the day.

It was early one misty morning in August as Charlotte was leaning over the tub in the laundry that her waters broke. She felt the warmth flood down the inside of her legs and her mouth gaped open as she stared down at the small puddle on the floor. She had been kept awake all night by cramping pains in her back, but even so it took her by surprise.

Sister Agatha, who had seen what had happened, swept over to her and tutted.

'Now look at the mess you've made,' she scolded, as if Charlotte had had some choice in the matter. 'Come away with you now. You'll have to go up to the first floor – but mop that mess up first.'

White-faced, Charlotte did as she was told. For weeks and months she had prayed for this moment to come, but now that it was finally here she was terrified and longed for her mother. Once the floor was mopped she returned the mop to the bucket and began to follow Sister Agatha from the room, but she had barely reached the door when the first contraction gripped her and she doubled over.

'Come along now, this is no time for play-acting,' the nun sneered. 'You've had the pleasure and now you must feel the pain, girl.'

Charlotte straightened as best she could and hobbled after the woman. She never knew how she managed to climb the stairs to the first floor, but eventually she made it – to be met by Sister Breda on the landing.

'Come along,' she said calmly. 'We need to prepare you.' She led Charlotte into a small room that contained nothing but a bed covered in a crisp white sheet and a trolley on which lay some evil-looking instruments.

'Let's be having that dress and your knickers off you,' the nun said as she bustled over to the bed.

'B-but what shall I put on?' Charlotte asked nervously as her eyes cast about for the sight of a nightgown.

'It's a bit late in the day to be displaying false modesty now,' Sister Agatha said coldly. 'I've no doubt you were naked when you conceived the bastard you are carrying, and now you can bring it into the world the same way.' She then left in a swish of black skirts as Charlotte eyed her with contempt. The nun didn't appear to have a compassionate bone in her body and yet she was a woman of the cloth. But then so was her father – and look at him!

Charlotte peeled her dress and sodden knickers off and lay down on the cold sheet. Soon afterwards, the real agony began and she had to grit her teeth to stop herself from crying out. This was pain as she had never known it and she was convinced that she was going to die. She only prayed that it might be soon. She was given no pain relief whatsoever and as the contractions grew stronger, she couldn't help but cry out in agony.

'Shush now,' Sister Maeve urged. 'You must put all your efforts into giving birth.'

Charlotte glared at her and bit down on her lip until she drew blood. Her hair had begun to grow again into curls that framed her face, but now they clung damply to the back of her neck and forehead.

By teatime the screams had given way to dull hiccuping whimpers as Charlotte's strength waned. Every half an hour or so, Sister Maeve would appear to check her and at last she began to roll her sleeves up.

'Now then, Eilish,' she said with authority. 'The baby's head is crowning. You must wait until I tell you, and then push with all your might.'

Charlotte groaned as another contraction arched her back and then she heard the Sister say as if from a long way off, 'Now, Eilish! Push *now*!'

Charlotte lifted her head and pushed with all her might, and as the contraction passed she dropped back onto the pillows in a pool of sweat and tears.

'I . . . I can't do it any more,' she mumbled.

'Oh yes, you *can*. We're almost there,' the Sister scolded as she leaned to look closer at the small dark head that was just visible between Charlotte's legs. 'Now when the next contraction comes, push again.'

Charlotte did her best to do as she was told but it was another half an hour before the Sister said, 'The next push should do it. Come along now!' She rested her hand on Charlotte's abdomen and as she felt the next contraction coming, she urged, 'Now, Eilish – one last effort. Push!'

With the last of her strength Charlotte heaved with all her might and suddenly the sound of a newborn baby's wail filled the room as the Sister held aloft a bloody little bundle of flailing arms and legs.

'It's a girl,' Charlotte heard her say as she sagged back against the pillows. The Sister wrapped and laid the child in a small bassinet that she had recently wheeled into the room before turning her attentions back to the mother.

'Hmm, you've torn,' she said. 'Still, there's nothing to be done for that. You'll just have to put up with the pain until it heals. But now let's get this afterbirth away and then I'll see to the infant.'

Twenty minutes later, when the afterbirth had been delivered, she threw a sheet over Charlotte's trembling body and marched away with the baby in her arms to bathe it.

Charlotte lay staring at the ceiling as she shivered with shock. The birth had easily been the worst experience of her whole life, and she knew then that she would definitely never have another child.

When Sister Maeve came back in some time later with the child swaddled in a plain white sheet, Charlotte turned her head away. It seemed so cruel to make them all care for the babies and feed them when soon they would be taken away to new homes.

'I don't want to see her,' Charlotte said dully.

Sister Maeve visibly bristled. 'It's right sorry I am to be hearing it but I'm afraid you have no choice in the matter,' she said crossly. 'You brought the child into the world and now it must be your

143

responsibility to care for her until her new mammy and daddy come to take her to her new home. Sure I haven't the time to be seeing to the poor little mite.'

Unceremoniously she thrust the child towards Charlotte, whose arms instinctively reached out to take her.

'I should warn you before you look at her that the child has a birthmark,' the nun now told her. 'And right on her face as well.' She clucked disapprovingly. 'It's not going to make it easy to find her a new home. Most of our parents want perfect babies, but there's nothing we can do about it. We must just pray that someone will take pity on her.'

Charlotte eyed the bundle in her arms warily as thoughts of the bodged abortion sprang into her mind. Could it be that the child was marked because of that?

Tentatively she drew back the corner of the sheet, and as she was confronted by a pair of startlingly blue eyes staring up at her, she gasped. Just as Sister Maeve had said, there was a red birthmark on the child's left cheek. It was almost heart-shaped, but even so she was beautiful, with a mop of fair hair and creamy soft skin. As she gazed trustingly up at her mother, emotions that Charlotte had never known coursed through her and a huge lump formed in her throat. This was her *daughter* – a real live little human being. It suddenly didn't matter how she had been conceived. She was here now and a part of her for all time.

Stroking the child's downy cheek, Charlotte smiled at her through a haze of tears wondering how she could ever have produced something so beautiful.

'Hello, little one. Welcome to the world,' she crooned softly as Sister Maeve bustled about collecting the stack of bloodied towels she had used during the delivery. The Sister glanced at her just once before disappearing off through the door, leaving mother and baby alone together.

Charlotte stared in awe at her new daughter. She hadn't even wanted to look at her, but now she could scarcely drag her eyes away from the child's little face. *I mustn't get attached*, she silently chided herself. *She'll be going to live with a new mum and dad soon.* She was shocked at the pain the thought brought, even though she knew it was inevitable. All of the indignities she had been forced to suffer over the last months had been leading to this moment. She had longed to get the birth over and done with so that she could escape and resume her life, so the emotions she was experiencing took her completely by surprise. Of course the child would be far better off with parents who could give her everything she wanted. And yet . . .

Sister Maeve bustled back in then and crossing to Charlotte, she snatched the sheet down and bared her breast.

'You should try and feed her,' she said impatiently.

As she brought the child's rosebud mouth to Charlotte's nipple the child latched on as if she knew exactly what she should do and began to suckle contentedly.

'That's good.' The Sister nodded her approval. 'Your milk will come in soon. You can feed her yourself for a few days and then we'll wean her on to a bottle. She'll need to be taking formula properly when her new parents come for her.'

'How long is that likely to be?' Charlotte asked timidly.

'Oh, I should think within a couple of weeks.' Sister Maeve began to tuck the sheets around her. 'That is, if we can find a couple who are prepared to take a child who is imperfect. The birthmark really couldn't have been in a worse place and no doubt it will get bigger as she grows.'

Charlotte focused on her baby. How dare the nun say that she was imperfect? Even with her birthmark she was easily the most beautiful baby that Charlotte had ever seen, and already the thought of giving her away was unthinkable. But what other option was open to her? Even if she managed to get them both out of there, how could she support herself and a child? Pushing the depressing thoughts away she concentrated on her baby, determined to enjoy every single second they had together. She would worry about tomorrow when it came, but for now she would just enjoy her daughter.

Eight days passed. Then, one day as Charlotte was changing her baby's nappy following a feed, Sister Agatha appeared in the door of her room on the first floor.

'Put the child in her crib and go and stand over there,' she said without preamble, pointing towards the corner of the room. 'There is someone here who wishes to look at the baby.'

Charlotte's stomach did a somersault and inside she started to cry silent tears. *No, no, it's too soon*, she told herself, but nonetheless she did as she was told. She had little choice.

A couple were ushered into the room and Charlotte surveyed them critically. The woman, who looked to be in her mid-twenties, was small and petite, with long dark hair coiled on the top of her head in loose curls that hung down to frame her delicate face. She was heavily made-up and she was immaculately dressed, as was the tall man at her side who was gripping her elbow protectively. He was fair with blue eyes, and when he glanced towards Charlotte he smiled at her nervously, obviously ill-at-ease.

'This is the child,' Sister Breda told them, urging them further into the room. 'As I explained, she does have a birthmark on her face but other than that she is perfectly healthy and well.'

The woman approached the cot and stared down at the baby, showing no sign of what she was thinking.

'What do you think, darling?' she asked her husband in a lilting Irish accent.

Looking even more uncomfortable, the man tugged at the collar of his shirt as if he couldn't breathe.

'It's entirely up to you,' he told her. 'Whatever you want, my pet.'

'Hmm . . .' The woman surveyed the baby as if she was eyeing up a piece of meat on a slab. 'I have to say the birthmark worries me. Little girls should be pretty without blemishes, shouldn't they?'

Charlotte's hands bunched into fists. Just who did this woman think she was anyway? Daisy, as Charlotte had taken to calling the baby, was beautiful with or without the birthmark – surely she could see that?

'Do you have any other babies we could look at?' she asked Sister Breda now.

The nun nodded. 'We do have one more but it's a little boy,' she told her. 'And you *did* specifically request a girl.'

The woman, who was clearly spoiled rotten, shrugged her slim shoulders. 'I know I did,' she agreed. 'You can dress little girls in such pretty clothes, can't you? But then I think we'll take a look at the boy, if you don't mind.'

Ignoring Charlotte and the baby as if they weren't there, she then turned on her dainty high heels and tripped from the room as her husband cast an apologetic glance towards Charlotte and scuttled after her.

The second they were gone, Charlotte raced back to the cot, lifted the baby into her arms and started to rock her to and fro.

'Don't you listen to what she said,' she murmured. 'I wouldn't want you to go to someone like her anyway. And you are beautiful – just you always remember it.'

As Charlotte stood holding her baby at the window later, she saw the young couple emerge onto the steps of the convent with a small bundle wrapped in a blue shawl in the woman's arms. She let out a sigh of relief. The woman had clearly decided on the baby boy and Charlotte thanked God for it. There was no way she would have wanted her to have her baby.

'There now,' she crooned. 'You're still here safe and sound with your mummy.' *But for how much longer?* a little voice whispered, and the thought of what lay ahead made Charlotte break out in a cold sweat. Every day was precious now and she knew that she must make the most of her time with Daisy, before the child was removed from her forever. It was a chilling thought.

Chapter Eighteen

Exactly one week later, Charlotte heard Sister Breda leading yet another couple along the landing and her blood ran cold as she clutched Daisy more tightly to her. The child was just slipping into a contented doze and as Charlotte stared at her daughter she began to panic. What if this was another set of would-be adopters come to look at Daisy?

The footsteps slowed outside her room and Charlotte's heart skipped a beat as Sister Breda pushed the door open and all her fears were realised.

'Put the child in her cot and stand over there,' she said, again pointing to the same corner.

Charlotte's lip trembled as she did as she was told and once in the corner she wrapped her arms tightly around herself. The nun floated into the room, her black skirts billowing, with yet another couple close behind her.

Unlike the first woman, this one had a kind face and she smiled at Charlotte sympathetically as she approached the cot. She was tall with short dark hair that curled around her face and blue eyes, and she was dressed in sensible shoes and a plain but smartly cut blue coat that emphasised the colour of her eyes. The man who followed was slightly taller than her with mousy-coloured hair and a ruddy complexion, and he was also plainly but smartly dressed in a dark grey suit, a white shirt and a striped tie. He too smiled at Charlotte.

And then Charlotte's worst fear became reality when the woman gazed down into the cot and gasped with delight.

'Why, she's truly *beautiful*, isn't she, David!' she murmured. She didn't even seem to notice the birthmark on the baby's cheek.

Her husband's face relaxed and he smiled as he followed his wife's eyes. 'She certainly is.' And then addressing the nun he asked excitedly, 'May we hold her?'

Charlotte recognised the couple's Midlands accent as Sister Breda nodded. 'Of course you may,' she told him, then turning to Charlotte she said shortly, 'Go to the kitchen and prepare some bottles for the child. I shall call you when you are needed.'

Charlotte hesitated, reluctant to leave her baby, but then seeing the look on the Sister's face she left the room on feet that felt like lead. As she closed the door behind her she saw the woman lift the child from her cot and tenderly cradle her against her, and the sight was almost more than she could bear. Daisy was *her* baby!

Down in the kitchen, she boiled the kettle and made up some bottles, then she waited impatiently for someone to come and instruct her to go back to her room. She was pacing the floor when Sister Breda appeared with a wide smile on her face.

'I have some good news for you,' she told her. 'The dear people have decided that they will take the child, even with her imperfection.'

'*No!*' The word shot from Charlotte's lips before she could stop it, and the smile slid from the Sister's face.

'Why, it's a *bad* ungrateful girl you are,' she admonished. 'You should be thankful that there are kind people who are prepared to live with the fruit of your sins.'

'They won't have to because I want to keep her,' Charlotte said with a note of desperation in her voice.

The nun had had this reaction from other girls many times before and her lips slid into a thin line as she drew herself up to her full height.

'That is out of the question.' Her eyes were steely as they fastened on Charlotte. 'The Kindlers are good people and they have come a long way. I am going to complete the necessary paperwork with them now, and whilst we are gone you may pack the baby's necessities and say your goodbyes. You will find a small suitcase in the bottom of the wardrobe. We shall be back to fetch her within the hour.'

Charlotte somehow staggered back along the landing just in time to see the couple and the Sister disappear through the door at the end of the corridor. The key then turned in the lock as she hurried back in to her baby. Daisy was lying in her cot gurgling contentedly as her little arms and legs waved in the air, and Charlotte's heart felt as if it was breaking. She took the suitcase out of the wardrobe, then carefully folded the nappies and tiny little nightgowns, and packed them into it, then fetched the bottles she had made up, and after wrapping them in some strips of linen, she placed them in the case too. And now it was time to say goodbye to her baby.

'I will never forget you,' she whispered brokenly as she kissed the soft curls on her head again and again. 'And wherever you are, I will always be thinking of you.'

Eventually the footsteps in the corridor sounded again and Charlotte could hold back the tears no longer. They gushed out of her eyes so fast that she was almost blinded.

The couple, who were looking decidedly uncomfortable now, came back into the room with Sister Breda.

'It is time,' the nun told her and held her arms out for the baby.

Charlotte clung to her daughter and a look of irritation flashed across the nun's face.

'Pull yourself together, Eilish. You always knew this moment would come. Let us not make it worse by creating a scene.'

'I call her Daisy,' Charlotte told the woman desperately, looking past the nun, and then she could only stand there mutely as the baby was tugged from her arms. Snatching up a shawl, Sister Breda tutted disapprovingly as she wrapped the child in it then crossed the room and handed Daisy to Mrs Kindler.

The woman looked towards Charlotte with an expression of sorrow on her face. 'I'm sorry you are so upset,' she said softly. 'But we will always do our best for her for you. She will be loved and wanted more than you could ever know. We have tried for a baby of our own for many years and had almost given up hope, but she is like a gift from God and I thank you from the bottom of my heart. Goodbye, my dear. And God bless you.'

She then turned and walked away as Charlotte slithered into a heap on the floor and sobbed uncontrollably, clutching a tiny bootee that was all she would ever have of her daughter now. All the pain and humiliation that had gone before was nothing compared to what she was feeling now, and with every ounce of her being she prayed that she might die because this agony was beyond bearing. Eventually she dragged herself up and stood staring down into the empty cradle.

Charlotte was shown down to her old room later that evening and she found Joan there.

'Aw'ight, mate?' Joan greeted her perkily. 'Your scrap gone an' all, 'as she? I heard you'd had a gel. A right flighty piece she was, the woman what took mine, as I fink I told you. An actress, by all accounts. Still, I dare say he'll be fine.'

Charlotte could well remember how upset Joan had been when her baby had first been taken away from her, but guessed that the girl was trying to put a brave face on.

'Where is Rebecca?' Charlotte asked now as she looked at the other empty bed.

'Had a miscarriage, from what the other girls were sayin',' Joan told her matter-of-factly. 'It seems that when it was over, her gran come to take 'er back 'ome, the jammy little sod.'

Charlotte sighed.

'Now come on,' Joan said bossily. 'There's no need to look so miserable. As yer once told me, the worst bit is over now an' we can start to think about gettin' out of this dump. You'll feel better about it in a couple of days' time.'

Charlotte doubted that very much but even so she nodded dully as she made her way to her old bed and sagged onto it. It seemed a lifetime ago since she had slept there and yet it was barely more than a couple of weeks.

'I called her Daisy,' she told Joan in a voice barely above a whisper.

'Yer daft bugger,' Joan chided. 'What was the point of that? Her new mum an' dad are bound to give her another name.'

'I know, but for the short time she was mine I wanted her to have a name and she'll always be Daisy to me,' Charlotte replied.

Joan's face softened as she saw her friend's distress. She had deliberately tried not to allow herself to get close to her own baby, but she had still felt devastated when he went – not that she would ever admit to it. But she could see how hurt Charlotte was.

As Joan sought for something comforting to say, Charlotte began

151

to feel in the gap in her mattress and she smiled weakly as her fingers closed around the sock she had placed in there.

'What yer got there?' Joan asked curiously.

'Oh, nothing.' Charlotte hastily pushed it back into place just as Sister Agatha appeared in the doorway.

'Into your nightclothes now, girls,' she ordered and they both immediately began to change. Seconds later they were both in bed and because she wasn't in the mood to talk, Charlotte immediately turned over and pretended to be asleep.

The next day Charlotte was sent back to work in the laundry and she went without complaint. She knew that she should be planning her escape, but the loss of her baby was still so raw that she couldn't think of anything but Daisy.

I'll find a way out, she promised herself. Just as soon as I get my strength back. She thought of the money she had tucked away in her mattress. At least she had the means to get away, which was more than many other of the girls here had.

As the day progressed, Charlotte noticed that Joan seemed quiet and distracted. Normally as soon as Sister Agatha was out of earshot she was whispering in Charlotte's ear, but today she kept her head down. Charlotte was actually grateful for the fact. Joan was usually full of fun, and Charlotte didn't feel in the mood for being happy. Her breasts were painful and leaking and she was still sore from the birth, but she knew better than to complain. There would be no sympathy forthcoming from Sister Agatha. During the time she had spent on the first floor with her baby her hands had begun to heal, but soon they were red raw and weeping again. Charlotte was so miserable that she didn't even notice, but gradually the hurt and pain turned to anger as she thought of her father. There was nothing she could do now about losing her baby, but she could get her revenge on him – and it was only the thought of escaping and doing just that which kept her going.

She moved through the day like an automaton, trying hard not to think about her baby, and it was a relief when they were finally sent to their room that evening.

Joan immediately climbed into bed and turned on her side, and

Charlotte did the same. It was Sunday the next day so at least she wouldn't have to have her hands in hot water all day, although she dreaded the thought of all the time she would have to sit in the chapel on the hard pews. She was just dropping off to sleep when Joan's voice came to her from the darkness.

'Eilish . . . are you awake?'

'Yes.' Charlotte turned over and looked towards Joan's bed.

'I er . . . just wanted to say that you've been a good mate to me while I've been in 'ere.'

It seemed a strange thing to say and Charlotte was mildly surprised. 'Well, thank you. You've been good to me too,' she answered.

'Well, the fing is . . .' Charlotte heard Joan gulp deep in her throat before rushing on, 'I just wanna say I'm sorry.'

'Whatever for?' Charlotte whispered. 'We've all done things we're sorry for, but you don't have to apologise to me.'

Joan fell silent and after a moment Charlotte shrugged and turned back over. Joan could be a very strange girl at times but perhaps despite all her brave talk she was missing her baby too. She gazed at the stars high in the sky through the window. Her baby was out there somewhere under those very same stars, and she prayed that she was being well cared for. It was her last thought before she fell asleep.

The following morning, the girls were surprised when Sister Breda came to wake them.

'Poor Sister Agatha is confined to her bed with a bad case of influenza,' she informed them. 'And right poorly she is too, God bless her. But come on now, girls. You need to get showered. We wouldn't want you to be late for Mass, now would we?'

Without Sister Agatha's watchful eye on them every second the day was somewhat more relaxed than usual, and when they were finally let out into the patch of garden, Charlotte slunk off and found a quiet corner to sit in and enjoy the late-afternoon sunshine. They would only have an hour and then they would have to go back to the chapel again so she intended to relish every moment.

Normally Joan would have joined her but she still seemed strangely distracted and was wandering up and down the length of the low wire fence like a cat on hot bricks.

Shrugging, Charlotte settled back on the grass and closed her eyes as she listened to the birds singing. All too soon it was time to go back to the next service again and the girls reluctantly followed Sister Breda along the bare corridors.

It was as they were all heading for the dining room for their evening meal that Sister Breda suddenly paused.

'Has anyone seen Joan?' she asked as her eyes flitted over them all. The girls all shook their heads and Sister Breda sighed with irritation. 'Go ahead, girls,' she told them. 'I've no doubt she's still loitering outside. That girl is a law unto herself, so she is.'

She hurried away and the girls moved on to take their seats in the dining room. They had barely sat down when Sister Breda rushed back into the room and after having a hasty word in the ear of the Reverend Mother, who was as usual seated at the top table, they both stood and left the room.

Charlotte frowned, hoping that something hadn't happened to Joan, then she stood and joined the queue at the food table but her eyes kept constantly straying to the door hoping for a sight of her friend.

'What do you think has happened to Joan?' one of the girls hissed to Charlotte as they sat back down with their meagre meal.

'I've no idea, but she's been acting rather strangely all day to tell the truth,' Charlotte whispered back.

There was still no sign of Joan by the time the girls were led to their rooms and by then the rumours were rife. Some of the girls maintained that she was ill in the sick bay whilst others were saying that she had run away. Charlotte had no idea who to believe. Getting undressed, she slipped beneath the thin scratchy blanket, very aware of the empty bed across from her. It felt strange and lonely without Joan and she just wished that she knew what had happened to her.

She tossed and turned restlessly until eventually Sister Breda came into her room and perched on the edge of her bed.

'I need to talk to you, Eilish,' she said gravely. 'And I want you to answer me truthfully. Did you have any idea at all that Joan was planning to run away? And if you did, do you know where she might be heading?'

'Run away?' Charlotte gasped. 'Why no, I didn't know anything about it.' Suddenly she understood why Joan had got so emotional with her the evening before. She must have been planning it.

The nun sighed and shook her head. 'She's a silly girl, so she is,' she muttered. 'And she'll not get far. The Reverend Mother has the Gardai out looking for her already. It's terrible trouble she'll be in when they find her and fetch her back.'

She then rose and left without another word as Charlotte lay there feeling shocked. Joan must have taken advantage of the fact that Sister Agatha hadn't been there to keep her eye on them that afternoon and somehow scrambled over the fence and escaped. But where would she go with no money and dressed in the convent uniform? She would stick out like a sore thumb. And then a terrible thought occurred to Charlotte and she began to tremble. Joan had seen her check the sock where she kept her money hidden on the day she had come back to their room following her baby's departure.

Sitting up in the fast-waning light she dug her fingers into the slit of the mattress and her stomach sank; there was nothing there. She delved deeper, thinking she must have been mistaken but still there was nothing. Every penny that she had hoped would get her safely home to England was gone. Joan had taken it, which would explain why she had apologised to her the night before. She must have been planning her escape even then.

A lump swelled in Charlotte's throat as a sense of despair stole over her, and yet still she prayed that Joan might get safely away.

Chapter Nineteen

It was almost a week since Joan had escaped and still there was no sign of her. Sister Agatha was now back in charge of the laundry following her bout of the flu and seemed to be in an even worse mood than usual, if that was possible. If one of the girls did the least thing wrong, she would bring the split cane whistling through the air and down onto their knuckles, and the girls were almost afraid to breathe for fear of putting a foot wrong.

Charlotte was beginning to think that Joan might have got well away by now and prayed that she was right. She was still smarting from the pain of the loss of her savings, and yet she could forgive Joan for what she had done. Desperate times called for desperate measures, and she knew that Joan had reached the end of her tether. There was no saying what the poor girl might have done, had she been forced to stay there any longer. Even so, Charlotte knew that when she made her own bid for freedom, it would be much more difficult without a penny to her name. Whilst the money had been safely stored in her mattress she had known that if she could just get out of the convent and make her way to the coast, she had sufficient funds to catch the ferry back to England. But now what would she do?

The thought nagged at her day and night, and as her body slowly recovered from the birth of her baby the need to get away returned tenfold. It was now early September and the weather was slowly changing. Each morning a thick mist floated across the grounds of the convent and thankfully it wasn't so stifling in the laundry any more – which was one blessing at least.

Charlotte was scrubbing at a sheet shortly after lunch one day when she noticed a nun enter the laundry and whisper in Sister Agatha's ear. The Sister drew herself up to her full height and scowled before sweeping down on Charlotte with a look on her face that could have curdled milk.

'Dry your hands, Eilish, and go to Sister Magdalene's office this instant. It seems that you have a visitor.'

Despite the disapproval on the Sister's face, Charlotte's heart soared. Who could it be? Was it her father or her aunt who had had a change of heart and come to set her free? Knowing them as she did, she dismissed that idea almost immediately. They would probably be quite happy for her to rot there indefinitely, so who was it?

Straightening, she wiped her soapy hands on her huge cotton apron before meekly following the Sister, aware of the envious eyes of the other girls tight on her as she passed them.

They walked silently through the labyrinth of dismal corridors until at last they stood in front of the door of the Reverend Mother's office.

The Sister tapped on it lightly, then opened it and ushered Charlotte inside. Sister Magdalene was standing behind her desk with her hands tucked deep into the sleeves of her habit and Charlotte could see a woman with her back to her sitting in the chair in front of her.

And then as Charlotte advanced into the room the woman turned and Charlotte's eyes lit up. It was Sheila, and she was smiling at her and looking very pretty in a lovely two-piece outfit in a soft shade of green with a string of pearls gleaming in the dull light at her throat.

The Sister who had escorted her there stood discreetly at the back of the room and it was she whom the Reverend Mother now addressed, saying, 'Could you take Eilish to the dressing room to collect her belongings, please, Sister? She will be leaving us shortly.'

Shock momentarily rooted Charlotte to the spot as she stared at the Reverend Mother open-mouthed.

'Well, are you going to just stand there all day?' the Reverend Mother snapped. 'Don't you want to leave us – is that it?'

'Oh . . . y-yes, I do,' Charlotte stammered.

Sheila was smiling broadly and she waved her hand at her, urging her to go with the Sister. Charlotte turned quickly then and stumbled away, terrified that she was asleep and that at any minute she would wake up to find this had been no more than a wonderful dream.

157

The Sister led her to a room and unlocked a small cupboard with Charlotte's name on it. Inside was her suitcase and the Sister nodded towards it, telling her, 'Hurry and get changed into your own clothes. I shall wait for you.'

Charlotte stripped off without a moment's hesitation. She had long since lost all sense of dignity in this place, and no longer worried about the Sisters seeing her naked.

She pulled the drab grey dress over her head followed by the coarse linen knickers and flung them into a heap on the floor, then sighed with pleasure as she lifted her own simple cotton bra and fastened it on. Next came her own panties and the skirt and jumper that she had arrived in. Everything was tighter on her now and she realised that she wasn't quite back in shape following the birth of her daughter. Thinking of Daisy brought a familiar lump to her throat but she blinked back the tears. There would be all the time in the world to grieve for her baby once she was well away from this place.

She then lifted her suitcase and sedately followed the Sister back to the Reverend Mother's office, breathing a huge sigh of relief when she saw that Sheila was still there. She was busily signing a form on the desk but when Charlotte entered the room she laid the pen down, straightened and pulled her gloves on.

'I think that's all then, isn't it, Reverend Mother?' she asked boldly.

'Yes, it is.' The woman inclined her head. 'May God go with you both and thank you for your more than kind donation to the convent.'

Sheila bustled towards Charlotte without another word, and addressing the other Sister she said imperiously, 'Would you kindly show us out, please?'

They left the room without a backward glance and Charlotte's knees started to knock together. Everything had happened so fast. What if it was some sort of cruel joke and they were going to be stopped at the door and shown back to the hated laundry?

But no, the front door was ahead of them now and another Sister was opening it for them and suddenly they were out on the steps in the watery sunshine. And then the door clanged shut behind them and Charlotte almost jumped out of her skin as the colour drained from her cheeks.

'It's all right, dear. Don't look so worried.' Sheila took some car keys from her handbag and hurried Charlotte down the steps. A shining Vauxhall Cresta was parked there and once Sheila had thrown Charlotte's case into the boot, she opened the front passenger door for her.

'Jump in,' she urged, and then teasingly, 'Unless you can't bear to leave the place, that is.'

Charlotte almost leaped into the front and slammed the door behind her as Sheila got into the driver's seat. The scent of new leather was in her nostrils and after the smell of the laundry it was a welcome change.

Sheila started the car and moved off down the drive, and still Charlotte held her breath. What if they wouldn't open the gates and let them out? But no, a nun was there with the gates held wide open for them, and once they had driven through them into a country lane Charlotte suddenly started to cry and couldn't stop.

Sheila drove on for some way then pulled to a stop and took Charlotte into her arms. 'There now,' she soothed. 'It's all over now.'

'B-but why? And how did you manage it?' Charlotte asked tremulously.

Sheila stroked her hair gently as Charlotte laid her head on her shoulder.

'Well, in answer to why, you didn't *really* think I'd just walk away and forget all about you, did you? And how? Let's just say that after I made a very generous donation to the convent the Reverend Mother was more than willing to let me take you into my care.'

'But I thought that they weren't allowed to let me go to anyone but family,' Charlotte choked.

Sheila pursed her lips. 'As you grow older you'll discover that money talks,' she told her grimly. 'But the main thing is you're out of there now and I'm going to take you back to my house for a time. Then we'll see about getting you home to England – if that's what you want, of course?'

Charlotte nodded vigorously at the thought of seeing her mother and her granny again. She had missed them both so much.

'Right then. Let's get going, shall we?' Sheila started the car again and as they drove past the rolling countryside she told her, 'By the way, my name isn't really Sheila, as you know. It's Marianne O'Connor. And I'm sure your name is not really Eilish?'

'It's Charlotte Hayes,' the girl told her, and they then drove on in silence until eventually the motion of the car rocked her off to sleep.

'Come on, sleepyhead! We're here.'

Charlotte started awake as Marianne gently shook her arm, and peering through the window she saw that they were parked in front of a smart townhouse that was three storeys high.

'This is my home,' Marianne smiled. 'It's on the outskirts of the city. I'd rather live in the country, to be honest, but this makes it so much more convenient for getting to work. But before we go in, there's something I must tell you. I have a housekeeper, Mrs Gallagher. She's a dear but she does love a good gossip. She believes that I've been travelling for the last few months and I have told her that you are the daughter of a friend of mine in England who is coming to stay for a little holiday. Do you think you can remember that?'

'Of course.' Charlotte smiled for the first time. After the confines of the convent, everywhere felt enormous and she was still struggling to believe that she was really out of there.

'Come on then. I'm sure you're ready for a decent meal and a real cup of tea,' Marianne grinned. 'Mrs Gallagher promised to have it all ready for you. I told her I was going to meet you off the ferry. Then tomorrow when you've had a good night's sleep we'll go shopping and get you some new clothes.'

'Oh no, I couldn't let you do that,' Charlotte objected quickly. 'You've done more than enough for me already.'

'Nonsense.' Marianne waved her objections aside. 'Now that my own daughter is away at university I really miss the shopping trips we used to have. Besides, I need some new clothes myself, so it will be a good excuse to get some.'

They both got out of the car and Charlotte followed her up the steps to a door that was painted a cheerful red with a heavy, highly-polished brass knocker on it. Marianne inserted a key into the lock and before she knew it, Charlotte found her feet sinking into a deep-pile pale grey carpet that stretched wall to wall the whole length of

160

a long hallway. The walls were decorated in a delicate shade of pink and the colour contrast made it appear warm and inviting and more than a little luxurious.

Marianne then beckoned her into one of the rooms that led off from the hallway and Charlotte felt as if she had stepped into another world. They were in a huge lounge the like of which she had only ever glimpsed in magazines before. This room was painted in shades of green, and a huge glittering crystal chandelier was suspended from the centre of a high ceiling that was edged with ornate plaster cornices. Comfortable settees covered in pretty cushions in various shades of green were dotted around an enormous cream marble fireplace, and expensive-looking ornaments were displayed on highly polished mahogany side tables that matched a massive mahogany sideboard which took up almost the whole length of one wall. At the windows, heavy velvet curtains were topped with fringed swags and tails, and the difference between this room and the one she had been forced to live in for the last few months was almost more than Charlotte could take in as she gazed around speechless.

'Do you like it then?' Marianne asked.

Charlotte smiled. 'How could anybody *not* like it?' she responded.

Just then, a grey-haired woman with a kindly smile entered the room and Marianne said, 'Ah, Mrs Gallagher. This is Charlotte, the young lady I told you would be staying with us for a while. You don't think you could rustle us up a nice cup of tea, do you? And a slice of your delicious sponge cake would go down a treat, if there's any going.'

Mrs Gallagher beamed at Charlotte and the girl warmed to her immediately. 'I can be havin' that ready fer yous in no time at all, so I can,' she said. 'An' I hope yous enjoy your stay here, Miss Charlotte.'

'Oh please, just Charlotte is fine,' the girl insisted, and patting the grey bun that was precariously perched on the back of her head, Mrs Gallagher nodded and shuffled away, closing the door quietly behind her.

'Mrs Gallagher is a real treasure,' Marianne confided, easing her shoes off. 'She's been with my husband and me since shortly after we were married and I really don't know how I would manage without her. When my children were small she was a nanny to them and it was wonderful to be able to carry on with my career knowing that they were in safe hands.' Her face dropped then. 'I feel very guilty about deceiving her as I have, and my husband too. But still, we all make mistakes and I've certainly learned by mine. I won't go making a fool of myself again, that's for sure.'

She gazed towards the window, and as Charlotte saw the pain in her eyes, she knew that Marianne was thinking of the baby she had given up. It was a pain that no amount of time would take away and something that she would regret for the rest of her life, just as Charlotte would.

'The Reverend Mother told me that you gave birth to a little girl too,' Marianne said eventually and Charlotte nodded. 'It was harder than I thought it would be, to let mine go,' Marianne whispered. 'Was it the same for you?'

Charlotte nodded again, too full to answer, but then Mrs Gallagher came back into the room pushing a tea trolley and the conversation was stopped from going any further.

'There's a good strong pot o' tea, a sponge cake an' some scones fresh from the oven,' she informed them. 'Oh, an' some of me homemade jam an' some fresh cream an' all. That should fill a hole till dinnertime. I've done your favourite steak pie fer dinner, by the way, Mrs O'Connor, an' crispy potatoes just the way yous like 'em.'

'You really are an angel, Mrs Gallagher,' Marianne sighed as she lifted the teapot, then smiling at Charlotte she added, 'That's as well as being just about the best cook in the whole world!'

Mrs Gallagher winked at Charlotte. 'Would yous just listen to the old flannel comin' out of her mouth? She knows be now that flattery will get her everywhere. But that's enough from me; I'll leave yous both to enjoy your tea now. Dinner should be ready in about an hour, if that's all right?'

'That's perfect,' Marianne assured her, and the elderly woman pottered away with a wide smile on her face.

'My husband has her wrapped around his little finger,' Marianne confided to Charlotte when the woman had gone. 'She'd stir his tea for him when he's home if I'd let her.' Again she looked guilty as she added, 'He's going to retire from the sea next year and then we'll get to spend a lot more time together.'

'Retire? Is he older than you then?'

'Well, yes, Donald is ten years older than me but he's not going to retire altogether. He'll take on a desk job, which means we'll have a more normal family life. I have a lot of making up to do,' Marianne added regretfully. 'Unlike you, I brought this whole sorry mess on myself. I just pray that the baby will be well looked after.'

She passed Charlotte a steaming cup of tea in a bone china cup and saucer, and as Charlotte sipped at it a look of pure pleasure passed across her face and she sighed contentedly.

'A bit different to that slop they served you in the convent, isn't it?' Marianne commented. 'At least I got to eat with the nuns. I used to look across at what you girls were served sometimes and wonder how you ever managed to stomach it. But that's enough of the doom and gloom now. You're out of there, thank goodness.'

'I really don't know how I'm ever going to repay you.' Charlotte bit into a slice of Mrs Gallagher's light sponge cake and almost groaned with ecstasy.

'You don't have to,' Marianne assured her. 'I just wish I could have helped all the poor lasses in there, but life is a cruel thing.'

Once they had finished their snack, Marianne showed Charlotte up to her bedroom, and again Charlotte was awestruck. Her room was at the back of the house and across from a park where swans were gliding on the smooth surface of a small lake. The furniture was a soft cream colour and like the downstairs there was a thick carpet on the floor, this time in pink. Pink flowered curtains hung at the high sash-cord window and a matching bedspread was smoothed across an enormous brass bed. Fluffy pillows were piled onto it and Charlotte could hardly wait to try it out.

'It's just *beautiful*.' She turned to Marianne and hugged her impulsively. The dear woman had thought of everything. A pretty lace-trimmed nightie as well as a pink candlewick dressing-gown were spread across the end of the bed and a selection of toiletries and a scented soap were placed on the dressing-table.

'After dinner you can have a soak in a nice hot bath and put lots of cream on your poor hands,' Marianne promised her thoughtfully.

163

'And whilst we're shopping tomorrow we'll nip into the hairdressers and get your hair styled for you. It actually suits you now that it's grown a little. But come along, dinner should be ready any time now, and Mrs Gallagher will have our guts for garters if we're late for it.'

Charlotte would never forget the meal that followed. The pastry on the steak pie that Mrs Gallagher had baked was so light that it melted in her mouth and the accompanying potatoes and vegetables were cooked to perfection. Just the smell of the meal made Charlotte's mouth water and she ate so much that she feared she would burst.

'I'm so sorry for being such a pig,' she apologised to Mrs Gallagher as the woman served her a third slice of pie.

Mrs Gallagher chuckled. 'Don't you dare say sorry to me for having a good appetite, my dearie,' she answered. 'There's nothing more satisfying than cooking for someone who appreciates your efforts. Now could you manage another roast spud an' all?'

The main course was followed by apple crumble and thick creamy custard, and Mrs Gallagher sighed regretfully as she served it. 'I always feel guilty, cooking one of these puddings when Mr Ronald's away at sea,' she told Charlotte. 'He loves me apple crumble, so he does. But then when he comes home I'll make him two the very first day.'

Just as Marianne had promised, the meal was followed by a lovely hot bath – and after all the days of being made to stand beneath a freezing cold shower, Charlotte really felt that she might have died and gone to heaven.

Before Charlotte went to sleep, Marianne tucked her into the wonderfully soft bed with its feather mattress and kissed her forehead gently. There was something irresistibly vulnerable about the girl, she thought. Perhaps it was the fact that she reminded her of her own daughter? Whatever it was, the woman was so pleased that she had gone and rescued her from that terrible convent.

'Goodnight dear, sweet dreams,' she whispered, but her words fell on deaf ears. Charlotte was already sound asleep and for the first time in many a long day, there was a smile on her face.

Chapter Twenty

Charlotte was disorientated when she woke the next morning and she blinked as she looked around the comfy bedroom, thinking again that she was dreaming. Appetising smells were wafting up the staircase, and despite the huge amount she had eaten the night before, she found that she was hungry again. She stretched and yawned then started guiltily as her eyes fell on the clock on the bedside table. It was gone nine in the morning, and at the convent she would have been hard at work by now. It was then that it hit her. It was *really* over. All the humiliation, the pain, the loss of the baby and all the indignities she had been forced to suffer were truly at an end, and the realisation brought the tears swelling in her throat. And then they came so forcefully that she was sure she would drown in them. They spurted from her eyes and she sobbed uncontrollably, rocking to and fro.

Marianne found her like this when she came up to collect her for breakfast, and without a word she wrapped her arms about the girl and let her cry all the pain out.

'That's it,' she soothed. 'Let it all go now. It's no good trapped inside.' Taking a handkerchief from the pocket of her skirt, she gently mopped at Charlotte's eyes until at last the sobs subsided and the girl went limp in her arms.

Marianne held her tight and told her, 'You needed to do that. But you should always remember that none of what has happened is your fault. The baby was forced on you.'

Charlotte sniffed and turned slightly to look at her. 'I should really be thinking of going home,' she murmured. 'I can't stay here taking advantage of your kindness. You've done so much for me already. I'd still be stuck in the convent if it wasn't for you.' She then went on to tell Marianne about the money that Joan had stolen from her, and how she had then had no idea how she was ever going to escape.

'At least while I had that tucked away I knew that I could get to the ferry and find my way home, but once the money was gone I was in real trouble. Even if I had managed to escape I would have had no means of getting back to England.'

'You mustn't judge her too harshly,' Marianne said. 'Being in that dreadful place was enough to make anyone do things they wouldn't normally do, and it worked out for you in the end, so let's hope that Joan is safe too. She wasn't a bad girl.' She then tilted Charlotte's chin and smiled at her. 'But now how about you go and get dressed and come down for some breakfast. Then we'll go off on that shopping trip, shall we? And as for staying here . . . Well, my children aren't due home for another couple of weeks yet, so let's get you feeling a little stronger and then we'll book you a ferry back to England. Meantime, would you like to telephone your mother to let her know that you are safe?'

Charlotte shook her head. 'No, I don't think so, thank you. There's so much explaining to do that I think I'd rather tell her what really happened, face-to-face. She believes I ran away from my aunt's, you see. And that isn't all . . .' She went on to tell Marianne about her father and the discovery she had made in his dark room, and as the tale unfolded Marianne's face became grim.

'You know that you must expose him, don't you?' she said.

'Yes, I do. If I'd done it when I first discovered it, none of this would have happened,' Charlotte answered regretfully. 'But there were so many things I was afraid of – my granny's health and how the disclosure would affect her for a start-off. She has angina, you see. And then there was my mother. She admitted to me that she had never really loved my father, had lost all feelings for him shortly after they were married. He was a bully of the worst kind and I think she is afraid of him. But I'm stronger now and I can face whatever happens when the truth comes out. I'll speak to Granny and my mum first and explain why I didn't tell them – and that will prepare them.'

'Good.' Marianne cuddled her again and then they sat for a time in silence, each drawing comfort from the other, until Mrs Gallagher called up to let them know she was about to serve breakfast.

* * *

Later that morning, Marianne drove Charlotte into Dublin and the shopping trip began. Marianne was more than generous and insisted on buying the girl three whole new outfits. Charlotte had always worn practical, hardwearing clothes rather than modern ones, and as she stared at the fashionable girl staring back at her from the mirror she could hardly believe that it was her. She had a new dress with a full swingy skirt tightly belted at the waist that showed off her slim figure to perfection, and two new skirts, as well as a pretty blouse with a Peter Pan collar and a lovely soft jumper made from Angora wool in a lovely shade of blue. Marianne then purchased for her a new coat, a new pair of court shoes and a selection of lovely underwear. Next stop was the hairdressers, and there Charlotte had her hair trimmed into a very becoming short style that framed her face. By the time she walked out of the salon she was loaded down with bags, hardly daring to imagine how much the shopping trip must have cost.

'It will take me forever to repay you for all this,' she fretted as Marianne led her into a smart restaurant for lunch.

Marianne chuckled. 'No it won't, because you don't owe me a penny. Call the clothes a treat. Perhaps you'll be able to do me a favour one day. Now what would you like for lunch?' Lifting the menu she began to study it, and realising that it would be useless to argue Charlotte did the same, wondering what she had ever done to deserve such a wonderful friend.

The next two weeks passed pleasantly, but as Charlotte's heart and body slowly healed she began to be impatient to see her mother and her granny again. She had missed them both more than she could say, and although she knew that her revelations about Bernard Hayes would hurt them, she felt now that they deserved to know the truth.

She said as much as she and Marianne were sitting in her comfortable lounge after dinner one evening and the woman was very understanding.

'In that case I shall get you a passage on a ferry,' Marianne told her. 'It's Thursday now, so how would leaving on Saturday suit you? I believe there is one that will take you into Liverpool, and from there you can get a train to the Midlands.'

Charlotte smiled at her gratefully. 'That would be wonderful – but I'll miss you,' she told her, and she meant it from the heart. They were both aware that, once Charlotte left, there would be little chance of them ever seeing each other again, since it would have caused too many questions. But after what they had been through together, the two women knew that they would never forget each other.

'I shall miss you too,' Marianne told her sincerely. 'But I shall always be glad that I met you and was able to help you. Never forget that.'

Late on Saturday afternoon, Marianne drove her to the port in Dublin after Charlotte had said a tearful goodbye to Mrs Gallagher, of whom she had become very fond. Marianne had booked her an overnight passage with her own cabin, so that Charlotte could sleep on the way, and she had also ensured that the girl had more than enough money to get her home once she reached Liverpool. All Charlotte's new clothes were packed away in a brand new suitcase that Marianne had bought for her, and after parking the car they walked together through the crowds that were streaming towards the ferry. The nights were fast drawing in now and already it was dusk as the wind from the sea whipped at their hair.

Ahead they could see passengers pouring up the gangplank onto the ferry, and they slowed their steps and faced each other.

'So – this is it then,' said Marianne, a catch in her voice.

'Yes,' Charlotte answered chokily, and then suddenly she dropped her case and flung her arms around Marianne's waist. 'Thank you *so* much for all you've done for me,' she wept. 'Without you I'd probably still have been stuck in that godforsaken place.'

The wind snatched at her voice as Marianne gave her a maternal cuddle.

'You just go and do what has to be done, and then make something of your life,' she said, stroking the girl's cheek tenderly. 'And who knows? One day we might see each other again.' But even as the words were spoken they both knew that it was highly unlikely.

A horn sounded then and Marianne lifted her case and handed it to Charlotte. 'Go on,' she urged. 'You need to get aboard. Now are you sure you have your money safe?'

Charlotte patted her new leather handbag, yet another gift from Marianne. 'Yes, it's in here. Goodbye . . . and thank you.'

Marianne gave her a gentle push in the back. 'May God go with you,' she said, and then Charlotte joined the queue and soon she was on the deck of the ferry scanning the faces on the dock for a sight of her friend.

The horn sounded again and slowly the gangplank was raised and the huge ferry shuddered into life. The sea was churning against its sides, black and choppy, but Charlotte didn't notice, she was too busy waving to Marianne. The ferry began to move sluggishly out to sea and the figures on the quay grew smaller until eventually they were nothing more than dots that were quickly swallowed up by the darkness.

Charlotte slowly lowered her hand then lifting her case she went to find her cabin. It was deep down in the bowels of the ship, and tiny. Even so there was a bunk and a small sink where she could tidy herself. The ferry was rolling alarmingly as it got further out to sea, but this time she had no fear of sailing. After what she had been through since coming to Ireland, a trip on a ferry was nothing. She was finally going home.

Chapter Twenty-One

The train drew into Trent Valley railway station late the following afternoon. From there it would be just a short bus trip into Bedworth, and then she would be home. As Charlotte stepped down from the train onto the platform she drew more than a few admiring glances. She had left as a naïve young girl and returned as a very attractive, smartly dressed young woman. Clutching her suitcase, she headed for the bus station in Bond Gate and soon she was on the last lap of her journey. Now as she thought of what lay ahead her stomach twisted into a knot but she kept her head high as she peered from the window of the bus.

Should she go home first or to her granny's? She decided that it would probably be better to face her parents first and get it over with. Half an hour later, the church and the vicarage came into sight. Her case was getting heavy by then and for the first time since she had left Ireland her steps faltered. But then she lifted her chin and, gripping the handle of her case tightly, she marched on. Her father wouldn't have started the evening service yet, so it was perfect timing.

As she moved down the familiar path she wondered why the vicarage was in darkness. Her mother would normally have a light on in the small lounge at the front of the building at this time, but perhaps she was in the kitchen at the back of the house. She and her father would have had their tea by then and her mother would no doubt be washing up. But as soon as she turned the corner she saw that the kitchen was in darkness too, and she frowned. The back door opened easily so she stepped into the room and snapped the light on – and gasped in shock. Her father had always been a stickler for everything being in its rightful place, but tonight the whole place looked as if a hurricane had swept through it. Dirty pots littered every surface and the floor looked as if it hadn't been mopped for months.

Placing her case down, Charlotte headed for the hallway. This too was unlit but she saw a light burning from beneath her father's study door. Taking a deep breath, she moved towards it – then before she could change her mind she rapped on it, opened it and walked in.

Reverend Hayes was sitting at his desk, and when he saw his daughter, he gaped in surprise.

'Charlotte! Wh-what are *you* doing here?' he said hoarsely.

Charlotte eyed him coldly. She had been gone for only a matter of months, but during that time he had aged considerably. The grey hair above his ears and at his temples had spread, and there was an air of dishevelment about him. 'I *live* here, in case you'd forgotten,' she spat, and then looking around she asked, 'Where's Mother?'

His eyes narrowed as he lifted the tumbler of whisky on his desk with a trembling hand and took a long swallow before answering, 'She's gone!'

'What do you mean, *gone*? Gone *where*?'

His lips stretched back across his teeth. 'She's left me – for another man, if you must know.' He glowered at her. 'And it's all *your* fault. She wouldn't believe that you'd run away from your Aunt Edith's and accused me of getting rid of you.'

'And she wasn't far wrong, was she?' He was no longer a figure to be feared, Charlotte thought – just a disgusting apology for a human being who didn't deserve the air he breathed. 'You would have left me to rot away in that convent for the rest of my life, but thankfully there are still good people in the world and someone rescued me.'

His face took on a sly look now and his voice became cajoling as he said, 'Of course I would have come for you. I just thought you would be better off with the nuns until after the birth of your bastard. I knew you were never overly keen on your Aunt Edith, and I thought you would be happier there. I did it for your sake, my dear.'

'You are a liar!' Charlotte hissed. 'And I'm glad my mother has left you. She should have done it years ago. You are a bully and you made her life hell on earth. And now I'm going to destroy you, because first thing tomorrow morning I shall go to the police and tell them *everything*.'

171

Stark terror raced across his features now. 'They'll never believe you. I am a well-respected man,' he blustered. 'Everyone is disgusted that your mother has left me to live in sin with that Brian Mason. She is nothing more than a whore!'

Charlotte's lip curled with contempt. 'They won't think that when they hear what I have to tell them. And they'll believe me all right,' she said with conviction. 'You see, I hid one of the disgusting pictures you took and you won't be able to argue your way out of *that*. The evidence will be there for them to see in black and white, and then they'll realise why Mother left you, and the tables will be turned. You'll be hounded out of town – if you're not sent to prison, that is. Personally I hope you are. You'll understand then what it was like for me to be locked away in that convent.'

'You wouldn't.' His voice held uncertainty.

Charlotte stared back at him for a moment before turning on her heel and heading for the door.

'Expect a visit from the police in the morning,' she shot over her shoulder, but once in the hall her shoulders sagged. She was terrified that he might follow her but thankfully there was no sound from the study. Keen to be gone now, she hurried upstairs to her room, and once she had put the light on she stared around it. Everything was just as she had left it and her heart ached to think of her mother, who must have prayed that she would come home. But there was not a moment to lose now if she was going to have her revenge.

Opening the wardrobe door, she rummaged about in a shoe box at the bottom and soon found what she was looking for amongst the little mementoes she had collected over the years. It was a photograph of her father and Andrew, and it left nothing to the imagination. Offering up a silent prayer of thanks, she tucked it into the pocket of her coat. All the way home she had worried that it might be gone. Had it been, it would have been her word against her father's, but the police could not argue with hard evidence.

Leaving the lights blazing, she ran from the room and raced downstairs into the kitchen, where she lifted her case and left the way she had come. It wasn't until she was outside of the vicarage gate that she slowed her steps and breathed deeply as her hands began to tremble. She glanced up and down the road. People were heading towards the church now for the evening service, so she quickly lowered her head and hastened on. She knew where Brian Mason lived and her heart beat faster at the thought of seeing her mother again. To get to his house she would have to pass her granny's, and it seemed silly to walk by without calling in to see her. Charlotte knew that the old lady would have been worried sick about her, and the thought of seeing her again lent speed to her feet.

One glance at her granny's cottage when she eventually reached it told her that something was different. The front garden, which had always been a colourful blaze of flowers, was neatly slabbed, and different curtains hung at the windows. The front door had been painted a different colour too, and it looked nothing like she remembered it. There was a light on in the front room and as Charlotte gazed in she saw a young woman with a baby in her arms pacing up and down the room. Perhaps Granny has gone to live with Mum and Brian, she thought as she hovered at the gate. She briefly considered knocking on the door, but then decided against it and set off again for Brian's house feeling slightly concerned.

Once she had turned into the road where she knew Brian lived, she hesitated. Was his the first house or the second? She couldn't be sure but there was only one way to find out. Marching boldly up the path, she knocked on the door of the first house and seconds later it was answered by a middle-aged lady in a pink nylon housecoat.

'Oh, I'm so sorry.' Charlotte flashed a becoming smile. 'I was looking for Brian Mason's house.'

The woman thumbed towards the house next door. 'That's all right, luvvie. It's that one next door you want.'

Charlotte thanked her and set off again, back down her path and up the one next door. Her hands were suddenly damp with perspiration as she wondered what sort of reception she would receive, but she didn't have to wait long to find out because almost the moment she'd knocked, the door was flung open and she was staring into her mother's astounded face.

'*Charlotte!*' A wealth of emotions scurried across the woman's features. Shock, disbelief, but most of all pleasure – and then suddenly the girl was in her mother's arms and they were both crying with delight at their reunion.

'I can't believe it,' Hilary sobbed. 'I'm afraid to blink in case you disappear and I've dreamed it.'

Charlotte sniffed and giggled. 'You haven't dreamed it, I'm really here,' she said shakily. 'But I'd quite like to come in, if you think Mr Mason wouldn't mind. I feel like I've been travelling forever.'

'Oh, of course! What am I thinking of?' Hilary almost dragged her across the doorstep as Brian appeared from the middle room.

'Brian, look!' Hilary cried, giving him an ecstatic smile.

He was smiling too as he held his hand out welcomingly. 'Well I'll be damned,' he chuckled. 'Your mum has dreamed of this moment every single day since you went missing. Come on in, pet. You are *so* welcome!'

Hilary snatched her case and dumped it onto the floor as she ushered Charlotte through a tidy front room into a middle room. A kitchen led off from that and Brian told them, 'I'm going to make a pot of tea and get you something to eat, lass. I bet you haven't eaten for a while, have you?'

When she shook her head he smiled good-naturedly. 'Right, I'll get on with it then. I'm sure you two have a lot of catching up to do.'

As the kitchen door closed quietly behind him, Hilary told her, 'Take your coat off, love, and come and sit down. I want to know everything that's happened to you. And of course I have a lot to tell you too about what's been going on here.'

Charlotte obediently draped her coat across the back of a chair before joining her mother on the sofa, where they held hands and stared at each other.

'So where do we begin?' Hilary asked, eyeing her daughter approvingly. 'You look beautiful and so grown up. I've been absolutely worried sick about you.' Her face became sad now as she relived the last few months in her mind. 'Your father had scarcely got back from Ireland when we had a call from your aunt saying that you'd run away, but I wasn't swallowing that for a moment.' She gave a shiver as the bad memories flooded back. 'That was when the trouble really started. I told your father I didn't believe a single word of it, and the very next day I went to Ireland myself. He did everything he could to stop me, but this time I wasn't listening. Of course when I got there, there was no sign of you, but I never ever believed the story that he and Edith cooked up. It just wasn't like you to do something like that, and when I got home your father and I had a blazing row.'

Hilary stood up and walked over to the window. She took a moment to compose herself, then came back and sat down. 'Your father wasn't used to me making a stand and it didn't go down very well at all, as you can imagine.' She sighed. 'He raised his fist to me but he soon backed down when I took a knife to him and threatened to use it if he touched me. A person can only take so much, but looking back I realise that was the beginning of the end. Soon afterwards I packed my bags and moved here to live with Brian – something I should have done years ago. But now tell me what *really* happened to you please. I need to know it all – and about the baby.'

And so Charlotte related what had happened, and as the story unfolded Hilary's face crumpled. Especially when she heard of the beautiful baby girl that Charlotte had given birth to.

'I called her Daisy,' Charlotte sobbed and it broke Hilary's heart. There was a measure of guilt there too, for hadn't she taken Charlotte to have the child aborted? Even so, she had had no idea that Bernard could be so very cruel, and her heart further hardened towards him as she thought of how her daughter must have suffered.

'Thank God for the wonderful lady who rescued you,' she whispered. 'And to think that there was nothing I could do! I shall never forgive myself for letting him talk me into allowing you to go to Edith's in the first place.'

'It wasn't your fault,' Charlotte said, gently squeezing her mother's hand. 'But I'm afraid that isn't all I have to tell you, Mum. You see – before I went away I discovered something about Father. I wanted to tell you about it but you were so rundown I was scared about how it might affect you.'

Hilary raised her eyebrows looking bewildered as Charlotte fumbled in her coat pocket and handed her the photo she had kept hidden all this time. And as Hilary stared down at it the colour drained from her face and she gasped, 'Dear God, no! It can't be true.' Her head wagged from side-to-side in horrified disbelief. And yet there was no disputing the evidence in her hand. She had always felt uneasy about her husband's obsession with the choirboys but never in her wildest dreams had she thought that he would be capable of something like this.

'I'm going to the police first thing in the morning,' Charlotte told her. 'I think he has gotten away with this for far too long, don't you?'

Hilary nodded mutely, too shocked to say another word. Brian bustled back in then carrying a tray laden with a pot of tea and a pile of ham sandwiches. Seeing the look on the women's faces, he placed it down and turned to leave again, but Hilary stopped him. 'Don't go, love' she said. 'I – I have something to show you.'

As she handed him the photograph, a look of pure disgust flitted across Brian's face. 'That man is nothing more than an animal. No – that's an insult. Animals would *never* behave like this,' he roared as colour burst into his cheeks, then calming himself he asked, 'What are you going to do about it, Charlotte?'

'I'm taking it to the police first thing in the morning,' she answered.

He nodded his approval. 'Good. Ever since your mother left him she's been seen as the scarlet woman by his loyal little congregation. It's about time they know what he *really* is and see what your mother had to live with. I just wish to God she'd never met him. But still, she's away from him now. You both are and that's the main thing. And Charlotte, there's a home here with me and your mum for as long as you want it.'

In that moment as he looked across at her mother, Charlotte could see how very much he loved her and her heart warmed at the sight.

'Thank you, but I thought I could perhaps go and stay at Granny's, although when I passed her cottage earlier on I noticed that there was a young woman in there. Is Granny living here with you and Brian now, Mum?'

A strange look passed between the couple and then Hilary steeled herself to say, 'No, love, she isn't. I'm afraid your granny passed away shortly after you went to Ireland.'

'*No!*' Charlotte shook her head in disbelief. 'She couldn't have – I never got to say goodbye.' Tears were spurting from her eyes now as Hilary hugged her comfortingly.

'I'm afraid it's true,' she whispered brokenly. 'Your granny hadn't been in very good health for some time, as you know, and one day her heart just gave out. It was very quick and peaceful, I promise you. In actual fact you are quite a wealthy young woman now. Your granny left all she had to you, and it's being kept at the solicitors in the town centre.'

'But she should have left everything to *you*! I told her that when she mentioned what she was planning to do,' Charlotte objected.

'No.' Hilary shook her head. 'It was me that asked her not to leave me anything. Your father would have taken every penny, and I hadn't left him when she passed away. It was after she died that I realised I didn't *have* to stay with him any more. You and Granny were gone, and suddenly it hit me how pointless my life was. I didn't have to play the part of an obedient wife any longer, and I'd got to the point where I didn't much care what people said about me.'

'Your mother doesn't need the money anyway,' Brian said as he patted Hilary's shoulder. 'Once she's divorced your father we're going to get married and move right away from here and start again – with you too, of course,' he added quickly. 'And I shall see to it that neither of you ever want for anything ever again. I've saved quite a bit over the years and I'm more than comfortable, so you just take the money and enjoy it.'

Charlotte felt as if the bottom had dropped out of her world. Her granny had always been such an important part of her life and now she would never see her again. She hadn't even been there with her at the end – and that was the hardest thing to bear. It was all too much to take in after what she had already gone through during the past months.

Now Brian pushed the plate of sandwiches towards her and smiled at her sympathetically, and she thought what a truly kind man he was. Somehow she knew that her mother was going to be happy with him from now on.

'There's a lot for you to take in,' he said softly. 'But try and eat something, love. Your granny wouldn't want to see you like this and you've got to keep your strength up.'

Charlotte dutifully lifted a sandwich and took a bite, not wishing to hurt his feelings but the food tasted like sawdust and stuck in her throat as she broke into a fresh torrent of weeping.

'It's all right,' he soothed as he dabbed at her cheeks with a large white handkerchief. 'In your own time. Me and your mum will make sure that no one ever hurts you again. You're safe now, I promise.'

His kind words only made her sob all the harder as she thought of her beloved granny and the baby she would never see again. And yet despite her grief, she felt that she had finally come home.

Chapter Twenty-Two

Shortly after the hasty snack Brian had made for her, Hilary showed Charlotte upstairs. Hilary was still reeling from what Charlotte had told her about her husband, and Charlotte was worn out after the long journey. The news of her granny's death had affected her badly and all she wanted to do now was try to lose herself in sleep.

When they got upstairs, the girl was amazed to see that they had a room all prepared for her.

'But this is lovely!' she exclaimed as she looked around at the comfortable, pretty bedroom.

'We got it ready for you shortly after I moved in with Brian,' Hilary told her, smoothing an imaginary crease in the pink satin bedspread. 'I knew that your father would break his neck to tell you where I was if you ever came home.' Looking deep into her daughter's eyes, she said, 'You don't think too badly of me, do you, pet? Brian really *is* a lovely man. I'm sure you'll like him as you get to know him better.'

'I don't think badly of you at all, Mum,' Charlotte retorted. 'In fact, I don't know how you put up with Father for as long as you did. And I like Brian already. He seems a genuinely kind man and he obviously loves you.'

Hilary's face brightened, making her look like a young girl again. 'He *does* love me,' she agreed. 'And he isn't afraid to show it. The last few months with him would have been just perfect, if it hadn't been for losing your granny and worrying about you. But you're home safe and sound now, and it's time for us to get on with our lives. I know that what you have to do in the morning isn't going to be easy, but for what my opinion is worth I think you are doing the right thing. It's time your father was exposed for what he really is.' She sighed heavily. 'And to think how he treated us all those years

– making out that he was perfect while all the time . . .' Her voice trailed away and Charlotte gave her a quick hug. And then Hilary was bustling about the room again, switching on lights and drawing the curtains against the dark night.

'Come on, miss,' she said bossily. 'You look all in. Get some sleep and we'll face tomorrow when it comes. The bathroom is the third door on the right along the landing. I'll give you time to have a nice soak then I'll bring you up a big cup of hot chocolate.'

'That sounds lovely,' Charlotte smiled, but once her mother had left the room she flopped onto the edge of the bed like a rag doll. She was home, but everything was different now – and after tomorrow . . . She scowled as she thought of what lay ahead but then pushed the thought away. Her mother was right. She would worry about that in the morning.

Please let me come with you, love,' her mother begged at the kitchen table the next morning. Brian had cooked them a wonderful breakfast before going off to work but Charlotte had been unable to do more than push the food about the plate. Her stomach was in knots but she was determined to go through with her visit to the police station.

'Thanks, Mum, but I'd rather do this alone,' she responded firmly, then seeing the worry etched on her mother's face she quickly added, 'I'll be home before you know it, and then it will be up to the police to take appropriate action. Once I've shown them that photo, it will all be over for Father bar the shouting.'

Hilary's lips set in a grim line. 'And serves him right too,' she choked. 'I've laid awake all night thinking about it and I still can't take it in.'

Charlotte rose from the table and went to fetch her coat, then after slipping it on and checking that she had the photo in her bag, she pecked her mother on the cheek.

'I shan't be too long,' she promised.

Unable to answer for the large lump that had formed in her throat, Hilary merely nodded. She had always thought of Charlotte as her little girl, but this was a young woman standing in front of her. A young woman with a score to settle.

'Good luck, love,' she said as she waved her off at the door and then Charlotte was striding away looking far more confident than she was feeling. Even so, her determination never wavered for a moment. What she was about to do was long overdue, and the sooner it was done the better.

She walked briskly with her head held high. It was a beautiful morning with white powder-puff clouds floating in the sky. Not at all the sort of day on which she would have expected to expose her father. Perhaps it should have been raining? she thought, as she moved along but then cleared her mind of everything apart from what had to be done.

Soon she was passing the alms houses, and shortly after that, the police station came into view. Charlotte's steps momentarily faltered but then, after taking a deep breath, she hurried on. In no time at all she was talking to the police officer on the desk, and after telling him that she had something of great importance to discuss, she was shown into a tiny cell-like room that contained nothing more than a table and three hard-backed chairs.

Several minutes passed, and then a sergeant joined her. 'Hello, Miss er . . . I am Sergeant Harwood. I believe you have something you wish to talk to me about?' he said politely.

'My name is Charlotte Hayes,' she informed him in a calm, clear voice. 'I am the daughter of the Reverend Hayes at Saint Sebastian's Church and I have something to show you.'

She withdrew the photograph from her handbag and placed it in front of him – and from that second on, everything seemed to happen in a blur.

An hour later, two police officers followed her into the vicarage, but it was soon apparent that Bernard Hayes wasn't there.

'He's probably over in the church,' she told them, and side by side they hurried out again.

As always, the door to the church was unlocked and Charlotte entered it first with the two policemen close on her heels. Once inside, they all blinked and slowed their steps. After the sunshine, the interior of the church was gloomy and it took their eyes a few seconds to adjust to it.

'He'll probably be in the vestry,' she told them as she started down the aisle, but then she stopped dead in her tracks and her hand flew to her mouth. Dangling from the thick wooden beam above the altar was a pair of legs.

'Stay here, Miss Hayes,' the older of the officers told her grimly as he pressed her down onto the hard wooden pew. 'We'll deal with this.'

Charlotte forced herself to breathe as the two policemen sprinted down the aisle. One of them was already on his radio asking for an ambulance, but she knew that it was too late. Even before they cut the figure down she knew that it was her father and that he was dead. Rather than face up to what he had done, Bernard Hayes had chosen to take the coward's way out. She watched the body drop lifelessly to the floor and just for a moment she had a glimpse of his face. His eyes were bulging and his tongue was swollen and lolling out of the side of his mouth. Pandemonium then broke out as two ambulancemen ran down the aisle and began to try to resuscitate him. Charlotte felt strangely detached from it all. She supposed that she should be crying – he was her father, after all – but she just felt numb.

Eventually she saw one of the ambulancemen shake his head at the sergeant, and then the man was striding back towards her.

'I'm so sorry, Miss Hayes,' he said hesitantly, 'but I'm afraid he's gone. It seems that your father's been dead for some hours.'

The sergeant had been in the force for many years and had dealt with some very strange cases in his time, but none as strange as this – and he could only begin to imagine how the young woman in front of him must be feeling.

'We'll have his body taken to the morgue at the George Eliot Hospital,' he informed her. 'And then perhaps you and your mother can decide which undertaker you would like to choose. I very much doubt there will be any need for a post mortem. It's very clear that your father took his own life. I'm so sorry, Miss Hayes.'

Personally he thought that things had turned out for the best. The press would have had a field day if the vicar had ever been arrested, but he still felt sorry for Charlotte. Poor girl, she was so pale she looked as if she had been drained of every drop of blood, which

182

was why he was so taken aback when she answered calmly, '*I'm* not sorry.'

She stared up at him with eyes old beyond their years. 'My father was a beast,' she said quietly. 'He did unspeakable things to young boys. One of them actually killed himself, and many more will probably never get over what he did to them. He deserved to die.' She then stood up and walked out of the church for the very last time. She knew that she would never go there again.

A police car drove her back to where her mother was staying, and the solemn-faced sergeant insisted on accompanying her inside where Hilary was nervously chewing on her nails and waiting for her.

She leaped up as Charlotte entered the house, and after she'd taken her daughter and the policeman with her into the lounge, she said hoarsely, 'What's happened?'

The sergeant coughed to clear his throat. Like everyone else in the town he had heard the gossip of how the vicar's wife had run off with a local man. She had been branded a whore, yet the woman staring at him now looked pleasant and perfectly respectable. But then there were always two sides to every story, as he had discovered long ago in this job, so now he told her, 'I'm afraid your husband is dead, Mrs Hayes. He hanged himself in the church.'

Hilary clutched at the edge of a table for support. 'I . . . I see,' she said falteringly. Just as Charlotte had a short time before, she supposed that she should be crying. Bernard had been her husband, but then it had been such a long time since she had loved him that she knew she would be a hypocrite to shed tears for him now. The only tears she had left were reserved solely for her daughter, who had suffered cruelly at his hands, and the innocent young boys he had corrupted, and she was horrified to realise that all she felt was relief. Bernard had thrived on the adoration of his congregation. He could never have stood their condemnation when his crimes came to light – so perhaps it was better for him this way.

'Is there anyone I can call for you?' the sergeant asked considerately.

Hilary nodded. 'Yes, please. Can you get in touch with Brian Mason – he works in the welding shop at Sterling Metals in Nuneaton. Oh, and perhaps you could ring Bernard's sister, Edith Hayes, for me? She lives in Ireland and I suppose we should let her know. There's a telephone in the hall, and a book with those numbers in it.' She pointed towards the hall with a trembling finger and Sergeant Harwood instantly left the room.

Ten minutes later he came back in and reported, 'Miss Hayes said to tell you she will be coming immediately. She will stay at the vicarage and she said to also tell you that she will arrange the funeral. Is that all right with you, Mrs Hayes? As his wife you are quite within your rights to arrange it yourself if you so wish.'

'No, let Edith do it,' Hilary sighed. Then: 'But what will happen now?'

'Well, there will have to be an inquest, of course, but going on the information we have, I should think it will all be very cut and dried. Now, would you like one of my officers to stay with you until Mr Mason arrives?'

Hilary placed a protective arm about Charlotte. 'No, we'll be fine,' she assured him. 'And . . . thank you.'

He shrugged. 'I'm afraid we haven't done much,' he answered, then he quietly left the room. They heard the front door close, and mother and daughter were finally alone.

Charlotte was staring off into space as she saw again in her mind her father's bulging eyes. It was an image that she would never be able to erase.

'Are you all right, love?' Hilary asked gently. It seemed such an inept question at such a time, but she couldn't think of anything else to say.

'What? Oh yes, I'm fine. But do you realise what this means, Mum?'

When Hilary stared at her uncomprehendingly, Charlotte went on, 'You're free now. You and Brian can get married if you want to and move away to make that brand new start you talked about.'

Hilary nodded slowly, 'Yes, I suppose you're right. We can all start again now, can't we? We'll all go together.'

Charlotte shook her head. 'No, you don't need me tagging along. I'm a big girl now and I've already decided what I'm going to do.'

Hilary looked horrified as she twisted her hands together. 'But you're all I've got left now. Of course we'll go together. I can't lose you again now.'

'You won't lose me and we'll always keep in touch,' Charlotte promised. 'But Granny wanted me to have a career. She suggested I'd be good at nursing, and more than ever now that's what I want to do. With the money that she left me I can afford to help support myself while I do my training. I think that's what she would have wanted. But first we need to get Father's funeral out of the way.'

Hilary snorted. 'Huh! If Edith is coming I doubt we'll have much of a say in that,' she said bitterly.

'And will that really be such a bad thing?' Charlotte asked, and again Hilary was shocked at how sensible and grown-up her daughter suddenly appeared to be. 'I've no doubt that you will be blamed for what happened – until the inquest. People will say that he killed himself because you left him. But once it all comes out they'll know the truth then. And I'm glad. Why should he be made into some sort of saint when he was really a devil?'

Hilary gnawed on her nail. Certain people had made her life hell since she had left Bernard. Now, as Charlotte quite rightly pointed out, they might change their opinion. She still didn't want to stay in Bedworth though. It held too many unhappy memories for her now.

Edith arrived the following day. The sergeant had given her Hilary's number and when she rang her, her voice was pure poison.

'I am at the vicarage,' she informed her. 'And I just wanted to tell you that I have all the arrangements for the funeral in hand. Bernard rang me on the evening before he . . . died, and he informed me that Charlotte is home. Is she with you?'

Hilary's feelings hardened as she thought of the part Edith had played in having her daughter locked away in the convent. She would never forgive her for that. 'Yes, she is,' she said fiercely. 'No thanks to you though, is it, Edith? Had it been left to you and Bernard, my daughter would still have been incarcerated in that hell-hole you tricked her into.'

'How *dare* you!' Edith cried indignantly. 'We did what we thought was in the slut's best interests. We couldn't have her bringing shame on the family.'

'If you think an illegitimate child – the result of rape – is shameful, I shudder to think how you'll feel when you've been to the inquest and heard what they have to say about your precious brother!' Hilary shot back, and she then slammed the phone down.

Charlotte had never known her mother to so much as answer Aunt Edith back before, and she felt proud of her. But even so the inquest was set for the following week, and they were both dreading it.

The inquest turned out to be every bit as awful as Charlotte had feared. As the information about Bernard's paedophilia became common knowledge, Edith was distraught and angry. The police had questioned a number of choirboys following Bernard's death, and now that he was no longer there to threaten them most of them confessed that he had done unspeakable things to them too. Edith forced herself to sit through it until a verdict of suicide was declared and then she stormed outside with her hands bunched into fists to wait for Charlotte and Hilary.

'This is all *your* fault! It's nothing but vicious *lies!*' she screeched at Charlotte. 'And those boys – why, they are lying too! You have forced them to say those evil, wicked things about my poor brother.'

Brian, who had been a tower of strength to both Hilary and Charlotte during these dark days, stepped in straight away.

'I understand this must be difficult for you,' he said reasonably, trying to placate her, 'but you saw the evidence of what he had done with your own eyes, Miss Hayes. When Charlotte arrived home and told her father that she was going to expose him, rather than face the consequences, he took his own life.'

Edith looked him up and down as if he was something vile stuck on the sole of her shoe before then turning her wrath full on Hilary. 'As for you – you *whore!*' she cried. 'How could you have the nerve to bring your lover along to your husband's inquest? My poor Bernard! No wonder the balance of his mind was disturbed after the way you treated him. He was a loyal, faithful husband to you and you left him without a second thought.'

'It wasn't quite like that,' Hilary defended herself, but Edith cut her words short.

'My brother will be buried tomorrow,' she snarled, 'and neither you nor that pathetic apology of a daughter of his are welcome'.

Her voice rose into a scream. 'I want you both to stay well away, do you hear me?' And with that she turned and marched away.

'Phew!' Brian placed his arms about Hilary's shaking shoulders. 'You always told me what a tartar she was but I'd never have believed she could be *that* bad. But how do you both feel about not going to the funeral?'

'It's for the best,' Hilary said quietly. 'I'd have looked an awful hypocrite if I'd turned up, wouldn't I? And it's going to be a witch-hunt, with all the papers there. I wonder how Edith will cope?'

'Let's think of it this way – that it's no longer our affair,' Brian suggested. 'And now, ladies, let's go home. It's over now and we can all get on with our lives.'

Turning, they linked arms and walked away with a feeling of relief. The worst was finally over.

Chapter Twenty-Three

Charlotte loaded another wrapped dish into a tea-chest, ready for the shifters, and joked to her mother, 'We won't be able to move in here soon.'

Hilary chuckled as she glanced around. Half the house was packed now and everywhere looked very bare apart from the Christmas tree that stood in one corner of the living room. Shortly after the New Year she and Brian would be moving to Leamington Spa. It was not a great distance away but far enough to ensure that the gossip wouldn't follow them. It was now a few days before Christmas, and recent weeks had not been easy for any of them. The local and national newspapers had had a field day with Bernard's story, and Hilary was suffering from nerves again; she hardly dared to set foot out of the door. Deep down she blamed herself for not realising that Bernard was abusing the choirboys, and every time she thought of young Andrew she was consumed with guilt. If only she had known she might have prevented his death. Admittedly, she was no longer regarded as a scarlet woman. In fact, people were now very sympathetic towards her and some had even approached her to say she should have left Bernard years ago. Others blamed her for living with such a man, even claiming that she must have known what he was up to. None of it made things any easier.

They had all agreed that they would wait until after Christmas before they started their new lives, and would celebrate Christmas and the New Year together as a family. In the meantime, Charlotte and her mother had enjoyed spending time together. It was funny now that Charlotte came to think about it, but already she regarded Brian as family and he would be even more so soon, because during the week between Christmas and the New Year, he and her mother were going to be married at Nuneaton Register Office. Hilary had fretted that it might look disrespectful, marrying again so soon after Bernard's death, but as Brian had sensibly pointed out, the marriage had been over for many years before she left him – so why wait? The way he saw it, Hilary deserved a little happiness now and he was determined that he would be the man to see she got it.

Both Brian and Hilary were sad that Charlotte had decided she didn't want to go to live with them, but they accepted that it was what she wanted, and were secretly very proud of her. The girl was ready to fly the nest now, and after all she had been through, they knew that she was capable of looking after herself. The money that her granny had left her was now safely deposited in her own bank account, and she was determined to start her nursing career.

It was obvious that Charlotte still mourned her baby, and that hurt Hilary more than she could say. Sometimes she would see a haunted look in her daughter's eyes as she stared off into space, and the woman would know that she was thinking of her child. Hilary would never forgive herself for trying to help Charlotte to terminate the pregnancy, but then everyone made mistakes – and this was one that she was going to have to learn to live with.

Charlotte had been to see her old friend Babs, who was now the mother of two small children, and they had greeted each other as if they had never been apart. It was Babs who had told her that Harry was now in prison for raping a fourteen-year-old girl. Charlotte wasn't really surprised after what he had done to her, and even felt a measure of satisfaction that he had finally got his come-uppance. At least while he was locked away he couldn't hurt any more poor girls. As far as she was concerned, it was just a pity they couldn't throw the key away and leave him to rot in jail. She was still convinced that he had played a part in her father's secret 'hobby', but of course she would never know now.

Standing with her hands on her hips, she looked around and declared, 'I think that's enough packing for today, don't you? How about we catch the bus into Coventry and do some Christmas shopping? I think we deserve a break. We could go and have a bit of lunch too while we're at it – my treat, or rather Gran's. We deserve a break.'

'I think that's an excellent idea,' Hilary said, wiping her hands down the sides of her skirt. 'Just give me ten minutes to tidy myself up and we'll get off.'

Hilary was still reluctant to venture into Bedworth town centre, but Charlotte could understand why. There were still people who were buzzing with all the latest gossip and developments, and both Hilary and Charlotte cringed whenever someone approached them to offer their so-called condolences. This was a part of their lives that they wanted to put behind them now, but they knew it would never happen as long as they stayed in Bedworth.

Charlotte was looking forward to the future with mixed feelings. Part of her couldn't wait, the other part was nervous about being all alone in the world. But then after what she had endured over the last few months, she was sure she would cope.

Two weeks ago, she had attended an interview with the Matron at King William's Hospital in London, and this had been followed by a short Maths and English test. Just yesterday, she had received a letter from the hospital informing her that she had passed, and been accepted as a cadet nurse. She would start her training in the New Year.

Mother and daughter spent a happy day together in Coventry shopping and admiring the pretty Christmas displays in the store windows, and when they got home they were in a happy frame of mind. It still felt strange to both of them to be able to come and go as they pleased. Reverend Hayes had always dictated where they went and when, and the newfound freedom was taking some getting used to. Brian was quite the opposite of Bernard, always pushing money at them and encouraging them to go out and treat themselves, and the more Charlotte got to know him the more she realised that he and Hilary were made for each other. Now she could go off on her chosen career with a clear conscience, knowing that her mother would be loved and cared for.

The pair arrived back laden down with shopping bags, tired but pleased to find Brian was home from work.

'Oh love, I'm so sorry.' Hilary looked flustered as she quickly took her coat off. 'We decided to go and do a bit of Christmas shopping and the time just seemed to run away with us. I meant to be home before you. I haven't even started the dinner yet.'

Brian chuckled as he filled the kettle at the sink and placed it on top of the stove to boil. 'Well, you're hardly on the clock, are you? And it's nice to see you both looking so happy. I can help you prepare the dinner now – but let's have a nice cup of tea first, eh? Did you buy anything nice?'

Again, Charlotte thought how kind he was and a warm little glow spread through her as she took her shoes off. She guessed they must have clocked up miles traipsing round the shops and her feet were aching. She watched her mother unloading their purchases and showing them to Brian, who inspected them dutifully with an indulgent smile on his face, and suddenly feeling in the way, she told them, 'I reckon I'll just go and have a quick bath before dinner, if you don't mind. That is unless you need me to help?'

'Of course we don't,' her future stepfather told her. 'You go and have a nice long soak. But drink this hot tea first. It will keep you going until dinnertime.'

Charlotte knew that she would never forget the Christmas she spent with her mother and Brian that year. It was perfect and so different to the ones in the past. Admittedly her father had always insisted on a turkey and all the trimmings, but this year as well as Christmas fare there was also laughter and an easy atmosphere. Even though they would shortly be leaving the house, Brian had insisted on decorating it and had strung paper garlands from the ceilings – something Reverend Hayes would never have agreed to. Bowls of holly with bright red berries were placed here and there, and with the lights on the Christmas tree twinkling in the corner, everywhere looked warm and inviting. They opened their presents together and Charlotte was touched to find that her mother had bought her many of the things from the list she'd been sent that she would need to start her nurses training: flat black lace-up shoes in a lovely soft leather, a special upside-down fob watch, a pair of round-ended scissors, a navy-blue cardigan, a pen and a small torch.

Charlotte had bought her mother a rather daring negligée set in a deep pink satin trimmed with lace. 'For your honeymoon,' she told her and Hilary blushed to the very roots of her hair. She had bought Brian a smart manicure set in its own leather wallet and he laughed when he opened it as he held out his hands, which were burned and scarred from the work he did in the welding shop. All the same he seemed very pleased with it and he kissed her soundly, declaring that he would treasure it.

Charlotte could not help but think of Marianne, and on Christmas Eve she had risked giving her a short phone call. Thankfully it was Marianne who answered; the woman was delighted to hear from her and she sounded very happy. Her family were all back together again, and like Charlotte she was trying to move on with her life. But Charlotte knew that also like herself, beneath her smiles was a heartache that would never go away.

This was Daisy's first Christmas, and as Charlotte pulled crackers and read out the silly jokes inside them on Christmas Day, she secretly wondered what her baby was doing. Would her new mummy and daddy have bought her lots of presents? Was she a happy baby? Were they looking after her properly? They were all questions that would never be answered, and she couldn't help but wish that things could have been different. Even so, she tried her best to leave the past behind and enjoy the present.

Hilary and Brian had prepared and cooked the Christmas dinner together; that in itself Charlotte found amazing. She could never remember her father so much as filling the kettle. Once the meal was over, Brian ushered the women away from the table and made them sit watching a film on BBC while he did all the washing up.

It was as they were sitting there, comfortably full and drowsy with the heat from the fire that Hilary squeezed her hand affectionately.

'Are you *quite* sure that I can't persuade you to come to Leamington with us, pet?' she murmured. 'You know that we would love to have you.'

Charlotte smiled. 'I know you would, Mum, and thanks, but I've done a lot of growing up this year and it's time for me to branch out on my own now,' she answered. 'I think Granny would have liked to think I was putting her money to good use and I can hardly wait to start my training now.'

Hilary sighed. Charlotte had changed so much over the months she had been away that sometimes she hardly recognised her now, she seemed so mature and independent. Not that this was a bad thing, but Hilary knew that she would miss her daughter dreadfully when she went off to London. It seemed so very far away, although as Charlotte had quite rightly pointed out, it was only a train ride.

Mid-afternoon, Brian produced a tin of Roses chocolates and a tray of fresh brewed tea, and both Charlotte and her mother groaned and giggled.

'I've heard of being fattened up for Christmas but this is ridiculous,' Hilary joked. 'I shall never get into my wedding outfit at this rate.'

'So what? I like a woman with a bit of meat on her bones,' Brian teased as he poured the tea.

Once more Charlotte glimpsed the love in his eyes and she was pleased for her mother, but not at all envious. After what Harry had done to her she knew that she would never trust another man for as long as she lived. Men like Brian were few and far between, and she determined to stay a spinster, answerable to no one. And then her thoughts returned to her baby again but she pushed them to the back of her mind, determined not to spoil Christmas Day.

The day before New Year's Eve, Brian drove them all to the Register Office in Nuneaton. Hilary looked lovely in a cream two-piece suit and a little hat with a tiny veil. Charlotte had tried to persuade her to have something more adventurous, but her mother had stood firm.

'I'm hardly a blushing virgin bride,' she said. 'To be quite honest I'd be happy to marry Brian in a paper bag. And I don't want any fuss and palaver either. I just want us to be married and then to come home.'

But on that point at least, Brian put his foot down and insisted on booking them all in for a slap-up meal at a posh restaurant in the town centre.

And so they were married, and although it was a very quiet ceremony with no one but Charlotte and two people they had called in from the street to act as witnesses, it was still a beautiful service, and the love that Hilary and Brian felt for each other was apparent on both their faces as they took their vows.

'It gives me great pleasure to declare that you are now husband and wife. You may kiss the bride,' the registrar said eventually and Brian was delighted to do just that as Charlotte looked on with a beaming smile on her face.

As they all came out of the Register Office door, Charlotte showered the newlyweds with confetti and Hilary giggled like a schoolgirl. She could never remember being so joyful in her whole life, and it showed.

'So then, Mrs Mason, how about we go and have some posh nosh for our wedding feast now, eh?' Brian teased, and linking arms with both Charlotte and Hilary he led them away feeling like the luckiest man in the world.

They had a sumptuous meal and returned to Brian's house in a radiant frame of mind. Brian had loved Hilary for so long that he could scarcely believe that she was finally his wife. Charlotte then retreated to her room, wishing to give the newlyweds some time on their own. She was in a pensive mood. In just five more days she would be leaving to start her new life in London, and although it was what she wanted, it was also a little daunting.

Hilary had begged her to let her go with her, but Charlotte had insisted that she was quite capable of managing on her own. After all, how hard could it be? Sighing, she began to pack a few things into the smart suitcase Marianne had bought her. Very soon now her life would change yet again.

Chapter Twenty-Four

The engine throbbed into life and a plume of steam and smoke floated along the platform as the guard hurried the length of the train, slamming doors. Then he blew his whistle and Charlotte waved frantically to her mother and Brain as the train slowly chugged forward.

'Goodbye, goodbye, I love you!' Hilary shouted as she ran alongside, holding on to her hat. And then the train picked up speed and she slowly became a speck in the distance, still waving.

When her mother and Brian had finally disappeared from sight, Charlotte sank back onto her seat and sighed. It was really happening now; she was on her way to begin her training. It was a cold and frosty morning in January 1958 and in just three days' time she would begin her first day as a cadet nurse at King William's Hospital, London. She patted her handbag, afraid to let it go. Inside was a sizeable sum of money that would pay for her lodgings in a B&B near the nurses' homes, which were all full. Hilary and Brian had drummed into her how rife pickpockets were in London, and now she was almost paranoid. She had already transferred another large sum of money from her bank account to one in London, in case her meagre weekly wages were insufficient.

As she stared from the window her thoughts returned to her baby and once again the pain cut deep, as did her resentment of men. She knew that she would never be able to form a relationship after what Harry had done to her, and its terrible consequences, and she hoped that her training would help to fill the hole inside her that Daisy had left.

'Going on holiday, are you, dear?'

Charlotte dragged her thoughts back to the present to see an elderly lady sitting opposite addressing her.

'No, actually I'm going to King William's Hospital to begin my nurses' training,' Charlotte replied.

'How exciting!' The woman patted the smart hat perched on the top of her thick grey hair, which was pulled into a tight bun. 'Will you be staying in one of the nurses' homes?'

'Unfortunately, they were all full, since I applied rather late for this intake. However, I'm going to apply to live in a boarding house near the hospital when I get to London, and then I'll look around for a little flat to rent.'

'Hmm, I just may be able to help you there,' the woman said, peering at Charlotte through thick-lensed glasses that were perched precariously on the end of her nose. 'It just so happens that I'm going to stay with my sister for a few days in her bed and breakfast establishment very close to your hospital. I believe she does accommodate some student nurses but you'll have to get permission from your Matron to stay there. It's very comfortable,' she hastened to add. 'and her rates are *very* reasonable.'

'Whereabouts is it?' Charlotte asked, intrigued.

'It's in Greville Street, off the famous street called Hatton Garden. Hop on a bus down Holborn and you could be at the hospital in ten minutes.'

'Really?' Although the street names meant nothing to her, for Charlotte this was like the answer to a prayer. 'Do you think she might have a room available?'

The elderly woman nodded. 'It's possible. Now, our Vera is very fussy who she takes in. But you look like a nice respectable young woman, and I'm sure she wouldn't object to having you there. She will telephone the hospital for you, to get permission. Oh, and by the way, I'm Mrs Preston.' The woman held her hand out and Charlotte shook it.

'Thank you very much, Mrs Preston,' she said politely. 'I'd love to come along with you and see if she has room for me.' And so it was agreed.

By the time the train chugged into Euston, Charlotte felt as if she had known Mrs Preston forever. The journey had passed pleasantly as they discussed everything from food to politics, and Charlotte could hardly believe her luck. It seemed that somewhere safe to stay had fallen into her lap.

The platform was heaving with bodies as the two women headed for the entrance, and there, just as Brian had warned, she was confronted with her first tramp.

'Can yer spare a few pennies fer a poor ex-serviceman?' He held his hand out imploringly but Mrs Preston stuck her chin in the air and glided past him.

'Ignore him, dear,' she told Charlotte imperiously. 'If you gave to every one of these so-called war veterans, you wouldn't have a penny to your name before you'd walked a mile in this city.'

Casting a guilty glance towards the vagrant, Charlotte clutched her case and pottered after Mrs Preston, who seemed to be walking a mile a minute.

Once outside, they walked down to King's Cross and caught a bus up Gray's Inn Road. Once they got off, Charlotte followed Mrs Preston through a maze of streets, having no idea whatsoever where she was. Not that it mattered. Mrs Preston obviously knew where she was going and strode purposefully along.

'It's not far now,' she told her. 'My sister lives just down here.'

They were passing huge buildings that seemed to reach into the sky. They were large three- and four-storey townhouses, and Charlotte looked about her with interest. Many of the houses had been turned into flats and bedsits, but as Mrs Preston stopped in front of one she told her, 'This is Vera's place. Her husband, Dr Isaac Manners, used to be a dentist, and have his practice downstairs, but sadly he passed away a few years ago. That's why she takes in the occasional guest to help pay the bills. Living in London can be very expensive, you see? She is on the list of approved landladies for King William's, so I'm sure she'll be happy for you to stay if you arrive with me.'

Mrs Preston mounted three steps and rang the doorbell. The door flew open and a woman who was the image of Mrs Preston but slightly younger appeared.

'Why Esme, you're here!' She looked genuinely happy as she grabbed her sister to her in a bear hug. Then, glancing over her shoulder at Charlotte, who was feeling rather self-conscious, she asked, 'And who is this?'

'I'm Charlotte Hayes,' she replied shyly.

'I met this young lady on the train purely by chance,' Mrs Preston explained, smiling kindly at Charlotte. 'And it turns out that she'll be starting at King William's as a cadet nurse in a few days' time. She told me that she would need somewhere to stay, since the nurses' homes are full, and of course I immediately thought of you, dear.'

'In that case you'd better come in,' Vera told them pleasantly as she held the door wide. 'I dare say you'll both be desperate for a cup of tea after your journey. Come along to the kitchen. You can leave your case there by the door for now, dear. It will be perfectly safe.'

Charlotte somewhat reluctantly did as she was told. She was still so nervous that she didn't want to let any of her possessions out of her sight, but then the woman seemed nice enough.

Soon she was seated at a large scrubbed table with a cup of tea and a slice of fruit cake in front of her. The kitchen was enormous and as the two women chatted and caught up on all their family news, Charlotte had a good look around. Everywhere was very clean, and she just hoped that she would be able to afford to stay there. The cost of accommodation would be much more expensive in London than it was at home, and she wondered how much Mrs Manners would be charging per night.

She didn't have to wait too long to find out because shortly afterwards Vera turned to her and said, 'I'm afraid the only room I have available at the moment is "up in the gods" as I call it, on the top floor. It's a bit of a trudge so if you like it I could let you have it for four pounds a week? That would include your breakfast and a main meal, depending on your shifts on the wards. How does that sound?'

It actually sounded very reasonable. Charlotte quickly calculated that after the cost of her board and with her bus fare to and from the hospital, she could probably manage on another seven and sixpence a week, which was roughly what she had estimated.

'Let me show you the room before you make your mind up, and if you decide to take it, I shall telephone the Matron.' Vera crossed to a large board that was covered in keys, and after taking one down she nodded towards the staircase, saying, 'It's this way.'

'I'll stay here,' Mrs Preston told them, kicking her shoes off and lifting her feet onto a kitchen chair. 'My bunions are beginning to complain, so I'm going to rest for a while.'

Charlotte followed Mrs Manners up a long narrow staircase that seemed to go on forever. A patterned stair-runner held down with brass stair-rods ran all the way up it, and like the kitchen everywhere looked neat and tidy.

Eventually they reached the fourth floor and Vera leaned against the banister rail as she breathlessly pressed the key into Charlotte's hand.

'It's that door there.' She pointed ahead. 'Our dental nurse used to live in it when my husband was alive. You go on in and see what you think while I get my breath back. Every time I come up to this floor I realise I am not as young as I used to be.'

Charlotte grinned and after inserting the key into the lock and opening the door she found herself in a pleasant room with a sloping roof on either side of it. It wasn't large, but there was more than adequate space for her to move around in.

A bed with a metal headboard stood against one wall and there was a large chest of drawers and a bedside table, as well as a table and chair in the window where she could sit to study in the evenings.

A wardrobe stood directly behind the door and the floor was covered in linoleum with a big rug at the side of the bed. A quilted satin bedspread in pale blue covered the bed, and gay flowered curtains hung at the window. A gas fire stood inside a small fireplace. Charlotte was curious to look out of the window from up here and she tripped across the room excitedly. The view almost took her breath away as she stared across the sooty rooftops of London. She could see St Paul's Cathedral! It was like being on top of the world.

'So what do you think? My other young ladies have been quite happy here,' said Vera, who had now come to stand in the doorway. 'I know it's a bit of a long haul to get up here, but it's peaceful for when you are reading your books, and for sleeping during the daytime after night-shifts.'

Charlotte turned to beam at the woman. 'It will be perfect,' she assured her. 'The climb doesn't concern me at all and I'd love to stay here.'

'That's agreed then,' her new landlady smiled. 'Jolly good. Now, I usually ask for a week's money in advance.'

After fumbling in her handbag for her purse, the girl carefully counted four pound notes out into the woman's hand.

'Right then, you can fetch your case up and make yourself comfortable whenever you're ready, dear. Personally, I don't envy you, having to cart it up all these stairs.'

Charlotte chuckled. 'Oh, I'm stronger than I look,' she assured her, and they went back down the staircase together, both feeling satisfied by the outcome.

Charlotte next saw Mrs Manners at dinner that evening. She had spent the afternoon unpacking her case and had also used the pay phone in the hallway to ring her mother to tell her that she had arrived safely and had found somewhere nice to stay near the hospital. Hilary had been hugely relieved. She still wasn't happy with the idea of Charlotte flying the nest but knew that she could do little about it. Charlotte was a young woman now.

The meal that Vera had cooked was delicious, and suddenly realising how hungry she was, Charlotte took full advantage of the fact. There was a home-made steak and kidney pie covered in pastry that melted in the mouth and a selection of perfectly cooked vegetables followed by a rice pudding sprinkled with nutmeg that Charlotte sighed over. As well as herself, Mrs Preston and her sister Vera there were also three more girls at the table and Charlotte glanced at them curiously, wondering where they all came from and what they were doing in London. No doubt she would soon find out, she thought to herself.

Once the meal was over, Charlotte offered to help clear the table but Vera shooed her away.

'You'll do no such thing, dear,' she told her in a horrified voice. 'You're a paying guest.'

Charlotte wandered back up to her room feeling at a bit of a loose end. It was very dark already and a little late to start sightseeing as she didn't know her way about yet. So eventually she decided on an early night and almost the second her head hit the pillow she was fast asleep. Her first night in London had begun.

At breakfast, only one of the girls she had seen the evening before was present, and Charlotte noticed that she was pushing the scrambled egg about her plate while looking rather green about the gills. Alarm bells instantly went off in her head.

Turning to her now, she said, 'Hello, I'm Charlotte. I didn't get to introduce myself last night.'

'Oh er . . . hello, I'm Lesley.' The girl looked uncomfortable but Charlotte was determined to find out a little about her, even though she knew it was none of her business.

'Are you working in London or here for a holiday?'

The girl looked even more flustered if that was possible and hesitated for a moment before stammering, 'Er . . . I'm just here for a little holiday.'

Charlotte didn't believe her for a minute, but she couldn't very well say that, of course.

The girl then scraped her chair away from the table, clamped her hand across her mouth and fled from the room without another word, leaving her breakfast untouched.

Charlotte shrugged as her thoughts returned to her own plans for the day. With the girl forgotten for now, she ate up her porridge and toast and marmalade, collected her bag and coat and set off through the smoggy streets to take a look at London.

By midday, Charlotte's feet felt as if they didn't belong to her. She was sure that she must have walked at least ten miles. She called into a café for a hot drink, since by now it was bitterly cold, and her hands and feet were numb. Gratefully, she wrapped her fingers about the steaming mug. Being a tourist was extremely hard work, she decided. Nursing would be easy by comparison.

By the time she returned to Greville Street, her nose was red and glowing, and Mrs Preston, who was passing along the hallway, chuckled.

'Crikey, you look like Rudolph the red-nosed reindeer, love,' she teased. 'Come on in by the fire and get warm. I'm sure our Vera won't mind you thawing out in her sitting room.'

It was as Charlotte was holding her hands out to the flames, hoping she wouldn't get chilblains, that she suddenly thought of the girl she had sat with at breakfast that morning. 'Do you know how Lesley is?' she asked. 'I thought she looked rather poorly.'

Mrs Preston shook her head. 'I have no idea. Vera once told me it doesn't do to get too involved with your lodgers. There are those that will take advantage if you do, so she just takes their rent and asks no questions, and as long as they are respectful and pay their money on time, and the student nurses follow the hospital's rules, she leaves them to their own devices. I do know that lass went out earlier on though, and came back looking like death warmed up. I passed her in the hall but she didn't speak, she just scuttled off to her room.'

'Sorry, I didn't mean to be nosy,' Charlotte apologised.

Mrs Preston shrugged. 'It's all right. It's no skin off my nose but if you take my advice you'll just worry about yourself while you're in London. A young girl like you needs to keep her wits about her. There are some bad things go on here, believe you me.'

Charlotte pursed her lips. Mrs Preston obviously thought she was an innocent young girl, but how she could have enlightened her. She wondered what the woman would say if she were to tell her about the time she had spent in the convent and the baby she had given birth to. But she pushed those thoughts firmly away. She really must try to forget the past. Unfortunately, it was proving rather more difficult than she had thought it would be, and she still had to stop herself from bursting into tears every time she saw a baby in a pram.

'So how did your day go?' the woman asked now and Charlotte sighed.

'I couldn't see too much in the smog, but it cleared eventually and I walked quite a long way, getting to know the area around here and around the hospital. It will help when I begin my course. There's plenty of bomb damage here still, isn't there – the same as back home in the country.'

Mrs Preston stretched her slippered feet out towards the fire. 'Ah well, mind how you go. You need to be careful in a big city like this.'

'I shall,' Charlotte promised and then she moved towards the door, telling her, 'I'll see you at dinner. Thanks for the warm.'

It was as she was passing a door on the third floor on her way to the attic staircase that she paused. She could distinctly hear someone crying and she wondered what she should do. After standing dithering for a moment, she gently tapped at the door. The crying stopped instantly but no one came to answer it. Charlotte moved on. Mrs Preston was right. She had enough worries of her own without taking on someone else's.

Lesley wasn't present at dinner that evening but Charlotte wisely didn't comment on it. Once the meal was over she decided to brave the cold again and go for another brisk walk. Wrapping up warmly in layers of clothes, she set off up Holborn Viaduct, passing the turn-off to the Old Bailey, until she came to St Paul's Cathedral. It was thrilling to get close to a famous landmark like this after only ever seeing it in pictures. It was as she stood there admiring the beautiful architecture that she became aware of someone next to her. Turning her head she saw a young man.

He smiled at her in a friendly fashion before commenting, 'It's quite breathtaking, isn't it?'

He was tall and quite good-looking with dark hair and blue eyes and Charlotte felt herself blushing.

'Yes, it is,' she said shyly.

'Have you been inside?'

Charlotte shook her head.

'Oh, that's a shame. Perhaps we could meet up back here tomorrow and go inside together?'

Anger surged through her. 'No, thank you,' she said coldly. 'I have an appointment tomorrow.'

'Then how about I take you for a drink? Your choice of venue, of course, and my treat.' He clearly wasn't going to be put off so easily, so Charlotte swirled about and stamped off, leaving the young man standing there with a bemused expression on his face.

How dare he try to pick me up like that? she fumed to herself, and then when she had put some distance between them she felt slightly guilty. Had she over-reacted? Perhaps he was just trying to be friendly. But then Harry had started off by being friendly to her – and look at the heartbreak that had led to. Men were all the same as far as she was concerned – except for Brian, that was – and she didn't care if she never set eyes on another male for the rest of her life.

It was coming up to 9 p.m. and she was on the third floor on her way back to her own room when she heard the crying once more. Making a decision, she took a deep breath and rapped sharply on the door.

'Is that you, Lesley?' she called and after a moment someone answered.

'Y-yes.' There was the sound of a key in the lock, and Lesley's tearstained face appeared through a gap in the door. Without her face powder and eyebrow pencil she suddenly looked much younger than Charlotte had taken her for.

'What's wrong?' Charlotte asked gently.

'I . . . I'm fine,' she choked.

'Well, you certainly don't look fine to me, so you can either tell me what's the matter or I'll go and fetch Mrs Manners.'

'Oh no – don't do that!' Opening the door wider, the other girl frantically ushered Charlotte into her room, after glancing nervously up and down the corridor. She was clearly in a panic but Charlotte stared at her steadily, hoping that she would confide in her. Instead, Lesley perched on the end of the bed and wrapped her arms tightly about her middle with a look of abject misery on her face. Charlotte's eyes took in the room, noting the soft leather suitcase standing against one wall and the pure wool coat hanging on the hook on the back of the door. Everything about Lesley's possessions spoke of quality, and Charlotte guessed that she had come from a well-to-do family.

'Have you run away from home?' she asked bluntly.

The girl hung her head. Eventually she replied, 'I – I had words with my parents, but I haven't run away.'

Charlotte waited for her to go on but the girl had closed up like a clam now, so she turned back towards the door. At least Lesley appeared to be a little calmer now.

'If you decide you need to talk, I'm up on the next floor,' she told her. The girl nodded but said nothing, so Charlotte left her sitting there and moved on to her own room. There was no way she could help someone who didn't wish to be helped, and she was tired now and more than ready for bed.

Chapter Twenty-Five

Charlotte's mouth was dry as she stood waiting outside Matron's office with a number of other girls. Some of them were giggling and joking but they didn't fool Charlotte for a second. This was a big day for all of them, the first day of their training, and she could hardly believe that it had finally arrived.

Eventually the girls fell silent as an enormous woman in a starched white cap and a nurse's uniform swooped over to them.

'Right, girls.' She peered closely at them one at a time as she clutched a clipboard with a list attached to it. 'I want you to answer your names as I call them out so that I know you are all present and correct. Is that clear?'

The girls nodded in unison as she began to shout out names, and once it was done she tucked the clipboard beneath her arm before ordering, 'Follow me now and no chatting. Remember that you are in a hospital.'

She marched off down the corridor with the girls following in an orderly line, and Charlotte felt a little disappointed. She hadn't expected the teaching staff to hang out a flag but she had expected a welcome of some sort. They filed past doctors in starched white coats, patients, harassed-looking nurses and porters until at last they came to a flight of stairs that they discovered led down to a rather dismal basement. It was full of lockers, some of which already had names on them, and they were told that this was where they would get changed for the duration of their training. There were also a number of large cardboard boxes strewn across the floor and the nurse began to open them one at a time.

'I am Matron's assistant, Nurse Baker,' she informed the girls. 'And I am now going to issue you with your uniforms. They are to be worn at all times whilst you are on duty, but *under no circumstances* must they be worn outside of the hospital. Do you all understand? You come in here each morning and evening to change.'

When the girls all dutifully nodded she began to call out names again, and as each girl stepped forward she looked her up and down, assessing what size she might be before rummaging in the boxes and throwing four clean but obviously pre-worn uniforms at her. Once all the girls had been supplied she told them, 'Get changed now, and I shall be back shortly to fetch you. You will find a number of empty lockers. Choose which one you each want. There are keys in all of them, so please keep them safe. I shall expect anyone with long hair to tie it back with a navy blue ribbon. Clips and slides are not acceptable, neither is any make-up or jewellery apart from a fob watch.'

When Charlotte put her uniform on it was at least two sizes too big for her but there was nothing she could do about it for now. She hastily slipped the navy-blue cardigan her mother had bought her for Christmas over the top of it and fastened her fob watch to the top pocket. She then tied back her hair, which was now almost shoulder-length again, firmly into the nape of her neck, and slipped her feet into her flat black shoes then waited for the nurse to come back and inspect her. There was no mirror in the basement and as the uniform was decidedly unflattering to say the least, Charlotte could only suppose that she must look a fright, as some of the other girls did.

By the time Nurse Baker came back to inspect them the girls had once more formed an orderly line and now she ushered them down yet another long corridor for their medicals. This was the part that Charlotte had been dreading. How thorough would the medical be – and would they be able to tell that she had given birth?

They were shown into a room with a small changing area and a toilet block, and ordered to strip off. Not so very long ago, Charlotte would have died of shame and humiliation if she had been forced to undress in front of other people, but the months at the Convent of the Sacred Mother, of being forced to shower naked with all the other girls had hardened her and she undressed without a qualm. The girls were then taken one by one in to see the doctor, who poked and prodded them and asked endless questions whilst scribbling on a chart.

At last it was over and the last girl to go into the doctor was dressed again. Charlotte was just thankful that the medical had not been as intrusive as she had feared. It was then that Nurse Baker reappeared.

'We shall now do a tour of the hospital,' she informed them. 'And then after lunch you will each be told where your work placements are and you will report to that department – so take note of where we are going.'

Charlotte soon realised that this would be much easier said than done. The hospital was huge, an endless labyrinth of disinfectant-smelling corridors that twisted and turned and all looked the same. Within minutes she was hopelessly lost, but judging by the confused looks on the faces of some of the other girls, she wasn't the only one.

First stop was the reception area, where busy receptionists were directing people to the ward or department they were looking for and answering a number of phones that never stopped ringing. Everyone who visited the hospital for whatever reason reported here, and the area was seething with people.

Next stop was the Bacteriology department where the girls were confronted with endless samples of blood, stools, urine and other unspeakable things. People in white surgical masks and gloves, swamped in white coats, were peering through microscopes at small glass culture dishes, and the smell was nauseating. Charlotte was relieved when they moved on to the next part of the department, which was marked Histology. In there were endless shelves loaded with jars full of formaldehyde, each containing different organs of the body. In one was the body of an aborted foetus and Charlotte's eyes filled with tears as she gazed at it. It had tiny arms and legs and even its face was clearly visible, although it was obvious that it had been aborted in the early stages of development. The girl standing next to Charlotte swayed as she dry-heaved, and Charlotte gripped her arm to steady her. It wouldn't do to have one of the new cadet nurses pass out at this early stage of the training.

Nurse Baker clucked her disapproval before shooing them out, and next they were shown into the Haematology laboratory. Every patient's blood sample, whether they be in- or out-patients was dealt with here. Specialised clinics were also held within this department for people who needed blood transfusions or those who were suffering from blood-related cancers such as leukaemia. The place was totally chaotic as disgruntled patients waited to see the doctor who had to deal with literally dozens of patients each day.

All of the girls were relieved when they were led out of there, and each was hoping that they wouldn't have to work in that department. But there was no time for discussion because now Nurse Baker clapped her hands together with authority to demand silence.

'Next I am going to take you into two different wards,' she informed them, almost as if she was offering to take them on a trip to the seaside. 'There you will be able to see the qualified nurses working first hand and see what a first-class job they do. Matron demands excellence and professionalism from her staff at all times. Nothing less will do.'

The girls glanced at each other uneasily as they followed Nurse Baker up a steep flight of stairs to the first floor. Here they were shown into a ward with beds set out in regimentally straight lines down either side; nurses in different coloured uniforms were flitting about seeing to the various needs of their patients.

Some were taking temperatures or blood pressures before recording them on the charts that hung on the end of every bed; others were behind drawn curtains giving patients a bed bath or a bedpan; another nurse went from bed to bed straightening the bedclothes. As one nurse hurried by with a bedpan on her way to the sluice room, catching Charlotte's eye she gave her an encouraging wink. Whilst all this was going on, domestics in dark blue dresses were steadily mopping floors and wiping the tops of the bedside lockers.

The Ward Sister, a very attractive blonde, hurried over to greet them. 'I apologise if it seems a little chaotic at the moment,' she said in a friendly fashion. 'We are preparing for the doctor's and Matron's visit. We have to have everything just so before they do their rounds.'

She looked down the length of the ward, clearly proud of it, and Charlotte warmed to her; she hoped that she might be placed on this ward. This Sister seemed to be pleasant at least, which was more than could be said for Nurse Baker, who seemed to be showing them around under sufferance.

209

'I have a few moments to spare so I'll explain about some of the cases we care for in here,' the Ward Sister said. 'We tend to care for people with chest complaints in this ward. Patients may have suffered coronaries or they may be asthmatic – although we also have patients who suffer from anaemia or diabetes.'

Charlotte listened intently as the Sister briefly described the kind of treatment some of her patients might be receiving. This was the part that interested her most, although as yet she had no idea if she would ever be able to qualify as a midwife – which would be her chosen career. She had given it a lot of thought and decided that if she was never to have any more babies of her own, at least this way she would be able to be close to babies.

The rest of the morning seemed to pass in a blur and eventually the girls were directed to the staff canteen where they were given an hour to have their lunch.

Charlotte found herself sitting next to the girl who had almost fainted in the Histology department earlier in the morning. As they ate their lunch they got into conversation.

'I'm Libby,' the girl introduced herself with a friendly smile. 'There's a lot more to this nursing lark than I realised,' she admitted through a mouthful of chicken soup.

Charlotte instantly took a liking to her. Libby was quite short with striking red hair that seemed to have a life of its own, a spattering of freckles spread across a rather cute upturned nose, and eyes that were a very pretty shade of blue. Charlotte immediately sensed that they would become friends.

'Where are you from?' she asked.

'Bradford.' Libby stuffed a stray lock of hair behind her ear; it was already escaping from the hairband she had tied it back with.

'I've been flat-hunting for two solid days since I got here,' she went on with a worried frown. 'I was late applying for a place at King Billy's, and all the rooms in the nurses' home were taken. I'm in one of the approved bed and breakfasts at the minute, but my savings won't last long at this rate. I need to find a cheap flat to share or I won't be able to stay. My parents are really hard-up, you see. They can't help out.'

Charlotte felt sympathetic, and then as a thought occurred to her she suggested, 'How about we found a flat to share?' Then flushing she rushed on, 'It's only a thought, of course. I mean, you don't know me from Adam and you might not want to—'

'Why, that's a wonderful idea,' Libby interrupted with a radiant smile. 'I doubt we'll have much time now until the end of the week, but we could start to look at the weekend if you like? A two-bedroom place would be perfect, but if we can't find one I'd be more than willing to sleep on a bed settee.'

And so it was decided, and as they finished their lunch the two girls discussed the different areas where they might try searching, hoping that their plan would be approved by the hospital. It would mean asking the Matron's permission and they agreed that they would go and see her together at the earliest opportunity.

After lunch, each of the new cadets was assigned a place to work and Charlotte found herself heading for the X-ray Department. She had been rather disappointed to find that cadets were not allowed to work on the wards apart from doing the more menial jobs like bed baths and cleaning. As before, the waiting room of the X-ray department was heaving with people. Some were on stretchers, some on crutches, and others were seated uncomfortably on the hard-backed chairs, their limbs covered in splints and bandages.

Anne, the departmental manager, met Charlotte at the entrance and hastily gave her a tour, explaining departmental rules and regulations as they went. In no time at all Charlotte's head was spinning as she tried to take it all in. There were five radiographers working there as well as Mr Wilson, the chief radiographer, who had his own secretary. It soon became obvious that the most important rule was to protect the staff from exposure to radiation. Anne pointed out that above each door was an oval red light; if it was switched on, it indicated that X-rays were being taken – and no one was allowed in. The radiographers who actually took the X-rays were all issued with heavy leaded jackets and protected by lead-lined screens within the rooms whilst X-rays were taking place. They all seemed a very friendly bunch and Charlotte felt that she was going to like working there.

Charlotte's job would be to file the X-rays into boxes in alphabetical order in a small room between the X-ray department and the

Casualty department, as well as seeing to the needs of any of the patients who might need to use the toilet or a bed pan whilst they were there. Charlotte wasn't too keen on that part of the job and wrinkled her nose with distaste as she was shown into the sluice room and directed how to use the steriliser. But even so she accepted that it was all part of nursing and soon got stuck in.

As well as her work in the X-ray department, Charlotte was told during the course of the afternoon that she would also have to attend lectures within the hospital – this in addition to being given day release to a local polytechnic where she would have to study basic biology, chemistry and physics as well as anatomy and physiology. Charlotte knew that she was going to be kept more than busy, and by the time her first day at King William's Hospital was over she was tired but happy. She and Libby had been to see the Matron during the afternoon break to ask for permission to search for a flat to share, and the woman had agreed to it, but only after a lengthy lecture on keeping safe, etc. Now Charlotte could hardly wait to begin the search.

She managed to find her way to the locker room where Libby was already changing out of her uniform. Once they were ready, the two girls left the hospital together chatting happily. On the main road they parted company and Charlotte hurried away to catch the bus back to Greville Street, wondering what Mrs Manners would be cooking for dinner that night. Her first day as a cadet nurse had left her as hungry as a hunter.

Chapter Twenty-Six

Charlotte arrived back at the lodging house to find Mrs Preston fastening her little hat on in the hall mirror with her suitcase packed and all ready to go by the front door.

'Ah, here you are, love,' she said cheerily. 'I'm glad I've seen you before I went. I'm off home shortly, but I hope I'll get to see you again.'

Charlotte felt quite sad to see her leave. Both she and Vera had been very kind to her during the short time she had been in London.

'So how did your first day go?' Mrs Preston asked now.

'Really well.' Charlotte had a spark of excitement in her eye as she told the woman some of the things she had seen and done.

'Well, that's good then, and I have a feeling you're going to make an excellent nurse,' the older woman told her approvingly. 'But now I really must go else I'll miss my train from Euston. I've already said goodbye to Vera. She's in the kitchen cooking the dinner, so come here and give me a hug.'

Charlotte willingly did as she was asked and once Mrs Preston had left she wandered through to the kitchen to see Vera. She was in the process of removing a leg of lamb from the oven and the smell made Charlotte's stomach rumble with anticipation.

'Ah, here you are,' Vera greeted her. 'Dinner will be ready in two shakes of a lamb's tail, and while you're eating you can tell me all about your first day at the hospital.'

Soon, Charlotte and two of the other girls who lodged there were seated in the dining room, along with a young couple who had arrived that day, but at a glance Charlotte saw that Lesley was missing.

Vera sighed when she mentioned it as she placed a big tureen of mixed vegetables in the centre of the table.

'She didn't come down for breakfast either and I haven't heard a peep out of her all day,' she said. 'Do you think I should go up and knock on her door and check that she's OK?'

'No, you finish serving the meal, I'll go and do it and tell her that dinner's ready,' Charlotte volunteered, and darted away, taking the stairs two at a time. She arrived on the third-floor landing slightly out of breath and tapped on Lesley's door.

'Lesley! Mrs Manners wanted you to know that dinner is ready.' She waited for an answer and when none was forthcoming she tapped on the door again, a little harder this time.

'Lesley? Are you in there?' Again there was no answer so eventually she turned and went back downstairs.

'She doesn't seem to be in,' she told Vera.

The landlady frowned. 'That's strange then because I haven't heard her go out,' she commented. 'But then again she might have gone while I was in the back room. I'll put her dinner in the oven and when she comes in later I can warm it up for her.'

Dinner was a pleasant affair. It turned out that the young couple had got married the day before and come to London for a short honeymoon. They had spent the day sightseeing and were all starry-eyed and love-struck. Charlotte supposed she should have envied them but she didn't. She had no plans to include a man, any man, in her life ever again. From now on she would make nursing her life.

After dinner she settled down in the comfortable sitting room to listen to the wireless, and then she phoned her mother and Brian to tell them all about her first day at 'King Billy's'. There was still no sign of Lesley and Charlotte had a bad feeling. She knew that what Lesley chose to do or where she chose to go was absolutely none of her business, but the girl had looked so ill and miserable the day before when she had spoken to her that Charlotte couldn't help but worry about her.

At nine o'clock when the other guests had all gone out, she went upstairs to tap on Lesley's door again and still receiving no answer she made her way back down to speak to Vera, who was reading by the fire.

'You don't think she's in her room and too ill to answer the door, do you?' she asked Vera fearfully.

'I suppose there is a chance that's the case,' the landlady said. 'I must admit she didn't look too chipper yesterday. I've got a spare key to all the rooms. Would you like me to go and check.' Vera hated to intrude on people's privacy when they were lodging in her house, but she could see how concerned Charlotte was, and it was making her feel anxious too.

'It might not be a bad idea,' the girl said in a small voice, and then she waited while Vera fetched the spare key to Lesley's room.

They went back upstairs together, and once on the third-floor landing Vera knocked sharply on the door. 'Lesley, if you're in there can you answer me, please? Otherwise I'm going to come in to check that you are OK.'

There was no sound but for the steady tick-tock of the grandfather clock downstairs, so after waiting for another few seconds, Vera inserted the key into the lock and opened the door.

Her hand instantly flew to her mouth and she gasped with alarm as Charlotte pushed past her. Lesley was lying on the bed in a pool of blood and she wasn't moving.

'Run down and phone for an ambulance,' Charlotte told Vera as she hurried over to take Lesley's pulse. She couldn't find one and she began to panic as Mrs Manners flew from the room. There was nothing she could do then except wait for the ambulance to arrive. Vera left the front door swinging open for them and shortly afterwards two ambulancemen raced up the stairs carrying a stretcher between them. They ushered Charlotte and Vera out on to the landing before closing the door firmly behind them.

'I couldn't find a pulse,' Charlotte shouted after them in a shaky voice but she doubted that they had heard her.

It seemed like an eternity but eventually the door opened and a grim-faced ambulanceman joined them.

'I'm afraid there was nothing we could do for her,' he told them. 'She's been dead for some hours, by the look of it.'

'*What*?' Vera was horrified.

'We can't be sure at this stage,' the man said cautiously, 'but it appears that she bled to death. I'm afraid I can't really say more than that.'

The floor seemed to rush up to meet Charlotte as she was suddenly transported back in time but she pulled herself together with an effort

215

as the man now asked, 'is there a phone I can use? We need to call the police.'

Vera pointed silently down the stairs and the man headed in that direction, leaving the two women to stare at each other in horror.

'Oh, why didn't I think to check on her earlier?' Vera fretted as she cried softly into a scrap of a white handkerchief. 'To die all alone like that. The poor, poor girl. Whatever is her mother going to think?'

'It isn't your fault,' Charlotte soothed her. 'If anything, it's mine. I spoke to her last night after I heard her crying and I left her to it. She told me that she'd had a row with her parents. Now I understand why. They probably threw her out when they discovered she was pregnant.'

'Pregnant?' Vera echoed, her eyes stretched wide.

'I can't be sure, of course.' Charlotte lowered her voice. 'But when I spoke to her last night she told me that after she'd had that row with her parents, she'd left home. She didn't exactly admit that she was having a baby, but I'll bet you she was. Didn't you notice how ill she looked every morning and how she couldn't face food?'

'Now that you come to mention it she did seem a bit picky,' Vera acknowledged. 'But I didn't put two and two together.'

'Hmm, I wouldn't mind betting that she'd come to London to get rid of it.' Charlotte scowled. 'I bet she went to someone for an abortion and it went wrong. I could be completely wrong, of course, and letting my imagination run away with me, but we'll see.'

They were still standing there some minutes later when sirens sounded in the street outside and two policemen joined them on the landing.

'Which room is the girl in?' one of them asked and when Vera indicated, he nodded solemnly before telling them: 'Would you mind going downstairs, please? We have the pathologist on the way and we will need to take a statement from you both later.'

Vera and Charlotte silently made their way downstairs and shut themselves in the sitting room. They could hear footsteps going up and down the stairs and eventually there was a tap at the door. The police officer to whom they had spoken earlier appeared and took a seat.

'Now, how much did you know about this girl?' he asked as he took a notebook from his pocket.

'Not an awful lot,' Vera told him tremulously. 'She was just lodging here and she didn't speak very much. She seemed to want to keep herself to herself, although she was a nice polite girl.'

'So what made you unlock her room?' he questioned and the landlady told him all about the concerns she and Charlotte had had about the girl.

The officer carefully recorded everything they had said in his notebook before telling them, 'Thanks for your cooperation. The ambulance is here to take her away now. But I'm afraid your room is in rather a mess.'

'Oh, don't worry about that.' Vera flapped her hand dismissively. The state of the room was the last thing on her mind at present. 'Poor lamb,' she choked. 'What will happen now?'

'We found her name and address amongst her belongings so my colleague is contacting her parents even as we speak. I dare say they'll visit you to collect her belongings, if you wouldn't mind putting them all into her case. It all seems very cut and dried, and I don't think we'll need to trouble you any further.'

When Vera raised her eyebrows he snapped his book shut and lowered his voice. 'I really shouldn't say anything but it will be common knowledge soon anyway and you both seem to have cared about the girl, so off the record I'll tell you that it looks like she went for a backstreet abortion that went wrong.' He shook his head regretfully. 'It appears that someone used a Higginson syringe on her and it ruptured her uterus, causing her to haemorrhage severely.' He sighed heavily. 'I've seen it too many times before, I'm afraid. Young girls who don't know how to cope so they take what they think will be the easy way out.' He then rose, telling them, 'I should stay in here for a while longer if I was you and give them time to remove the body.'

Vera thanked him, and once he had gone she sank down into her chair again hardly able to take it all in. It seemed such a criminal waste; a young life like that just snuffed out. There was the sound of something being manoeuvred down the stairs and both women shuddered. It was probably the ambulancemen bringing poor Lesley's body down on the stretcher.

'Men are such *bastards!*'

217

The words spewed out of Charlotte's mouth before she could stop them and the landlady was shocked. Charlotte seemed such a well brought-up young lady; Vera never dreamed that she would even have heard such a word, let alone be capable of using it.

'Sorry,' Charlotte muttered, her cheeks stained a dull red. 'It's just made me so angry. Why didn't the man who got her into that condition stand by her?'

'I doubt we'll ever know the answer to that.' Vera patted the girl's hand and then they sat there until the house was silent again.

As Charlotte lay in bed that night, tears trickled down her cheeks in the darkness as she thought of Lesley and all the other girls she had seen back in the convent. They had all made a mistake but they had been forced to pay a terrible price for it, herself included. Seconds later she was thinking of her baby again, and as she remembered how Daisy had felt cradled in her arms, she could almost smell her. That lovely baby smell of milk and talcum powder.

Why was it so difficult for young girls to get a legal abortion, she wondered. If only things were easier for them, so much tragedy could be averted. And as she lay there, her desire to become a midwife grew stronger. One day she would fulfil her ambition, and if somewhere along the way she could help a young girl like Lesley, who was in no position to bring a child into the world, then so be it.

Chapter Twenty-Seven

Charlotte tried her best to put what had happened to Lesley to the back of her mind. She had to, if she was going to focus on her studies and succeed in achieving her ambition.

On Saturday morning she met Libby bright and early and they set off flat-hunting together. They had brought lots of pennies for phone boxes, to dial the numbers on postcards in sweetshops and elsewhere, advertising vacant properties in their price-range. As the day wore on, however, they became disheartened.

'My God, you wouldn't leave a dog in there,' Libby said in disgust as they ran down the steps of one particularly revolting place. 'Did you *see* the mould around the bath, and the walls were running with damp!' Then glancing at her watch she sighed. 'We just have time to look at a couple more then I shall have to go back to my digs and get ready for work. Where do you think we should try next?'

Charlotte studied her notes. 'Well, there's this one here.' She stabbed her finger at an advertisement that she had scribbled down. 'But it's in Soho, and everyone knows that it's a bad place.'

'Beggars can't be choosers, and I'm not fussed if you're not,' Libby groaned. 'Come on, it can't be any worse than some we've looked at, and it is a two-bed place. I think we're going to have to lower our sights a little or we'll never find anywhere – not in the areas we've been looking in up to now, anyway.'

They had done a complete tour of the area around the hospital, but the only flats that were half decent were way out of their price range. The war had destroyed so many buildings, and there was a housing shortage – that was part of the problem.

Getting off the bus at Tottenham Court Road, the two girls made their way to the address in Soho. The street it was in was rather dismal, and they passed clubs advertising topless dancers displayed on posters outside. But the girls kept their eyes averted and hurried on. It was gone four o'clock in the afternoon now and frost was beginning to form on the pavements as the light faded fast.

'I think this it,' Charlotte said eventually as she peered at a number on a tall townhouse just off Soho Square. It looked very dilapidated but they supposed it was worth a look now that they were there.

Charlotte rang the bell at the side of the door but it didn't work, so she rapped loudly on the door sending a shower of flaking paint fluttering onto the pavement.

They heard shuffling footsteps approach and seconds later an old woman who looked like a witch peered out at them.

'Yes – what d'yer want?' she barked ungraciously.

Libby gulped before saying politely, 'Hello, we've come to enquire about the flat that you're advertising.'

The old woman, who was dressed from head to foot in black, narrowed her eyes and peered at them more closely. Her wispy grey hair was wild and straggly, and her face had so many lines on it that Charlotte couldn't even begin to imagine how old she might be.

'An' could yer pay the rent on time?' The woman puffed on her cigarette and drew an old black shawl more tightly about her scrawny shoulders.

'Oh yes,' Charlotte assured her. 'My friend and I are cadet nurses at King William's Hospital and there would be no problem with the rent.'

'Hmm, well I suppose it's better than takin' in any more street girls,' the woman said ungraciously. 'Can't trust those Toms, not for a bleedin' minute. They'd nick everythin' you owned if you didn't keep yer eyes peeled an' yer wits about you. I dare say you'd better come in and 'ave a look at the place. My name is Lil – that's all you need to know. The owner is a Maltese gentleman – an' you don't wanna get on the wrong side of him!'

Suddenly Charlotte wasn't so sure that she wanted to see the flat but it would have appeared churlish to walk away now so she glanced resignedly at Libby and they stepped into the hallway. It was almost as cold in there as it was outside and the paper on the walls was peeling and grubby. She could feel the faded linoleum sticking to the soles of her shoes and there was an overpowering smell of cats, but she kept a smile plastered to her face as the woman showed them up a steep staircase to the first floor.

When she eventually shuffled to a stop outside one of the doors that led off a long landing she fumbled with a large bunch of keys before inserting one into the lock.

'This is it.' She waggled a nicotine-stained finger at them warningly. 'You can have a look around then come down an' tell me if you want it or not. But keep yer 'ands off the stuff in there, or I'll 'ave yer. An' the rent will be five pound ten shillins a week. A month up front, just in case you does a runner.'

As she poddled away, Libby looked distressed, and whispered, 'Crikey, I don't have that much money on me. That's eleven pounds each!'

'But I do if it's right for us,' Charlotte assured her. 'Come on – we may as well have a look at it now we've come this far.'

They stepped warily into a fair-sized room that had obviously been used as a lounge-cum-dining room. An old settee was shoved against one wall and two wooden chairs stood next to a table that was leaning dangerously to one side.

'Blimey, this lino is more holy than righteous,' Libby sniggered, but Charlotte was looking at the place through different eyes.

'At least it's a fair size,' she pointed out. 'Most of the ones we've looked at up to now haven't had room to swing a cat around in. Let's look at the rest of it before we make a decision.'

They moved across the room towards two small single bedrooms and a bathroom that left a lot to be desired. The smell in there was appalling and Libby held her nose and grimaced.

'Whoever stayed here last didn't believe in doing much cleaning, did they?'

'It's nothing that a bit of Ajax and elbow grease couldn't put right. Now let's have a look at the kitchen.'

That room proved to be a bit of a disappointment, since it was very tiny, but even so there seemed to be everything they needed in there – a small cooker, a sink and a number of rather battered pans that had obviously been left by the last occupant. They were all absolutely filthy but even so Charlotte was smiling by now.

'You know, I think we could make this really nice,' she said

221

optimistically. 'The walls are bare plaster, so all we'd need to do is paint or whitewash them. Then we could put new lino down and get some secondhand furniture from somewhere. I could buy some curtain material too and run us up some curtains, if I invested in an old sewing machine. I used to be quite handy with a needle. What do you think?'

Libby shivered as she stared around. 'That's all well and good, but it isn't in the best neighbourhood, is it? And I don't like the sound of the owner.'

'I know,' Charlotte agreed, then added sensibly, 'But we already know that we can't afford the rents in the better areas. And there is a serious housing shortage in London, so . . .'

'Hmm . . .' Libby chewed thoughtfully on her lip for a moment before coming to a decision. 'All right then', she said, 'if you're quite sure, let's take it.'

They went downstairs and gave Lil a two-pounds deposit. After promising to return with the rest of the month's rent the next morning, they came back out into the fresh air. Charlotte was feeling excited. Admittedly the flat needed a lot of work doing on it but it would be the first home of her own.

'I hope we've done right,' Libby fretted as she remembered the abominable smell in the toilet.

'Of course we have. Once we get in there we'll have it cosy in no time,' Charlotte said confidently. 'In a month's time you won't recognise the place and we can move in as soon as we like once we've paid the rent. When would suit you?'

'Well, it would have been nice if we could have had time to do it up first, but to tell the truth I'm getting dangerously low on funds so it's the sooner the better.'

'In that case why don't we start tomorrow morning?' Charlotte suggested. 'If we don't do it then we won't get another chance until next Saturday at least, what with working.'

'I suppose you're right,' Libby said dismally. She wasn't feeling anywhere near as happy about the move as Charlotte was, but knew that it made sense. If she didn't get somewhere cheaper to live soon her few savings would be depleted and she'd have to go home with her tail between her legs, which was the last thing she wanted. By taking the flat, she might just be able to scrimp along on her wages.

The two girls parted company then as Libby had to hurry away to her digs to get ready for her evening job. Charlotte went back to Vera's, keen to share her good news with her.

'Why, that's wonderful, dear.' The landlady was genuinely pleased for Charlotte as the girl chattered on about her new flat. 'I'll miss you though. You haven't been a bit of bother. I just wish all my guests were as easy as you. It does sound as if this place you're going to needs a bit of doing up though and I might be able to help you there. You see, I've got a couple of single beds going begging. I've been storing them in the outhouse and I'd be pleased to get rid of them. I dare say they'll be better than the ones that are in the flat. I've also got some odd pairs of curtains knocking about, if you're not too fussy about the colour.'

'Oh, we're not,' Charlotte assured her hastily. 'Anything would have to be an improvement on what's there already and Libby and I would be more than grateful for them.'

'In that case, my bridge partner Audrey who lives just down the road might get her husband to bring them round to you. He's got a van, you see, and I'm sure he wouldn't mind.'

Charlotte flung her arms around the woman and kissed her soundly on the cheek. 'You are an absolute angel,' she smiled.

Vera blushed at the compliment. She just hoped that Charlotte would be all right now that she was branching out into the big, wide world. London could be a dangerous place for naive young girls. Poor Lesley was a prime example, although Charlotte did seem to have her head screwed on right. In fact, in some ways she appeared to be much older than her years, and the dentist's widow often wondered what had happened to make her that way. Not that she would ever dream of asking. She had discovered long ago that it didn't do to get overly involved with her paying guests. And that even applied to young Lesley.

Charlotte could scarcely sleep that night after phoning her mother and Brian to share her good news. Luckily she still had just about enough cash left to pay the month's rent but then she would need to go to the bank to withdraw a little more to do the improvements on the flat. Vera's offer of curtains and two beds would be a great

223

help, but as she lay there she listed all the other things that she and Libby would need, such as china and cutlery for a start-off, and then bedding and some paint. The list was endless but she was sure they would manage it between them.

The next morning she was up bright and early, and packed, ready to go. Once she had finished her breakfast, the landlady handed her a sealed envelope.

'What's this?' Charlotte asked curiously.

'Well you paid the next week's rent in advance on Friday, and you've only been here for two nights – so that's the rest of it back,' Mrs Manners said briskly.

'But I can't take this,' Charlotte objected.

Vera flapped her hand dismissively at her. 'Oh yes you can,' she insisted. 'That will buy a lot of the bits and bobs that you're going to need for your new home, so don't look a gift horse in the mouth. And hurry up with that cup of tea now. Michael, my friend Andrey's husband, will be here with his van any time, and as soon as you've helped him load those beds on and the curtains he'll give you a lift to the new place. Make sure you pop in to say hello if you're nearby – you're always welcome, dear.'

The landlady sighed enviously as Charlotte tripped happily away. Oh, to be young with my whole life in front of me again, she thought to herself, then marched briskly away to the kitchen to prepare for her charlady's visit.

'Is that you, Libby?' Charlotte shouted when someone tapped at the door of the flat later that morning.

'Well, who were you expecting – Tony Curtis?' Libby quipped.

Charlotte laughed as she hurried over to open the door. Libby dragged her case inside then looked around. Charlotte had already scrubbed the glass in the windows and hooked up a pair of Vera's cast-off curtains. Although they were a bit long, they looked lovely.

'What do you think?' Charlotte's cheeks were glowing. 'The lady where I was staying gave them to me and there's a pair each for our bedrooms too. Aren't they smashing?'

'They certainly improve the look of the place.' Libby fondled the soft velvet. The drapes were in a lovely shade of light gold, slightly

224

faded along the seams, which was why Vera had taken them down, but they were still in nice condition and a million times better than the tatty old rags that had hung there before.

'Now do you see what I mean?' Charlotte asked as she spread her hands. 'Just hanging a new pair of curtains has helped. Think of how it will look when we get around to painting the walls and getting some decent bits of second-hand furniture. And Vera has given us a bed each too. The man who gave me a lift here has taken the old ones away. Come and see.'

Libby had to admit that the beds were very nice and she began to feel a bit better. She had spent the whole night fretting about whether or not they had done the right thing, but Charlotte's enthusiasm was infectious and she was beginning to feel more optimistic already.

'I've started scrubbing the kitchen now,' Charlotte informed her then. 'But I reckon if we nip over to Petticoat Lane before it closes, we might be able to get some paint there and lug it home on the bus. We could make a start after we get back from the hospital each night – except for the nights you're working,' she added. 'So what colour do you fancy for the lounge?'

Libby grinned good-naturedly. 'Why don't we stick to cream or white throughout? We can put anything with those colours and they won't clash with my hair!'

By teatime they were back at the flat with all their purchases. Before beginning the hunt round the market, the friends ate saltbeef sandwiches and cheesecake at the Jewish deli, and drank strong tea at a stall. Fortified, they'd managed to find three large tins of magnolia-coloured emulsion at a knock-down price, as well as a box of crockery and cutlery. At the bedding stall, they'd purchased a stack of blankets, sheets and two new pillows. The market trader had got his young son to whistle up a black cab 'for the young gels', and Charlotte paid the fare back to Soho.

It took quite some time to unload all the goods, under the beady eye of their new landlady, who was clutching a copy of a Sunday paper and a glass of Guinness, and then at last they were inside their new house, with the door closed. The cab driver, Morrie, had given the girls a hand and refused the tip Libby tried to give him.

'I think we ought to make a start on the painting in here as soon as we've got our breath back,' Libby decided. 'And incidentally, from now on I'm going to call you Lottie, Charlotte is much too long-winded.' The girl seemed to be almost as excited as Charlotte now. 'And once we've got this room shipshape, I'm going to paint my room pink,' she added.

Charlotte smiled. She had a feeling she was going to enjoy sharing a flat with Libby and suddenly the future looked brighter.

Chapter Twenty-Eight

January 1964

'Off out again, are you?' Charlotte asked as Libby appeared from her bedroom in a bright red tent dress covered in enormous yellow flowers.

Libby flicked the bell sleeves aside so that she could apply her pale lipstick in the mirror that was suspended above the electric fire.

'Yep, I'm seeing Gavin again tonight.'

Charlotte looked up from the papers she was studying. 'Sounds to me like you're getting quite serious with this one,' she commented teasingly. At least he'd lasted over a week, which was a lot longer than most of Libby's boyfriends did.

'Not on your life,' the other girl denied hotly. 'I'm too young to be tying myself down, but there's nothing wrong in going out and enjoying yourself, is there? We're only young once. You ought to try it yourself sometime, Lottie.'

'Oh, don't start that again. You sound like my mother,' Charlotte groaned. 'I'm quite happy studying in my spare time, thank you very much. I'll never get to be a midwife if I don't work hard at it.'

They were both now State Registered Nurses and Libby was more than happy with that status, but Charlotte was still determined to attain her dream of becoming a midwife.

'So what do you reckon?' Libby asked now as she twirled in front of Charlotte to show her latest new dress off.

'It's very nice. Another Mary Quant, is it?'

Mary Quant was a designer who sold her fashions from a boutique called Bazaar in King's Road, in Chelsea. It was fast becoming a parade ground for the fashionably young and Libby loved her designs. So much so that Charlotte often teased her that she must spend at least a quarter of her wages in that shop every month. Mind you, she was well aware that soon all that could change again. Up until a few months ago Libby had favoured the hippy trend that was also very fashionable. Her hair had been long and flowing and she had always seemed to be weighed down with beads. Before that she had hung out with the teddy boys, but since going out with Gavin, who was a confirmed Mod, she had drastically changed her image.

'Yes, it is.' Libby pulled her comb through her close-cut hair. Her other heroines were Jean Shrimpton, and another model who had recently burst onto the scene called Twiggy. A young, waiflike-looking girl, she seemed to be on every billboard they passed.

'So where are you off to tonight then?' Charlotte asked now as she chewed the end of her pencil.

Libby pulled her coat on and wrapped a long scarf around her neck. 'We're going to the cinema to see *Billy Liar*. I really fancy that Tom Courtney.' Then as a horn sounded outside she flew across to the window. 'It's Gavin,' she shouted across her shoulder. 'See you later, Lottie.'

The door banged resoundingly behind her and crossing to the window, Charlotte tweaked the curtain aside and saw Gavin sitting on his Lambretta wearing a duck-green hooded parka and blowing into his hands. Seconds later Libby appeared and after clambering up behind him she wrapped her arms around his waist and they roared away.

Charlotte dropped the curtain and returned to her studies. It seemed as if she and Libby had lived here forever and she was very content, although her life was very different to that of her flatmate. Whilst Libby was happy to go out every chance she got, Charlotte kept herself very much to herself. Occasionally she would spend a weekend with her mother and Brian in their lovely home in Leamington, or visit the cinema with Libby, but other than that, apart from going to work at the hospital she barely went out. It wasn't because she was short of invitations. Any number of young men had invited her out on a date during the years since she had lived with Libby, and her friend would get very frustrated with her each time she turned them down.

'You'll never meet Mr Right at this rate,' she chided gently, but

Charlotte would simply reply: 'I don't *want* to meet Mr Right, thank you very much. I'm quite happy on my own.'

For a time Libby had actually wondered if her friend might have lesbian tendencies but that idea soon went to the wall. Charlotte just didn't seem to be interested in either sex, which Libby thought was a shame. With her long blonde hair and sparkly blue eyes, Charlotte was a very attractive girl and she could have been stunning if she'd only taken a little more interest in herself. Even so they got along fine and Libby was happy with their arrangement, as was Charlotte.

Crossing to the record-player that Libby had bought in John Lewis up by Oxford Circus, Charlotte lifted the needle and turned it off. As usual Libby had had the Beatles' latest LP record *With the Beatles* blaring out. The Beatles were a young group from Liverpool and Libby loved them, especially George. Charlotte quite liked them too, but not whilst she was studying. Her favourite was Paul. She then went to the small fridge that they had recently purchased and got herself a bottle of Coca Cola before returning to her studies, and before she knew it she had forgotten about everything else.

Two hours later she yawned and stretched. Then she looked around the sitting room. She and Libby had left the flat in Soho almost two years ago and now rented this one in Bethnal Green in the East End of London. This area and the docks had been cruelly bombed during the Blitz, leaving devastation where people's homes had once stood. But now blocks of flats were rising from the rubble, the beautiful old townhouses that had survived the war blending effortlessly with the new builds.

The new place was a lovely flat in a Georgian terrace that spoke of bygone splendour, and Charlotte loved living there. She had seen it advertised on a noticeboard at the hospital, and when she and Libby had gone to view it they had both fallen in love with it at first sight. It was bigger than the flat off Soho Square and in much better condition, so they had decided that it was worth the extra rent it would cost them. They had both loved their little flat in Soho, at least in the daytime. But setting foot outside at night had been another matter entirely, and Charlotte had lost count of the times she had been propositioned by men. After dark, of course, it was a red-light district.

During the time they had lived in the new flat they had added to the furniture they had already bought and now it was a very comfortable home; Charlotte couldn't see a time when she might ever want to leave it. She had also moved to work in the London Hospital in Whitechapel, an easy walk away from Bethnal Green, and she was enjoying being there too. She had become quite friendly with one of the young doctors, and Libby was always teasing her about it.

Joseph Branning was a quiet soul, and much like Charlotte he tended to keep himself very much to himself. They had got talking purely by chance when Charlotte had had no choice but to sit next to him in the staff canteen one lunchtime. All the other seats had been occupied and she had looked at him apologetically before asking, 'Would you mind if I sit here?'

'Be my guest.' He had pulled the chair out for her and their friendship had grown from there, although Libby found it hard to accept that anyone could have a man as a friend without becoming romantically involved with him.

'You should snap him up before someone else does,' she would scold Charlotte. 'He's quite a dish with those big brown eyes and that lovely dark hair.'

Charlotte would smile and say nothing. Joseph had never acted as anything less than a gentleman to her, which was partly why she liked him. But she did worry about him sometimes. The other doctors seemed to shun him, and every time a promotion came up he never seemed to be considered for it, which Charlotte felt was a shame. He was remarkably conscientious about his job.

Now she tidied her textbooks away and was just about to snap the light off before going to bed when Libby stormed in and threw her bag onto the chair that Charlotte had just vacated.

'*Men!*' she snarled as she snatched her bag up again and fumbled in it for her cigarettes and lighter. 'Bastards, the whole lot of them!'

'Hmm, do I detect trouble in paradise?' There was a twinkle in Charlotte's eye as she smiled ruefully at her friend.

'You could say that.' Libby lit a cigarette and inhaled the smoke deeply. 'I shan't be seeing *that* twerp again.'

Another one bites the dust, Charlotte thought but she was too tactful to say it. Instead she offered, 'How about I make you a nice hot cup of cocoa? It will help you to sleep.'

'Thanks!'

Charlotte headed off for the kitchen. No doubt Libby would tell her what she and Gavin had rowed about tomorrow; tonight she was just too tired to listen so she wouldn't ask. Libby could ramble on for hours when she was in the mood and Charlotte had to be up at six the next morning.

Libby was still in bed when Charlotte crept out of the flat the next morning and headed for the hospital.

Already the market in Whitechapel was teeming with people setting up their stalls, and some of them shouted a greeting as Charlotte hurried by, keen to get out of the bitter cold. A thick frost coated the pavements and she had to be careful not to slip. It wouldn't do to arrive at the hospital as a patient instead of a nurse.

Once inside the main hospital she went straight to the locker room where she began to change into her uniform. Two other nurses were there changing too behind the next set of lockers and Charlotte's ears pricked up when she heard one of them mention Dr Branning.

'Yes, I overheard Sister saying that he'd been passed over for promotion yet again,' she heard one of them say. 'It's no wonder though, is it? They reckon he's as bent as a nine-bob note. He only needs to put a foot out of line and they'll get rid of him altogether. He stands no chance of ever becoming a surgeon. I mean, it's illegal, isn't it? The surgeons are looked up to, aren't they? And most of them are respectably married. Whoever heard of a homosexual surgeon? Shame though 'cos he seems like a decent enough sort of bloke. Apart from *that*, of course. Ugh, just thinking about it makes my blood run cold. It ain't natural, is it?'

'Well, I think it's a damn waste to womanhood,' the other girl said jovially. 'Fancy a nice-looking chap like that being a pansy! I wouldn't kick him out of bed if he had normal urges, I don't mind telling you.'

The voices receded then as the women left the locker room and Charlotte dropped heavily onto a bench as shock coursed through her. Joseph a *homosexual*? But then it made sense in a way and could explain why he had never made a pass at her.

231

She shook her head to clear it before hurrying away to the ward she was working on. Perhaps it was all just rumours and wild speculation?

It was during the afternoon break that she next saw Joseph. He came to join her in the canteen.

'Afternoon, Nurse Hayes,' he said politely as he took the seat next to her. 'How are things?'

'Pretty busy to be honest,' she told him. 'We've had two emergencies come in this afternoon, which is why I'm late taking my break. I had to prep them both for immediate surgery.'

Charlotte found herself staring at Joseph from the corner of her eye, wondering if what she had heard was true. He was a remarkably good-looking man, but just because he didn't bother with women didn't make him a homosexual, surely? If that was the case, they might say the same about her because she never bothered with the opposite sex either, and yet she certainly had no leaning towards women.

'I heard some nurses chatting in the locker room this morning,' she said casually. 'They were saying that you'd been passed over for promotion again.'

Joseph shrugged, but colour crept into his cheeks. 'Yes I was, but I'm getting used to it by now.'

Charlotte felt sorry for him. She knew how hard he worked and wondered why, even if what the nurses had said was true, something like his sexual tendencies should affect his job? But then she had worked in hospitals long enough to know that surgeons were revered. The Matron and the surgeons were treated like gods and their reputations had to be without blemish. As a thought suddenly occurred to her she asked, 'Are you doing anything tonight?'

When he raised his eyebrows she felt herself blushing. 'I'm not chatting you up or anything like that,' she said quickly, 'but my flatmate is out most nights and I thought you might like to come round for dinner. I don't usually bother cooking just for myself and it would be nice to have a night off studying – but only if you haven't got anything else planned,' she added lamely, suddenly wondering if this was such a good idea after all.

She fully expected him to decline the invitation so she was surprised when he smiled and answered, 'That would be really nice. Thank you. Would you like me to bring anything?'

She was embarrassed now and croaked, 'Just yourself – and perhaps a bottle of wine?' She hastily scribbled down her address. 'Shall we say about seven thirty?' She was standing up now and he nodded.

'Thank you. I shall look forward to it.'

Charlotte scuttled away like a scalded cat and didn't slow her steps until she was entering the ward. *What the hell made me to do that?* she questioned herself. But she had no time to think about it before the Sister bore down on her and before she knew it she was running around like a headless chicken.

On the way home that evening she called in at the butcher's and bought two fat juicy lamb chops. She then went into the greengrocer's and got a cabbage, some carrots and potatoes.

Libby was getting ready to go out when she got in and seemed in a much better mood than the night before.

'Are you all right?' Charlotte asked cautiously.

Libby threw back her head and laughed. She was wearing a pinafore dress tonight, yet another of Mary Quant's creations.

'If you mean am I heartbroken over Gavin, the answer is no,' she answered. 'There are plenty more fish in the sea. He was too full of himself by half, if you want the truth. In fact, I reckon I'm going to give men a miss for a while. I'm going out with a nurse from St Bart's tonight. We're off boogying. Why don't you come?'

Charlotte avoided her eyes as she carried the groceries to the kitchen. 'Actually I have someone coming round for dinner.'

Libby had been in the process of putting her coat on but now she paused to grin. 'Oh yes? Man or woman?'

'It's a man, if you must know,' Charlotte said peevishly, deeply embarrassed. 'But it's not what you think. He's just a friend.'

'Oh, that would be the elusive Dr Joseph then, would it?' Libby's eyes were sparkling with mischief. 'I reckon I might hold on to meet him at last.'

'No – don't do that,' Charlotte said much too quickly. 'I'm already wondering why I bothered to invite him in the first place, but I felt sorry for him. He's just been passed over for another promotion. It's such a shame because he's very hardworking.'

'Mm, I *bet* he is!' Libby smirked.

Charlotte lifted a towel and lobbed it at her friend. 'Clear off,' she said with a smile. 'And mind your own business.'

Libby chuckled and seconds later the door closed behind her and Charlotte began to scoot around trying to get everything ready.

Joseph arrived punctually at seven thirty clutching a bottle of wine and looking very uncomfortable.

'I forgot to ask you what you were cooking so I brought red wine. I hope that's all right?' he said as Charlotte ushered him into the flat.

'That's fine, thank you. I've cooked us some lamb chops. I hope you like them?' She had changed into a plain black dress and brushed her hair until it shone, and he thought how different she looked out of her nurse's uniform

'It just so happens that they're one of my favourites,' he assured her as he followed her into the kitchen and glanced around. She certainly kept a very tidy home. There didn't seem to be a thing out of place, which made him feel rather guilty as he thought of his own home. He had never been the tidiest of people.

Charlotte poured them each a drink then left him in the lounge while she hurried away to serve up the meal.

'Umm, that was quite delicious,' Joseph told her an hour later as he rubbed his stomach appreciatively. 'I haven't had a meal like that since I left home. My mother was a good cook too.'

'Do you get to see her often?' Charlotte asked.

'Unfortunately she died when I was fifteen.' She saw the pain flicker briefly in his eyes.

'And what about your father?'

'Oh, he left my mother and me when I was quite young.' The young doctor pursed his lips. 'It was just as well. I think he might have killed one of us eventually if he hadn't. He was a bully. After Mother died I lived with an elderly aunt until I came to London to study. She still writes to me occasionally, but other than her I'm on my own.'

'My father was a bully too,' Charlotte said in a low voice, and the common bond seemed to break the ice between them, although Charlotte was cautious about how much she told him. There were still many things that she found just too painful to discuss, even with Libby.

Before she knew it, it was ten o'clock and glancing at his watch Joseph said guiltily, 'Goodness me, look at that. It will be time to get up before we go to bed. I must be going, but thank you for tonight, Charlotte. I've really enjoyed it. I don't get to go out much so it was a real treat.'

'Neither do I, we shall have to do it again,' Charlotte said and she meant it. She had found him remarkably easy to talk to.

She saw him to the door, and after clearing up, she went to bed in a happy frame of mind. Whether Joseph was 'queer' or not, she had enjoyed his company.

Chapter Twenty-Nine

Over the next two months, Charlotte's and Joseph's friendship blossomed. She was aware that they were being gossiped about at the hospital but she didn't much care. They were just friends who enjoyed each other's company – and what could be wrong with that? Joseph had never been anything other than a perfect gentleman and Charlotte didn't want more. At least once a week now they had dinner together, either at her flat or his, and sometimes they even went to a restaurant to eat. Occasionally they made a trip to the cinema too, and twice they had been to the West End to see a show. Charlotte had expected Libby to pull her leg about it or tease her at least, but for some reason, Libby seemed preoccupied and had taken to staying in. It was almost as if the roles had been reversed and Charlotte started to worry about her.

It was one day in March when Charlotte got home from her shift at the hospital that she finally asked, 'Is anything wrong, Libby? You haven't seemed yourself for a while. I thought you were going to the Marquee Club tonight to see the Yardbirds.'

Libby was curled up in a miserable heap on the settee listening to a Kinks record. The kindness in Charlotte's voice made her eyes instantly fill with tears. She hesitated for a second and then muttered, 'I'm not going now. Oh, I've been such an idiot, Lottie! I'm in a real mess and I don't know what to do.'

The tears came then in floods as Charlotte sat down next to her and took her hand. There was a sick feeling in the pit of her stomach because she had a horrible intuition that she knew what was coming.

'Are you pregnant?' she asked gently.

The tears fell faster as Libby buried her head on Charlotte's shoulder. 'I-I think so. I've missed two periods now and I'm usually as regular as clockwork. Oh Lottie . . . What the hell am I going to *do*?' Her voice was heavy with despair.

Charlotte's heart went out to her.

'Well, I suppose the first thing we should do is get it confirmed.' She was trying to be practical, but Libby shook her head vehemently.

'I can't do that. If I go to my doctor's, it will be on my records – and that's the last thing I need.'

Charlotte could see her dilemma, but could think of no other option. 'The problem is, you can't hide it forever if you *are* pregnant,' she pointed out.

'I know – and that's where I hoped you would be able to help me,' Libby sniffed. 'You *are* training to be a midwife – couldn't *you* examine me?'

Charlotte chewed on her lip. 'I suppose I could,' she said uncertainly. 'I'm not fully trained yet but I think I know enough to tell you if you are pregnant. It's rather unethical though.'

'But who is going to know apart from us?'

Charlotte saw the desperation in her friend's eyes and gave in. 'All right then, go into the bedroom and lie on the bed. I'll just get my coat off and wash my hands and I'll be right with you.'

Libby scuttled away to do as she was told as Charlotte's stomach tightened into knots. She really wasn't happy about this at all, and yet she hated to see Libby so upset and didn't want to let her down.

Half an hour later Libby sat with her arms wrapped about her waist rocking to and fro, a stunned expression on her face. Every instinct had warned her that she was pregnant, but actually having it confirmed made it seem more real somehow.

'Are you quite sure?' she asked in a shaky voice that was little more than a whisper.

Charlotte nodded. 'I'm afraid so. All the signs are there – swollen tender breasts, morning sickness, the works.'

Libby stared off into space. 'Then I have no option but to get rid of it, do I?' she said.

'Oh, now just hold on a minute.' Charlotte was horrified. 'If you were thinking of getting a back-street abortion, you can forget it. You wouldn't believe some of the things I've seen in the maternity ward. Young girls with their insides so mangled they will probably never be able to carry another baby. Then there's the high risk of infection if you go to those people. Most of them live in squalor—'

She stopped abruptly when she saw Libby staring at her thoughtfully.

'But *you* could do it,' she said softly.

Charlotte gasped. '*Me?* Why would I risk my career to do something like that?'

'Because you care about me,' Libby said stubbornly. 'And I'm sure you'd do a better job of it than these idiots you've been telling me about. Please say you'll at least consider it, Lottie.'

Charlotte stared down at the floor, her mind racing. There was a measure of truth in what Libby said. She was well into her training now and she knew what to do – but what if something were to go wrong? If anything should happen to Libby, she knew that she would never be able to live with herself, and her career would be up the creek without a paddle. But then she thought of Lesley, and a vision of the poor girl lying in a pool of blood floated in front of her eyes.

'All right then, I'll think about it,' she said cautiously. 'But I'm not making any promises. Now I must go and get ready. I'm meeting Joseph in half an hour and we're going out to grab a bite to eat. Will you be all right here on your own?'

'Of course.'

Charlotte saw the hope in her friend's eyes and it tore at her heart, but it was a very risky thing Libby was asking her to do. And then, as she quickly changed into a smart black skirt and a pretty blue Laura Ashley blouse, her mind raced back to all the other poor girls she had been incarcerated with in the convent. Wouldn't it have been better if someone had done for them what Libby was suggesting, rather than having to go all through the pregnancies just to have their babies torn away from them, as Daisy had been torn away from her? As always, thoughts of her beautiful girl brought tears springing to her eyes, but Charlotte hastily removed the pins from her hair and dragged a brush through it before racing away, not wishing to be late for her date with Joseph.

'Come on then, spill the beans,' he said as they sat in a small restaurant by Aldgate East station. 'You've hardly said a word since we met and you're pushing that risotto around the plate as if it's poison.'

'Sorry.' Charlotte flushed. 'It's er . . . well, Libby has a problem and she's asked me to help her with it and I don't know what to do.'

'I see.' Joseph took a sip of water. He had never seen Charlotte so quiet and guessed that it must be something serious. 'Is it anything that I can help with?'

Charlotte shook her head miserably. She longed to confide in him, but what would he think of her if he knew what she was contemplating? He was a doctor and it was his job to save lives, not take them away.

'All right then.' He nodded ruefully towards her uneaten food. 'How about I pay the bill and we go and find somewhere quiet to have a drink?'

Charlotte nodded gratefully as he waved the waiter across. Back out in the street, she tucked her arm into his and they strolled along in silence for a time. That was one of the things she had come to love about Joseph. He didn't expect anything but friendship from her, which was just as well because Charlotte knew that this was all she had to give now.

'How about this place?' he asked eventually, pausing outside the doors to a rather rundown-looking public house. She stared absently up at the sign, *The Dog and Duck*, and nodded. The mood she was in, one place was as good as another. In fact, she wished she had stayed in.

Once inside, they made their way through a fog of cigarette smoke to a table in the far corner, and then Joseph hurried away to get the drinks.

When he came back, he placed a brandy in front of her – and seeing her surprise, he grinned. 'Purely medicinal. I thought you looked like you could do with it.'

It was then that the need to share what was bothering her became overwhelming, and leaning towards him she whispered, 'What do you think of young women who have illegal abortions?'

She had expected him to look shocked but instead he said calmly, 'I think that sometimes, for various reasons, they feel as if they have no choice in the matter. Is that what this is about, Lottie? Is Libby pregnant?'

When Charlotte nodded he sighed. 'And she's asked you to get rid of it, has she?' Another nod as he lifted his glass of ale and took a swallow. 'Is there no chance of the father standing by her?'

'No. They were never serious about each other and they finished weeks ago.'

'And what about her parents – wouldn't they help her out?'

'No chance.' Charlotte sipped at her brandy and shuddered as it burned its way down her throat. 'She is the eldest of a huge family and her father is a bit of a one, by all accounts. Libby did any part-time jobs she could all through her final years of school to save enough to have the opportunity of becoming a nurse, and I know it would destroy her if she had to go home with her tail between her legs now.'

Joseph studied her face intently, and after a while he said, 'Then you have to decide if you dare to help her.'

'What – you mean you wouldn't think badly of me?' she gasped.

He shook his head as he swirled the ale around in his glass. 'No, I wouldn't. I've seen too much suffering in my career to condemn anyone who is trying to help someone.' He sighed. 'Just today I visited a cancer patient on the ward. He's terminal and very near to his end, the poor old chap. He's in indescribable pain and he begged me to put an end to his suffering. And do you know what? I was very tempted to do just that. All I would have needed to do was increase his dose of morphine and he would have been gone in minutes – peacefully. He wouldn't even have known about it. Instead, he faces a wicked death. I couldn't help him, of course, because he was in hospital, but it's different with Libby. No one else knows, do they?'

'No.'

'Then you must do what you think is right.'

Neither of them had ever discussed much of their private lives, but from the little she had told him, Joseph had assumed that Charlotte had led rather a sheltered, privileged life – the only child of a vicar and his wife until her father had died and she had come to London to begin her nurse's training. He thought it rather strange that she could show such empathy for a young single pregnant mother-to-be. Surely she would have been protected from all that?

As if she could read what he was thinking, Charlotte took a

deep breath and said, 'I think it's time I told you a few of my little secrets.'

When he looked puzzled, she rushed on, 'The thing is, Joseph . . . I'm not quite what I appear to be. You see, some years ago I found myself in a very similar position to Libby, after I was raped.'

He looked shocked but she could see the sympathy in his eyes, and now that she had started she was keen to make a clean sweep of it, and so there in the little back-street spit and sawdust pub she told him everything, the words tripping over each other.

'And so you see, somewhere I have a little daughter,' she finished hoarsely as the tears spilled down her cheeks unchecked. 'And I wouldn't wish this kind of heartache on *anyone*. Not a day goes by that I don't think of her and pray that she is happy and safe.'

'Oh, Lottie!' Joseph scarcely knew what to say. And here he had been thinking that Charlotte was one of the privileged few.

He took her hand gently and stroked it as he tried to digest all that she had told him. 'I suppose that explains why you never have a boyfriend?' He looked at her quizzically and she nodded.

'I shall never have a relationship with a man again – not *ever*,' she declared. 'Except with you, of course,' she added hastily. 'But we are simply friends and I can cope with that. You make no demands on me.'

She watched different emotions flit across his face as he struggled with himself. She had bared her soul to him. Did he trust her enough to do the same? He decided that he did and now it was his turn.

'The thing is, Lottie, you must have heard the rumours about me that go around the hospital? Well, the truth of the matter is I could never be more than a friend to you because those rumours are true. I am not physically attracted to women. I realised it when I was quite young and all my friends were getting girlfriends. It was as if they were trying to outdo each other and get the most notches on the bedposts, and I found it all rather repugnant. Do you understand what I'm trying to tell you?'

'Are you explaining that you are a homosexual?'

He bowed his head in shame and nodded. 'Yes, I am,' he said, 'but I don't flaunt the fact. I did briefly have an affair with a teacher at my school and I adored him, but of course he soon moved on to someone else: there were plenty of boys to choose from. That's when I promised myself that from then on, I would become celibate. Trouble is I'm only human and now I do have one special . . . er . . . friend, but we are very discreet. As you have noticed, the other doctors at the hospital have their suspicions and that's why I keep getting passed over every time a promotion comes up. They expect the surgeons to be happily married, their characters without blemish.'

Now it was her turn to squeeze his hand. 'We're quite a pair of misfits, aren't we?'

He chuckled, but it was a sad sound. 'Yes, I suppose we are, but we just have to get on with it.' Glancing at the clock, he saw that it was nearly closing time.

'Goodness me.' He drained his glass. 'I think I'd better get you safely home.'

At the door to her flat he lifted her hand and kissed it tenderly. 'It's a shame there aren't more non-judgmental people in the world like you, Lottie Hayes,' he said. 'Please, think carefully about what Libby has asked you to do. I'd hate you to go ahead with this and then torture yourself afterwards. You've been through quite enough as it is in your short life. Even so, I believe you will do what you think is right and for the best reasons, and I'll be behind you whatever your decision. Goodnight, my dear.'

'Goodnight, Joseph.' Charlotte stood for a while and watched him striding away with his coat-tails flapping about his legs in the breeze. Then she opened the door to the flat and slipped inside. She had some very serious thinking to do.

Chapter Thirty

Three nights later, Charlotte returned home after her shift at the hospital to what appeared to be an empty flat.

'Libby? Are you in?' she called as she slid out of her coat.

'Y-yes, I'm in here.' The voice came from the bathroom.

Charlotte went over and tapped at the door, asking softly, 'Are you all right in there?'

When there was no answer she pushed the door open a little. A wall of steam met her, and for a moment she couldn't see anything. But then she made out Libby lying in a scalding hot bath clutching a half-empty bottle of gin.

'What the hell do you think you're doing?' She covered the space from the door to the bath in two seconds flat and yanked the plug out as Libby started to wail.

'I heard someone say that this was a good way of getting rid of unwanted babies.'

'Then you heard someone say wrong,' Charlotte scolded. 'Gin and hot water is just an old wives' tale. Now let me help you out of there and come through to the kitchen. I'll make you some coffee. If you've drunk all that gin you're going to need it.'

When Libby was seated, shame-faced and tipsy in the kitchen, Charlotte shoved a mug of black coffee towards her. 'I'll do it,' she said quietly and Libby started to cry again, but this time it was with relief.

'Are you still quite sure that this is what you want?' Charlotte asked Libby as she placed the instruments she had borrowed from the hospital into a stainles-steel dish – all sterilised. It was almost a week since her friend had first asked her to help her, but now Charlotte was prepared to go through with it. The way she saw it, she didn't really have a lot of choice. If she didn't do it, Libby would go to someone who would, and they might butcher her.

'I'm sure.' Libby looked absolutely terrified but determined. She could see no other way out of her predicament and just wanted it to be over now. 'But Lottie – if anything should go wrong, no one will ever know of your involvement. I'll say I had it done in some back street and your name wouldn't be mentioned.'

'Well, let's just hope it doesn't come to that.' Charlotte was even more nervous than Libby was, but also quietly confident that she could do this procedure successfully. Now she looked towards her friend and suggested, 'Should we get it over with then?'

There was a large waterproof sheet on Libby's bed – also borrowed from the hospital – and Charlotte had covered it with a thick layer of towels.

As Libby climbed up onto the bed, Charlotte went away to scrub her hands, and when she came back she told her, 'Pull your legs right up and then let your knees flop open.'

Once Libby had done as she was told, Charlotte lifted one of the lethal-looking instruments from the dish. 'Now this is going to hurt but you must keep absolutely still,' she warned her. 'Are you ready?'

Libby stared up at the ceiling and nodded as Charlotte bent over her. Seconds later, the girl gasped as a searing pain tore through her, but she clenched her teeth and forced herself to remain still. This was agony as she had never experienced it before and tears squeezed out of the corner of her eyes. It seemed to be going on forever, but at last Charlotte straightened and told her, 'That's it.'

'I–is it over?' Libby groaned, her face the colour of putty.

'This part is, but the next part will be even more painful.' Charlotte stroked her finger gently down Libby's cheek. 'Come on, we'll get you into a nice hot bath now. That will soothe the pain a little.'

She helped Libby through to the bathroom where the water was already run and assisted her to climb into the bath as Libby leaned on her heavily.

'I'll go and get you a stiff drink now,' she told her once the girl was settled. 'I bought some brandy on the way home hoping it might ease the pain a little.'

Within seconds she was back and pressing the drink into Libby's trembling hand.

Libby took a great gulp of it and choked before spluttering fearfully, 'What's going to happen now?'

'We just have to wait for everything to come away. It shouldn't take too long. A few hours at most, I should think.'

They sat in silence as the little bathroom filled with steam. Each time the water grew cooler Charlotte topped it up with more from the hot tap, and slowly Libby began to relax until suddenly she let out a low growl of pain and grasped her stomach.

'Ouch! Oh, it *hurts*.'

'It's all right. This is what should happen,' Charlotte soothed, but it broke her heart to see her friend in such pain, especially when she knew that she was responsible for it. Slowly the bathwater turned red and Libby's whimpers increased to dull growls of agony.

'Come on, we need to get you onto the toilet.' Charlotte almost manhandled the girl out of the bath and then held her in her arms as Libby's unborn child slithered out of her. It was over and Charlotte prayed that God would forgive her for what she had done as Libby sobbed uncontrollably.

For the next few days whenever Charlotte wasn't at work she watched over Libby like a mother hen, but thankfully there seemed to be no signs of infection and she started to heal although she was very quiet. Charlotte plied her with nourishing food and insisted she rest.

She had just got to the hospital one day and changed into her uniform when she bumped into Joseph as she came out of the locker room straightening her cap. One glance at the strained look on her face told him all he needed to know. Taking her elbow, he steered her around the corner out of the way of prying eyes and said quietly, 'Judging by the look on your face, you went ahead with it then?'

Charlotte dropped her head and nodded.

'And how is she now?'

'She's on the mend,' she answered subduedly, by no means proud of what she had done.

He squeezed her arm. 'Then it's best forgotten now.' His voice was kindly and it helped her to know that he didn't condemn her for what she had done. Over the time they had known each other, Dr Joe Branning had become a very valued friend. So much so that she couldn't imagine her life without him in it now.

'So how about I come round to your place tonight with enough fish and chips for all of us?' he suggested. 'I dare say Libby could do with a bit of cheering up as well. It can't have been easy for her.'

'We'd like that.' Charlotte flashed a grateful smile then watched as he strode away before turning and hurrying on to the maternity ward where she was still training. Just one more year and she would be a fully qualified midwife, but it was strange to think that she had taken a baby's life before she had even delivered one.

Libby slowly recovered and began to go out again, although she never fully regained her old sparkle. Then in June she met a young man. He was a porter at St Bart's and suddenly all Charlotte heard was the name Carl. It was, 'Carl says this,' or 'Carl went there.'

Charlotte had a funny feeling that Libby was well and truly smitten, and her suspicions were confirmed the following November when she came home from work one evening to find her flatmate pacing the floor in their sitting room.

'You'll wear a hole in the lino if you don't slow down,' Charlotte teased as she walked into the kitchen to fill the kettle. It was bitterly cold outside and she was longing for a good strong brew and half an hour off her feet.

Libby followed her and leaned against the dresser with her arms folded.

'I have something to tell you,' she began nervously, and when Charlotte stared at her she rushed on, 'As you know, Lottie, I've been seeing Carl for some time now and the fact is – there's no easy way to tell you this – he's asked me to marry him and I've said yes.'

'Why, that's absolutely wonderful news!' Charlotte hurried over to give her a hug.

'Yes, it is,' Libby agreed. 'But what about you? How will you manage the rent here all on your own? Do you think you could get someone else in to share with you?'

Charlotte balked at the very idea. Since her stay at the convent she had allowed herself to get close to no one apart from Libby and Joseph, and had made no friends at all, which was just as she liked it.

'Oh, so *that's* what you were looking so worried about!' she chuckled. 'Of course I'll manage. My wages will be going up in another few months when I qualify as a midwife, and until then I still have quite a lot of my granny's money put aside to keep me going.'

Relief washed across Libby's face. She had been terrified about telling Charlotte that she would be leaving her. They'd been through so much together and Libby knew that she was going to miss her.

'So when did this happen then?' Charlotte was eager to hear all about it now.

'Just tonight when he walked me home from work.' Libby's eyes were sparkling. 'And he's taking me to Hatton Garden to buy me a ring on Saturday.'

'And when is the big day to be?'

'Ah well, I shall have to ring my mum and tell her about it before we go ahead with deciding on that,' Libby said sensibly. 'But we don't want a big wedding. Just a quiet Register Office do will suffice, and we're thinking sometime in March. There doesn't seem to be any point in a long engagement if we're both sure that this is what we want. And we are. I never dreamed I'd meet someone as wonderful as Carl and I couldn't have if you hadn't . . .' Her voice trailed away as they both thought back to the abortion Charlotte had performed on her earlier in the year.

'I still feel terribly guilty every single time I think about it,' Libby muttered, serious again now. 'But what sort of life could I have offered a baby?'

'You have to stop thinking about it now and look to the future,' Charlotte said compassionately. 'We both did what we thought was best, and whether we were right or wrong, we can't go back. What's done is done. But you will keep in touch when you're married, won't you?'

'Of course I will, always,' Libby assured her, excitement sparking in her eyes again. 'But first we have a wedding to plan. What sort of outfit do you think I should have?'

They spent the rest of the evening talking about weddings, and when Charlotte finally went to bed she was happy for her friend but also sad at the thought of losing her. *Still*, she consoled herself, *at least I still have enough to be financially independent, and soon I shall be fully qualified.* On that comforting thought she drifted off to sleep.

Libby and Carl were married late in March 1965, and as Charlotte heard them exchange their vows, a lump formed in her throat. They looked so happy and she was pleased for her friend. Libby's parents and siblings had travelled to London for the wedding but were due to return home on the train later that afternoon. Her mother was a short plump woman with a kindly face and fluffy brown hair, and Charlotte took to her straight away although she wasn't so sure about her father. A wiry little man who was half the size of his wife, he spent the whole time tugging at his shirt collar and fidgeting uncomfortably, but even so it was a joyful occasion and as the happy couple emerged from the Register Office, Charlotte showered them with confetti. Husband and wife then posed on the steps for photos that the groom's father took on an old Kodak Brownie camera.

Libby then tossed the small posy that Charlotte had insisted she should have high into the air and Charlotte flushed to the roots of her hair when it landed smack in her arms.

'Ooh, looks like you two are going to be next!' Libby's mother said archly as she looked towards Charlotte and Joseph, who had also attended the wedding. They certainly made a handsome couple and they seemed to be very fond of each other.

Charlotte and Joseph exchanged a glance. If only Libby's mother could have known the truth about them both . . . But of course they accepted that to onlookers they must appear as a couple. Thankfully the moment passed as they all piled into taxis and went to a restaurant in Spitalfields for dinner. Libby was positively glowing with happiness and looked truly beautiful in the smart two-piece suit that Charlotte had helped her to choose. It was cream, and with it she wore a neat little hat with a veil that sat coquettishly on the side of her head. When they had first begun to hunt for the bride's outfit, Charlotte had done her best to persuade Libby to go for a long white Ossie Clark gown, but now she was forced to admit that she looked just perfect. And Carl, who was also very smart in a new navy suit, white shirt and striped kipper tie, looked like the cat that had got the cream.

Libby, Charlotte and Carl had spent the previous week transferring all Libby's possessions to Carl's flat, which was off St John Street, quite close to St Bart's where they both now worked. Charlotte somehow knew that they were going to be happy. But it was sad to think that after today she would be all alone. She would never experience the happiness that Libby had. Pushing the thought away, she determined to enjoy the rest of the day and that was exactly what she did.

Eventually Joseph escorted her home. It was early evening by then and Libby and Carl had left for a three-day honeymoon in Southend.

'Will you come in for a coffee?' Charlotte asked at the door to the flat. The thought of going in alone was daunting.

'Actually I had no intention of leaving until I'd had one,' he teased, sensing that she was feeling a little abandoned.

Once inside, Charlotte hurried away to put the kettle on as Joseph loosened his tie and collapsed into a chair.

'It was a lovely wedding wasn't it?' he remarked when Charlotte returned with two cups of Nescafé. He chuckled then. 'It's quite ironic really,' he went on. 'Here's Libby and Carl embarking on a new life, and mine as I've known it is about to change too.'

'Why's that then?' Charlotte kicked her shoes off with a sigh of relief and curled them beneath her on the settee.

'It's my flat. I got notice to quit this morning in the post just before I left for the wedding.' He sipped at his drink. 'It seems some high-flying property developer has bought our block and is going to turn our flats into luxury apartments so we residents are going to be out on our ears.'

Charlotte's brain went into overdrive. 'Why don't you move in here with me?' she blurted out. 'You could have Libby's old room and we get along together well enough.'

Joseph almost choked on a mouthful of coffee. 'I couldn't do that,' he gasped as he mopped at a stain on his shirt with a clean white handkerchief. 'Crikey, there's enough gossip flying around over us, as it is. That would really blow my chances of ever becoming a surgeon if they discovered that I had moved in here. They'd assume that we were living in sin and you'd be branded a loose woman.'

'I suppose you're right,' Charlotte conceded. But it seemed such a shame. They got on so well together and she felt comfortable with Joseph because she knew that he would never make any sexual demands on her. She grinned ruefully. 'Ah well, it was just a thought. Pity though that you've got to look round for a new place when there's an empty room going begging here.'

'I entirely agree, but thanks for the offer. It would have been quite nice to have someone to share things with. But then you and I aren't like other people, are we? There's going to be no happy ever after for either of us. We're misfits – you because of what you've been through and me because of my sexual preferences. Life can be harsh at times, can't it?'

'Yes, it can,' Charlotte murmured as a picture of Daisy floated in front of her eyes. 'Very harsh.'

Chapter Thirty-One

For the next week, Charlotte spent every spare minute she had helping Joseph to flat-hunt, but without success. They were well into the Swinging Sixties now, and suddenly London was *the* place to be, which had made the rents climb sky high.

'My God,' Joseph groaned as they made a hasty exit one evening from a particularly grotty pad they had viewed off the Clerkenwell Road. 'That place must be a cockroachs' paradise. It should be condemned.'

Charlotte giggled. 'It was pretty gruesome,' she agreed. 'But let's call it a day for now. I don't know about you but I'm starving. We had three deliveries on the labour ward today and I didn't get to have any lunch.'

They hopped on a bus back to Whitechapel and soon they were seated in a small Italian restaurant that they favoured. Joseph had gone very quiet and Charlotte stared at him over a plateful of Spaghetti Bolognese.

'Are you OK?' she enquired.

'Yes.' He stared down at his food before saying, 'I've had an idea and I've been toying with it for a few days, but I'm not sure how you'd feel about it.'

'So try me.'

He gulped deep in his throat before going on. 'Well, the thing is, when Libby got married you offered me her room, but we both realise that if I moved in with you it would cause a scandal.'

She nodded.

'I think I might have found a way around it. What I mean is . . . if we were to get married, no one would bat an eyelid, would they?'

Charlotte's fork hit the plate with a clatter. 'You want us to get *married*?'

'Well, it would only be for the sake of appearances,' he said hastily. 'I mean, we'd have separate bedrooms and everything. As you rightly said, we do get on, don't we – and you've always told me you don't want to get married in the ordinary sense.'

'I don't,' she said with conviction as her mind raced. What Joseph had suggested actually made sense when she came to think about it. Marriage would give them a cloak of respectability and ensure that neither of them was ever lonely. But it was such a huge step . . .

'What do you think?' he asked tentatively.

'I can see the sense in it,' she admitted. 'But we'd both have to be very sure.'

'Oh, I know that.' He looked troubled. 'And of course, if ever you *did* meet anyone who you felt romantically inclined towards, we could get a divorce.'

Marriage, divorce! Charlotte's mind was spinning.

'I'm going to have to think long and hard about this,' she told him.

Joseph dug into his lasagne. 'Of course, and don't feel that you're under pressure in any way. I won't think any the less of you if you decide that you don't want to. I'd quite understand and I hope that it wouldn't affect our friendship.'

'It won't,' she promised. 'But what would I tell my mother and Brian?'

'You wouldn't need to tell them anything,' he answered sensibly. 'To everyone else we would just be a normal couple getting married. People are used to seeing us out and about together, and I think it's caused quite a bit of confusion.' He chuckled. 'Until you and I became friends, the rumour that I was a raving poofter was going around the hospital like wildfire. But now they don't know what to think.'

Charlotte smiled now too. 'Yes, and I think they all thought that I was rather strange too, because I never had any boyfriends.'

'So there you are then. I rest my case!'

'I suppose it *could* work. You might even get your promotion if you were married,' she said musingly. 'I'll think about it.' And they then both pretended to turn their attention back to the food in front of them, although they seemed to have lost their appetites now.

* * *

After dropping a chaste kiss on Charlotte's cheek when he saw her to her flat later that evening, Joseph hurried away. With her mind in turmoil, Charlotte let herself into the darkened flat and stood looking about. Everywhere seemed so empty without Libby and she missed having someone to chat to. But even so, what Joseph was suggesting was a huge commitment. She had made a conscious decision never to get romantically involved with a man, *any man*, ever again. She had been determined that from now on she would be entirely self-sufficient and concentrate on her career. But what she hadn't reckoned with was the loneliness. Oh, her mother and Brian were always at the end of the phone admittedly, and when she found time to visit them for the odd weekend they always made a fuss of her, but that wasn't like having someone here in London; someone to come home to.

A picture of Joseph's handsome face flashed in front of her eyes as she dropped heavily into a chair without even bothering to put a light on. There had been a time when almost every nurse in the hospital had set her cap at him – until the rumours about him being a homosexual had started to circulate, that was. Strangely Charlotte had never thought of him in a romantic light, he had just developed into a very dear friend, almost like the older brother she had never had. And he *was* remarkably kind and easy to get along with. She realised that she had a lot of soul-searching to do.

A week later, Charlotte was no closer to reaching a decision. She had seen Joseph on a number of occasions but he hadn't mentioned the subject of marriage again, which she was grateful for. He wasn't the sort of man to persuade her into doing something she wasn't happy about. Sometimes she even wondered if she had imagined the whole thing. Had Joseph really proposed to her? For the majority of the time she could see the sense in his suggestion. At other times she realised that she would be making a huge commitment to a man whom she didn't love – at least not in the way a wife was supposed to love her husband. But then if she was to go through with it, theirs would be no ordinary marriage anyway. It was more like an arrangement between friends that would suit them both.

She decided to make a list of the things she liked and disliked about him, so grabbing a pencil she chewed thoughtfully on the end of it for a moment and began.

Likes

The way he always makes me feel safe when I'm with him.
The smell of the Old Spice aftershave he wears.
His dry sense of humour.
His kindness and compassion.

Dislikes

?

She drew a blank on this one, which didn't make things any easier whatsoever. It was at times like this that she wished she had someone to talk to and confide in, but apart from Libby there was no one. It certainly wasn't something she could discuss with her mother. She knew that Hilary would have been distraught at the thought of her daughter entering into a loveless marriage – but surely even that would be better than being faced with a life of loneliness?

She finally reached her decision the following day. It happened as she was hurrying home from work following a very long shift on the maternity ward. She had watched two beautiful babies being born that day and could hardly wait now for the time when she would be responsible for bringing the children into the world herself. She was very close to becoming a qualified midwife. Her thoughts as usual when she was off duty were full of Joseph and her head was down as she rushed through the teeming streets. And then suddenly someone tugged at her handbag and she instinctively clung onto it as she looked up into the dilated pupils of a young man who appeared to be high on drugs, or drunk at the very least.

'Let it go, you stupid bitch,' he screeched as Charlotte wrestled with him. 'Else I'll knock your fuckin' 'ead off.'

'No! *Go away!*' Charlotte screamed, praying that someone would come to her assistance. Couldn't people see what was happening, or did they just not care?

And then he punched her smack on the nose and she was so shocked that it knocked her off balance and she fell heavily to the ground, releasing her hold on the bag. The youth turned to run, but before he had a chance, someone caught him by the scruff of the neck and shook him as a dog would shake a rat.

'Why, you little lowlife. Haven't you got anything better to do than pick on women half your size?'

Charlotte looked up through a haze of tears to see Joseph dangling the lad with his feet off the ground. He dropped the bag and Joseph threw him away from himself in disgust.

'Go on – be off with you, and think yourself lucky I haven't marched you straight off to the nearest police station,' he shouted after him as the youth sprinted away.

A small crowd was gathering by then as Joseph stooped to pick up her bag and help her to her feet. Blood was pouring from her nose and she felt dizzy.

'Are you all right?' His face was creased with concern as she unsteadily swiped the hair out of her eyes and brushed her coat off.

'Y–yes, I'm fine,' she managed, glancing at her knees and the holes in her stockings. 'I just want to go home.'

Taking her elbow, Joseph gently walked her to the kerb and hailed a cab.

'B-but I'm almost home now,' she objected.

'So you are, but you're not up to walking there after the shock you've just had. I want to get you home and check you over,' he said in a tone that brooked no argument.

As a black cab pulled up at the kerb he shepherded her inside then passed her his handkerchief. 'Hold that on your nose,' he instructed, and she gratefully did as she was told, wondering what she would have done if Joseph hadn't happened along.

'It was lucky you came by when you did,' she told him shakily.

'It wasn't luck – I'd just been round to your flat,' he informed her as he placed a protective arm about her shoulders. 'When you weren't in, I guessed you'd be working late so I decided to come and meet you. It's getting so that it's not safe for a woman to be out on her own around here any more.'

Still badly shaken she merely nodded as the cab wove its way in and out of the traffic until it finally came to a halt outside her flat. Joseph quickly paid the driver before ushering her inside her home and pressing her into a chair.

'Now you sit there,' he ordered her. 'I'm going to make you some hot sweet tea and then I'm going to check those cuts on your knees. You must have fallen quite heavily.'

'They're only grazes,' she told him in a small voice, but actually she found it was quite nice to have someone fussing over her.

He was back in no time and once she had finished her tea he lifted her skirt and undid her suspenders. Colour burned into her cheeks. 'Wh-what are you doing?' she said.

He glanced up at her. 'I can hardly have a proper look at those knees with laddered stockings stuck to them, can I?' he answered calmly. She felt herself relax. Joseph had gone into doctor mode and she could have been anybody. Just another patient that needed treating.

He bathed her knees free of any dirt and grit and nodded with satisfaction when he saw that they were indeed merely grazed.

'There are no deep cuts, so they should heal nicely,' he commented. 'Right – let's have a look at that nose now.' Tilting her chin, he then examined her face before telling her, 'Well, luckily it doesn't appear to be broken, but I'm afraid you're going ot have two lovely shiners in the morning.'

'Oh, no! What shall I tell them at work?' Charlotte groaned as she raised her hand to one of her eyes. It was swelling nicely and was very tender.

Joseph rinsed his hands in the bowl of water he had placed at her side. 'You won't need to tell them anything because you won't be going anywhere for a few days.'

'But—'

He glared at her. 'There will be no buts. You're staying at home until I say you're well enough to go back to work, and that's an end to it.' He wagged his finger firmly at her and she grinned despite herself.

'Now,' he went on, 'I'm going to run you a nice hot bath. I'm then going to make you a snack, and once I've got you tucked up in bed

I shall stay the night in Libby's old room – if you have no objections. I certainly don't want to leave you alone after what's happened.'

Charlotte was actually quite relieved. The experience with the handbag snatcher had unnerved her more than she cared to admit, and it would be nice to think that there was someone there with her.

'That will be nice. But I'll have to make the bed up.'

'I am more than capable of doing that myself,' he said primly. 'Where are the sheets and blankets?'

'In a chest in Libby's old room.'

'Right, consider it done – but first I'll get that bath on the go for you.'

Charlotte leaned her head back against the cushions and smiled meekly. Joseph could be quite masterful when he chose to be.

Two hours later she was tucked up in bed with a hot-water bottle listening to Joseph pottering around the flat turning lights off.

He had just one week left until he had to vacate his flat, but suddenly she knew that it wasn't going to be a problem. In the morning she would tell him that she would accept his proposal of marriage.

'Are you quite sure about this?' he asked anxiously over breakfast.

She nodded, realising that she must look a terrible sight. Just as Joseph had predicted, she had two black eyes this morning and her nose was swollen too, which didn't make for a very pretty picture.

He had cooked her two soft-boiled eggs, but even opening her mouth made her wince with pain.

'Yes, I'm sure,' she said quietly and he squeezed her hand across the table and grinned from ear to ear.

'Why, that's wonderful news!' He suddenly became serious. 'Just so long as you realise that this will be a marriage in name only.'

Charlotte shrugged. 'It's the only sort of marriage I would want,' she answered truthfully. 'After what Harry did to me I never want to get close to a man again – not in that way, at least.'

Joseph was saddened. Charlotte was such a beautiful young woman. He was sure she could have had any man she set her cap at, but it was obvious that her scars went deep. He glanced at the clock then and hastily began to fiddle with his tie.

'Look, I shall have to shoot off otherwise I'm going to be late for work,' he told her. 'But we'll talk more this evening. I'll come back as soon as I've done my shift and I'll bring us something to eat. Meanwhile I don't want you stepping foot outside of this flat. Do you hear me, Nurse Hayes?'

Smiling ruefully, she fingered her swollen face. 'Yes, Doctor Branning. I'm hardly going to venture far looking like this, am I? Do you think you could just ring the ward for me and tell them what's happened?'

'Consider it done.' He shrugged his long muscular arms into the sleeves of his jacket. 'And when I come back I'll bring some ointment for your knees as well. We can talk about the plans for the wedding then too.'

He plonked a perfunctory kiss on the top of her head and seconds later the door slammed behind him. Charlotte bit her lip. She had just agreed to become Joseph Branning's wife and she had absolutely no idea at all if she had done the right thing. Only time would tell.

Chapter Thirty-Two

'So what are you going to tell your mother and your stepfather?' Joseph asked that night as they balanced Chinese takeaways on their knees.

'I've been thinking about that all day.' Charlotte swallowed a mouthful of beansprouts. 'And I've come to the conclusion that it might be best not to say anything at all until we've done the deed.'

When Joseph raised an eyebrow she explained, 'If we were to tell them, Mum would want a big fuss. I am her only child, after all, so she'd probably want a long white dress and a veil and all the works. I'm afraid I'd feel rather a hypocrite going through all that palaver given the circumstances, so it might be better if we just slipped out and did it quietly at the Register Office and then told them when it's done and dusted.'

Joseph could see the sense in what she said but he still felt quite guilty. After all, every girl dreamed of a big white wedding, didn't she? But then Charlotte wasn't every girl. And this was no ordinary wedding.

'Well . . . if you're quite sure that you could settle for that,' he said.

She nodded. 'I am quite sure. In fact, I don't even want to tell Libby. She'd be as bad as my mother for wanting a bit of a fuss.'

'In that case I'll call in at the Register Office and see how soon it can be done.'

He made it sound almost like going to the dentist, and Charlotte grinned. 'At least give this face time to heal,' she chuckled. 'I don't want to look like the Bride of Frankenstein.' And then on a more serious note she told him, 'You know, if ever you wanted to be with your er . . . friend permanently, I wouldn't mind.'

Joseph lowered his eyes. As it happened, he was very fond of the man that he saw from time to time, but they both knew that their feelings could never come to anything. He was another doctor at the hospital who to all intents and purposes was a respectable married man, and Joseph knew that he would never risk his marriage and career by 'coming out'.

'The same goes for you. If you were ever drawn to another man who could make you happy in the normal sense, I would agree to a divorce immediately. You might just decide that you want another child.'

Charlotte snorted. 'Huh! There's about as much chance of that happening as a snowball's chance in hell, but it's nice that we can be honest with each other. No, Joseph, there could never be another baby for me. The cradle will stay empty if I can't have Daisy in it.'

They then ate the rest of their meal in silence as they each contemplated their future together.

Two nights later, Charlotte answered the door to find Libby standing there with a worried frown on her face.

'So it *is* true,' she said appalled, as she stared at Charlotte's distorted face. 'I heard someone say that you'd been attacked and I couldn't rest until I came around to see for myself. What happened?'

Charlotte told her about the bag-snatcher over a glass of wine.

'The bastard, attacking a defenceless woman!' Libby seethed. 'Thank God that Joseph came along when he did or Lord knows what might have happened.'

She was so incensed that Charlotte couldn't help but smile. Libby had changed her image yet again and now her hair was done in a bouffant style and flicked up at the ends. She had so much eye make-up on that she resembled a Panda, but then that was Libby. As Charlotte had discovered, she was a slave to fashion.

'I'm on the mend now,' she told her optimistically. 'And I'll be back at work next week, so there's no real harm done.'

Libby became very quiet then and as she thoughtfully swirled the wine around her glass, Charlotte sensed that there was something else she wanted to say.

'What is it?' she asked bluntly.

Libby flushed. 'Actually it's this young nurse at work. She's a friend of mine and I'm afraid she's gone and got herself pregnant. Oh Lottie, the poor kid is absolutely terrified about having to tell her parents, and so . . . well, I know its a cheek, but I wondered if you could . . .'

'You wondered if I could give her an abortion?' Charlotte said dryly as her stomach flipped over.

'Yes, that's about the long and the short of it,' Libby answered lamely. 'I wouldn't dream of asking you under normal circumstances, but the thing is, it wasn't her fault. She went to a party, see, and someone slipped something into her drink. I don't really need to tell you the rest, do I? The poor girl is frantic and talking about going for a back-street job. I've explained to her how dangerous this would be, but I think she'll go through with it if you can't bring yourself to help.'

'I see.' Charlotte poured herself another drink. Under these circumstances would it really be so very wrong to help the girl? 'And how far gone is she?' she asked now.

'She's just missed her second period. Her father is a well-known politician and she's terrified about what will happen if this news should leak out.'

'Then in that case I suppose I could help her . . .' Pictures of all the lost souls back in the convent were flashing once more before Charlotte's eyes. All those girls' lives could have been so different if someone had helped them. Hers could have been too, if her father and her Aunt Edith had not betrayed her. Thoughts of them made the bitterness swell in her chest again but she pushed the feelings aside.

'Just let me get back to work and then I'll borrow the things I need from there,' she told Libby. 'Can you bring her around here – shall we say next Wednesday night? I have Thursday off so she could stay here until it's all over and I'm sure that she's OK.'

'You're a pal, Lottie; she'll be so relieved and grateful.' Libby hugged her. 'I feel awful for asking you, but I knew you'd understand. Thank you.'

Charlotte briefly thought of telling Libby about the wedding, but changed her mind. The fewer people who knew about it the better until it was all over, and then hopefully not too many questions would be asked.

261

When Libby had gone, Charlotte began to think of the girl who would be coming to visit her the following week. It seemed strange that she was studying to bring babies into the world by day yet taking their lives away by night. This would be the second abortion she had performed, but she didn't feel guilty about it. The babies that were delivered in hospital were wanted more often than not; Libby's and this girl's babies might have ruined their lives if they had gone ahead with the pregnancy. Convinced that she was doing a kindness, Charlotte tried to put it from her mind. She had quite enough to think about for now as it was.

Charlotte returned to work the following Monday. The bruises on her face were fading by then and she managed to disguise them with make-up. The Ward Sister asked her how she was, but other than that no one made a fuss or commented on her being off. Charlotte was now literally just weeks away from sitting her final exams, and if she passed them she would then be a qualified midwife and all her years of hard work would have come to fruition. It was an exciting prospect and she was determined to succeed.

Joseph took her out for a meal that evening but she didn't really enjoy it. By then she was painfully aware of what she was going to do to Libby's friend in less than two days' time now. She briefly thought of telling Joseph about it but decided against it. He had been very understanding about the abortion she had performed for Libby, but he might not be quite so accepting of her performing one for someone who was a virtual stranger.

Joseph picked up on her mood and put it down to pre-wedding nerves. It was clear that Charlotte's mind was elsewhere, so he avoided any talk of the wedding and as soon as they had eaten he dropped her back at her flat with a kiss on the cheek before hurrying away.

Libby arrived punctually with her friend at seven on the dot on Wednesday as arranged. Greta, as the girl introduced herself, was a bundle of nerves as Charlotte ushered her into the flat.

Like Charlotte, she was a tall natural blonde, with a heart-shaped face and the deepest blue eyes that Charlotte had ever seen. She was also remarkably well-spoken, and it was instantly apparent that she had had a very good middle-class upbringing. Her eyes flicked nervously about the flat as she perched on the very edge of the settee with her hands folded primly in her lap.

'You don't have to look so frightened,' Charlotte told her encouragingly. 'I'm sure everything will be fine, and in less than twenty-four hours' time it should all be over. But are you completely sure that you want to go through with this?'

'Oh *yes*.' Despite the girl's terror she nodded vigorously. The alternative was just too terrible to think about. Her parents would disown her if they ever found out that she was pregnant, even though it had been none of her doing.

'Then I just need to ask you a few questions before we begin.' Charlotte went through the list of things that she wanted to ask and when the girl had answered to the best of her ability, Charlotte led her to Libby's old room which she had all prepared and ready for her.

'I need you to strip off from the waist down and lie on the bed,' she told her as Libby looked on fearfully. All this was bringing back memories that she had tried in vain to forget.

'Do you want me to stay and help?' Libby asked now.

Charlotte patted her hand understandingly. 'No, you wait out there. You can run the bath if you want to do something. It shouldn't take long.'

Greta left early the next morning in a cab that Charlotte had called for her. The unborn child had come away from her in the early hours of the morning, and she had held on to Charlotte and sobbed with relief and regret.

'I shall never be able to thank you enough,' she told her with genuine feeling. She was still sore and in considerable pain, but at least it was all over now. 'My life as I know it would have been over if I had been forced to go on and have the baby.'

'Well, you must try and put it behind you now. Just take the painkillers as I told you and in a few days' time you'll start to feel better.' Charlotte hugged her as she saw her into the cab then hurried away to tidy the flat up, hoping once again that she had done the right thing. Joseph was going to start moving some of his things in later that evening, and at the moment Libby's old room looked like a bloodbath. It wouldn't do for him to see it like that.

'You seem a lot chirpier tonight,' he commented as he heaved a box containing some of his medical journals into the hallway later that evening.

'Yes, I am.' Charlotte picked up some of the lighter luggage and took it to what was to be his room, which was now spick and span once again.

'Good, because I have some news for you. I've managed to get us a slot to get married at the Register Office.'

'*Really?* When?'

'At one o'clock, a week this Saturday. How does that sound to you?'

Charlotte gulped deep in her throat. She hadn't expected it to be quite so soon, but then if they were going to go ahead with it, she supposed there was no point in delaying.

'That sounds fine,' she assured him as her mind went into over-drive. A week on Saturday! She hadn't even been shopping for an outfit yet. Not that it was that important. She doubted that Joseph would notice what she wore. It was hardly going to be a conventional wedding, or marriage for that matter.

'I was lucky enough to get a cancellation,' he went on. 'I thought that if I'm going to be living here within the next few days, it was a case of the sooner the better. We don't want to set tongues wagging any more than they already are, do we?'

'No, I don't suppose we do, but being called Mrs Branning is going to take some getting used to.' She grinned suddenly. 'But come on, let's get your things put away and then we can eat. I've cooked us a shepherd's pie.'

'That's what I like to hear,' he teased. 'You're domesticated already.'

The following week, Charlotte had a shopping trip to Carnaby Street, and in a small boutique there she found a suit that she felt would be just right for the wedding. It had a fitted skirt that just skimmed her knees, and a short jacket with threequarter-length sleeves that fastened with two large buttons at the front. It was ivory and actually very simple, but it put Charlotte in mind of a Dior one she had seen Jackie Kennedy wearing on the television and she fell in love with it at first sight. To go with it she bought a pair of cream high-heeled shoes and a matching bag. Then on the way home she wondered why she had gone to so much trouble. There would be only Joseph to see it and she was sure that he wouldn't much care what she wore.

Later that day he moved the rest of his things in and she found that she quite liked having him about the place. He was more than willing to do his fair share of the housework and the cooking, and she felt that the arrangement would work well.

In no time at all the big day arrived and Charlotte was surprised at how nervous she felt as she prepared to go to the Register Office. She dressed and took especial pains with her make-up before joining Joseph in the lounge, where he was staring from the window waiting for the cab he had ordered to arrive.

'Why you look lovely, my dear,' he told her when she emerged from her bedroom. 'Here, let me pin this onto your jacket for you.'

She was touched to see that he had bought them both buttonholes: a carnation for him and a pale pink rose for her. 'Should I have got you a posy too?' he asked, looking concerned.

'Not at all,' Charlotte assured him. 'Under the circumstances I scarcely think we need to go over the top, do you?'

He looked guilty then. 'You know, you don't have to go through with this,' he told her. 'If you want to change your mind it isn't too late and I'd quite understand.'

'I don't want to,' she assured him as the cab's horn sounded outside. Then snatching up her new bag from the chair she asked with a grin, 'Shall we go and get married?'

An hour later they stood on the steps of the Register Office looking slightly bemused.

'Crikey, that was quicker than a trip to the dentist's,' Charlotte quipped as she fingered the thin gold band on her finger. They had asked two people off the street to stand in as their witnesses and now they could hardly believe that they were really husband and wife. In name at least.

'Er . . . what shall we do now?' Joseph looked slightly ill-at-ease

265

as he folded their marriage licence and placed it in his pocket. 'Would you like to go for a meal or something?'

'Actually, I wouldn't mind just going home, if that's all right,' Charlotte answered. 'I've got so much swotting to do with this final exam coming up that I really ought to get down to it.'

'In that case, would you mind very much if I went out for a few hours? My friend, the doctor I told you about, is in the city today and he asked me if we could meet up. But only if you don't mind, of course. I haven't made any definite arrangements until I knew what you wanted to do. It feels rather strange to marry you one minute and then rush off and leave you the next.'

'You go. I can make my own way home,' Charlotte told him, wondering if this was the strangest marriage that had ever taken place. She had just become Mrs Joseph Branning and now her husband was about to go off to meet his male lover.

'I'm a very lucky man to have met you, Mrs Charlotte Branning.' He kissed her lightly on the cheek before sprinting away, to be gobbled up by the crowds, and then Charlotte turned and set off in the opposite direction.

Chapter Thirty-Three

December 1968

The snow was fluttering down steadily outside the smart apartment window in Marylebone as Charlotte and Joseph sat down to dinner together one bitterly cold evening. They had moved there almost eighteen months ago following Joseph's promotion to surgeon at the Royal London Hospital, and Charlotte loved the place. It was very grand compared to the flat they had shared in Bethnal Green when they were first married, and during the time they had lived there she had totally refurnished and decorated it to her own taste. The address was just around the corner from Harley Street, and they both felt at home there.

Hilary and Brian had been to stay with them the week before, and so Charlotte and Joseph had been forced to share a bedroom for appearances' sake. They had been reluctant to let Charlotte's parents know that theirs was anything other than a conventional marriage, but it hadn't been a problem. They were completely at ease with each other and Charlotte loved Joseph devotedly as she might have loved an older brother. Their marriage had been a complete success and suited them both down to the ground.

At least once a week, Joseph set off to meet his lover whilst Charlotte pottered around the flat, enjoying a few hours on her own; she accepted it as part of their life together. She was aware that, had she wished to have a relationship, Joseph would have given her his blessing – but her feelings towards men had not changed, and she was quite happy with the way things were. The gold band on her finger kept the wolves at bay, and she found that being married to a well-respected surgeon had its perks. Wherever she went she was treated like royalty and Hilary and Brian loved

Joseph too, although they had been shocked at the speed of the wedding.

'I bet you any money you like she's pregnant,' Hilary had told her doting husband indignantly when they had first been informed that Charlotte was married, but as the months went by and no baby was forthcoming she had been forced to eat her words. At first she had felt quite resentful of the fact that she had been cheated out of attending her only daughter's wedding, but then as she got to know her son-in-law and saw how well he treated her daughter and how happy Charlotte appeared to be, she had forgiven them both and come to love him.

'Yes, my daughter is married to a well-known surgeon in London,' she would boast, and Brian would look on with an amused twinkle in his eye.

Now that their visit was over and they had gone back to Leamington, the flat felt strangely empty. They had all gone to see the controversial musical *Hair* at the Shaftesbury Theatre with its shocking, full-frontal nudity, and for a boat-trip on the Thames as well as visiting Madame Tussaud's Waxwork museum. It had been fun, and Charlotte was in a contented mood as she served the meal. That day, she had delivered healthy twin boys and a lovely baby girl, and was still smiling as she recalled the delight on the parents' faces at first sight of their offspring. The thrill of delivering a healthy baby never seemed to wane. She loved being a midwife and never regretted her choice of career for a second. Of course, there were days when things went wrong, and it wasn't such a nice job. Just the day before, she had delivered a stillborn baby boy and she had cried with his parents although there was nothing at all anyone could have done to prevent it. But for the most part she was content and very well respected, even though she was one of the youngest midwives on the maternity unit.

Now after placing a bowl of roast potatoes in the centre of the table she sat down and glanced at Joseph. He looked preoccupied and she asked, 'Is everything all right, love?'

'What?' He dragged his thoughts back to the present and forced a smile. 'Oh yes – everything's fine, thanks. What sort of a day have you had?'

Charlotte immediately launched into a description of the babies she had delivered but after a while she sensed that he wasn't listening to her. He was pushing his food around his plate which was strange in itself. Joseph usually had a very healthy appetite.

'Look,' she said eventually, 'it's more than obvious that something is bothering you. Can't you share it with me, Joe?'

They usually shared everything, and Charlotte guessed that it must be something very important.

'As a matter of fact . . . there is something.'

Charlotte set her knife and fork down as she waited for him to go on and gave him her full attention.

'It's er . . . Michael. I met him during my lunch-break today and he told me that he's being transferred to a hospital in the Midlands – the George Eliot in Nuneaton. Do you know of it?'

'I do, actually. Bedworth, where I was brought up, is quite close to it,' Charlotte said as her heart ached for him. Michael was his doctor friend and the love of his life. It was all so sad.

Like Joseph, Michael hid behind the façade of being a respectable married man, knowing that he and Joseph could never openly be together. Charlotte had met him and his wife socially on a number of occasions and liked them both immensely, although she had sometimes felt sorry for Elsa, Michael's wife, who had no idea whatsoever of her husband's tendencies; they had even had two children together. A dainty little woman with amber eyes and dark hair, she had an infectious laugh which Charlotte found appealing. But now Michael was leaving and Charlotte knew that Joseph would be bereft without him.

'I'm sorry, Joe.' The words seemed so inadequate but she could think of nothing else to say. Instead, she leaned across the table and squeezed his hand.

He shrugged. 'It's just one of those things, isn't it? Michael and I go back a long way but we'll just have to accept it.'

'Unless you could get a transfer there too,' she said hesitantly. She hated the thought of leaving her life in London, but if it made Joseph happy she would be prepared to move. After all, they must need midwives in Nuneaton as well as here.

He shook his head. 'I've already made enquiries,' he confessed rather sheepishly. 'But there's only one post going begging – although . . .'

'Although what?'

'Well, there is a vacancy for a GP at a practice in the town.'

'But you are a qualified orthopaedic surgeon,' Charlotte objected. 'Wouldn't it be a bit of a demotion, becoming a GP?'

'Not at all.' Joseph was looking at her hopefully now. 'In fact, I'd quite like a change,' he rushed on. 'To be honest, being part of a surgical team can be very political sometimes – you know, hierarchial – and I'd like to try something completely different. It would mean going on a few courses, but it shouldn't be a problem. But only if you were prepared to move – and if you could get a job too,' he ended rather shame-facedly.

Charlotte quietly stood up and walked across to the window, glancing around the room as she went. There was a wall-to-wall fitted Axminster carpet on the floor, with a dark brown background and large orange flowers scattered all across it. Charlotte could clearly remember the day the carpet fitters had come to lay it; she had thought it was the height of luxury. A Dralon three-piece suite covered in orange cushions was set out around the television set, and crushed velvet curtains hung at the windows. In the corner, the Christmas tree that she and Joseph had chosen from the market the night before was now standing in a sturdy bucket covered in baubles, with its twinkling fairy-lights lending a cosy feel to the room. She had made this apartment into their home.

Tweaking the heavy net curtain aside, she looked down into the street below. Taxis and cars were whizzing by and the pavements were teeming with people, many of them loaded down with bags as they did their Christmas shopping. The whole place was alive with sounds and smells that she instinctively knew she would never find anywhere else. She loved living in London . . . but she also loved Joseph too, in her own way.

'Can I have until after Christmas to think about it?' she asked.

Joseph nodded eagerly. 'Of course. You can have as long as you like, and— Well, I don't want you to feel that you're being bullied into anything. I shall stand by whatever you decide.'

She nodded before walking into the kitchen to fetch the dessert she had bought from the baker's on the way home. Their main course was cold now.

* * *

270

Their Christmas was spent quietly at home. They cooked a traditional Christmas dinner with all the trimmings and when it was eaten they curled up on the settee together and watched *The Wizard of Oz* and ate chocolates until they were sure that they would burst.

On Christmas evening they took a brisk walk hand-in-hand, and no one seeing them would ever have guessed that they were anything other than a normal, happily married couple. They were deeply attached, and easy in each other's company – but now Charlotte found herself faced by yet another dilemma. Did she love Joseph enough to follow him back to the Midlands or was it time to make a life here by herself? Part of her baulked at the thought of being so close to her hometown. What if Harry was out of prison and back there and she should bump into him? And Daisy – her beautiful Daisy – was somewhere in the Midlands too, but Charlotte was sensible enough to realise that she could pass her on the street and not even recognise her now. Her baby girl would be coming up to eleven years old now.

It was not an easy decision to reach.

The following evening, Joseph was called into work to perform an emergency operation after a traffic accident, and Charlotte found herself at a loose end. There was nothing on the television that she wanted to watch so she wrapped up warmly and took a stroll down Regent Street, to Piccadilly Circus and then along the Embankment. Everywhere was unusually quiet, but then it was Boxing Day and Charlotte guessed that most people would be at home with their families. The snow was still falling softly, making the normally grubby streets look unusually clean and fresh, but it was bitterly cold and she had just decided that she would head for home when she heard a noise coming from a large cardboard box on the inside of the pavement. It had sounded like someone crying.

Pulling her scarf more tightly about her throat she peered through the snow, calling, 'Hello? Is anyone there?'

The noise stopped abruptly so Charlotte inched closer. She could see the opening of the box and what appeared to be a young girl huddling inside it.

'Are you all right?' Throwing caution to the winds Charlotte bent down and extended her hand but the girl shrank away from it.

'Go away! Leave me alone!' There was a catch in her voice and Charlotte scowled. The poor thing must be freezing in there. She knew that some people slept rough under Waterloo Bridge, but they were a community who kept themselves to themselves.

'Don't you have anywhere to go?' she asked but got no reply.

Charlotte waited patiently.

For a time it seemed that the girl wasn't going to answer her but then she cautiously stuck her head out of the box, and in the flickering light from the streetlamp, Charlotte saw that the girl looked barely older than fourteen at the very most. Her hair was flattened to her head with damp and she was shivering uncontrollably.

'Have you eaten today?' Charlotte asked, and when the girl shook her head Charlotte straightened up before saying, 'Then you'd better come with me.'

The girl hesitated before slowly crawling out of the box to stand in front of her. She looked so sad and pathetic that Charlotte's heart went out to her. 'Look, why don't you come home with me?' she suggested kindly. 'You could have a bath and something to eat, and I'm sure I could find you some dry clothes. They'll be a bit big for you, but at least they'll be dry.'

Again the girl hesitated but then she inched closer, and Charlotte hailed a taxi.

Back in the warmth of the Marylebone apartment, the girl's eyes stretched wide with surprise as she stared about the cosy room.

'Cor, this is lovely,' she said between chattering teeth, moving nervously from foot to foot.

'I'm glad you like it but I want you to get out of those wet clothes before you catch your death of cold,' Charlotte told her. 'I'll run you a bath and then when you're warm and dry, we'll see about getting you fed. Come along.' She knew that she was mad for allowing a complete stranger into her home. She was probably a street girl and a thief, but it was Christmas, after all, and no one deserved to be alone at such a time.

Whilst she was running the bath she collected a spare dressing-gown and nightie and laid them across the chair in the bathroom.

Then going into the girl she told her, 'It's all ready for you. Take as long as you like.'

The girl hovered uncertainly, torn between taking a warm bath and making a run for it. The bath won in the end and she trotted off to the bathroom hardly daring to believe her luck. Charlotte put some chicken soup on the top of the oven to heat and cut some thick slices of crusty bread before spreading it generously with butter; then she sat back and waited.

The girl emerged half an hour later with her cheeks glowing and her hair freshly washed as she clutched Charlotte's dressing-gown about her.

'Thanks for that,' she mumbled as she eyed Charlotte warily.

'Right, you look like a good meal wouldn't go amiss.' Charlotte carried the soup and the plateful of bread and butter to the table and the girl sidled onto the chair. Charlotte could almost see her mouth watering and she finished the lot in seconds. Charlotte refilled her dish and again the food vanished.

'That was just the job, missus. Real good grub. Thanks a lot.' The girl rubbed her stomach, and leaned back in her chair as Charlotte sat down opposite her.

'So how about you tell me how you came to be sleeping in a box by the river on this cold night, especially so close to Christmas?' she said softly.

The girl stiffened and for a moment Charlotte thought she was going to clam up but then she shrugged.

'I'm pregnant,' she said bluntly, and her eyes welled with tears which she angrily swiped away. 'I live in Stepney wiv me mum an' dad, but when Mum found out I was up the duff she told me to clear off before me dad found out. He'd kill me stone dead if he knew.'

Charlotte stared at her sympathetically. It was the old story – yet another young girl with a baby on the way that would ruin her life.

'Me name's Annie, by the way,' the girl told her now as she rubbed at her nose with the back of her hand, and then she rushed on, 'There's nine of us in our 'ouse in Stepney, and 'alf the time me mum don't know where the next meal is comin' from. Dad's a boozer, see? So I decided . . .' she lowered her eyes and flushed . . . 'to go on the game an' give the money I made to Mum. It worked for a time and kept us goin' till I slipped up, but now . . .' Her voice trailed away.

'How old are you, Annie?' Charlotte asked gently, appalled at what she was hearing.

'I'm fourteen, nearly fifteen.' The girl sighed deeply. 'I was plannin' on workin' in one of the clubs up Soho when I left school, but I don't know what's goin' to happen to me now. I ain't even got the money to get rid of it.'

'But you wouldn't have to pay,' Charlotte told her. 'Surely you know the Abortion Act came into effect this year? It's legal now, but you would need to get consents from two doctors before the operation.'

Annie's head wagged from side to side. 'Two doctors? Nah, I couldn't do that. I'd be too ashamed.'

'Then I could take you. Would that help, if someone was with you?' Charlotte offered.

Again the girl said adamantly, 'No, thanks all the same but I'd rather . . .'

'You'd rather what?' Charlotte asked with concern as she saw the girl's growing agitation.

'I'd rather do away with myself than have to do that.'

'Oh Annie, you can't *mean* that!' Charlotte was horrified and the girl was openly crying now.

'I do – I *swear* it. I've been thinkin' of ways to do it an' all.'

Charlotte's mind was working overtime. Here was yet another victim, and somehow she sensed that the poor kid meant what she said.

'Then perhaps I could help you,' Charlotte said quietly. 'I'm a midwife, you see. But only if you *really* want to get rid of the baby, that is?'

'Oh, I *do*.' Annie's eyes were popping. She could hardly believe her luck. If only she could get rid of the baby she could go back home and she'd be more careful in future. She'd learned a lesson she wouldn't forget in a hurry.

'But why would you do that for me?' she then asked suspiciously. 'I ain't got no money to pay you.'

'As I've just explained, you don't need to pay for abortions any more. And let's just say that once I found myself in your position,' Charlotte replied. 'I went through with having my baby, only to have her taken off me shortly after she was born. It changed my life and I wouldn't wish the agony I've gone through on anyone.'

Her mind was racing ahead now. Joseph was likely to be gone all night so the chances were, if she helped this girl, Annie could be gone by morning and he need never know about it.

'Do you want me to help you then, or will you consider going through the proper channels?'

'I'd let you do it,' the girl said immediately, and so without another word Charlotte rose and began to collect the things she would need.

Very early the next morning Charlotte escorted the girl down to the foyer of their apartment block. Annie was pale and shaky, but the worst was over now and she was dressed in some clean clothes and a coat that Charlotte had given her.

She pressed some money into the girl's hand and smiled sadly. 'Get yourself a cab home with that,' she urged. 'You're still weak and you'll need to take it easy for the next few days, but for goodness' sake just tell your mum that you've got a bad period. If you're unlucky and get an infection, go straight to a hospital and tell them you had a miscarriage. If anyone ever knew what I had done, my career would be finished.'

'Ta.' Annie suddenly hugged her. 'I reckon you've saved me life. I won't forget this. Ta-ra now.'

Charlotte watched the girl step out onto the snowy street then hurried away to remove all signs that Annie had ever been there. What Joseph didn't know he wouldn't worry about.

Chapter Thirty-Four

'I've been making enquiries and it seems that there is a vacancy for a midwife on the maternity unit at the George Eliot hospital,' Charlotte told Joseph early in the New Year.

They had been hunting for bargains in the January sales and were just emerging from Selfridges, clutching several bags. Charlotte was more than ready to walk the short distance home and put the kettle on.

'Really?' Joseph stared at her with hope shining in his eyes. 'Does this mean that you might consider moving there?'

In his usual considerate way he had not mentioned the move once all over Christmas. He would never pressure Charlotte into doing anything she wasn't happy about, but she knew him well enough by now to know that he had thought of little else. She could see it in his eyes every time she looked at him. Michael had already left London, and Charlotte sensed that Joseph was missing him. The two men had always been very discreet about their relationship, meeting once a week in a small hotel down in South London. Charlotte had accepted it without question. She had known from the day they married that Joseph was involved with a man and she had never let it trouble her. Their marriage had worked well for both of them and they were surprisingly fond of each other. So much so that Charlotte could not imagine her life without him now; which was why she had decided to go along with his suggestion.

'I've already applied for the post,' she told him, and saw his whole face light up – attracting more than a few admiring glances from women who were passing by. Joseph really was a remarkably handsome man. Marriage and security suited him. He could have had the women falling at his feet, but Mother Nature had made him prefer men.

'*Really?* Do you mean it?' He lifted her off her feet and swung her around as if she weighed no more than a feather there and then in the middle of the busy street, and people who saw him do it thought what a perfect couple they made. If only they could have known the truth.

'In that case I shall need to apply for the family doctor post.' His eyes were bright with excitement.

'And we'll have to look for somewhere to live. I think we should buy a house now. How would you feel about that? I have quite a bit saved up and we could easily afford the mortgage.'

Now it was Charlotte's turn to get excited. Their very own house – it sounded wonderful! They could perhaps find one with a nice little garden and then she could have some pets. She had always loved animals but had never been in a position to have any. Her father had forbidden it, and since moving to London she had always lived in rented accommodation. Perhaps it was time to put down some roots?

The couple walked down Oxford Street, their minds full of the changes ahead. Both agreed it was a good start to the New Year.

Over the next weeks they spent every weekend in Nuneaton and eventually found a house that was just perfect for them. It was a small three-bedroomed detached property, quite close to the hospital where Charlotte would be working, and they fell in love with it at first sight. It was quite a modest house, but to Charlotte it was a palace. The garden sloped down to the banks of the canal, and although the house was dated inside, Charlotte was full of ideas of what she would do to it. Both she and Joseph had been successful in getting their new posts, and now it was just a matter of handing their notice in and packing.

Suddenly Charlotte found herself looking forward to the move. After all, as much as she loved their apartment in London, it was still only a rented property – but the house in Nuneaton would be theirs. It was a thrilling prospect.

They moved in the first week of April. Charlotte had now passed her driving test and treated herself to a Mini some months before, and so she drove them to Nuneaton with a furniture van following on close behind.

When the van was unloaded and the removal men had gone, with a fat tip tucked into their top pockets, Joseph opened a bottle of champagne.

'To the new house!' he said as the cork popped, and he poured the fizzing liquid into mugs. They hadn't unpacked the glasses yet but it didn't matter. They duly toasted their new house and their new jobs, then set about unpacking some of the boxes, wondering how they had managed to accumulate so much stuff. Neither of them was due to begin their new jobs for another two weeks and Charlotte was determined to spend the time settling in.

Within a week everything was unpacked, but the house looked very bare.

'We ought to go shopping for some more furniture,' Joseph remarked as he glanced around the sparsely furnished lounge.

'I quite agree, but first I want us to get a dog.' Charlotte grinned at him. 'The lady next door was telling me that there's a place in Caldecote where they take in stray dogs. I think we should go and have a look first thing tomorrow.'

'If that's what you want,' Joseph agreed indulgently. Charlotte didn't often ask for anything, and on the rare occasions when she did he found it hard to refuse her.

They set off bright and early the next morning and found the sanctuary easily. It was a lovely sprawling old house with a large kennels at the side of it, and the gentleman who greeted them could not have been friendlier.

'I don't want one too big,' Charlotte explained to him, 'because I shall be working. But I'll be close enough to get home to check the dog during my lunch-hour so he won't be left alone all day.'

'Hmm.' The man patted his chin thoughtfully. 'I don't actually recommend anyone who works having a dog,' he disclosed. 'The dogs tend to get lonely if they're left alone for too long. But if you were to take *two* dogs, that would be a different matter entirely. They keep each other company when you are out then, you see?'

'Two!' Charlotte looked taken aback, but she could see the sense in what he said. She mulled the idea over.

'As it so happens I might have just the two you're looking for,' the man went on with a cheeky grin. 'They came in last week. It was a very sad case. An elderly lady owned them, but sadly she passed away and as they've never been parted I'd like to place them together.'

'Oh, what sort are they?' Charlotte asked.

'They're little Westies – cute as buttons and friendly as they come.' He chuckled. 'Between you and me, the wife has taken a real shine to them and I reckon she'd keep them herself if I gave her half a chance. Would you like to see them?'

Charlotte glanced at Joseph and when he grinned she nodded. 'Yes, please.'

Mr Treadwell, as the man then introduced himself, led them towards a long low building from which the sounds of dogs barking was coming. Once inside Charlotte's eyes filled with tears. Pens ran the length of either side, and they were almost all full of dogs of every shape and size who flung themselves at the wire doors to attract their attention.

'Oh dear,' Joseph muttered ruefully. 'I can see us going home with half a dozen at this rate.'

They walked on until Mr Treadwell stopped in front of one particular pen, saying, 'Here they are then.' After fumbling with his keys he opened the door and the next moment two furry snow-white little bodies hurled themselves at Charlotte and began to lick every inch of her that they could reach.

Mr Treadwell chuckled. 'Meet Milly and Max,' he said. 'It looks like they've taken a shine to you already.'

Charlotte's heart melted at the sight of them. The dogs were adorable and she knew that she could love them.

'Oh Joe, they're just gorgeous,' she breathed, as she dropped to her knees to hug and pet them. 'I don't think we need to look any further. They're just perfect. May we have them – *please*?'

Joseph scratched his head. 'Looks to me like we don't have much choice in the matter,' he commented with a smile. 'I think they've already decided they're coming home with us.' He then went off with Mr Treadwell to fill in all the necessary paperwork and half an hour later, Milly and Max were in the back of the Mini on their way to their new home.

Charlotte was positively bubbling with delight and Joseph was pleased to see her looking so happy. They called into a pet shop and bought beds, dishes, food, toys and anything else they thought the new additions to the family might need, and then before they knew it the dogs were racing around the lawn of their new garden with their tails wagging furiously.

'Life doesn't get much better than this,' Charlotte sighed blissfully as she stood with her arms crossed, watching the dogs frolicking on the lawn.

Joseph felt a sharp pang of guilt. She looked lovely standing there with the sun turning her hair to spun gold. Charlotte was a beautiful woman yet she was totally unaware of the fact, which was part of her charm. He knew that she would have made a wonderful mother and often felt sad for her. She deserved a real husband and a real marriage. But what she had gone through in her early years had left mental scars and he knew that she would never have any of those things. She had put up barriers that no normal man would ever be able to cross, and staring at her now he thought it was a crying shame.

Within a week, Milly and Max were well and truly settled in and Charlotte couldn't imagine being without them. All the pent-up love that she had kept locked inside for her baby for so long was poured onto her pets and Joseph knew that she adored them.

On the morning that she started her new job at the hospital, she wept when she had to leave them and Joseph was concerned.

'You don't have to work if you don't want to, Lottie,' he told her kindly. 'I earn more than enough to keep us both and I'd be quite happy for you to stay at home.'

Charlotte bristled as she swiped away her tears. 'I appreciate the offer,' she told him indignantly. 'Thanks, Joe, but I have worked hard to become a midwife and as much as I hate to leave the dogs I have no intention of giving up on my career just yet. I'm just being silly, I suppose. I'm sure Milly and Max will be just fine.'

He shrugged helplessly. There didn't seem to be much else he could do.

Charlotte settled into her new job in no time at all and quickly formed a routine. In her lunch-hour each day she would rush home to spend it with Milly and Max and the arrangement seemed to work so well that she soon wondered why she had ever worried in the first place.

Almost before they knew it, they were into summer. She and Joseph took the dogs for long leisurely walks along the canal in between redecorating their house, and Charlotte began to enjoy the slower pace of life. In fact, to her surprise she found that she didn't miss London at all!

It was one evening when Joseph had gone off for his weekly meeting with Michael when there was a knock on the front door. Charlotte sighed impatiently. She was in the middle of painting the skirting boards in the back room ready for the new carpet she had ordered that was due to be laid the following week, and she resented the interruption.

Laying the paintbrush down, she headed for the front door wondering who it could be. She certainly hadn't been expecting visitors. When she opened the front door she found Elsa, Michael's wife, standing on the doorstep, and she flushed with embarrassment. She was dressed in an old pair of paint-spattered jeans and a T-shirt, and was very aware that she looked a total wreck, whereas Elsa looked immaculately groomed as usual.

'Why, Elsa, how lovely to see you,' she gushed, trying her best to hide her surprise. 'Do come in and do please excuse me being in such a mess. I wasn't expecting visitors. I'm painting in the back room.'

To her surprise, Elsa swept past her into the lounge without a word of greeting, her face tense.

Charlotte awkwardly closed the door behind her then rubbing her hands down the sides of her jeans she asked, 'Is anything wrong?'

'*Wrong?* How can you stand there so calmly and ask me that?' Elsa was clearly agitated as she fumbled in her handbag, withdrew a cigarette and lit it.

Charlotte waited quietly, her heart in her mouth. She had an awful feeling that she was going to hear something that she didn't want to.

Elsa dragged deeply on her cigarette, then gazing at Charlotte through a haze of smoke, she asked, 'Have you *any* idea at all what our husbands have been up to?'

'I er . . . what do you mean?'

'I mean that our husbands have been seeing each other,' Elsa spat. 'Do you understand? They are *lovers*!'

'Oh.' Charlotte wasn't sure how she should react. Should she tell the truth or deny all knowledge of it?

'They are together even as we speak,' Elsa rushed on. 'But for the last time. I shall tell Michael that I want him to leave, and that if he continues to see Joseph I shall expose them for what they are – *homosexuals*.' Her eyes filled with tears now and her hands began to shake. 'We've been married for seventeen years – *seventeen years* – and I've given him two lovely children. I had no idea what was going on until today. Can you believe that? I must have been blind.' The tears spilled over now and raced down her cheeks. 'I thought we were happy,' she said brokenly. 'But all the time I must have been just a front for him.'

'I'm sure that isn't true,' Charlotte objected gently. 'Michael loves you, anyone can see that, and he adores your children.'

'But obviously not as much as he adores your husband!' Elsa was alternating between despair and anger, and Charlotte felt at a total loss. What could she say to ease the poor woman's pain? She herself had gone into her relationship and marriage with Joseph knowing exactly where she stood, but it must have come as a terrible shock to Elsa.

'Let me go and get us a glass of wine,' she said weakly, and now Elsa almost snapped her head off.

'A glass of wine? Do you *really* think a glass of wine is going to make this situation any better? It would have been bad enough to find out that Michael was having an affair with another woman – but *a man*! How am I ever going to hold my head up again? And what am I supposed to tell my children? "Oh I'm so sorry, darlings. Daddy is leaving because he has a *boyfriend*"?'

Her eyes narrowed then as she studied the guilty look on Charlotte's face and her mouth dropped open. 'Oh my God – you *knew*, didn't you?'

Charlotte nodded miserably. There seemed no point in lying now. The mood Elsa was in, she was bound to drag it out of her anyway.

'But I . . . I don't understand.' Elsa dropped heavily onto the nearest chair, shock mirrored in her eyes. 'How could you marry him, knowing this about him?'

'It's a bit of a long story, and even if you don't need that glass of wine, I certainly do.' Charlotte scuttled away and returned minutes later clutching a bottle of red wine and two glasses whilst Milly and Max looked on with their ears down. They had picked up on the atmosphere and sensed that something was wrong.

She poured out a large glass each then slowly began to explain how she had met Joseph when she was working at the Royal London Hospital. 'He admitted that he was homosexual,' she told Elsa. 'I knew that he had someone he was close to, but I didn't know at that time that it was Michael. Ours has always been a marriage of convenience. What I mean is we don't . . . you know? We have a platonic marriage and it works for us. I often wondered if you knew about their relationship too, but I never liked to ask you.'

'But why would a beautiful woman like you tie yourself down to a queer?' Elsa asked incredulously.

'I suppose we were just two misfits who came together for the companionship,' Charlotte told her in a small voice. 'Something happened to me when I was very young and after that I knew that I would never get married, not *properly* married. And then I met Joseph and I enjoyed his company so I thought, why not? It was better than facing a life of loneliness.'

Elsa shook her head in disbelief. It was all so much to take in. Her whole world had just fallen apart in more ways than one. 'So you are sitting there calmly telling me that their relationship doesn't disgust you?'

'We can't help the way we are made. I accept Joseph for what he is,' Charlotte answered quietly.

'Well, *I* won't accept it.' Elsa's eyes were blazing with fury now. 'Unless . . . you could see your way clear to helping me out with another problem I have, that is.'

As Charlotte gazed at her blankly Elsa rushed on, 'The thing is,

I've just found out that my teenage daughter is pregnant.' She gulped deeply but forced herself to go on. 'It came as quite a shock. Catherine is just fourteen years old and very bright. We were hoping that she would go on to university when she finished boarding school, but now . . . Well, I don't have to tell you that her life will be ruined if she goes ahead with this, do I? So the long and the short of it is, if you will help her out of her predicament, I will let Michael go quietly. If you don't, I shall expose both him and Joseph, and they will both lose their reputations as well as their jobs. No doubt you would too.'

'But that's blackmail,' Charlotte said hotly.

'Oh come now, that's rather melodramatic, isn't it? You're a midwife, for goodness' sake! You must know what to do. My life with Michael is over, but surely you wouldn't want my daughter's life to be over too before it's even properly begun?'

'But you could get an abortion done legally,' Charlotte objected.

Elsa snorted. 'Oh yes? You know what it's like in the medical profession – it's a small world and everyone knows everyone. Her secret would be out.'

'But there is such a thing as patient confidentiality,' Charlotte pointed out desperately.

'Yes, you're quite right, there is – for Joe Bloggs off the street – but not when there's a doctor's daughter involved!'

Charlotte stared back at the woman, seeing no way out. It was obvious that Elsa meant every word she said.

'Very well then,' she agreed eventually. 'I'll do it – but only because you leave me no choice. Bring her round here tomorrow evening at seven o'clock.'

Relief washed across Elsa's face as she placed her glass down and rose. She looked like a woman with the weight of the world on her shoulders, and Charlotte couldn't help but feel sorry for her. What with her daughter's pregnancy and discovering about her husband's homosexuality, she must be going through hell.

'Couldn't you find it in your heart to accept Michael for what he is?' she asked softly. 'Your marriage has worked up to now. Does this really have to change it?'

Elsa stared at her as if she had taken leave of her senses. 'I could never bear to let him touch me again now,' she breathed in disgust. 'If you choose to live with a freak, then that's up to you. Goodnight, I shall see you tomorrow evening.'

And then she swept unsteadily from the room, leaving Charlotte reeling with shock.

Chapter Thirty-Five

Joseph was home early that evening looking as if the end of the world had come. He was surprised to see Charlotte curled up on the settee with Milly and Max, nursing a large glass of wine and looking not a lot happier than he felt.

Charlotte broke the silence. 'I've had a visit from Elsa . . . She knows about you and Michael.'

Joseph was appalled. He had always tried to keep that part of his life away from Charlotte as much as he could, but now she had been dragged into it.

'I'm sorry,' he muttered shamefacedly. 'Was she very angry?'

'I'm afraid she was, but I've just realised she didn't tell me how she found out.'

'She came across a note I sent to him in one of his jacket pockets when she was getting it ready to go to the dry cleaners.' Joseph looked the picture of misery. 'It just said what time I would be meeting him and where, so she went along to the hotel and made a few enquiries. I hadn't signed my name so Elsa assumed that he was having an affair with another woman. When she found out that it was me he met there each week, she challenged him about it and he broke down and admitted everything.' Joseph ran a hand distractedly through his thick hair. 'Apparently she'd had her suspicions that he was having an affair for some time – since long before we left London. I suppose it was because he went out at the same time on the same night every week. We should have been more careful, but unfortunately it's too late to do anything about it now. He doesn't think we should see each other again and Elsa has told him he has to leave. She's asked for a divorce so he's staying in a hotel tonight. Everything is such a mess and I'm just sorry that you've had to become involved.'

'I'm afraid it's even worse than that.' Charlotte took another gulp of wine. 'It turns out that their daughter, Catherine, is pregnant and Elsa has told me that if I don't get rid of the baby for her she'll tell everyone why she's kicked Michael out.'

'But that's blackmail!' Joseph went at least three shades paler. 'I won't let you do it.'

'Oh, so you're prepared to risk all three of us losing our careers in medicine and our reputations, are you?' Charlotte snapped more sharply than she had intended to. 'I don't have a choice, Joseph. If this leaks out we'll all be ruined, and she won't take the girl for a legal abortion because she's too scared of word getting out . . .' Strangely, Charlotte had felt no guilt about the young girls she had helped up to now. Their lives would have been ruined had she not helped them. But since abortions had been legalised she had thought that she would never have to do it again.

Seeing the sense in what she said, Joseph clenched his fists with frustration. Just a few hours ago everything had been perfect, but now it was ruined and the life they had shared happily together was at risk.

'It doesn't seem right or ethical that you should have to do this,' he said.

'Well, it won't be the first time I've done it, or the second if it comes to that,' she shrugged. 'I was hoping that now abortion has been legalised, I would never be put in this position again, but what choice do I have? I've seen too many young girls' lives ruined through unwanted pregnancies and I don't feel at all guilty for helping them. It's not as if I'm doing it for gain . . . But what about you and Michael? I know how much he means to you.'

'That's well and truly over now,' he said. 'As much as Michael thinks of me, he'll put his family first. He adores his children – and his wife, if it comes to that. I have to accept that we won't see each other again. I don't want to make things any worse for him. I'm just hoping that once Elsa is over the initial shock, she'll take him back.'

'Huh! I wouldn't count on it,' Charlotte remarked caustically. 'Think about it – I went into this marriage fully aware of your relationship with Michael. But Elsa feels that she's been betrayed in the worst way possible, that all her married life has been a sham – and can you really blame her?'

'I suppose not,' Joseph mumbled miserably, and then turning he went upstairs leaving her to her thoughts; there seemed precious little else to say now.

'She *will* be all right, won't she?' Elsa fretted the next evening as Charlotte ushered her and her daughter upstairs. She had everything ready for them and just wanted to get the night over and done with now. Catherine was a younger version of her mother. Tearful and terrified, she looked so vulnerable that Charlotte couldn't help but feel sorry for her. Elsa didn't look much better, her eyes were red-rimmed from crying and she was a bag of nerves, nothing at all like the happy, sophisticated woman that Charlotte remembered. She was still wearing the clothes she had worn the night before, and with her face devoid of make-up she seemed to have aged overnight.

'Let me explain what's going to happen,' Charlotte said as she guided Catherine into the spare bedroom where the bed was made up with a waterproof sheet. She quickly told them what she was going to do and what would happen afterwards, and Elsa turned so pale that Charlotte was afraid she was going to faint.

'It might be better if you waited downstairs,' Charlotte suggested, but Elsa shook her head.

'No, I want to stay with her. Will it take long?'

'Just a matter of minutes,' Charlotte assured her. 'And then we wait until the foetus comes away from her. It should all be over by morning.'

Elsa's face hardened then as she glanced around and spat, 'And where is *he*?'

'It's quite all right. Joseph is staying elsewhere tonight. You won't have to set eyes on him,' Charlotte said steadily. 'But now let's get on with it, shall we?'

By three o'clock in the morning a very shaken Catherine was sitting on the settee sipping hot sweet tea with the ordeal behind her.

'I suppose I should thank you,' Elsa said coldly.

Charlotte was not offended by her tone. The woman had gone through so much in the last couple of days that it was no wonder she scarcely seemed to know if she was coming or going. 'There's

288

no need to,' she replied. 'Just take your daughter home now, give her painkillers and get her to rest for a few days.'

With a curt nod the woman guided the girl out of the door and towards her car.

As Charlotte closed the door behind them, she sighed with relief. Catherine had screamed so loudly that Charlotte had been terrified that the neighbours would hear. They might well have done, but if they commented on it she would tell them that a friend who had had a terrible nightmare had been staying for the night. That should satisfy them. She yawned now as she slowly climbed the stairs to clean up the mess. She was due at work in less than five hours' time but she wanted to put the house to rights before Joseph returned the next morning. Hopefully she would have time for a quick nap before her next shift.

Whilst Charlotte was with Catherine, Joseph stared morosely from the window of a motel less than three miles away. The rain that had been threatening all day was now pouring down in torrents. 'My Boy Lollipop' was throbbing through the thin adjoining wall, but he heard and saw nothing as he stared sightlessly into space. He had suffered agonies of guilt all day about what Charlotte was being forced to do. Was it time to end their relationship? he wondered. And yet the very thought of living without her filled him with dread.

Joe had known since a very young age that he was different to other boys. When they had become attracted to girls *he* had found himself becoming attracted to *them*, and even then he had known that it was wrong. But there was nothing he could do about it. Once in his early teens he had walked a girl home from a school dance and kissed her. He wanted to be normal – to be like the other boys – but the kiss had done nothing for him at all, whereas when he saw other boys in the showers after PE he would become aroused and have to turn away from them to hide his erection. He had gone through every kind of agony because of his sexual preferences and felt like a misfit; an outcast. And then Charlotte had come along like a breath of fresh air and made no demands on him. All she had wanted was companionship and friendship, and for the first time in his life she had allowed him to appear to be a normal man to the outside world. He had never been like Michael, who was able to find pleasure with either sex. But then he knew that Charlotte would not have wanted that. She had made it clear from the very beginning that she never wanted a man in her life in the sexual sense ever again. And so they had fulfilled a need in each other, but now he wondered if it was enough.

He had spoken to Michael that very morning on the phone in the privacy of his office at work, and for the first time had realised that he could never be as important to him as his wife and family were. Michael was a broken man, bereft at losing his wife and children, and he had made it categorically clear that their affair was well and truly over. But to Joseph, Michael had been everything.

So what now? he asked himself. Should he release Charlotte from her commitment and spend the rest of his life alone, or could they go on as they had before? He determined to let her make the ultimate decision and abide by whatever she decided. He owed her that much at least.

Over the next few days, the couple had endless heart-to-heart talks and eventually they decided that they would try to go on as before. To the outside world what they shared might have been classed as weird, but in their own way they loved each other.

Four weeks later, Charlotte heard on the grapevine that Elsa and Michael were back together and she was glad for them, although she felt sorry for Joseph. Of course, no one knew why they had broken up in the first place. Elsa had been true to her word there. Charlotte guessed that their relationship might never be the same again, but she hoped for the sake of their children that they would make it work. She and Joseph went on as before too, just as they had agreed, but somehow the sparkle had gone out of him now and she wondered if it would ever return. They still had their home and their dogs, their careers and even each other up to a point, and both of them realised that this was going to have to be enough.

Chapter Thirty-Six

Just two months later, Charlotte hurried to the locker room one evening to get changed following a long shift to find a young student nurse sobbing her heart out there.

She paused then crossing to her she asked kindly, 'Boyfriend trouble, is it?'

The girl, a pretty brunette with amber eyes, sniffed and nodded. 'You could say that. He's dumped me because I told him—'

'You were pregnant?'

The girl's eyes widened as she stared back at Charlotte fearfully.

'And I suppose now you want to get rid of it and try to forget that this ever happened?'

Another nod.

'Then why don't you have a termination?'

'I've already been to the doctor but he refused me one on medical grounds. I – I have a slight heart murmur. Our doctor is of the old school. He believes that babies should be born in wedlock and made me feel like something that had crawled from under a stone. I was so ashamed, I couldn't bring myself to go to another doctor now.'

'But why didn't you get yourself on the pill?' Charlotte asked.

The girl shrugged. 'Same reason as I didn't want to go to the doctor about this, I suppose. He's so old-fashioned and he would have condemned me for sleeping with a boy before marriage.'

'Then I suggest it's time you changed your doctor,' Charlotte told her matter-of-factly.

The girl broke into a fresh torrent of tears then, and despite having promised herself she would never perform another abortion, Charlotte felt herself softening. She scribbled down her address and passed it to the girl.

'Look, have a think about it, and if you're still quite sure this is what you want, come to my house at seven o'clock on Wednesday evening. I might be able to help you. Oh, and be prepared to stay the night.'

The girl looked as if she had just had all her prayers answered. 'What – you mean you'll really help me?' she asked incredulously. When Charlotte nodded she leaped up and hugged her fiercely. 'Oh, thank you!'

'It must be strictly on a private and confidential basis, though. No gossiping!' Charlotte warned her sharply. 'This is my career at stake if word got out.'

'I understand,' the girl answered earnestly, stuffing the address into her coat pocket. 'Goodnight – and God bless you.'

She hurried away as Charlotte stood there with the words ringing in her ears. *God bless you*. But would He? She would be taking yet another life. But then she would be giving the girl *her* life back. When she looked at it that way, she really couldn't believe that she was doing anything wrong. The babies that she aborted were not going to be loved or wanted and planned for, like the ones she delivered in the hospital on a daily basis, so surely she was doing a kindness?

'I'm not standing in judgement of you,' Joseph told her worriedly when she explained what she intended to do and asked him if he would mind staying at the motel again overnight. 'But you do understand that if you were to get found out, you could go to prison? Especially if something went wrong.'

'It won't go wrong,' she said confidently. 'I know exactly what I'm doing – and who else has this girl got to turn to?'

He shrugged, feeling seriously concerned now, but he didn't argue. There would have been no point. Once Charlotte had made her mind up, there was no changing it.

To Charlotte, the first Christmas in their new home was just about as perfect as it could be. Hilary and Brian came to stay with them for a few days the week before, and begged Charlotte and Joseph to go back to Leamington to share Christmas with them, but Charlotte was determined to spend this first Christmas in her own home. Hilary accepted her decision with good grace. Charlotte was a very independent woman now and devoted to her career. She had an air of confidence about her and was highly respected in her job, and Hilary was proud of her although she did drop more than the odd hint that it would be nice to have some grandchildren, which made Joseph's cheeks glow.

'Oh, there's plenty of time for that. I still have a lot of work to do on the house yet.'

Charlotte passed it off but Joseph felt guilty nonetheless. He was sure that Charlotte would have made a wonderful mother but that would never happen whilst she stayed with him. Even so she seemed quite happy with things the way they were, and as long as that continued, who was he to rock the boat? Hilary and Brian obviously had no idea that their marriage was anything less than conventional and that was how Charlotte wanted it to stay.

They went for long walks along the frozen canal with Milly and Max, collecting sprigs of holly covered in fat red berries, and Charlotte put the Christmas tree up in the middle room and covered it in twinkling fairylights. Joseph had paid to have a smart new tiled hearth fitted in that room with an electric fire and everywhere looked warm and inviting. On Christmas Day they stayed in together and had a traditional Christmas lunch, and if there was a faraway look in Joseph's eyes sometimes as he thought of Michael, Charlotte chose not to comment on it.

February 1975

The next five years passed in the blink of an eye. Thankfully, Charlotte wasn't called on to perform abortions now as the new birth pill became more easily available. Some young girls were even opting to go ahead with keeping their illegitimate babies now and Charlotte was sure that this was a sign of changing times. There was no longer the stigma still attached to unmarried mothers as there had once been, although many narrow-minded people still frowned on them.

Everything seemed to be changing. Just that week Margaret Thatcher had been appointed as the first woman Prime Minister of the United Kingdom.

'I'm still not sure that a woman will be up to the job,' Joseph remarked one evening as he read about her in the newspaper.

'Oh, you're just old-fashioned,' Charlotte shot back. 'Times are changing, Joe, and personally I think for the better. Why *shouldn't* women have as good jobs as men?'

Charlotte was now thirty-five years old and at the peak of her chosen career. She had long since lost count of the number of babies she had delivered, but she still got a thrill each time she helped a new little soul into the world, especially when the babies were wanted. She still thought of her own baby all the time and found it hard to picture what she might look like. Daisy would be a young woman now and Charlotte hoped that she was happy wherever she was.

Charlotte and Joseph had added another dog, a springer spaniel they named Ben, to their family, plus two cats called Pickles and Mustard, and Joseph often joked that the place was turning into an animal sanctuary. They had found the cats as tiny kittens, abandoned along the banks of the canal when they took the dogs for a walk one day, and Charlotte had taken them home and nursed the frail little creatures back to full health. Ben had just turned up on the doorstep one day, a bag of bones, with his coat matted and with the most soulful brown eyes that Charlotte had ever seen. Needless to say he had quickly joined the fold too and now they all lived together in harmony.

On the whole both she and Joseph were content and if either of them felt that there was something missing in their lives they never mentioned it.

Charlotte had just got in from work one evening when the phone rang. Joseph was doing a late surgery at the practice where he worked in Riverslade Road, so Charlotte hurried to answer it, laughing at Pickles and Mustard as they rolled around the floor together on the way.

'Hello,' she said after she had lifted the receiver.

'Charlotte – is that you?'

She instantly recognised her stepfather's voice and the smile slid from her face. He sounded upset. 'Yes, it's me. Is everything all right, Brian?' For no reason that she could explain, her heart began to thud as she waited for him to answer.

'Well, actually, no it isn't. It's your mum. She's had a heart attack and they've rushed her into the Royal Hospital in Leamington. I think you should get there as soon as you can, love. I'm afraid it isn't looking good and I'm just going there now.'

'I'll be there,' Charlotte choked as shock washed through her like iced water. She slammed the phone down and slid her feet back into the shoes she had kicked off only seconds before. Then she hastily wrote a note for Joseph, snatched up the keys to the latest Mini and raced outside, leaving all the house lights blazing. Unfortunately, she hit all the rush-hour traffic so it took her an hour and a half to get to the hospital, and then another ten frustrating minutes before she could find which ward they had taken her mother to. She was shivering with cold by then as she hadn't even waited long enough to put her coat on.

'Mrs Mason has been admitted to the Coronary Intensive Care Unit,' the highly made-up, snooty receptionist behind the desk eventually informed her, and Charlotte raced away without even thanking her, looking for signs that would lead to the unit along the way.

At last she located it, only to find that the double doors were locked. She pounded on them and eventually a nurse appeared.

'My mother came in a short while ago,' she babbled breathlessly. 'Mrs Hilary Mason.'

'Oh, I see. You'd better come in.'

Why did the nurse look so sad? But Charlotte was too intent on finding her mother to give it much thought.

'Would you mind waiting here for a moment?' the nurse said now. 'I'll go and fetch Sister to have a word with you.'

She hurried away and it was as she was standing there nervously wringing her hands together that Charlotte became aware of the sound of someone crying. Without waiting for the nurse to return, Charlotte walked round the corner, where she saw Brian. He was sitting on a hard plastic chair with his face in his hands, and her stomach did a somersault. Why wasn't he in with her mother?

'Brian?'

He started at the sound of her voice and before she knew what was happening, he had jumped up and wrapped her in his arms.

'I'm so sorry, love,' he sobbed. 'But you're too late . . . She's gone.'

295

Charlotte felt the ground rise up to meet her, and had it not been for Brian's arms around her she was sure she would have fallen flat on her face. As a nurse she was no stranger to death. She had delivered babies who had died in their mother's arms within minutes of them being born, and stillborn babies who never took a breath – but this was different. This was her mother, and the pain she was feeling was almost unbearable.

'B-but I came straight away.' She shook her head in disbelief. 'I would have been here sooner, but it was the traffic you see . . .' She realised that she was babbling but seemed unable to stop herself.

'Shh,' he soothed as he stroked her hair gently and again it struck her what a wonderful man Brian really was. Even in grief he was trying to put her feelings first.

'If it's any consolation to you, it wouldn't have mattered how quickly you came. She had already gone when I got here after ringing you, and I was only a matter of minutes after the ambulance. It was a massive heart attack. They said it would all have been over in seconds, so that's something at least. I couldn't have borne to see her suffering.'

He started to weep again. Great wracking sobs that shook his sturdy body and they clung together for comfort.

Shortly afterwards, they were shown into Hilary's room. The nurses had washed her, and lying there she looked so peaceful that Charlotte could almost believe that she was merely asleep; that at any second she would wake up and give them one of her lovely smiles.

'She was very proud of you, you know,' Brian said brokenly as he stroked his wife's hand. It was already cooling and he could hardly believe that she had really gone from him.

'It's so unfair,' Charlotte said shakily. 'You made her so happy, Brian, but you had such a short time together.'

'Ah, but the thing is, I would rather have had the short time I spent with her than a whole lifetime with someone else.' He wiped his eyes. 'You see, your mother was the only woman I have ever loved so I consider myself to be a very lucky man. We packed more love into our marriage than most people could experience in a lifetime. I don't know how I'm going to go on without her.'

'Don't talk like that,' Charlotte begged as a cold finger ran up her spine. Brian was calm now, too calm to be natural. 'I want you to come back to stay with me and Joseph tonight. I wouldn't want you to be on your own.'

He shook his head. 'I appreciate the offer, love, really I do, but if it's all the same to you I'd rather be on my own if you don't mind.'

The door swung open then, cutting their conversation short, and Joseph appeared looking flustered and concerned. He had arrived home shortly after Charlotte had set off for Leamington and immediately followed her.

He instantly hugged Charlotte and patted Brian on the back before saying awkwardly, 'I'm so sorry. I'll wait outside while you say your goodbyes and then I'm going to get you both home. You can leave your cars here – neither of you will be fit to drive. A couple of my colleagues will come back with me tomorrow to collect them for you.'

But Brian held up a hand. 'Thanks for the offer, Joseph, but I'd rather drive home by myself if you don't mind. I already said my goodbyes before Charlotte arrived so I'll leave you to it now.'

He bent and kissed Hilary's cold cheek tenderly then with a nod at Charlotte and Joseph he left the room.

'I'm not happy about him being all on his own,' Charlotte fretted. She couldn't shake off the terrible sense of foreboding that had wrapped itself around her like a cloak.

'I'm afraid you don't have any say in the matter,' Joseph pointed out. 'Grief affects everyone differently and if Brian wants to be alone we should respect his wishes.'

The journey home was a nightmare. Charlotte hugged herself miserably as memories of her mother flashed in front of her eyes.

She was very proud of you, Brian had told her, but what had Hilary had to be proud about really? Charlotte was evaluating her life now and she didn't much like what she saw. She had almost gone through with an abortion at an early age then gone on to give birth to an illegitimate baby that was then taken away from her. Then she had met Joseph who was a homosexual and she had entered into a marriage of convenience with him because it suited them both and because she was frigid. Admittedly she had worked hard to attain her dream of becoming a midwife, but how would her mother have felt had she known of all the babies her daughter had illegally aborted? Admittedly, she hadn't performed any abortions for some time now. But even so, the more she looked back on her life the less there seemed for anyone to be proud of.

Joseph tried to reach Brian all the next morning on the phone to discuss the funeral arrangements whilst Charlotte sat locked in her own little world of grief.

'I shall go over there in the next hour if he doesn't answer soon,' he said worriedly, but he didn't have to because shortly afterwards the police from Leamington rang and Charlotte could tell by the look on Joseph's face as he took the call that it was yet more bad news. Somehow she had been expecting it.

'It's Brian, isn't it?' she said as he placed the phone down.

Joseph nodded. 'I'm afraid it is, love. The neighbours have been calling around all day to try and check on him but they couldn't make him answer the door, so eventually they rang the police, who broke in. Brian is dead too. It appears that he took an overdose shortly after getting home from the hospital last night. I'm so sorry. If only I'd listened to you and made him come home with us, this wouldn't have happened.'

'It's not your fault,' she answered. 'I think Brian knew what he was going to do. But at least they're together again.'

Joseph was at a loss what to say to her. He knew how much her mother and Brian had meant to her, and now they were both gone.

'I'll make all the necessary arrangements,' he promised. 'Just leave everything to me.'

She nodded numbly. And then it hit her. Joseph was all she had left in the world now – and her animals, of course.

Chapter Thirty-Seven

December 1990

Charlotte bent to stroke the dogs before going off to the hospital. Sadly, Milly, Max and Ben had long since passed away, but the house was still bulging with animals that she had adopted. Snatching up her coat, she planted a swift kiss on Joseph's cheek. She knew that it would probably be late that evening before she saw him again, as he was on call that evening.

'See you later, darling.' He returned the kiss affectionately and as she hurried out to her car she found herself thinking how lucky she was. She and Joseph had knowingly entered into a very unconventional marriage, yet somehow it had worked for them and they had grown together over the years. Looking back, she could see they had started to grow closer after the death of her mother and Brian. Joseph had been her rock, organising the funerals down to the very last detail. The only thing that had spoiled his carefully made arrangements had been the arrival of her Aunt Edith, like the Bad Fairy, at the funeral. It had shocked Charlotte to the core to see her there in the church, and to this day she had no idea how the woman could have learned about their deaths. Possibly someone she had once known back in Bedworth was keeping her informed. She was just as hateful as Charlotte remembered, gloating over the double grave – until Joseph had given her her marching orders, that is.

'Have you no respect?' he had asked her coldly.

'Why should I have respect for that *whore*? She deserved to die,' the embittered spinster had spat. 'It was she who caused my dear brother's death, God rest his soul – her and that floozie daughter of hers.'

When she had pointed a trembling finger in Charlotte's direction,

Joseph had taken a firm grip of her scrawny elbow and almost dragged her out of the churchyard, warning her in no uncertain terms what would happen if she ever dared to so much as show her face again. Luckily she hadn't, but it had taken Charlotte a long time to get over the deaths, compounded by her aunt's appearance, and throughout that dark time Joseph had been there for her, dependable and solid as a rock.

Eventually she had begun to mend and come to terms with her loss, and now she was a very well-respected senior midwife; Joseph's practice was thriving too. They spent all their spare together, never happier than when they were in each other's company, which as far as Charlotte was concerned just went to show that sex was only a small part of a marriage, and she was quite content without it. In fact, she was sure that could she still have had Daisy, her life would have been perfect.

On one particular day, by the time Charlotte was due to go home she had delivered four little souls into the world, and one of the births had not been easy. The delivery team were pleased when an emergency caesarian was avoided. She was tired as she walked out of the hospital and down to the car park. It was dark and bitterly cold, and she could hardly wait to get home and have a good strong cuppa and a warm in front of the fire.

'*Please* help me, missus. Me friend gave me your address an' I'm desperate.'

Charlotte stared at the woman who was clutching at her arm as if her very life depended on it. She had been so intent on getting to her car that she hadn't noticed the woman lurking about.

'The thing is, me old man is in nick an' he's due out next month,' the woman whined. 'If he finds out I'm havin' another nipper that ain't his, he'll kill me stone dead. It were Grievous Bodily Harm that put 'im away in the first place.'

Charlotte drew the woman into the shadow of the hospital. The last thing she wanted was this. How on earth had word leaked out about her helping those poor young girls? She had sworn them to secrecy. Should she pretend not to understand? But the woman did look desperate, poor thing.

'I've already got six kids that I can scarcely afford to feed.' The woman was crying pitifully now. 'An' I know I've been a silly cow. I should 'ave kept me legs crossed but yer get lonely when yer old man's away. Please help me, I *beg* yer. Another baby will kill me, I know it will. I'll pay yer, honest I will. I mean, I ain't got a lot but I'll get the money together somehow.'

Charlotte sighed and looked more closely at her. The woman was probably in her late thirties but the hard life she had led made her appear much older. There were worry lines on her face and she was shaking with fear.

'Couldn't you go to your GP and arrange a termination through the proper channels?' Charlotte asked. There was something about this woman that made her feel nervous.

Her eyes wild and terrified, the woman gabbled, 'Oh no, I couldn't do that. Me bloke might get to find out about it an' then I'd be done for. You're me last hope.'

Charlotte shook her head. 'I'm sorry, but I really can't help you,' she told her firmly. 'I'm sure your husband will never know about it if you go through the proper channels. A doctor has to respect patient confidentiality. I suggest you make an appointment at the earliest opportunity, and now if you'll excuse me I really do want to get home.'

She made to walk by the woman who began to cry broken-heartedly now and Charlotte paused. She hated to see anyone so upset and the poor thing really was obviously terrified of her husband.

Eventually she said reluctantly, 'Very well then. Come to my house at seven o'clock next Wednesday evening and I'll talk to you. I'm not promising anything, mind, but be prepared to stay there for a few hours at least. And you'll need to arrange for someone to care for your children. Here's my address. But don't say a word to anyone. *Anyone*, do you understand?'

'Oh God bless yer.' The woman grabbed Charlotte's hand and kissed it. 'I'll get me sister to look after the nippers an' don't worry. I'll not breathe a word to a single livin' soul.'

'See that you don't,' Charlotte replied, and then she turned and walked away. It had been a long time since she had performed an abortion. The woman had made a mistake, but then no one was perfect – so should she be made to suffer for it at the hands of a violent husband? And would helping just one more person be such a terrible thing? The woman was clearly in a desperate plight.

'I wonder if you would mind staying at a hotel on Wednesday evening?' Charlotte said the next evening as she and Joseph sat at supper together. She had given it a lot of thought and decided that she would help the woman – but this would be the very last time. Ever.

Joseph had been off work that day with a streaming cold and she hated to kick him out, but what else could she do?

'Oh Charlotte, no!' His voice was heavy with cold and with concern. He had never interfered before, but it had been such a long time since then, and it was completely unnecessary to do things this way now. Why take the risk? Anyway, he felt so dreadful he didn't relish the thought of a night in a draughty hotel room.

She felt guilty as she looked at his streaming eyes and nose. 'Well, I suppose you could stay if you were prepared to keep out of the way in your room,' she said doubtfully.

'Couldn't you just refuse to do it? Abortions are legal now, and this just doesn't make sense.'

Charlotte lifted her chin with the look of determination that he knew so well. 'I've already agreed to it, and if you met the woman you'd see why,' she informed him. 'She's had a bit of a fling while her husband has been in prison and has ended up pregnant. Her man is due out soon and apparently he's very violent. She's terrified of what he'll do if he finds out, and on top of that she has six children already. How could I *not* help her?'

'It sounds to me like she's an older woman who should have known better,' he rapped out. 'She's hardly some naïve kid, is she, and we could lose everything if you ever got found out! It bothers me that she approached you. Surely she could arrange it through her doctor?'

'She's far too afraid to do that and I want to help her. Mind you, I haven't actually agreed to do anything. I just told her to come round and said that I would talk to her. If I can persuade her to do it legally, I will.'

Joseph sighed resignedly, feeling too unwell to argue but he wasn't at all happy about it.

'Very well then, I'll keep out of the way,' he muttered and the subject was closed.

As arranged the woman arrived punctually at seven o'clock on Wednesday evening, looking absolutely terrified.

'I'm Florence, by the way. People call me Floss.' As she introduced herself, her eyes swept around Charlotte's immaculate little house, which was a palace compared to her home.

Charlotte noticed that her coat, which was a faded red, was worn and shabby and her shoes were down at heel. She was stick-thin too and looked as if she hadn't had a solid meal in months.

'How about we have a cup of tea before we talk?' Charlotte suggested, feeling sorry for the woman despite her misgivings. 'Put your coat over there and make yourself comfortable. I shan't be long.'

Floss shrugged her skinny arms out of the sleeves of her coat and flung it over the back of an armchair, not bothering to pick it up when it landed in an untidy heap on the floor. She had more pressing things to concern herself with at present.

When Charlotte returned some minutes later with a tray of tea and biscuits she found the woman fondling the ears of her latest addition, Sadie, a little Yorkshire terrier.

''Ow do yer manage to keep the place so nice an' neat wi' all these pets?' the woman asked.

Charlotte chuckled. 'Oh, I have a very tidy-minded husband which helps enormously, and I *don't* have six children!' she told her. 'Now help yourself to some tea and biscuits, and then we'll talk, shall we?'

The woman picked up the china cup and saucer and sipped at the tea as she eyed Charlotte warily. She certainly wasn't what Floss had been expecting. Word had it that she was knocking on fifty but no one would have guessed it. She was still a very attractive woman. For some reason Floss had pictured a fifty-year-old midwife as being plump and matronly, but instead Charlotte was slim and her lovely fair hair had barely a streak of grey in it. She wondered briefly if she should come clean and tell Mrs Branning the whole truth, but dismissed the idea immediately. She was so close now to getting this whole sorry mess over and done with . . . and if the woman knew,

303

she would surely refuse to go ahead with it. Things would work out all right – they had to.

'I . . . I'm ready,' she said some minutes later, placing the cup and saucer carefully back on the tray with a trembling hand. She didn't relish the thought of what lay ahead one little bit.

'So, have you thought any more about what I suggested, about seeing your doctor?' Charlotte asked.

The woman's head wagged from side to side. 'I ain't doin' that!' she said emphatically.

'Very well. Follow me then and we'll get you examined.' Charlotte had everything ready for the procedure just in case, although she still had grave misgivings. She couldn't quite put a finger on it, but something felt wrong.

The woman followed Charlotte up the stairs to a little room that overlooked the garden at the back of the house. The whole of the stairs and even the landing was wall-to-wall carpet and she could feel her feet sinking into it. It was a far cry from the holey lino back at her own place.

'So how far gone did you say you were?' Charlotte asked as the woman undressed and clambered onto the bed, eyeing the covered dish full of instruments Charlotte had ready with dismay.

'I didn't – but I'm about two months.' The woman flushed guiltily.

Charlotte began to gently probe around the woman's stomach and after a moment she straightened up.

'I'd say you were four months at the very least, and that puts a whole different light on things,' she said. 'I'm sorry, Floss, but I dare not go ahead. At this late stage there is a greater chance of complications. It could be very dangerous.'

Panic flared in the woman's eyes. 'You've *got* to do it!' she gasped. 'Me old man will be 'ome in the blink of an eye an' if I ain't got rid of it by then I'm done for.'

'I'm sorry,' Charlotte repeated, 'but there is far too much risk involved. You might even be over the time for a legal abortion.'

Floss's face hardened. 'You *will* do it,' she said ominously quietly. 'Otherwise I might just have to pay a visit to the local cop shop an' have a little whisper in their ears. I know enough about you to get you 'ung, lady, so you just get on wi' it *now*.'

Charlotte stared at her in stunned disbelief. 'Haven't you understood a single word I've said?' she snapped, ignoring the woman's threats. 'I'm telling you that this would be incredibly dangerous. Do you *really* want to risk your life?'

'I ain't got no choice. I'm riskin' it anyway, if my Jem finds out.' The woman's head dropped back onto the pillow and Charlotte knew that she was beat. If she didn't see it through, this woman might just carry out her threat and then everything she and Joseph had worked so hard to achieve would be over. Their life together, their jobs, their home, everything. The scandal would be immense. She shuddered and wondered why she had ever got herself into this position in the first place. Hadn't her gut instinct warned her against it? Why hadn't she listened to it? But it was too late for regrets now. All she could do was get on with it and pray that things went well.

She washed her hands thoroughly in the bowl of hot water she had ready, very aware that Joseph was just along the landing in his room, then lifting a lethal-looking instrument from the stainless-steel dish she told the woman, 'I'm afraid that this is going to hurt, but you *must* keep still.'

Floss nodded then took a deep breath as Charlotte leaned over her. She felt the cold steel slide inside her most private part then indescribable pain tore through her and she forced her knuckles into her open mouth to stop herself from crying out. It seemed to go on forever but then she felt warmth on her inner thighs and Charlotte told her, 'That should do it.'

Floss watched Charlotte drop the bloodstained instrument back into the bowl and wash her hands again as agony ripped through her.

She felt as if her insides had gone through a shredder but she remained silent until Charlotte told her, 'Come on, we'll get you into a hot bath now. It should help to ease the pain until the baby is ready to come away.'

As Charlotte helped her across the landing she was concerned to see that Floss was bleeding heavily and dripping blood onto the carpet. She shouldn't be losing so heavily yet, she thought. Within seconds of lowering the woman into the bath the water turned crimson. Floss's eyes were rolling in her head with the pain, but

Charlotte had to admit that she was being very brave. Not that she had much choice. The damage was done now and there was no going back.

This is going to be the very last time I *ever* do this, Charlotte vowed to herself solemnly as she pulled the plug and let the bloody water gurgle away. She hurried away for towels but no matter how many she placed between Floss's legs they instantly turned red. She was losing far too much blood.

'I think we'd better get you back onto the bed so that I can take a look at you,' Charlotte said quietly, and when there was no reply she glanced at her patient's face. Panic set in then. Floss was unconscious, and her breathing was slow and raspy.

'*Joseph!*' Her scream echoed along the landing, setting all the dogs barking, and seconds later Joseph appeared, tying his dressing-gown about his waist.

'Jesus Christ!' He took in the situation at a glance and dropping to his knees he grabbed the woman's wrist and took her pulse. 'She's slipping away,' he said. 'Run and fetch my black bag.'

Charlotte almost tripped over her own feet in her haste to do as she was told.

'Pass me my stethoscope,' he ordered, every inch the doctor now.

All fingers and thumbs she fiddled with the clasp of the bag and passed it to him, and as he listened to the woman's chest, Charlotte could see the fear on his face too.

'We have to get her flat on the floor,' he told her urgently, and between them they somehow managed to manhandle the woman out of the bath. Within seconds the floor was covered in blood that spread in a pool about their knees as they bent over her.

Joseph placed the heels of his hand on her chest and began to compress it there before holding her nose and blowing into her mouth, but it was soon clear that this was doing no good at all.

'I need to get some adrenalin into her.' Pushing Charlotte aside he grabbed a syringe from the side of his bag and a small phial containing a clear liquid, but before he had had time to load it he heard Charlotte give a sob.

'Joseph . . . I think she's stopped breathing.'

He dropped the syringe and felt for a pulse but there was nothing.

He began to compress her chest again and then again and again, until eventually Charlotte laid her hand gently on his arm.

'Joe,' she said brokenly as tears slid down her cheeks. 'You can stop now – she's gone.'

He sat back on his heels, sweat standing out in beads on his forehead as he stared despairingly at the lifeless body in front of him.

'Wh-what happened?' Charlotte was in shock and her face was almost as pale as the woman's now.

Joseph sighed. 'I can't say for sure but it looks to me like her heart gave out.'

The silence was deafening as they sat there trying to take in what had happened. It was Charlotte's biggest nightmare come true. Floss was dead – and it was all her fault.

'What do we do now?' she asked eventually.

'I suppose we shall have to call for an ambulance,' Joseph said. 'We can't leave her lying here, can we?'

Charlotte's heart was beating so fast now that she feared it was going to explode from her chest. 'I *knew* I should never have done it,' she lamented. 'Right from the first second she approached me I had a bad feeling about it. Abortion is legal now,' she rambled on as she hugged herself. 'The other girls I helped – well, they had nowhere else to turn and I couldn't bear to think of them enduring the pain and humiliation that I had to suffer. But Floss – I told her to go through the right channels, that she was putting herself at risk, but she gave me no choice. She was threatening to expose me and we would have been ruined.'

As Joseph looked at her, sympathy raced through him. Charlotte was not a bad person and he knew how much she still grieved for the child she had lost. He couldn't let this destroy her, he just couldn't.

'I suppose we could get rid of the body?' he said shakily.

Charlotte's head snapped up as she stared at him in disbelief. 'What do you mean?'

Joseph was trying to think straight but it was hard, what with his bad cold and the recent trauma. 'Well, no one knows that she was coming here, do they? We could drop her body into the canal at the bottom of the garden and hopefully the current will carry her away from here.'

Charlotte had thought that she knew Joseph inside out but now she looked at him as if he was a stranger.

'Think about it,' he said, as he took her shaking hands in his. 'If she's found here, you're done for – and possibly me too. Everything you've worked for all these years will be gone – *everything*. And all because you tried to help her.'

'When I examined her I found out she was much further on than she'd admit to,' Charlotte told him now. 'So I told her it would be dangerous – unethical – to go ahead with it, but she said that if I didn't she would go to the police. Somehow she knew that I had done this before and I was so scared that I went ahead. I wish to God I hadn't now. If she'd had a saline abortion at the hospital, she'd still be alive. Her poor children Joe!' She started to cry.

Joseph felt compassion for his wife. After all, wasn't he as bad? He had known what she was doing but he had never tried to prevent it.

'I suppose we could try it,' Charlotte said guardedly now. She could see the sense in Joseph's suggestion, as horrible as it was. If she was found out he would be in trouble too and she couldn't bear that.

'Good girl.' He patted her hand. 'Now go and fetch a sheet. We could wrap her in that.'

Charlotte stumbled away and returned minutes later clutching a clean white sheet fresh from the airing cupboard.

They wrapped the body in it as best they could, then he told her, 'You hold her feet, I'll carry her top end.'

Floss had only been a skinny little scrap of a woman, but they soon discovered that a dead body was actually quite heavy. Somehow they managed to manoeuvre the corpse down the steep narrow staircase and into the middle room. The animals were all sleeping in their baskets, but looked up as they part-dragged and part-carried her to the back door where they lay her on the kitchen floor.

Joseph was wheezing and out of breath by then. 'We can't attempt it yet,' he said sensibly, blowing his nose loudly. 'We've got to wait until the early hours of the morning when we're sure that the neighbours are asleep. Meantime we've got to scrub this place to within an inch of its life. There mustn't be a drop of blood left anywhere.

You go and start on the bedroom and the bathroom. Bundle up the towels and everything that you've used, and when we've disposed of the body I'll start a bonfire in the back garden. There will be nothing left to show that she's ever been here. By morning it will be just a pile of ashes.'

Charlotte trudged off to do as she was told, feeling as if she was caught in the grip of a nightmare. She methodically scrubbed every inch of the bathroom until it sparkled and then she cleaned the carpet on the landing before going into the bedroom and doing the same there, bundling up the waterproof sheet and the towels as Joseph had told her to. And then there was nothing to do but wait, and they sat together and watched the minutes of the clock ticking away until two in the morning.

'I think it should be late enough now,' Joseph announced grimly. 'Come on, let's get it over with.'

Panic gripped her and she clutched at his arm. 'Oh Joe, I don't know if I can go through with this.'

He stared at her sternly. 'What other option is there? If we don't, our lives will be in ruins. Now hold yourself together. It will all be over soon.'

He inched the back door open and listened, sighing with satisfaction when nothing but the sound of the night creatures greeted him. A quick glance across the fence assured him that the neighbour's house was in darkness so he nodded at Charlotte and together they carried Floss awkwardly down the garden path. A thick frost had settled on the grass, making it slippery, and they had to tread carefully but at last they reached the end of the long garden. It was pitch black here and Charlotte could no longer see Joseph's face but she heard him when he whispered, 'All right – now lower her into the water as gently as you can then I'll push her further out into the current if I'm able to.'

There was a gentle splash as Floss's poor damaged body hit the water, then Joseph pushed with all his might and they saw the sheet float gently out towards the middle of the canal. And then the current caught at it and as it drifted away they saw it disappear beneath the surface.

'Right, now let's get those things burned,' he said, his teeth chattering with the cold.

They crept back up the lawn keeping a watchful eye on their neighbour's bedroom windows as they went, and soon after they had the soiled towels and bedding piled in a corner. Joseph splashed some petrol over them and struck a match, and seconds later the flames roared into life, sending a shower of sparks up into the black sky.

'Let's get back inside,' Joseph whispered. 'They'll be burned to ashes in no time – there's no point in standing out here watching them and catching our deaths of cold.'

Shock was setting in now and Charlotte nodded numbly as she stumbled up the garden behind him. She could barely see where she was going for the tears that were spurting from her eyes, and she just couldn't believe that Floss was really dead.

'What do we do now?' she asked fearfully once they were inside as Joseph pressed a glass of brandy into her trembling hand.

'We do nothing.' His mouth was set in a grim line. 'But I want you to promise that you will *never ever* do this again, Lottie. I always had a horrible feeling that things would go wrong one day, and one death on our consciences is more than enough to cope with. In our professions you and I are supposed to *save* lives!'

'I couldn't refuse,' she answered in a small voice. She wished that she could turn the clock back, that she had refused to go ahead with the abortion, but it was too late now. What was done was done and there was no going back. Somehow they were going to have to pray that they were not connected to Floss's gruesome death, but worse still, they were going to have to learn to live with what had happened.

Chapter Thirty-Eight

It was gone seven o'clock in the morning before Charlotte and Joseph retired to their rooms, but Charlotte was up again half an hour later. She was far too upset to sleep and at eight o'clock she rang work to tell them that she wouldn't be in as she was sick. There was no way she could have faced anyone just yet. She was sure that they would be able to see what had happened if they so much as looked at her. Did *I* kill her? she asked herself over and over again It was a tragedy, and as she thought of the six children who would be waiting for their mother to come home, the guilt was almost unendurable.

Joseph got up at nine but neither of them could face any breakfast. He took the dogs for a walk down the lawn to check that all the bloodied bedding and towels were properly burned, and when he came back he reported that there was nothing left of them but ashes. It should have made Charlotte feel better but it didn't. Nothing could, and she knew that she would never forgive herself for what had happened.

It was just after ten that morning when a loud rapping sounded on the front door. Charlotte looked fearfully at Joseph and asked, 'Are you expecting anyone?'

He shook his head. 'No, I'm not, but just go and answer it and act naturally. It's probably just someone selling something.'

She wiped her sweaty palms down the slides of her old jeans and then lifting her chin she strode to the door with a fixed smile on her face.

'Hello, may I help—'

'*All right, where is she then?*' An enormous woman cut her words short as she pushed Charlotte aside and strode into the room, her eyes flicking from one place to another.

'Excuse me?' Charlotte snapped indignantly. 'Just who do you think you are, to come barging into my home like this?'

'I'm Floss's sister, that's who I am,' the woman replied. 'All night I've been lookin' after her kids. I've packed 'em off to school an' she still ain't home – so where is she?'

'I think you m-must have m-made a mistake,' Charlotte stuttered. 'I . . . I don't even know anyone by the name of Floss.'

'Don't spin me that bullshit!' the woman exploded. 'An' don't get comin' yer hoity-toity voice wi' me. Our Floss told me exactly where she were goin' an' I know all about yer.'

'And just what is that supposed to mean?' Charlotte was panicking now and trying her best not to go to pieces.

Luckily, Joseph came to the doorway dividing the two rooms just then and the woman turned her wrath on him. 'Are *you* gonna tell me where our Floss is?' she demanded. ''Cos I'll tell yer now – I ain't leaving 'ere till yer do.' She then roughtly elbowed him aside and strode into the back room as Joseph and Charlotte exchanged a worried glance. Floss had promised Charlotte that she hadn't told anyone where she was going, but she had obviously been lying.

They hastily followed the woman into the room and now Joseph said gently, 'I'm sorry, Mrs er . . . but I'm afraid you must have made a mistake.'

''Ave I 'ell as like.' The woman's eyes travelled the room looking for a sign of her sister, and suddenly she gave a triumphant shout. Before they knew what was happening she had bent down and grabbed something from the floor behind the easy chair.

'So if our Floss ain't been 'ere, 'ow do yer explain *this* then?' As she brandished the faded red coat in the air, Charlotte's stomach did a somersault.

She saw the defeat on Joseph's face and the stoop of his shoulders and said desperately, 'Well, actually she *was* briefly here last night, but she left soon after she arrived. You obviously know that she wanted me to er . . . help her, but when I pointed out the dangers she changed her mind and left.'

'Oh yeah? Wi'out her coat? Yer must think I'm fuckin' thick,' the woman stormed. 'Now yer can save the rest o' yer lies fer the police.' And with that she banged out of the house, still clutching the coat.

'Look, it's her word against yours,' Joseph said without conviction.

312

'Who is going to believe the likes of her above you? Just stay calm and deny everything.'

But Charlotte shook her head wearily. 'No, Joe, I can't. It's gone too far for that now,' she told him. 'To be honest it's almost a relief. I was finding it very hard to live with what I'd done. I shall just tell the truth, but I don't want you dragged into it. None of this was your fault. All you did was try to help her.'

'But I'm as involved as you are,' he pointed out. 'I knew what you were planning to do and I did nothing to stop it. And then when everything went wrong I helped you to dispose of the body. It was even my idea. But there's still time for you to get away if you go now. Just go anywhere and I'll get some clothes and money to you as fast as I can.'

She smiled at him. It was just like Joseph to put her before himself, which was why she was so very fond of him.

'No,' she whispered. 'I've done the crime and now I must pay the price.' And so saying she settled down on a chair and waited for the police to arrive.

'Mrs Charlotte Branning?'

Charlotte nodded, as she stared up at the detective in front of her.

'I would like you to accompany me to the station for questioning regarding the disappearance of Mrs Florence Watts.'

'May she have a solicitor present?' Joseph asked. He had already phoned one and asked him to be on standby as it happened.

'Of course.' The detective then turned his attention back to Charlotte and she rose without a word and followed him from the room out to the waiting police car.

It felt as if they had been questioning her for hours and now her eyes felt gritty from lack of sleep. The detective who had taken her to the police station was now convened in the next room with the solicitor who had sat with her throughout the questioning, and she just wished that it could all be over.

She had told them everything, apart from Joseph's involvement in the incident, and she just hoped that he would have the common-sense to say that he had been ill in bed in another room and had known nothing about it. The way she saw it, Joseph was innocent and shouldn't be made to suffer for her mistake.

When the detective next entered the room his face was set in grim lines. 'Charlotte Branning, I am arresting you for the murder of Florence Watts. You have the right to remain silent, but it may harm your defence if you do not mention when questioned something which you may later rely on in court. Anything you do say will be given in evidence . . .'

His voice droned on but Charlotte was no longer listening. She was now being formally arrested, which she had expected. Even now divers would be searching the canal for Floss's body, and she was glad. The woman deserved a proper resting-place.

When all the formalities were finally out of the way, the detective looked towards the sergeant who stood at the back of the room and nodded. The man instantly snapped his notebook open and waited.

'Now then, Charlotte, the fact that you've admitted Mrs Watts died in your home will help when the case comes to court but there are still a few things that don't quite add up.'

When Charlotte stared at him blankly he continued, 'You say that you managed to lift her body out of the bath then you dragged her down the stairs and across the garden to the canal, and then you threw her into the water. Is that so?'

When Charlotte nodded he stroked his chin thoughtfully. 'I'm afraid that doesn't quite ring true. You are not a big woman, and you would have had to be very strong indeed to lug a dead weight all that way on your own.'

She looked away to avoid his eyes. She had told him everything that had happened from the first time she had set eyes on Floss until the night of her death. The only thing she had omitted to tell him was about Joseph's involvement, and she was determined to keep her husband out of it at all costs. That was why his next words had her eyes popping with shock.

'It's strange then that your husband, who has been in the next room for the last two hours being questioned, is telling a slightly different story.'

'You have Joseph *here*?'

He nodded solemnly. 'Yes, we do, and he admits to helping you dispose of the body.'

'I made him do it,' she said, desperate now. It was strange; she scarcely cared what happened to her any more, but she very much cared about what happened to Joseph. After all, none of this sorry mess was his fault.

'So you are admitting that your husband was involved up to a point then?'

She screwed her eyes tight shut as she nodded miserably. There was no point in trying to cover it up any more.

'Now that you know the whole story, can I go home?' she asked.

'I'm afraid you won't be going home for possibly a very long time,' he said gravely. 'We will be holding you in custody until the first court case and then the judge will decide whether or not to grant you bail.'

'And my husband?'

'He may possibly be allowed home after questioning but I'm afraid he's been charged with trying to pervert the course of justice. He will probably be bailed to appear at the police station at regular intervals until his trial comes to court.'

Charlotte dropped her face into her hands and cried as if her heart was going to break. How could things have gone so terribly wrong?

Floss was recovered from the canal early the next morning. Her body had been carried almost a mile away from Charlotte's home on the currents. She was immediately taken to the hospital so that a post-mortem examination could be performed.

Detective Bruce visited Charlotte in the cell beneath the police station where she was being held to tell her the results, and it was the first bit of good news she had to cling on.

'The post mortem and medical records have revealed that Florence Watts had a weak heart,' he told her. 'So it appears that the illegal abortion you performed on her wasn't wholly responsible for her death, although of course the haemorrhaging and shock to her body wouldn't have helped her condition.' He glanced at Charlotte sternly over the top of his glasses before going on, 'Because of this, your charge will be reduced from murder to manslaughter.'

'I see,' Charlotte answered tonelessly.

'Apparently her doctor warned her after the birth of her fifth child that another pregnancy could kill her, but she chose to go on and have a sixth baby – and then of course she was pregnant again when she came to you for help.' He paused. 'That's the good news but I'm afraid there is some bad news as well. Mrs Watts's sister has named another woman on whom you performed an illegal abortion, and she in turn has named another. I can't believe that an intelligent woman like you who is a qualified midwife could have been so stupid. Surely you must have known the risk you were taking?'

'They needed help,' Charlotte said calmly, showing no signs of remorse whatsoever. 'If I hadn't helped them they would have no doubt gone to some grotty back street where they ran the risk of being butchered or dying from an infection.'

'But isn't that exactly what you are?' he asked coldly. 'These women could have had their abortions done legally, had they visited their GP. Did they pay you?'

'No, they did *not*! And the women I helped, apart from Mrs Watts, had no recourse to legal abortions. Suicide was sometimes the only other option. Mrs Watts herself was in fear of her life from her violent husband.'

'Even so, I'm afraid however good your intentions were, what you did was illegal,' Detective Bruce answered. 'And now if you'll excuse me I have to get on. Hopefully you will appear in court sometime next week, now that we have the results of the post mortem.'

'When can I see my husband?' Charlotte asked as he turned to leave and he paused. As far as he was concerned, what she had done was sinful. It made a mockery of the career she had chosen, but even so she seemed such a kind polite woman that it was hard to dislike her.

'I'll see if he can call in and visit you for half an hour tomorrow,' he promised and then he was gone and Charlotte was left to stare at the four bare walls.

'The newspapers are having a field day with it,' Joseph informed her glumly the next afternoon. 'It's plastered all across the front pages. "'Respected Midwife by day, Illegal Abortionist by night.'"

He faced her across the table, painfully aware of the officer who was standing in the background listening to everything they said. He desperately wanted to reach out and take his wife's hand to comfort her, she looked so lost and so out of place there, but he had been warned before entering the room that there must be no physical contact of any kind.

She shrugged; she had gone past caring what people said about her now.

'Never mind about that,' she said. 'How are you?'

He sighed. 'According to my solicitor I might get anything up to five years.'

Charlotte was horrified. 'But that's *awful!* And what will happen to the animals? Who will look after them while we're gone?'

He lowered his eyes. 'I'm afraid I'm going to have to find new homes for them, Lottie. I don't have any choice.' His eyes implored her to understand. 'They can't look after themselves, can they? And I'd rather do it in advance than have to let the RSPCA go in and take them all away to pounds if I get sent down. According to my solicitor I could be in court within a month.'

'Oh, Joe, what have I done to us all?' she sobbed and he could only look on helplessly. He knew how much Charlotte loved their pets. On them she poured all the love she should have poured onto the daughter who had been torn away from her. But he had no choice but to go ahead with his plan now. There was no going back. From anything.

Chapter Thirty-Nine

'Have the jury reached a verdict?'

'Yes, Your Honour.' The appointed jury spokesman stood and, avoiding Charlotte's eyes, stared at the grim-faced judge.

'And do you find the defendant guilty or not guilty?'

'Guilty, on all charges.'

Charlotte's heart sank as the judge now looked towards her.

'Having listened to all the evidence, I accept that you did not intend to kill Mrs Florence Watts, but even so the operation you performed illegally on her, inadvertently led to her death. You then tried to dispose of her body. I also have to take into account the other abortions that you performed illegally in the past. You are a disgrace to the profession that you chose to embark on, and therefore I sentence you to fifteen years in prison with the recommendation that you do not serve less than ten years. Take the prisoner down.'

Charlotte clutched at the front of the witness-stand as the floor rushed up to meet her. *Fifteen years!* It seemed like a life sentence, but then she had not expected to get away with what she had done lightly. *But fifteen years!* She would be an old woman before she was released.

A hand on her elbow dragged her thoughts back to the courtroom and she turned to look into the cold eyes of a policewoman. She was handcuffed before being led down some steep steps into the cells below. She went quietly. At the bottom, the policewoman removed the handcuffs and shoved her none too gently into a cell where she sank onto the hard bed in a daze. If only she could have spoken to Joseph it would have made things so much easier, but he was already serving five years in Winson Green Prison in Birmingham. With luck he would be out in half that time if he behaved, which she had no doubt he would. But what would he come out to? His career was in tatters and it was all her fault. He had already been struck off the Medical Register and she knew only too well that he would never be allowed to practise medicine again. The last time he had come to see her before standing trial, Joseph had assured her that their home would be safe at least. The solicitor he had appointed would be in charge of his bank account and would pay the household bills while he was inside.

Poor Joseph, life had dealt him yet another cruel hand. And all because he had tried to help her. She knew that she would never be able to forgive herself for the pain she had caused him.

She had no concept of time as she sat there on the hard bed staring at the bare plastered walls. Names had been scratched into them by other people who had been locked up in there and she studied them absently. *Jonno was 'ere! Suzie luvs Mikky!* She counted twenty-four different ones before she gave up. And then the sound of the cell door being unlocked brought her out of the trance-like state she had slipped into and she looked up to see two uniformed officers staring in at her.

'Come along, Mrs Branning,' one of them said. He was a tall man with a face that looked as if he had been in more than his fair share of brawls. His nose was flattened and spread across his cheeks and she wondered if he was a rugby player. He was certainly the right build for it. He advanced on her and clipped the handcuffs on again before attaching them to his own wrist and she had the urge to giggle. Did he expect her to try and get away? She would probably have lasted two seconds flat.

'We have a van waiting outside for you,' he informed her as she stood and meekly followed him from the cell; the other officer fell into step behind her.

'Where am I going?' she dared to ask.

He answered her civilly enough. 'To Holloway Prison in London. You'll be travelling with another woman who has been sentenced today.'

So she was going back to London. It hardly seemed five minutes since she and Joseph had left there to start their new life in the Midlands.

She was led out of the back way into a high walled area behind the courthouse where she saw a large police van parked with iron bars across the back windows. Tall metal gates led into the yard and she was horrified to see a small cluster of newspaper reporters gathered there. The second she appeared, the cameras began to flash and one of the journalists shouted, 'Is it true then, Mrs Branning, that you and your husband were in a marriage of convenience? Is he really a homosexual?'

She lowered her head and tried to ignore them. How could they have found out? She and Joseph had always been so careful to keep their secret. Had someone they knew told about them? A picture of Elsa flashed in front of her eyes but she instantly dismissed that idea. As far as Charlotte knew, she and Michael had rebuilt their marriage many years ago so she would never have risked Michael's name becoming involved. There was too much at stake. But then perhaps it wouldn't have been that hard. Once the press and the police got on your trail there was no stone left unturned. In fact, it would have been easy if they had gone to London and listened to the rumours that had used to circulate about Joseph at the Royal London. Poor Joseph. She knew that this would be the ultimate humiliation for him.

Another thought occurred to her. Could Aunt Edith have had anything to do with this? She had always blamed Charlotte for her brother's death, and this was just the sort of thing she would do to exact her revenge. But no, Charlotte supposed that she was letting her imagination run away with her.

Two officers were in the process of trying to manhandle another woman into the back of the van, but it was not proving to be an easy task as she was fighting and screaming at them. 'Get yer 'ands off me, yer *bastards*!' she screeched as they tried to hold her. 'I've told yer, ain't I? It were me old man dealin' the drugs, not *me*.'

'You've told us all right, Veronica,' one of the guards muttered wryly as he wrestled with her. 'And I seem to remember you telling us the same thing the last time you went down for a stretch.'

At last they heaved her into the back of the van and beckoned Charlotte over. 'Now don't you kick off as well,' the guard warned her. 'We've got our hands full with Vonnie here.'

Charlotte climbed silently into the van, glad to escape the reporters, and took a seat opposite the woman, wincing as the heavy doors slammed shut behind her.

'Lousy filthy swines!' the woman muttered, then as she looked at Charlotte her eyes goggled. 'Ere, ain't you the woman that's been plastered across all the papers fer the last few months?' she asked, and then without waiting for an answer, 'The one what were a midwife up at the 'ospital by day an' did abortions by night?'

Charlotte sighed heavily. The woman made it sound as if she performed abortions on a daily basis and she couldn't even bring herself to answer her.

'Huh! A little Miss 'Igh an' Mighty, are yer?' the woman sneered. 'Yer'll soon get that knocked out o' yer where you're goin'. The types you'll be mixin' wi' in Holloway will soon cut yer down to size.'

'I didn't mean to appear rude,' Charlotte told her in a small voice, 'but the stories in the newspapers have been highly exaggerated.'

'Oh, so yer sayin' yer *didn't* kill that woman then?'

'Not deliberately.' Charlotte really didn't know why she was even bothering to try to explain. 'The woman that died had a weak heart but she didn't inform me.'

Veronica sniffed, grudgingly deciding to give Charlotte the benefit of the doubt. After all, the newspapers always blew stories up out of all proportion, as she knew to her cost.

Now she sagged back against the cold metal walls of the van and thankfully she had soon dropped into a doze, leaving Charlotte to her own thoughts. Pictures of all the people she had loved and lost in her life flashed in front of her eyes. Her granny, her mother and Brian, and of course her darling little Daisy, and now she had lost Joseph and her beloved pets too. She wondered how Joseph would cope in prison. He was such a gentle man, she prayed that he would be able to bear it and then she started to cry and didn't stop until much later when they had arrived at Holloway Prison.

The van pulled through enormous metal gates into a small area in which stood yet another high set of gates. Once the first set of gates had closed resoundingly behind them the second set were opened and she was driven into a large courtyard. As the guards helped her down from the van she looked up at the bleak façade of the building and her chest constricted. It was like being placed back in the convent in Ireland and suddenly panic set in. The next fifteen years of her life was about to begin – if she could survive it.

The first letter from Joseph arrived three weeks after she began her sentence. He told her that he was well and that he hoped she was too, but other than that he said very little, and reading between the lines Charlotte could only guess at how unhappy he was. Guilt stabbed at her afresh, and she felt helpless. He should never have been locked away but there was nothing she could do about it. She herself was adapting . . . but only just. The hours she spent locked in her cell seemed endless, but even that was preferable to having to mingle with the other prisoners.

Thankfully she had a tiny cell to herself at present and she was grateful for that at least. The food, whilst tasteless, was edible, and an improvement on what she had been forced to eat in the convent, but even so she knew that she was losing a lot of weight. Some of the other prisoners had shown an interest in her but thankfully she had not crossed paths with Veronica again. She had heard it whispered that the woman in the next cell, who caused havoc on the wing on a regular basis, was in for life after microwaving her baby to death because it kept her awake one night. Another woman just a few cells further along was in for stabbing her husband to death when she had discovered that he was having an affair with her best friend. After killing him, she had then cold-bloodedly gone along to her friend's house and stabbed her to death too with the same knife.

The horror stories were endless but Charlotte did her best not to listen to them and kept herself to herself as much as she could. Once a week she was taken along to the prison library where she would stock up with enough books to keep her occupied until the following week. For an hour each afternoon the inmates were allowed into the exercise yard, a bleak walled area with nothing but the sky above to look at. And there were also various courses that the prisoners could do if they so wished, but Charlotte preferred to remain in her cell. The only times she could not avoid being with the other women were at mealtimes and showertimes, and these were the times that she hated the most.

She knew that the others were curious to know what she was in for. Most of them bragged about the crimes they had committed but so far Charlotte had managed to avoid telling anyone anything. All she wanted was to be left alone to serve her time, but that proved a lot easier said than done. And then came the day she had dreaded when she entered the library to find Veronica there, chatting to some of the other inmates.

'Ah, I wondered where you'd been hidin' yerself,' Vonnie greeted her as if she was a long-lost friend, and then turning to the person next to her who looked more like a man than a woman, she told her, 'This is the one to see if ever yer find yerself up the duff – not that you've got much chance o' that happenin' in this place.' She winked. 'She's a bit 'andy fer gettin' rid of unwanted pregnancies, ain't yer, ducks!' She chortled then as if she had made some huge joke. 'Trouble was, the last one she did it for snuffed it an' Miss Innocent 'ere tried to get rid o' the poor sod by chuckin' her body in the cut. Ain't that so? An' that ain't all – accordin' to the papers, the chap she were married to was a bleedin' shirt-lifter. What do yer make o' that then? He's in Winson Green, an' if what they were sayin' about 'im is true, I bet 'e's havin' a whale of a time. He won't go short o' takers in there!' She threw back her head and roared with laughter as Charlotte died inside.

A silence had fallen and she could feel everyone's eyes on her, but she already knew that if she didn't make a stand these women would make her life hell on earth. And so turning to Veronica, she eyed her coldly before saying, 'As it happens I *did* throw a body into the canal. I've never denied it. And do you know what? Once I get out of here I wouldn't be averse to doing it again – if anyone upset me enough.'

The laugh died on Vonnie's lips now as she eyed Charlotte cautiously. She had seemed such a meek woman on the journey to the prison, but then they said the quiet ones were always the worst, so perhaps it would be as well if she let the subject drop. Vonnie was a typical big-mouthed bully, always happy to harass those weaker than herself, but now that Charlotte had stood up to her she deflated like a balloon.

'No offence meant,' she muttered. 'After all, none of us are innocent. We wouldn't be in this bleedin' flea-pit if we were, would we?'

When Charlotte continued to stare at her boldly, she quickly turned to the woman behind her and began to talk of other things. Meanwhile Charlotte began to look along the shelves at the books, outwardly as cool as a cucumber, but could they have only known it, she was dying inside. As if he hadn't got enough to contend with, it seemed that the whole world now knew that Joseph was gay. He had always kept it such a closely guarded secret and she wondered how he would cope with it. It was just another cross for her to bear.

The next two and a half years passed interminably slowly as Charlotte fretted about how Joseph was faring. His letters came as regularly as clockwork once every month and she always replied to them by return of post, but truthfully after receiving the first one he might as well not have bothered writing. Each one told her nothing more than that he was well and he hoped that she was too. And then at last the one she had been longing for arrived. He was being let out early the following month for good behaviour. He promised that as soon as he was home he would get a visit or pass and come and see her, and Charlotte cried with relief for a solid hour. Not for the fact that she would be having her first visitor, but because Joseph would finally be a free man again.

She began to count the weeks, then the days and even the hours . . . and at last the day came when a prison warden stood in the doorway of her cell and told her, 'You've got a visitor, Branning. Get yourself down to the visiting room.'

Charlotte's legs shook like jellies as she pushed her hair behind her ears and quietly followed the warden down the curved metal staircase. She was aware of some of the other prisoners' curious eyes on her but she ignored them. She had grown good at doing that and for the most part now they left her well alone, which was just what she wanted. The time she had spent in the convent shut away from her family had stood her in good stead and helped her to cope with this latest incarceration. It had given her the strength to survive and she knew that now she could see Joseph again, things would become easier.

She was led into a large room where tables with a chair on either side of them were placed in neat regimental rows. Many of the tables were already occupied. Mothers, husbands, sisters and daughters sat opposite the prisoners they were visiting with strained looks on their faces. And then she saw him and the breath caught in her throat. It was definitely Joseph, but not the man she remembered. This Joseph was skeletally thin and his smart clothes hung off his lean frame. His face was etched with lines that she couldn't remember being there before and a large scar that was well healed now curved from the corner of his right eye to his chin. His lovely thick hair, always one of his best features, was thin now, so much so that she could see his scalp through it, and it was snow-white and straggled across his collar. He obviously hadn't shaved for some time either and a beard was forming on his chin, giving him a slightly wild appearance.

She forced a smile as she approached the table and sat down opposite to him. 'Hello,' she said softly and he smiled back. The action made the skin surrounding the scar stretch and he looked grotesque.

'Hello, Lottie.' He was thinking that she too had changed. In fact, he would never have believed that anyone could change quite so much in less than three years. Charlotte had always looked much younger than her age but now he found himself staring at what appeared to be an elderly woman. The skin beneath her eyes was dark and lined, and her once thick mane of golden hair was now scraped back into a tight ponytail at the nape of her neck. It was hard to believe that Charlotte was only in her early fifties. Now she could have passed for someone in her mid-sixties.

'You look well,' he forced himself to say.

'So do you.' They both knew that they were lying, but what else could they say?

She was the one to break the silence that had settled between them when she asked, 'What happened to your face?'

'What – this?' His hand rose self-consciously to stroke the ugly scar. 'Oh, it's nothing. I er . . . slipped in the shower.'

They both knew that he was lying but Charlotte didn't contradict him. He must have had a terrible time in jail if the scar was anything to go by. There was so much she wanted to say, but she was painfully aware of the close proximity of the other tables and so she stayed on safe ground and asked, 'How is everything at home?'

'Fine,' he assured her. 'The gardens were rather overgrown but I'll soon pull them back into shape. It will give me something to do.'

'And have you tried to get another job yet?'

'I've applied for a couple, but I haven't been successful as yet,' he said cautiously. 'But you don't have to worry about money. The elderly aunt of mine who I lived with for a time died while I was . . . away, and she's left me more than enough to keep us going for years.'

'Oh!' Charlotte could vaguely remember him mentioning his aunt many years ago. But it was obvious that he found talking about his family painful and so she had always avoided it. Now she was stumped for something to say and although it was wonderful to see him a free man again, she suddenly wished that visiting time was over.

'Joseph, I want you to do something for me,' she told him now as she looked away from him.

'Of course. What is it?'

'I want you to promise that you won't visit me here again,' she said. 'Because of me I think you've seen enough of prisons to last you a lifetime, but I would be grateful if you'd continue to write to me.'

'Are you quite sure that this is what you want?' His eyes were full of pain and she could scarcely bring herself to look at him.

'I'm quite sure. I want you to go away and try to forget about me until I come home again. Try and rebuild your life.'

They both knew that this was going to be a lot easier said than done, especially Joseph. He had felt like he was living in a goldfish bowl ever since he had been released. The neighbours' curtains would twitch if he so much as set foot outside the door, and everyone was avoiding him as if he had the plague. If he walked into a shop everyone would stand aside and become silent while he was being served. But he could cope with all that. As far as he was concerned, he was as guilty as Charlotte was. He had known about the illegal abortions she had performed and he had never tried to stop her. It was Charlotte he was most concerned about now though. She looked so frail and he wondered if she would survive her sentence. It was up to him now to make sure that she still had a home to come back to if she did.

'Very well then, if that is what you want. But I'll write every single week.'

She blinked back tears as she squeezed his hand. 'Thank you. Please take care of yourself.'

She nodded towards a warden then and they came to escort her back to her cell. She looked over her shoulder just once. Joseph was still sitting there with his head bent, tears trickling down his cheeks. It was a vision she would retain in her mind for all the other long lonely years she had left to serve.

Chapter Forty

In 2008, Joseph's letters stopped arriving. Charlotte was worried sick. She continued to write to him on a weekly basis, but when three months had gone by and she still had not heard from him, she decided to contact his solicitor. She had met Mr McKenna on a number of occasions in the past and hoped that he would be able to tell her if anything was wrong.

Once her letter had been posted she waited with trepidation for his reply and the following week it arrived. She immediately knew that it was from him by the solicitor's stamp on the corner of the envelope. It had already been opened, as was all the prisoners' mail, but she withdrew the sheet of paper eagerly and began to read it.

Dear Mrs Branning,

I am writing in answer to your letter dated 13 June 2008. As you may appreciate, I no longer see a great deal of your husband since his release from prison, but after making a few enquiries on your behalf I am sorry to report that it seems that his mental health has deteriorated somewhat over the last couple of years.

I actually called to see him at your home recently at his request, to make some amendments to his will, and I was quite concerned to find that he appears to have become rather eccentric and reclusive. However, on this occasion he spoke quite rationally and was able to make his wishes known.

I am so sorry I cannot be of more help to you, but may I suggest that it might be more appropriate if you wrote to his GP with your concerns?

Yours sincerely,

L. McKenna

Charlotte stared at the sheet of paper as if it had bitten her. What did Mr McKenna mean? Eccentric and reclusive? Joseph's social skills had always been second to none; they had had to be. He had dealt with the public on a daily basis when he was a doctor.

She briefly considered contacting their GP as Mr McKenna had suggested, but dismissed the idea almost immediately, knowing that it would be a waste of time. No doctor would ever discuss a patient with another person, even a family member, without the patient's consent. And then it came to her. A long time ago she had asked Joseph not to come and see her again, but now she would write and tell him that she had changed her mind. At least that way, if he decided to come she would be able to see how he was for herself.

She wrote the letter the very same day and handed it to one of the wardens to be posted – then she waited, every single day seeming like a lifetime. She knew that it would be at least a week after Joseph received the letter before he could get here. He would have to apply for a visit or pass and go through all the red tape before he was allowed to come – if he chose to come, that was.

Every visiting day for the next two weeks she was on tenterhooks as she waited expectantly in her cell for a warden to come and say that she had a visitor, but each time she was disappointed. And then at last a warden appeared in the doorway on the third week and announced, 'You have a visitor, Branning. Follow me.'

Charlotte's heart raced as she followed the warden to the day room. Her eyes flicked over the heads of the other prisoners and their visitors until they found him. He was sitting at the far table right at the back of the room and he looked slightly confused, as if he wasn't quite sure what he was doing there.

'Hello, Joe.' She sat down opposite him and he stared at her blankly for a moment but then he smiled and just for a second she saw a glimpse of the man he had once been. She briefly wondered where the unpleasant smell was coming from before realising with horror that it was emitting from Joseph. But he had always been such a clean person! He had lost even more weight and now looked as if he had shrunk.

'Are you looking after yourself?' she asked before she could stop herself.

He shrugged. 'Of course.' His face broke into a grin then. 'The neighbours call me Holy Joe now because I've started going to church. It's warm in there.'

'Oh, Joseph!' He was barely making sense and she felt useless knowing that she couldn't be at home to care for him.

'And I've taken on another two dogs,' he went on. 'Bella and Woolly. They keep me company, you see.'

'That's wonderful.' She tried to sound cheerful for him, but tears were stinging at the back of her eyes. She was painfully aware that people were wrinkling their noses and looking towards them, but she ignored them and focused her attention on the poor wreck of a man sitting in front of her. And to think that it was she who had brought him down to this level. She knew that it was going to be even harder to live with herself after today, seeing him first hand.

She hurried away then to the small drinks counter at the end of the room and bought them both a cup of tea; hot, sweet and strong enough to stand a spoon in, just as she remembered Joseph liked it.

He slurped at it noisily and again she was shocked. Joseph's manners had always been impeccable but they certainly weren't now. Looking at the state he was in, she dreaded to think what their house might be like. But that wasn't her main concern. A house was just bricks and mortar. She could soon get it to rights again once she was home. It was Joseph that she was more worried about.

Since being in Holloway she had kept her head down and been a model prisoner, and the prison governor had already talked to her and told her that if she continued that way she would definitely get an early release for good behaviour. But even if that came about it was still two long years away and she wondered if Joseph would survive on his own for that long. Things seemed to be far worse than she had thought and she was desperately frustrated and concerned for him.

When it was time for him to leave she clung to his hand and asked him, 'You will come again, won't you?'

He had been staring absently into space but now he looked at her and said, 'Oh yes, if you want me to. I like coming on the train.'

He made it sound like a day out and she despaired as

she determined to speak to the prison social worker at the earliest opportunity. Perhaps they could organise someone to go in and keep an eye on him for her? It was worth a try at least.

'Goodbye, dear.' He leaned across the table and kissed her on the cheek now and she almost gagged at the close proximity of him as the unwashed stench of him smacked her full in the face.

'Goodbye, take care of yourself.' She watched him join the rest of the visitors who were leaving and shuffle away, and now the tears that she had managed to hold back trickled down her cheeks as she was led away back to her cell.

The prison social worker that she spoke to a few days later was very understanding and promised to do what she could, but she could make no promises. With that Charlotte had to be content. There was no more she could do.

The next two years passed painfully slowly, but at last she was summoned to the prison governor's office and she received the news she had been praying for.

'You will be released on the twenty-third of November, Mrs Branning.' He said a lot more but after hearing that, the rest of his words flew over her head. It was less than two months away and she would be home in time for Christmas with Joseph.

His visits had been spasmodic and each time he had come to Holloway over the last two years she had seen further signs of deterioration in him. But she would change all that once she got home, of that she was determined.

'Thank you,' she said, and the governor smiled. Despite the terrible crime for which she had been incarcerated, he had always found Charlotte Branning to be a nice woman and he hoped that things would work out for her once she was released.

'You will of course be on probation for the remainder of your sentence,' he went on to explain. 'And before you leave, a probation officer will be allocated to you in your area. You will have to report to them on a monthly basis, and should you get into trouble again during that period you will be returned to prison to serve the remainder of your sentence. I have to point that out to you, Mrs Branning. Are you prepared to abide by these terms?'

'Yes, sir,' she answered without hesitation. She knew that once she set foot out of that place she would never again return. She had learned by her mistakes.

And so now all she had to do was tick off the days on her calendar and they passed interminably slowly.

Less than two weeks before her release date she was summoned to the governor's office yet again. She assumed that he wanted to speak to her about her probation so it was a shock when she entered his office to find him looking very grave-faced.

'Sit down, Mrs Branning,' he said without preamble and sensing that something was badly wrong, Charlotte dropped onto the chair in front of his desk.

'I'm afraid that I have some very bad news for you.' He glanced at her sympathetically as he steepled his fingers. 'I have just had a phone call from your husband's solicitor. He informed me that your husband was involved in a very serious accident late last night.'

'But he's all right, isn't he?' Panic began to set in as Charlotte stared back at him.

'I'm afraid not. He stepped out into the road, into the path of an oncoming car, and was knocked down. They pronounced him dead on arrival at the hospital. I'm so sorry, Mrs Branning.'

Charlotte was stunned. It couldn't be true! She was due to go and look after him in less than two weeks' time. She was going to make it up to him for all that she had put him through. He just *couldn't* be dead. This must be some sort of cruel joke. But even as she stared at the governor's face she knew that it was true. Joseph was gone and she would never be able to put right the wrong she had done him now.

'Because of the extenuating circumstances I am going to propose that you are released in time to attend his funeral,' he went on. 'Mr McKenna assures me that he has all the arrangements in hand. Meantime I would like to offer my sincere condolences. It is most tragic.'

He nodded towards the warden who was standing at the back of the room, and as Charlotte rose unsteadily to her feet she allowed the woman to guide her back to her cell. Her head was reeling as she tried to take in the news. She and Joseph had never been married in the conventional sense, but even so he was all she had, and now she was completely alone. Suddenly going home and being released from prison didn't seem so important. She had become institutionalised over the years and she felt safe here. Once she was out she would be all alone in the big bad world and it was a frightening thought.

'Will you be all right?' the warden asked when they reached the door to her cell.

Charlotte nodded.

'Very well – but if you need anything, just come and find me.' This particular warden, a great Amazon of a woman with hands like hams and muscles that would have put a body-builder to shame, had always had a soft spot for Charlotte. She just wished that all her charges could be as polite as Charlotte was. She had never caused her a single bit of bother in all the time she had been there. 'I'll leave your cell door open,' she ended lamely. What could you say to a woman who had just been told she would never see her husband alive again? She silently slipped away, leaving Charlotte alone with her grief.

The following day, Charlotte was summoned to the governor's office again and he told her, 'Your husband's funeral will take place next Friday, Mrs Branning, and so we are going to release you on Thursday, the day before.'

'Thank you,' she muttered.

'Is there anything you would like to ask me?' he questioned, and when she shook her head he nodded. 'Very well, you may go.'

And so it was that the following Thursday morning she found herself standing outside the gates of Holloway Prison with the small case she had arrived with clutched in her hand. Mr McKenna had forwarded her some funds for the train and bus fares home – far too much, she thought, but she was grateful to him. The street seemed to be teeming with people and everywhere looked enormous. Traffic was flashing past at an alarming rate and petrol fumes hung on the air. They were all sights and smells that she had forgotten and she felt very small and insignificant. Her heart began to thud with panic. The social worker had told her that she would need to catch a 91 bus to get to Euston station and she looked frantically for a bus stop, wishing that they would just reopen the gates to the prison and let her back in.

Charlotte was painfully aware that her clothes were very outdated as she looked at the women passing by, but that was the least of her concerns. There were several young women pushing prams while smoking and talking into mobile phones, and some of them stared at her curiously as she forced herself to shuffle forward. She broke out in a cold sweat despite the bitterly cold day. She wondered if it had ever been as cold as this outside before she was admitted to prison. She was used to a cell that was maintained at a regular temperature and her teeth began to chatter. The task of getting home suddenly seemed insurmountable and she felt as if she was trying to get to the other side of the world rather than up to Nuneaton.

The bus and train fares were the next thing to shock her. They had risen alarmingly since she had been locked away and she realised why Mr McKenna had sent her so much. Two pounds for a bus-ride! Eventually she arrived at Euston and nervously queued to buy a ticket. Even the train seemed to travel faster than the speed of light, and the seating arrangements were all so different to what she remembered.

But at last she was seated and she stared nervously from the window as the train chugged towards Nuneaton.

When she finally stepped down onto the platform after a journey that had taken less than two hours, she headed for the exit and looked around her. Once more nothing was as she remembered it. A taxi rank stood outside now and the bus station opposite had been extensively modernised. All she wanted now was to get home but first she must take a taxi to visit the solicitor, Mr McKenna, to pick up the keys to her house.

He was kindness itself, and after giving her a further sum of money to tide her over and her house keys, he told her about the funeral arrangements.

She thanked him for all he had done for both herself and Joseph, and he shook his head sadly.

'I'm just sorry that I couldn't have done more,' he told her sincerely.

'Your husband was a highly intelligent man and it was sad to see him waste away. But now you must think of yourself, Charlotte. Joseph wanted you to be all right. I have his will here and I will read it to you following the funeral tomorrow. Rest assured that he left you very well financially provided for. Good day, my dear – and don't hesitate to get in touch if I can be of further assistance.'

Once Charlotte had left Mr McKenna's office she was so exhausted that she decided to take another taxi home – but when it pulled up outside her little detached house, she could hardly recognise it. Through all the long lonely years she had spent locked away from the world, she had dreamed about this house but now it looked nothing like it had when she had left it.

Hastily paying the taxi driver, she stood at the gate staring down the length of the front garden. Once there had been a neat lawn on one side of the paved path that led to the front door, and the borders had been a riot of colour with as many different plants as she could squash into them. Now it was nothing more than an overgrown tangled mess. She wasn't even able to see where the path was any more and the weeds were waist-high in places. Looking beyond the garden, she glanced at the windows. All of the curtains at the front were firmly drawn and the windows looked grimy and dull. The brass door knocker that she had always taken such a pride in was tarnished and she wondered how Joseph could have survived in such a mess. But then the inside would be better than this, surely?

As she pushed the gate open it squealed in protest on its rusty hinges, then she gingerly picked her way to the front door and inserted the key. It was late afternoon by then and the light was almost gone outside, but it was even darker inside and her hand fumbled along the wall for the light switch as she kicked the door shut behind her and placed her suitcase down. Her first glance of the front room had her gasping with dismay. Her beautiful Dralon suite was covered in dog hairs and dirt, so much so that the colour was almost indistinguishable. Moving on to the middle room which had served as their dining room she found that things were no better there. The teak table that she had always kept so highly polished that she could see her face in it was strewn with plates full of half-eaten meals, and half-empty cups. It was a mass of scratches and rings where hot drinks had been stood on it and she knew that no amount of polishing was ever going to restore it to its former glory. If she had thought that the first two rooms were bad, the kitchen proved to be a disaster area and she gagged at the smell in there before fumbling with the key in the lock and throwing the back door wide open. There were overflowing bags full of rubbish scattered across the floor and piles of newspapers everywhere she looked.

'Oh Joseph,' she muttered brokenly. 'How could you have lived in this?'

A quick glance down the back garden showed her that this was every bit as badly overgrown as the front, and she felt overwhelmed as she wondered how she was ever going to get it habitable again. And then her eyes fell on two large dog dishes half-full of rotting food and her stomach flipped. Hadn't Joseph mentioned on one of his visits that he had taken in another two dogs to keep him company? She seemed to recall that he had called them Bella and Woolly. But where were they now?

It was then that there was a loud banging on the front door, and drawing herself up to her full height, she hurried away to answer it.

A young woman with two dogs on a lead was standing there and she looked Charlotte up and down, making colour rush into her cheeks.

'You Mrs Branning?' she asked in a none too friendly voice.

Charlotte nodded mutely.

'Oh. Well, I'm your neighbour. I moved here three years ago and these are your hus— late husband's dogs. His solicitor told me that you would be home soon and asked me if I would look after them till you arrived. Well, here they are anyway. They're your responsibility now.'

'Oh thank you.' Charlotte took the dogs' leads from the woman's hand. 'But do let me pay you for their keep.'

'The solicitor sorted that,' the woman said coldly, and turning on her heel she walked away without another word.

'Thank you again,' Charlotte shouted after her but the woman never even looked over her shoulder.

Closing the door softly she now looked down at the two dogs. They were actually the weirdest-looking mutts she had ever laid eyes on, and at a glance it was clear that they could lay no claims to being pedigrees. One of them was quite large, a dull brown colour with short hair and ears that seemed to have a life of their own. The other was much smaller, with long fluffy hair, and at first glance it put her in mind of a Jack Russell terrier although on closer inspection she saw that the floppy ears and long tail were nothing like the breed's.

Even so, she was glad of their company. They appeared to be the only possible friends she might have at the moment, so dropping to her knees she stroked them simultaneously.

'So which one of you is Woolly then?' Instantly the little one's tail began to wag and it licked her hand. 'Ah, so you must be Bella?' Now the older one looked up at her from soft brown eyes and she knew that she was going to love them. 'Come on, let's go and see if Joseph has any tins of dog meat in the cupboard for you.' Clearly knowing their way about, they followed her through to the kitchen and after she had managed to wash their dishes and scrabble about in the kitchen cupboards she eventually found some dog biscuits and fed them.

'I'm afraid you'll have to manage with them for tonight,' she apologised as they wolfed the meals down in record time and drank the water she gave them. 'But tomorrow after the funeral I'll go shopping and get you some proper food.'

The strain of the day was catching up with her now and she was desperately tired, so after settling the dogs into their baskets she climbed the stairs to her old bedroom.

As she threw the door open and clicked on the light she was shocked to see that it was exactly as she had left it on that long-ago morning following Floss's death. Her nightdress was still neatly folded on the pillow although everything was covered in a thick layer of dust now. Her perfume bottles still stood in a tidy row on the dressing-table, and a quick inspection of the wardrobe showed her clothes still hanging there although the moths had had a field day and many of them were in tatters.

She had become used to noise going on all around her. It had

337

never been quiet in the prison, even at night. But now the silence and loneliness closed in on her, and lowering her head she wept. It was some homecoming – but then she knew that she deserved nothing more.

Chapter Forty-One

The following morning dawned damp and dismal and Charlotte's eyes felt heavy as she dragged herself out of bed and went downstairs to let the dogs out. They greeted her like a long-lost friend before tearing off down the garden with their tails wagging furiously. Pulling her dressing-gown more tightly about herself, she stared around at the filthy kitchen. It was going to take months to get the house back to any standard of cleanliness, but today she had more pressing things on her mind, namely attending Joseph's funeral. Glancing towards the shelves on the far wall that he had put up for her to house the saucepans, she could see and hear him in her mind as he had been then. They had been so excited about their new house, and nothing she had ever asked him to do had been too much trouble for him.

'Are they to Madame's satisfaction?' He had bowed as she inspected them and she could remember giggling.

'They'll do for now – but only just,' she had teased. It seemed such a long time ago now.

She found the kettle and filled it at the sink before putting it on to boil, making a mental note that the cooker was one of the first jobs on the agenda. It was covered in grease at least half an inch thick and she felt nauseous just looking at it. She made a pot of black tea and fed the dogs some Rich Tea biscuits, which had gone soft, and which she'd found in the back of the cupboard. Then a glance at the clock told her that it was time to start getting ready for the funeral.

Mr McKenna had informed her that the hearse would come to the house with a car following for her to travel in on the way to the church. Panic set in as she wondered what she should wear. She doubted very much if any of the things hanging in her wardrobe would be salvageable. However, she found a black jumper and skirt that had survived the moths: they would just have to do. She was just in the process of ironing them when the phone rang. She was mildly surprised that Joseph still had a phone, knowing how reclusive he had become, but she hurried to answer it anyway.

And then as she lifted the receiver a voice she had hoped never to hear again echoed down the line.

'Getting ready for your darling husband's funeral, are you?' it cackled.

Charlotte's blood ran cold. 'Aunt Edith' she gasped. 'How did you know where I lived?'

'I know *everything* about you,' the woman hissed. 'Since you killed your father I've made it my business to know.'

'I *didn't* kill my father!' Charlotte protested but her aunt's words cut her short.

'You might as well have put the noose around his neck yourself – and then you have the downright hypocrisy to go and marry a homosexual when you branded your own father a *pervert!*'

'Joseph was a good man!' Charlotte responded, and then as things began to fall into place: 'It was *you* who told the press about Joseph when I was tried, wasn't it? But how did you find out that he was a—'

'Filthy homosexual?' Her aunt chuckled but the sound held no mirth. 'It wasn't hard to work it out. I followed you to London, and after telling some of the nurses you worked with that I was your loving aunt, they eventually confided that you were seeing a doctor who was suspected of being a homo. And yes, it was me who told the press about him. And it was also me who drove him to become a recluse once you were safely locked away. I hounded him until he was afraid to set foot out of the door, spoke to the neighbours – made sure that every last one of them knew what you had done, and what he was. They all know now what a farce your marriage was. And all those poor babies you killed, eh? Before they ever got the chance to draw breath! But now you are paying the price. You're all alone in the world, aren't you? Just as you deserve to be.'

'You are a truly wicked woman,' Charlotte said quietly. 'Now just leave me alone.'

She slammed the phone down but her hand was trembling and

she had an awful feeling that she hadn't heard the last of Edith Hayes by a long shot. She had not seen or heard from her since the day of her mother's and Brian's funeral, and had prayed that she never would again. It was her aunt's fault that she had lost her lovely baby girl, and now the vicious woman was back to haunt her again, as if she hadn't done enough damage already. On the odd times that her aunt had crossed her mind, Charlotte had assumed that she would be dead by now. She must be well into her nineties Perhaps it was just her hatred of her niece that was keeping her alive? *But what can she do to me now?* Charlotte asked herself. *She's done all she can.* She forced her aunt from her mind then as she raced away to finish getting ready.

Later that day, Charlotte moved a pile of newspapers from the easy chair with an embarrassed smile so that the solicitor could sit down.

Flustered, she spread her hands and apologised, 'I'm so sorry about the mess, Mr McKenna. I'm afraid Joseph rather let the house go while I was away.'

'Don't worry about it.'

As he stared across at her, the man couldn't help but feel sorry for her. She had committed a terrible crime, there was no getting away from it, but she had paid the price now and he hoped that she would be left alone to live the rest of her life in peace. Looking at how frail she was, he doubted that it would be a very long life. She looked as if one good puff of wind would blow her away, and he knew that Joseph's funeral had been a great strain on her, although he admired the dignified way she had conducted herself throughout the service.

'So shall we go on to Joseph's will now?'

Lowering her head she nodded and so taking a deep breath he withdrew a legal-looking document from his briefcase and began, 'This is the last will and testament of Joseph William Branning made on this day . . .'

As his voice droned on, Charlotte did her best to concentrate, but all she could see in her mind was a picture of poor Joseph's coffin being lowered into the grave. It had hit her then that he was really gone forever and she had wished that she could just slip into the grave with him. What did she have to live for now anyway? Especially if her aunt was going to come out of the past to haunt her.

'. . . And so the long and the short of it is, Charlotte, you are now a fairly wealthy woman. The house is paid for and there are fifty thousand pounds in the bank.'

She started as she pulled her thoughts back to the solicitor. *Fifty thousand pounds*? It sounded like an immense fortune to her. At least she wouldn't have to worry about an income. After the pension and the possible benefits that the prison social worker had informed her she was entitled to, Charlotte doubted that she would even need to touch it. She had never been a spendthrift and had no intentions of changing the habits of a lifetime now, but it would be nice to know it was there safe in the bank, should she ever need it. Bless him; it was just like Joseph to make sure that she had been provided for.

'I – I don't know how to thank you for all you have done,' she said as calmly as she could, and Mr Mckenna smiled as he snapped his briefcase shut. It had been an abysmal funeral with only Charlotte and himself to mourn the poor man's passing and now he was keen to get back to work and try and put it all behind him.

'I am only glad that I could be of service to you,' he said. 'Good day, Mrs Branning – and good luck.'

She saw him to the door, then sinking onto the settee, she sobbed for a solid hour. Eventually the whimpering of the dogs made her pull herself together. Joseph had loved them and it was her responsibility to care for them now. That was the least she could do for him. After quickly drying her eyes she collected her purse and made for the door. There was a shop on the corner and she desperately needed to do some food shopping, for herself as well as for the dogs. She left the house, only to find a little huddle of women standing by her neighbour's gate.

''Ere she comes,' one of them said spitefully, loud enough for her to hear. 'Makes you wonder 'ow she can face anyone don't it, after what she's done? All that blood on her 'and's, eh? An' I ain't just talkin' about Floss's, God rest 'er soul. But all them little unborn babies. We just got rid of a queer out of our street an' then end up wi' a murderer instead. It makes you wonder what the world is comin' to!'

Charlotte forced herself to move on as her heart pounded in her chest. This was why Joseph had turned into a recluse, because of how they had all treated him. It was as she reached the corner that a familiar figure came hobbling into sight. 'Aunt Edith,' Charlotte said, as she came abreast of her. The sight of the elderly woman barely surprised her.

The woman eyed her with malice. 'Yes, it's me. I thought I'd come to say goodbye. I'm going back to Ireland tomorrow, now that I've done what I came to do.'

'So it was *you* that spoke to those women, was it?'

The old woman nodded. She had never been attractive when she was younger, but now she looked positively hideous. It was clear that she was almost crippled with arthritis and she was leaning heavily on a stick, but even that hadn't deterred her from getting what she considered to be her revenge for her brother's death.

'Don't you think we have all suffered enough?' Charlotte asked softly.

Edith shook her head. 'You could *never* suffer enough for what you did to my dear Bernard,' she spat. 'And those back there,' she waved her cane across Charlotte's shoulder, 'they'll never give you a moment's peace for as long as there is a breath left in your body. I can go away and die easy now, knowing that you'll get your just deserts.'

With that she turned and hobbled away, leaving Charlotte at a loss.

She arrived home to find raw eggs thrown against her front door and somehow she knew that this was only going to be the beginning.

It was the following night when Charlotte was sitting with the dogs that a knock sounded on the front door and when she went to open it she found a police officer standing there.

'Mrs Charlotte Branning?' he enquired, as he removed his cap and stepped inside.

She nodded fearfully.

'Are you the niece of a Miss Edith Hayes?'

Another nod.

'Then I am sorry to inform you that your aunt suffered a major heart attack this evening and died after being taken to the George Eliot Hospital. She was staying at a hotel in town and the landlord who runs it found your address amongst her possessions.'

'Oh!' So her aunt had died all alone. She supposed she should feel sorry for her but found it difficult.

'Are you Miss Hayes's only surviving relative?' he asked now and she replied, 'I am.'

'Then may I ask if you will take control of the funeral arrangements?'

'I'm afraid not. If you would ask the hospital to contact a funeral director, I will pay all costs.' Charlotte really didn't feel as if she had much choice in the matter.

'But won't you want to do that yourself?' The police officer looked perplexed.

'No,' Charlotte said firmly. 'My aunt and I were not on good terms, so I shan't be attending the funeral. She can be buried at Saint Sebastian in Bedworth, where my father, her brother, is buried as soon as possible. Just send me the bill.'

'Very well.' The officer reversed towards the door. There was no doubt about it; there were none so strange as folks.

Within a month of being home, Charlotte had been branded as 'the witch'. If she tried to work in the front garden children taunted her across the fence, so she stopped going out there and left it to grow even more wild. And if she visited the shop during the day, women hurled abuse at her. And so she took to visiting the corner shop late at night just before it shut when there was less possibility of people being about. She ventured into town just once, to take out a thousand pounds in cash to hide in the house, and passing a toy shop she saw a doll in the window that put her in mind of her baby. It had blue glass eyes and blonde hair, and Charlotte hastily bought it and called her Daisy.

Soon Charlotte found that it wasn't so bad to stay in all the time now that she had her baby and the animals to talk to, and her life settled into a pattern. Occasionally a stray cat or dog would venture into the garden and Charlotte would immediately adopt them. She never did get around to clearing out the house. After all, there was only her to see it and she found that she could live in it quite comfortably as it was, although she did make an effort to sort the back garden out so that the dogs could exercise there. Within months of being out of prison, Charlotte felt as if she had never been away.

Chapter Forty-Two

'Hello, Mrs Branning, my name is Cheryl Morris and I'm from social services. May I come in and talk to you for a while?'

Charlotte eyed the young woman on her doorstep warily as she yanked her old cardigan more closely about her.

'What for?' she asked abruptly.

The young woman looked slightly embarrassed. 'Well . . . actually we have received a number of complaints from the neighbours and local people concerning the number of animals you have and the fact that they rarely see you out and about. I'm here really just to check that you're OK, but it would be much better if you allowed me to come in so that we could talk properly.'

Charlotte paused before opening the door a fraction wider and beckoning the woman inside. The girl blinked as she entered the room. There was snow on the ground outside, but the curtains at the front-room window were tightly drawn, making it appear very dark. She followed Charlotte towards the back room, moving her hand along the wall to guide her as she went, and as they entered it, the over-powering smell of cats and dogs almost took her breath away.

A gas fire was lit in the hearth and three dogs of varying sizes were curled up in front of it. There were cats asleep on the two easy chairs and more on the table, and some of them raised their heads to stare at her as she entered the room. They clearly weren't used to visitors. But Cheryl Morris noticed that they all appeared to be very well fed and cared for, which was more than could be said for Mrs Branning. The old lady was as thin as a rake and looked incredibly frail although her voice when she spoke was refined. Cheryl knew that she was about sixty years old but she looked much older.

'So . . .' Cheryl plastered a smile to her face as she brushed her long brown hair across her shoulder. 'May I sit down?'

Charlotte lifted a fat ginger tom cat off one of the easy chairs and nodded, so the young social worker took a seat.

'I really just wanted to check that you were all right,' she said kindly. 'I understand from your neighbours that you don't go out a lot?'

Charlotte eyed her visitor warily. 'I don't need to, apart from to do a bit of shopping. There's no crime in that, is there?'

'No, no of course not,' Cheryl assured her. 'But I wondered if you were aware that there are lots of places for people your age to go if you wanted to. We have a lovely centre in the town where you could go daily for a hot meal if you wished, or if you found that too much, we could actually deliver meals to you.'

'I am quite capable of getting my *own* meals, thank you very much,' Charlotte replied haughtily. 'And I am still able to get about if I wish to. The fact is, I don't like to go out.' She nodded towards the front window. 'The people hereabouts have not been kind to me since I came home from . . . well. They call me names and throw things at my house. I've lost count of the times I have had bricks through my front window.' She lifted her doll and cradled it against her scrawny chest. 'I have my Daisy here and my pets, and as you can see they are all very well cared for.'

'Oh, I don't dispute it,' Cheryl told her quickly, looking around at the vast menagerie of animals. They all looked totally contented. It was actually Charlotte that she was more concerned about. She was speaking lucidly enough admittedly, but the way she held the doll as if it was a real baby was slightly disturbing. She spoke about it as if it was a real baby too. Could it be that she was in the early stages of dementia? The old woman's clothes hung off her skinny frame but they looked clean, even if they were many years out of fashion. And her snow-white hair was tidy too, arranged in a neat bun at the back of her head. Cheryl's eyes settled on a framed photograph sitting on top of the television set of a handsome young man with vivid blue eyes and thick dark hair.

'Is that your husband?' she asked now, and as Charlotte followed her eyes her face softened and Cheryl realised that she must once have been a very beautiful woman.

'Yes, that was my Joseph.' Charlotte sighed sadly. 'He was such

347

a good man, but again the people around here were not kind to him.'

'Why was that?'

Charlotte pursed her lips. 'Because they didn't understand him,' she said.

She often thought that her dear Joseph had been born at the wrong time. Nowadays it seemed that it was almost fashionable to be gay, but back when he was a young man it had been something to be ashamed of, and illegal, to boot. It was the same with unmarried mothers. Now there was no stigma whatsoever to a young woman who wished to keep her baby out of wedlock, but back when she had had her Daisy . . .

As her mind drifted back in time, Charlotte stared down into the doll's glassy eyes and her own filled with tears. All these long lonely years, and she had never been able to forget her. Never been able to come to terms with the fact that her child had been torn from her arms. It was a constant pain that had never gone away, and she accepted that it never would now. But if she could only see her daughter just once, even for a few minutes, then she knew that she would die happy. It was never likely to happen – it would take a miracle now – but she still lived in hope.

'They called my Joseph Holy Joe,' she said now. 'And when he stepped out of the house they hurled abuse at him, just like they do at me.'

Cheryl was actually aware of Charlotte's past. She knew that she had been in prison and why, but she still couldn't help but feel sorry for her. After all, she had served her time so why couldn't the locals just leave her to live whatever time she had left in peace? People could be so cruel.

'Are you claiming all the benefits you are entitled to?' she asked then. Perhaps she could help Mrs Branning that way. So many elderly people didn't realise what they were entitled to.

Charlotte eyed her coolly. 'I have never claimed a single benefit in my whole life,' she stated. 'And I *certainly* have no intentions of starting now. My husband and I worked hard. He was a well-respected surgeon and family doctor and I was a highly qualified midwife. I have probably brought more babies into this world than you have had hot dinners, my dear. We looked after our money so that we would never be a drain on the state, which is more than can be said for some nowadays. You only have to listen to the news on the television to hear how many people claim benefits. It's appalling and no wonder that our country is in such a mess. Why doesn't the Prime Minister send all the asylum-seekers packing for a start-off?'

Not wishing to get into politics, Cheryl said hastily, 'Well, are there any bath aids or anything at all that we could provide you with that would make your life easier?'

'Nothing at all, thank you.' Charlotte was a proud woman and it showed. It was obvious that she just wanted to be left alone.

'Very well then – if you are quite sure. But if there is anything at all that I can help you with, at any time, don't hesitate to phone me. I'll write my number down for you here – look. And it would be lovely if you would allow me to come and see you again, just to check that you are all right,' she added hastily as she scribbled on a small card and handed it to Charlotte.

Charlotte stared at the young woman suspiciously. She was tempted to tell her to clear off and never come back, but it had been quite nice to have someone to talk to, even if it had only been for a very short time.

'Very well then,' she said cautiously as Cheryl rose to leave. 'I'll see you to the door.'

'Goodbye then, Mrs Branning,' Cheryl said warmly when Charlotte opened the front door for her. 'It was lovely to meet you.'

Charlotte inclined her head before closing the door behind her visitor then she peered down at the card in her hand. Apart from Mr McKenna, Cheryl Morris was the first visitor to step over her doorstep since she had come out of prison. It was a funny old world, there was no doubt about it.

The weather conditions worsened over the next month and Charlotte found it increasingly difficult to get out to the shop. But of course she would not ask for help. Her pride was too great for that, so a couple of times a week she ventured out late at night across the treacherously slippery pavements. According to the weather forecasts she listened to on the television it was the worst winter they had had for years and she could well believe it. The frost on the pavements didn't thaw even in the day, and it was so cold that she took to sleeping in the one room downstairs with her animals, with the gas fire on low. The snow came intermittently, making even Charlotte's overgrown garden look clean and bright. Then it would clear and the frost would set in again until she wasn't sure what was the worst, the snow or the frost.

Cheryl Morris called to see her once again in February, and this time Charlotte admitted her without a qualm and even made her a cup of tea.

'How are you managing with your shopping?' Cheryl asked as she dipped a ginger nut into her tea. With the number of animals Charlotte had, she knew that it must be hard to carry enough food for them all, let alone any for herself.

Fiercely independent, Charlotte hesitated before admitting, 'Well, it is a little awkward with the weather being so bad. The tins of dog and cat food are very heavy, as you can imagine.'

'Then write me a list and I'll pop out and get some for you in the car,' Cheryl offered pleasantly. 'I'm not due back in the office for another threequarters of an hour so I have more than enough time.'

She had noticed that Charlotte had developed a rather nasty cough and she was concerned about her. The woman could be very prickly and standoffish but Cheryl liked her for all that and sensed a gentle soul beneath the hard façade that she presented to the world. From what she could make of it, Charlotte had been forced to become hard to survive. No one had helped her or shown her any compassion – that was a fact.

'I can manage,' Charlotte objected, but Cheryl wasn't going to be put off so easily.

'Why should you have to manage when I'm offering to do it for you?' Her eyes twinkled with mischief. 'I'm not going to run off with your money, you know? I'll even bring you a receipt. Now write me a list, please.'

And so Charlotte did just that, chewing on her lip in consternation as she watched Cheryl drive away in her car. She had managed so well on her own up to now that it went sorely against the grain to accept help of any kind from anyone.

Cheryl was back in no time, loaded down with bags which she helped Charlotte to unpack in the small kitchen. 'That's twenty tins of Pedigree Chum, twenty tins of Whiskas and two big bags of dry food for dogs and cats. That should keep your lot going for a while.' She glanced at Charlotte apologetically here. 'I forgot to ask you what sort they liked so I bought chicken and tuna. I hope that's all right?'

When Charlotte nodded and smiled, her whole face was transformed and once again Cheryl glimpsed the pretty woman she must once have been. Old age could be a very cruel thing. Once they had gone through the bags and Cheryl had given her the change from £50 she shot off back to work, leaving Charlotte with a warm glow inside her. Obviously not all people were bad.

The next time Cheryl called to see Charlotte was early in March, and when she tapped on the door the dogs began to bark furiously. But though she stood there for what seemed like forever, no one came to answer it. Cheryl frowned. Perhaps Charlotte had gone out to do her shopping?

'Mrs Branning!' She knocked on the door again, louder this time, before resorting to shouting through the letterbox. 'Are you in there?' Above the noise of the dogs she thought she heard someone answer but she couldn't be sure. Eventually she walked around to the side of the house and tried the gate, sighing with relief when she found that it wasn't locked.

She banged on the back door this time and was rewarded when she heard Charlotte shout, 'Come in! The door is unlocked.'

She found the old woman in the back room sitting in a chair with her foot propped up on a stool and looking far from well.

'Whatever has happened?' she asked with concern.

'Oh, I slipped in the yard and hurt my ankle,' Charlotte answered irritably. 'I don't think it's broken. I think I've just sprained it but it's very frustrating more than anything.'

Cheryl took her coat off. 'Then tell me what needs doing. Have the animals been fed?'

When Charlotte shook her head the young woman slipped away and began to open some tins of dog and cat food, then when they

351

were all eating she went back into Charlotte and asked sternly, 'And when did you last have something to eat and drink?'

'I'm not sure,' the old woman admitted. 'But I don't really feel like anything, to be honest.'

She started to cough again and Cheryl frowned. She was obviously far from well, but being the stubborn old bird she was, she wouldn't admit it. The young woman went back into the kitchen, but a quick search of the cupboards revealed that there was very little food in the house. It must have been days since Charlotte last did any shopping.

'Right.' Cheryl dragged her coat back on. 'Give me some money and I'll go and get some shopping in for you. You're almost out of all the basics – you need tea, sugar and milk, and that's before we start on any food for you. You don't even have a slice of bread here.'

Charlotte opened her mouth to object but Cheryl stared at her sternly as she fetched Charlotte's purse from the sideboard and handed it to her. 'Don't bother to argue because I intend to go whatever you say,' she warned.

Charlotte handed her three ten pound notes. 'Just get what you think then,' she said meekly and once Cheryl had gone she leaned back heavily in the chair wondering how much longer she could manage on her own. It was getting harder every day, and sometimes it was an effort just to get out of the chair. But she had to go on somehow for the animals. What would happen to them if anything happened to her? Grasping Daisy, she began to rock her gently to and fro as a tear squeezed out of the corner of her eye and trickled down her cheek.

'This doesn't look good,' Cheryl's boss remarked as she read through the report about Charlotte that Cheryl had written later that week.

'It isn't good,' Cheryl agreed glumly. 'I'm getting increasingly worried about her. She doesn't seem to be managing very well at all at the minute. I'm even having to go and fetch her pension for her now from the post office – not that I mind, of course.'

'Do you think we should be doing a full assessment on her to decide if we think she can live alone any more?' Brenda Smith had been the manager of the social services team that dealt with elderly people for many years. She was a kind, compassionate lady and could see that Cheryl had taken a shine to the woman.

'I suppose we should,' Cheryl said doubtfully. 'But I don't think Charlotte will take very kindly to it. She's very independent.'

'Even so, we have to put her welfare first. From what you've told me the house is very outdated and she has all those animals to look after. Has the doctor been in to see her?'

'I wouldn't think so. But she has a wicked cough, and with only one room in the whole house heated I worry about her. Between you and me, I think she's taken to sleeping downstairs with the animals because it's warmer there. I saw some blankets she'd tried to hide behind a chair. And of course she can't get about either, now that she's hurt her ankle.'

'Go in and visit her again,' Brenda advised, 'and see if you can persuade her to let the doctor call in and check her over. Meantime I'm going to advise a full assessment.'

Both of them were aware that they might be beginning a process that would change Charlotte's life as she had known it forever. It was very sad, but in their job they knew that they sometimes had to do what was necessary for the elderly people they cared for, even if it meant taking them out of their own homes. Cheryl sincerely hoped that this wouldn't be the case for Charlotte. She doubted that she would survive long without her menagerie. They were her whole life.

It was two weeks later before Charlotte finally agreed for the doctor to visit and when he did she didn't at all like what he had to tell her.

'You have pleurisy,' he informed her gravely as he folded up his stethoscope after examining her. 'And if we don't get you into hospital pronto it's likely to develop into pneumonia. It's gone too far for me to treat you at home. And that ankle doesn't look too good either,' he added. 'You can't possibly get about on that on your own. I wouldn't be surprised if it wasn't broken and I want it X-rayed as soon as possible.'

'I am *not* going into hospital,' Charlotte barked, but then a severe bout of coughing stopped her from managing to say any more. Cheryl was hovering in the background feeling upset and guilty. She hated to see Charlotte looking so afraid, but she seemed to be deteriorating by the day and Cheryl feared what might happen to her if she was left to her own devices. She had a sneaky suspicion that Charlotte wasn't eating properly any more, apart from when she herself called in to make her a meal. Of course, that wasn't part of her job description, but she had a sneaky soft spot for the old woman.

'And what will happen to all my animals if I go into hospital?' Charlotte asked now.

The doctor glanced at Cheryl and she gulped before replying, 'Don't worry about them. I'll see that they're well taken care of, I promise.'

Charlotte's shoulders sagged and all the fight seemed to go out of her as she stared around at her animals with tears in her eyes. Deep down she knew that she couldn't look after them properly any more. She also feared that if she once left the house to go into hospital, she might never return to it again. They would stick her in an old folks' home somewhere to die.

'So, can I phone an ambulance for you then, Mrs Branning?' the doctor asked.

She nodded numbly. Suddenly she didn't want to fight any more.

Chapter Forty-Three

June 2011

'So how are we feeling today then, Mrs Branning?' Beth asked as she breezed into the room. She had just spent a long weekend off duty with her family, and she was in a happy mood. Moving closer to the bed, she gently stroked the doll that Charlotte was clutching. 'She's very pretty,' she said kindly, almost as if she was speaking to a child. 'Does she have a name?'

Charlotte remained tight-lipped. She was past caring now and couldn't see the point in talking any more. She had nothing to say, although she had been tempted to talk to this young woman sometimes. She had been in the nursing home since being allowed to leave hospital, and she was aware that she was never likely to return to her home or her animals again, which meant she had little left to live for now.

Beth sighed before smoothing the quilt on Charlotte's bed. 'We're having a little fete here down in the day room on Saturday,' she told her conversationally. 'If you're feeling up to it I could take you down there in a wheelchair. That would be nice, wouldn't it? Much better than being stuck up here between these four walls all the time. There's going to be a table-top sale and my mum is going to bring my two children along. You'll be able to meet them then. I've got two – Aaron, who is eight, and Jody, she's four. They're a right handful, I don't mind telling you, but I wouldn't be without them. Oh, there's going to be a cake stall too and a raffle and all manner of things going on.'

As she chattered on, Charlotte thought what a delightful young woman she was, so kind and compassionate, just as she had once been before life kicked the stuffing out of her. Beth flitted around the room like a butterfly straightening and dusting this and that until she glanced around and sighed with satisfaction.

'There we are then, Charlotte,' she grinned. 'Your room is all shipshape again. Now what can I get you? How about a nice cup of tea – or would you prefer coffee?'

'Tea,' Charlotte said before she could stop herself, and Beth's face lit up. It was the first word she had ever heard the old lady say, and she saw it as a major breakthrough.

'Right you are, then – tea it is. It's two sugars, isn't it? And I'll see if I can't find you a couple of nice chocolate biscuits to go with it while I'm at it.'

Once in the kitchen she told her friend Nadine excitedly, 'Charlotte just spoke to me!'

Nadine was on her tea-break and she snorted. 'Stone the crows! How'd you manage that then?'

'I just asked her if she wanted tea or coffee and she answered tea.' Beth flicked the kettle on with a broad smile on her face and got a small tray out. 'I know it's not much but it's a start, isn't it?' She rooted about in the cupboard for biscuits as Nadine grinned indulgently.

'I don't know how you do it,' she laughed. 'All the oldies seem to take to you.' Her face became serious then. 'Isn't it today that the doctor comes in with the results of her brain scan?'

Charlotte had been suffering from terrible headaches and had been taken to the hospital the week before for a scan and some tests. The only way they had guessed she was suffering was because she would flinch when they opened her curtains and let in the light each morning, and then clutch her head and groan softly. But she hadn't complained, bless her.

'I think it is, but I doubt we'll get told the results,' Beth answered. 'The doctor will probably talk to the nurse and the manageress about it. I just hope it isn't anything too serious, that's all.'

She quickly poured boiling water into the small teapot she had prepared, and after checking that she had everything, she lifted the tray and shot across her shoulder, 'See you later then. Have a nice break, and if you go out for a crafty fag don't let the boss catch you.'

Charlotte was lying exactly as she had left her and Beth helped her up onto her pillows before pouring her tea for her.

'There you go then. I must be off now else the manageress will have my guts for garters. See you later, Charlotte.'

As Beth bustled out, Lottie grinned. She could remember when she herself had been full of energy, but that seemed like an awfully long time ago now. Once she had delivered five babies all in one shift. She could see them now in her mind's eye, each one of them very precious and a minor miracle. Three girls and two boys, they had been. She was sure she must have run at least ten miles that day, checking on first one expectant mother before rushing off to check on the next, all of them at different stages of labour. Over the years she had lost count of the number of babies she had brought into the world, but she tried very hard not to think of the ones she had aborted. And yet even now she knew that she had done it with the very best of intentions. She had just wanted to help the desperate girls who came to her. Was that really such a sin?

Leaving her tea untouched, she snuggled further down into the bed taking her doll with her. She was the nearest she would ever get to her real Daisy now and the knowledge still broke her heart.

It was the following morning and Charlotte was secretly pleased when Beth came in to open her curtains.

'The hairdresser is in today,' the young woman told her pleasantly. 'She comes in once a week. Wouldn't you like to come down to the day room and get your hair done?'

When Charlotte shook her head, Beth did not persist. 'All right then. I'll just get your brush and I'll do it for you. Then we'll get you washed, eh?'

As she drew the brush through Charlotte's long hair she asked, 'What colour was it when you were young?'

'It was blonde. Almost the same colour as yours,' Charlotte told her.

Beth stifled a grin. Things really were looking up. Charlotte was actually talking to her now.

'And I bet you were a right bobby dazzler too,' she teased.

'I suppose I had my moments.' Charlotte clammed up then. It wouldn't do to get too close to anyone, but Beth was remarkably easy to talk to.

Another two days passed and Charlotte couldn't help but notice that Beth was unusually quiet, so eventually she asked, 'Are you all right, dear?'

Beth sighed and managed a weak smile. 'Sorry . . . yes, I'm fine. It's just that we found out last night that my husband, Craig, is going to be made redundant. He works as a fork-lift driver at a factory on the Bermuda Industrial Estate, but they're cutting back on staff. We were saving up to buy a house. We live in a rented one at present, but I dare say our savings will have to keep us afloat now. It's a bit of a worry but I'm sure we'll manage. And at least I'm working, so that's something.'

Charlotte squeezed her hand sympathetically. Everything was so expensive nowadays; she sometimes wondered how young families managed. Thankfully she had not had to worry about money. Joseph had left her with the house paid for and a hefty inheritance, but she had lived so frugally that she had barely had to touch it and had existed on her pension for the majority of the time.

'I'm sure he'll get another job,' she murmured.

Beth sighed. 'I hope so, but jobs are pretty thin on the ground at present, aren't they? Still, that isn't for you to fret about. I shouldn't bring my worries into work, I'm sorry.'

'Don't be. I like you to talk to me,' Charlotte said softly. 'And actually, I've been thinking about what you asked me earlier in the week – about coming to the fete on Saturday. I think I might like to, after all.'

'Why, that's wonderful.' Beth looked genuinely pleased. 'I shall wheel you down to the day room myself, and introduce you to my family. I'm sure you'll get on with my mum. She's lovely.'

'It's a date then.' And strangely, Charlotte found herself looking forward to it.

Saturday morning was bright and sunny, and as Beth got Charlotte washed and changed she was very excited. 'The weather couldn't have been better for the fete,' she said, lifting the hairbrush. 'Because it's so nice we've decided to have a bouncy castle outside in the gardens for the children and some of the stalls are going to be put up outside too. It would be a shame to be stuck inside on such a lovely day.'

Charlotte was actually feeling quite apprehensive about going downstairs now and wishing that she had never agreed to it. It had been a long, long time since she had faced a crowd of people and the thought of it filled her with dread.

'To tell the truth I'm not so sure that I'm up to it,' she said timidly. 'What if one of my headaches comes on?'

'Then I shall whip you back inside and get you some of your tablets,' Beth promised. 'Now don't go backing out on me, Charlotte. I've been looking forward to this all week.'

Charlotte sighed, knowing when she was beaten. Beth was such a kind young woman, she didn't want to let her down, and perhaps it wouldn't be as bad as she expected. After all, no one would know her from Adam at the fete. But she had a nasty suspicion that the staff here in the home did know her history. They would have access to her notes and suddenly she didn't want Beth to think badly of her.

'I – I'd like to explain something to you,' she said awkwardly. 'The thing is, I dare say you know that I've been in prison and why.'

'That's none of my business,' Beth assured her kindly, but Charlotte shook her head.

'All the same I want to tell you why I did what I did.' She licked her dry lips as Beth looked on sympathetically. 'A long time ago I was placed in a home for unmarried mothers, and once my baby was born they took her away from me.' Even now after all the long years, as she thought of her daughter, Charlotte's eyes misted with tears. 'After that I had sympathy for girls who found themselves in my position,' she forced herself to go on. 'Abortion was illegal back then, and so I considered that by performing an abortion for them I was doing them a service. If I hadn't helped them they would no doubt have gone to someone who didn't know what they were doing and risk infections and all manner of things. At least I knew how to do it properly, with minimum risk. And then once abortion became legal I didn't think I would need to do it any more . . . but then there was someone . . . well, I'm sure you know what happened the last time, but I didn't want you to think I did it lightly. It was a terrible tragedy.'

Beth's eyes were full of tears too now as she patted Charlotte's hand. 'Thank you for confiding in me, Charlotte,' she whispered. 'But try not to think about it any more. It's all behind you now.'

Charlotte sniffed. 'You – you can call me Lottie if you like. Joseph always called me Lottie.'

'In that case, Lottie it is, but now let me go and get a wheelchair for you.' Beth stood back and smiled. 'And you look lovely in that new cardigan and skirt I got for you. How about we put your pearls on too? It *is* a special occasion, after all, isn't it? And I haven't seen you wear them since you arrived here. It seems such a shame for them to just lie in their box.'

Earlier in the week, Charlotte had given Beth some money to go and get her a new outfit, and she had chosen well, although it felt quite strange to be wearing clothes that actually fitted her again. Now Beth fetched a box from the drawer of Charlotte's dressing-table and when Charlotte sprang it open a lump formed in her throat as she stared down at the perfectly matched string of pearls within. Joseph had bought them for her one birthday and she had always loved them.

As Beth fastened them for her she smiled approvingly. 'There, the blue of that cardigan exactly matches your eyes. Now let's go down, shall we?'

She helped Charlotte into the wheelchair and seconds later she was pushing her along the first-floor corridor towards the lift. As Charlotte was wheeled along she had to admit that the home was beautiful. Thick carpets covered the floors and all the furnishings and curtains had been carefully co-ordinated, a different colour in each room. Her own room was decorated in various shades of green and she found it very calming. Again she had Mr McKenna to thank for being there. He had insisted that he chose where she would go when the social services department had informed him that Charlotte was no longer fit enough to live alone. And now he paid the home her rent each month and managed her money for her. He had also ensured that all her beloved animals were rehomed. She didn't have to do a thing and she was more grateful to him than he would ever know.

As the lift took them down to the ground floor, Charlotte clutched the arms of the wheelchair and panic began to set in. How would she face all those people? The lift doors opened and instantly everything was chaotic. People were milling about everywhere she looked, and some of the other staff called a greeting to Beth as they too wheeled people in chairs towards the garden. As Beth rolled her out into the bright sunshine she blinked. It had been a while since she had been outside and she felt vulnerable in such a large open space. The sky seemed to go on forever, a lovely shade of blue with fluffy cottonwool clouds floating across it, and the garden seemed enormous, the borders around the neatly mown lawn full of flowers of every colour and size.

She felt a pang of guilt as she thought back to the front and back gardens at her house. Once upon a time they had looked like this. But after she came out of prison, she had been too afraid to venture out to the front to tend it, for fear of people hurling abuse at her, and apart from keeping it reasonably cut down enough for the dogs to exercise in, she had left the back garden to its own devices. Mr McKenna had suggested that it might be wise to put the house up for sale. After all, as he had pointed out, with a little TLC it could make a lovely family home again, but Charlotte was reluctant to get rid of it as yet. Perhaps she would consider it in the future.

'Now then,' she heard Beth say as she slowed the wheelchair and looked around the brightly coloured stalls. 'I wonder if my crew are here yet? My mum and Craig promised to be here early. I'll bet the kids are over on the bouncy castle.' She manoeuvred the chair in that direction and then laughed. 'Yes, it's just as I thought – look. There are my two little demons in the queue.'

'Which two are they?' Charlotte asked as they drew closer, but Beth didn't have any need to answer because suddenly the children started to wave and their faces lit up.

'Mummy!'

They were lovely children – blond and blue-eyed, and they looked remarkably like their mother.

A young man with a friendly face was standing next to them and he instantly extended his hand, saying, 'Ah, you must be Charlotte. Or should I call you Mrs Branning? I don't want to appear forward, but Beth talks about you all the time.' He leaned closer with a twinkle in his eyes as he whispered, 'Between you and me, I think you are one of Beth's favourites.'

'Lottie will be just fine.' Charlotte warmed to him straight away. He was tall and dark-haired and quite attractive, although by no means handsome in the traditional sense. His mouth was a little too wide and he was slightly overweight, but his smile more than made up for that.

'So where is Mum then?' Beth asked him, glancing around.

He chuckled. 'The last I saw of her, she was haring off to help on the tea stall, but she's not far away.'

'In that case I'll leave the children in your capable hands and go and see if I can find her, so that I can introduce her to Lottie.'

'Yes, ma'am!' He touched his forehead in a mock salute and gave a silly little bow as Beth affectionately cuffed him around the ear. Then she expertly turned the wheelchair and for the next twenty minutes, she wheeled Charlotte from stall to stall, seeing the various goods for sale. There were quite a number of them and the atmosphere was light. One stall was full of homemade jams and pickles. Another was selling mouthwatering-looking cakes. There was a white elephant stall full of bric-à-brac that people had donated, and a second-hand book stall. Staff from the home were milling about selling raffle tickets to anyone that would buy them. The sound of children's laughter and music hung on the air and Charlotte slowly felt herself beginning to relax. Everyone was so pleasant that she found she was actually enjoying herself.

Beth eventually told her, 'I reckon it's time for a tea-break now. I don't know about you, but being out in this sun has made me thirsty. Let's go inside to the tea stall, shall we, and see if my mum is still serving on it. She loves to help out whenever we have a fete.'

The large French doors at the back of the home had been propped open and a long trestle table had been erected in the dining room. Behind it a number of women were busily making cups of tea, coffee, and squash for the children, and they were all obviously enjoying themselves if the sound of laughter was anything to go by.

'There's my mum – look.' Beth proudly pointed towards a fair-haired middle-aged woman on the far end of the stall who was carefully loading a number of drinks onto a tray for the customer to

362

take outside. 'We'll go over there and wait for Mum to serve us, eh? She makes a mean cuppa.'

Once again the wheelchair took off at a surprising speed and within seconds they were in front of Beth's mother. She didn't see them straight off as she was busy taking money and counting out change. Charlotte watched her, thinking how alike she and her daughter were. Beth was like a younger version of her, with the same ready smile and the same slim build. The woman was still very attractive for her age and looked a happy sort of soul.

'So,' Beth said quite loudly, 'what does a body have to do to get a cuppa round here? The service is appalling. You just can't get the staff nowadays.'

Recognising her daughter's voice, the woman smiled and turned – and as she did so, Charlotte felt her blood run cold. On her left cheek was a birthmark and it was almost a perfect heart shape.

'Lottie, meet my mum.' Beth introduced her. 'Mum, this is Lottie . . . Lottie, this is Daisy.'

Charlotte didn't hear any more. She had dropped back in her wheelchair in a dead faint.

Chapter Forty-Four

'That's it, Lottie. Just take nice deep breaths now.' The resident nurse was hanging over her with a look of concern on her face, and as she swam into focus, Charlotte realised that she was lying on her bed back in her room.

As she turned her head slightly she saw that Beth and her mother were there too, looking anxious.

'Oh, Lottie, you nearly scared me to death,' Beth choked, stepping forward. 'What happened?'

Charlotte swallowed before saying weakly, 'Sorry, dear. It was probably too much sunshine. I'm not used to it.' But her eyes were fixed on Beth's mother, who was standing close behind her.

She too came over, and gently taking Charlotte's hand she teased, 'I don't usually have that effect on people, Lottie. Are you feeling a little better?'

'Y-yes, thank you.' Charlotte clung on to her hand as if she would never let it go as she studied the birthmark on the woman's cheek more closely. She knew that she must appear rude, but she couldn't help it. She had never seen another quite like it in her life. And the woman's name – Daisy – could it be a mere coincidence? She looked to be about the age that her Daisy would be now too.

'You remind me of someone,' she said cautiously now. 'Do you mind very much if I ask what your maiden name was?'

'Not at all.' Daisy flashed a charming smile. 'My maiden name was Kindler, but unfortunately both my parents are dead now. We lost Mum just last year and Dad five years ago. It was a terrible blow. They were wonderful people.'

Charlotte gulped and pressed her eyes closed as the room swam around her once more. There could be no mistaking it now. This woman, this lovely, kind woman, was her baby. The baby that she had spent her life pining for. And so miracles really could happen.

'I think we ought to leave her to rest now,' Charlotte heard the nurse say then. 'I've already phoned the doctor and asked him to pop in and take a look at her, but she's had a big day and I think she needs some quiet time now.'

'Of course.' Daisy leaned across her and asked gently, 'May I come and see you again, Lottie, when you are feeling better?'

'Yes. I'd like that.'

The three women left the room and on the landing they met the doctor just coming out of the lift. He had come immediately he received the nurse's call and now he looked at her gravely before asking, 'How is she?'

'A little better,' the nurse assured him. 'It came on quite suddenly. She seemed to be enjoying herself and then she just went out like a light.'

'I'm afraid you can expect more of that,' he told her.

When Beth and her mother raised their eyebrows questioningly the nurse told him, 'I think they should know now, Doctor. Beth is Lottie's named nurse and she'll need to be told eventually anyway, so that she'll know what to expect.'

The doctor looked towards the two women before telling them, 'I'm afraid the tests and the brain scan that Mrs Branning had recently in hospital revealed that she has a brain tumour. Because of the position of the tumour and her age it is inoperable, so from now on all we can do is try to control her headaches with drugs and keep her as comfortable as possible.'

Beth clapped her hand across her mouth as tears stung at the back of her eyes. 'Oh no – but that's awful! And Lottie is such a dear soul. Does she know?'

The doctor nodded. 'Yes. She asked me to be honest with her, and so I told her everything.'

Daisy placed her arm comfortingly about her daughter's shoulders, distressed to see her so upset.

'Well, at least you know now, love, and we shall do all we can to make whatever time she has left as happy as possible. I can start to come in and spend a little time with her a couple of times a week at least, if you think she'd like it.'

'How long has she got?' Beth asked bluntly.

The doctor shrugged. 'How long is a piece of string? The tumour is quite large and is growing rapidly, so I should say three or four months at most, but then truthfully you can never tell. She could go on for a bit longer than that.'

'I see.' Beth was heartbroken. She was used to seeing the old people she cared for pass away, but there seemed to be something special about Charlotte.

'Anyway, I'd better get in and give her the once-over,' the doctor said now and after nodding courteously at them all, he slipped away into Charlotte's room.

The next three days passed interminably slowly for Charlotte as Beth was not in work. Every time the door opened she would look towards it hopefully, and each time another member of staff came in she would be disappointed. But then at last on the fourth day, Beth appeared like a ray of sunshine. There were so many questions that Charlotte wanted to ask her but she knew that she must tread softly until she got the lie of the land. She hadn't even decided yet if she would tell Beth and Daisy who she was.

'I liked your mother,' she said sincerely as Beth helped her out of bed into the bedside chair. 'And I'm so sorry I passed out on you like that.'

'Don't be silly, we all have our off days.' Beth tucked a cushion behind her and smiled. 'But it was still a lovely day, wasn't it?'

'It certainly was.' Beth would never know just how lovely it had been for her. She waited a moment as Beth began to tidy her room before saying slyly, 'I was quite shocked at the family resemblance between you and your mother, dear. Blond hair and blue eyes must run in your family. I noticed that your children have them too. Were your grandfather or your grandmother fair as well?'

'Actually we don't get our looks from our grandparents, God rest their souls,' Beth answered easily. 'My mum and both her brothers were adopted, as it so happens. Gran never made a secret of it and was honest with them from as early as they could understand. She told them that they were all very special because she and Grandad had chosen them, but that they had all had other mummies before she took them home. I think it's right to be honest with children, don't you?'

Beth continued dusting the dressing-table as she chattered on. 'Mum came from a convent for unmarried mothers in Ireland, by all accounts, and Granny never forgot her real mother. The poor girl was heartbroken by all accounts when Granny and Grandad took Mum away, and she told them that she had named Mum Daisy. They liked the name so much that they decided to keep it.'

The young woman paused as she stared musingly off into space. 'I can't imagine how awful it must have been for her to have to give her own baby away, can you? Mum often thought of trying to trace her apparently, as she got older – but then she decided against it. As she pointed out, her birth mum was probably happily married by then with another family to care for, and Mum didn't want to upset her. Besides that, she adored my gran and grandad, so all in all things turned out OK.'

'That's good then,' Charlotte said quietly as her mind raced back over the years. There had been a time shortly after moving back to the Midlands that she had thought of trying to trace her baby too. Joseph had been wonderful and had told her that he would help and support her all he could, but then commonsense had taken over and Charlotte had realised that it would be like looking for a needle in a haystack. The Midlands covered a large area, and anyway, even if she had found her, what effect might it have had on the child? And so she had abandoned the idea – but oh, to think her beloved Daisy had been so close to her all this time! Her mouth had gone quite dry and she felt the urge to cry again, but she knew that she mustn't. Beth had just described a very happy family unit and she didn't want to do anything to spoil that. She would keep her secret and just be content to know the truth herself.

'Did your mum mean what she said when she offered to come in and see me?' she asked innocently.

Beth nodded. 'Yes, she did. In fact, I'm sure she said that she was going to pop in this afternoon.'

'I'll look forward to that then.' And Charlotte meant it.

* * *

Over the next two months Daisy became a constant visitor and Charlotte lived for the days when she saw her. The more she got to know her, the prouder she became. Daisy had a heart of pure gold and loved her family unreservedly. Charlotte found it hard to take in that she now had not only a daughter but a granddaughter and great-grandchildren.

And then came the day when Daisy asked her, 'Would you like to come to tea on Sunday, Lottie? Craig could fetch you in the car. I'm doing a barbecue for the family and we'd love you to join us.'

Charlotte felt as if she was going to burst with happiness. Things could not get much better than this. If only she could get rid of these damned headaches, everything would be perfect – but then she knew that this was highly unlikely and that her days were numbered now.

'I'd love to,' she said, but first she had another appointment to keep with Mr McKenna, who was calling in to see her the next day at her request.

'So how are you then, Mrs Branning?' Mr Mckenna asked when he arrived for their appointment.

'Oh, I can't grumble,' Charlotte answered as she patted the seat at the side of her. 'Now look – there's something I'd like you to do for me. But first, though, I have to tell you a little story so that you will understand.'

Half an hour later Mr Mckenna shook his head in amazement. 'I shall do what you've requested immediately, Mrs Branning,' he promised. The story she had just told him of a young naïve girl locked away in an Irish convent for unmarried mothers was heartbreaking. 'And thank you for confiding in me. That was an astonishing story, and I'm honoured that you wished to share it with me. You really are quite some lady. I shall have the amended documents here first thing in the morning for you to sign. But why don't you tell Daisy and her family who you really are?'

'Because I don't want to hurt them,' she said softly. 'They've managed without me all these years, and I might not be long for this earth – so things are best left as they are. At least I know the truth and now I can die happy. I consider that I have been very fortunate.'

Charlotte's eyes grew teary as he rose and shook her hand warmly and once he had gone she looked out of the window sightlessly with a broad smile on her face.

Craig came to collect her on Sunday as promised and insisted on wrapping her up like a mummy before he wheeled her out to the car. 'Strict orders from Beth,' he informed her. 'She doesn't want you catching cold.'

Daisy's house was a modest but tidy semi-detached property which was remarkably close to Charlotte's house. It seemed incredible to think that her daughter had lived so near to her all that time and she had never known it.

Daisy's husband, John, was charming and made her feel so welcome that within minutes of being there, Charlotte felt as if she had known him for years. Aaron and Jody, Beth's children, were delightful little imps and Charlotte chuckled and almost burst with pride as she watched them scampering about getting into mischief.

Daisy cooked hot dogs and beefburgers, and Charlotte was sure that a meal had never tasted so good while Beth looked on happily. She had never seen Lottie looking so happy – or eating so much for that matter.

The view from Daisy's back garden was breathtaking: it looked out across Coton and almost all of Attleborough.

'When anything happens to me I want to be buried in Coton churchyard with my Joseph,' Charlotte suddenly said out of the blue.

Beth became serious. 'Then I hope it isn't for a very long time,' she said.

Charlotte smiled sadly. She was no fool. The headaches had been getting increasingly worse over the last weeks. But strangely, death held no fear for her now. She had found not only her daughter but a whole family, and she had loved every second of the time she had spent with them.

'I want to tell you something,' she said now. 'And it's simply this. You and your mother have made me feel a part of a real family, and I love you all for that.'

Deeply touched, Beth took her hand in her own and stroked it. 'Why, thank you, Lottie. That's a lovely thing to say and we all love you too, as it happens.'

As the afternoon shadows lengthened it became chilly and Craig offered to run Lottie back to the home. She was feeling rather unwell by then, with the beginnings of another headache stabbing behind her eyes, and she kissed them all soundly before leaving.

Nadine, Beth's friend, was on duty that evening and after Craig had seen her safely back to her room, Nadine helped Charlotte to get washed and changed into her nightgown and into bed as she listened indulgently to her chattering on about what a perfect afternoon she had had.

'I think Beth and her family have really taken a shine to you,' she smiled as she tucked the blankets about Charlotte's scrawny legs.

'They're all *wonderful*,' Charlotte said dreamily. 'And I'm so, so proud of them.'

Nadine frowned, thinking this rather a strange thing to say. You could almost believe that the old woman was talking about her own family. But then her mind was probably wandering a little. It happened to a lot of old people in the home eventually.

'Now then,' she said when she had checked that there was nothing else that Charlotte wanted, 'shall I tuck Daisy in next to you?'

Charlotte eyed the doll before shaking her head. 'No, thank you, dear,' she said with a smile. 'I don't need her any more. Just turn off the light on your way out, would you? I'm tired now. Goodnight.'

'Goodnight, Lottie.' Nadine paused at the door. She had never known Charlotte to go to sleep without her doll before, and for no reason that she could explain, she felt uneasy. She shrugged, convinced that she was just being silly, and clicked the light off before softly closing the door behind her.

Charlotte smiled into the darkness and then wrinkled her nose as she sniffed at the air. Wasn't that Old Spice aftershave she could smell? The one that Joseph had always favoured? Suddenly she had the feeling that he was very close, and with her mind full of happy thoughts, she closed her eyes.

Epilogue

'But this is almost identical to the letter that I've received,' Beth said in confusion to Daisy as she glanced at the letter in her hand. It was from Mr McKenna, Charlotte's solicitor, and addressed to her mother. She had received a similar one herself only that morning.

I would be most grateful if you could call to see me at your earliest convenience regarding the estate of the late Mrs Charlotte Branning, he had written.

'What do you think he wants?' Beth asked, baffled.

'She's probably left us each a little keepsake in her will,' Daisy answered. 'And I wouldn't be surprised if she hadn't left you her string of pearls. She knew how much you liked them and it would be just like her to do something kind like that.'

Beth nodded as her mind drifted back to finding Charlotte dead in bed the morning following the barbecue. It had been a terrible shock for her and, whenever she could snatch a moment alone, she had cried on and off for the rest of the day. And yet, Charlotte had looked so peaceful. She was even smiling, so Beth hoped that her end had been pain-free.

Both she and her mother and their husbands had attended Charlotte's funeral the day before, and Beth was pleased that she had been able to carry out Charlotte's last wish of being buried with her husband in Coton churchyard. Joseph had been buried in a double plot and Beth had ensured that they reopened the grave so that his wife could lie with him. She knew it was what Charlotte had wanted and hoped that wherever they were, the couple were finally reunited.

Now she missed the old woman every single time she set foot in the home, and some of the joy had gone out of working there. Not that she had much choice in the matter. Craig's job was gone now and they had to make every penny count. They had already eaten heavily into the money they had managed to put away, and with their savings went all hopes of putting down a deposit and buying their own home.

'Well, I suppose if Mr McKenna wants to see us it would make sense if we went together,' Daisy said now.

'How about tomorrow morning then?' Beth suggested. 'It's my day off and Craig is at home to watch Jody.'

'About eleven o'clock?'

Beth nodded. 'All right then, leave it with me and I'll ring Mr McKenna and check that the time is convenient for him.'

Daisy gave her daughter a hug then. She hated to see her looking so sad.

Beth hastily swallowed the rest of her tea before rising. 'Must be off,' she told her mother. 'I've got to pack Charlotte's things up today and I'm not looking forward to it one bit. We have a new resident due any day and the manageress wants to put her in Charlotte's room.'

Daisy frowned, knowing that it wouldn't be an easy job for her daughter to do. 'Would you like me to come and help, if I'm allowed?' she offered.

Beth hesitated but then shook her head. 'Thanks for the offer but no, I'll be fine.' And she set off, dreading the job ahead.

The next morning an efficient-looking young woman ushered Daisy and Beth into Mr McKenna's office. He was expecting them and he stood up to shake their hands warmly, noting that they both looked rather bewildered as to why they should even be there.

'The late Mrs Branning thought very highly of you both,' he told them once they were seated. 'Which is why she summoned me a short time ago to make some amendments to her will. With your permission I will read it to you now.'

The two women exchanged a puzzled glance before nodding and so Mr McKenna proceeded: '"This is the last will and testament of Charlotte Branning made this day . . ."'

They shifted uncomfortably in their seats until eventually he said,

'"To Mrs Beth Malone, my string of pearls that she always admired. May she wear them in good health and think of me from time to time with fondness".'

Beth promptly burst into tears and her mother hastily handed her a handkerchief, but the solicitor's next words had their eyes popping. '"Also to Beth, my home and the sum of ten thousand pounds which will go some way towards turning it into the family home I always hoped it would be".' Beth opened her mouth to protest, but Mr McKenna hadn't finished yet. '"And to Mrs Daisy Barrett I leave the remaining sum of money in my bank account which will total approximately thirty thousand pounds, and all the rest of my worldly possessions, with my love and gratitude for the great kindness she extended to a lonely old woman".'

'B-but I can't take that,' Daisy spluttered. 'I've done nothing to deserve it.'

'And neither have I,' Beth added.

Mr McKenna smiled. 'Oh, I think Mrs Branning would disagree with that,' he said kindly. 'That dear lady had a very hard life. Far harder than you could possibly believe. She was always on the outside looking in, but you two made her feel a part of a real family, if only for a little time, and that meant the whole world to her. Take her legacy and enjoy it. It is what she wanted.'

'In that case, thank you we will,' Daisy said softly, and taking her daughter's hand they left the solicitor's office side-by-side.

Beth's mind was racing. She had visited Charlotte's home twice to collect things that Charlotte had said she needed. It was run down and outdated admittedly, but already Beth could see the children playing in the garden there and she and Craig making it into their own little palace. *God bless you, Lottie, wherever you are*, she silently prayed. *You've just made my dreams come true, our very own home*. She then flashed her mother a radiant smile.

Mr McKenna sighed as he watched them walking down the street from his office window. He still wondered if Charlotte shouldn't have told them of her true identity and had encouraged her to do just that – but she had been adamant that they should never know who she really was, so he must respect her wishes. Just thinking about the life she had led made him feel sad, but then at least she had discovered her daughter and a whole new family she had never known existed in the end, and just for a short time he had watched her blossom.

And now her legacy would change their lives forever, and for the better. He had a feeling that they would use it wisely, which just went to show: you just never knew what life had in store for you.

Now you can buy any of these other **Rosie Goodwin** titles
from your bookshop or *direct from the publisher*.

FREE P&P AND UK DELIVERY
(Overseas and Ireland £3.50 per book)

The Bad Apple	£8.99
No One's Girl	£8.99
Dancing Till Midnight	£8.99
Moonlight and Ashes	£8.99
Forsaken	£8.99
Our Little Secret	£8.99
Crying Shame	£6.99
Yesterday's Shadows	£5.99
The Boy from Nowhere	£5.99
A Rose Among Thorns	£6.99
The Lost Soul	£8.99
The Ribbon Weaver	£5.99
A Band of Steel	£5.99
Whispers	£5.99
The Misfit	£5.99
Tilly Trotter's Legacy	£8.99
The Mallen Secret	£8.99
The Sand Dancer	£8.99

TO ORDER SIMPLY CALL THIS NUMBER

01235 400 414

or visit our website: www.headline.co.uk

Prices and availability subject to change without notice.